Kate Chopin

Kate Chopin was born in St. Louis in 1851. She began writing after her husband's death in 1883, supporting herself and her six children with the publication of stories in the leading popular magazines of the day. Her first novel, *At Fault,* a pioneering work in the sympathetic treatment of the then almost taboo subject of divorce, appeared in 1890. *Bayou Folk,* her first collection of stories, was published in 1894 and gained her immediate national fame as an outstanding local-color writer. But her second story collection, *A Night in Acadie,* in 1897, began to depart from this popular and financially rewarding literary vein by presenting unconventional heroines whose views and actions were in sharp conflict with the morality of the day. With her novel, *The Awakening,* in 1899, Kate Chopin achieved what was to prove her literary masterpiece and her ultimate break with popular taste. The novel was widely denounced and banned from bookstores and library shelves, and the author consigned to oblivion. Shunned by friends and publishers alike, Kate Chopin died in 1904, seemingly forgotten. *The Awakening,* however, survived—to give its author a permanent and important place in American literature.

The Awakening
and
Selected Stories
of
Kate Chopin

EDITED
AND WITH AN INTRODUCTION BY
Barbara H. Solomon

A SIGNET CLASSIC
NEW AMERICAN LIBRARY

TIMES MIRROR
NEW YORK AND SCARBOROUGH, ONTARIO
THE NEW ENGLISH LIBRARY LIMITED, LONDON

Copyright © 1976 by The New American Library, Inc.

Library of Congress Catalog Card Number: 75-37380

SIGNET, SIGNET CLASSICS, MENTOR, PLUME AND MERIDIAN BOOKS are published *in the United States* by The New American Library, Inc., 1301 Avenue of the Americas, New York, New York 10019, *in Canada* by The New American Library of Canada Limited, 81 Mack Avenue, Scarborough, Ontario M1L 1M8, *in the United Kingdom* by The New English Library Limited, Barnard's Inn, Holborn, London, EC1N 2JR, England

First Printing, April, 1976

2   3   4   5   6   7   8   9   10

PRINTED IN THE UNITED STATES OF AMERICA

Contents

Introduction

St. Louis evenings in the spring of 1899 must have seemed far less soft and balmy than they had for many a year to Kate Chopin, who had just seen the publication of her second novel, *The Awakening*.[1] Perhaps even the lights of the elite houses she had known so long seemed to glitter with an indifferent hardness, for the appearance in print of her most recent work had brought her harsh criticism and condemnation, as well as ostracism from many of those who had always formed the close-knit world of St. Louis society. The reaction of outrage to this novel ought not to have been a surprise to its author. From the beginning of her literary career, Kate Chopin had been told by editors that they would be glad to accept her stories if only she would tone down the women she wrote about.[2] Exactly a decade before she finished *The Awakening*, her first completed tale had contained certain objectionable materials, according to the two editors who read it. Subsequently, Chopin destroyed the tale, so that we have been left only the title—"A Poor Girl."

During the same year, 1889, the first two of her stories to be published, "Wiser Than a God" and "A Point at Issue," established the kinds of subject matter which would occupy the author over the next decade. Each explores a range of feminine experience in its depiction of an unconventional heroine who attempts to make intelligent choices about the lifestyle she wishes to adopt. In "Wiser Than a God," Paula Von Stoltz rejects George Brainard's offer of marriage because, as she attempts to explain to him, "it doesn't enter into the purpose of my life." And amazingly for that era, Chopin's heroine does not live to rue the day she rejected the handsome and wealthy young suitor—does not send for him

[1] The second novel in order of composition, *Young Dr. Gosse*, is no longer extant.
[2] Per Seyersted, *Kate Chopin: A Critical Biography* (Baton Rouge: Louisiana State University Press, 1969), p. 68.

to beḡ forgiveness for valuing her art and work more than his love.

In the second tale, "A Point at Issue," the heroine, Eleanor Gail, has chosen to marry Charles Faraday, but their union, both agree, must be tailored like a garment which never chafes or restricts, but provides comfort with ample room for growth and development:

> In entering upon their new life they decided to be governed by no precedential methods. Marriage was to be a form, that while fixing legally their relation to each other, was in no wise to touch the individuality of either; that was to be preserved intact. Each was to remain a free integral of humanity, responsible to no dominating exactions of so-called marriage laws. And the element that was to make possible such a union was trust in each other's love, honor, courtesy, tempered by the reserving clause of readiness to meet the consequences of reciprocal liberty.

An outraged town discovers how unconventional the couple can be, for their married life is to begin with a long separation. After the honeymoon trip, Eleanor remains in Paris to study French while Charles returns to America. Their subsequent discovery of the limitations of marital trust and their decision to end the separation seem less important than their original idealism and view of marriage as an unfinished, incompletely defined institution. For the Faradays, being husband and wife means the continual making of new decisions, not the mechanical playing of ancient roles.

Very likely, the Faradays' recognition of the need for personal freedom within marriage was a reflection of the relationship between Kate Chopin and her understanding husband. Married in 1870 to Oscar Chopin, Kate O'Flaherty left the St. Louis of her active girlhood to live in the city which was her husband's home, New Orleans. She left behind the home where she had been raised by three widowed women—a mother, grandmother, and great-grandmother. Her mother, Eliza Faris O'Flaherty, was descended from French families that had settled in America in about 1700. Kate's father, born in Ireland, had become a well-to-do merchant after emigrating to America, first to New York and then to St. Louis in 1825. After a brief first marriage (his wife died in childbirth), Thomas O'Flaherty married Eliza Faris in 1844. Katherine, born in 1851, was the second of their children. The comfortable and pleasant childhood of Kate Chopin was abruptly shattered on a day which must have begun as a festive occasion. Along with other influential community leaders, Thomas O'Flaherty was aboard a ceremonial train making its inaugural run over a newly-built section of the Pacific Railroad when a collapsing bridge caused a catastrophic train wreck. O'Flaherty was among twenty-nine victims killed in the accident. Katherine, who was only four, had lost her devoted and vigorous father.

From the age of nine until she was graduated at the age of seventeen, Kate attended the St. Louis Academy of the Sacred Heart. A year later, she met Oscar Chopin, who was twenty-five and had left his native New Orleans to work at a St. Louis bank.

Of Oscar's character not a great deal is known. One important element, however, in the formation of his attitudes toward the treatment of women may well have been the harshness of his father toward his mother. The relationship between Victor Chopin and his wife became so strained that for a period in the 1850's Oscar's mother left his father's household. The elder Chopin's cruelties also extended to the slaves he owned, and at one point in Oscar's life, the father tried to get the son to act as overseer of slaves who were chained together at their work in the fields. The boy would have none of it. Perhaps instructed by his father's inadequacies as a human being, Oscar was all the more sympathetic to his young wife's need for personal freedom and independence. At any rate, from the earliest days of her marriage, Kate appears to have retained a good deal of her liberty and to have been thoroughly supported by her husband when she chose to dress or act somewhat unconventionally.

Recorded in her diary during the couple's European honeymoon are some of Kate Chopin's descriptions of the numerous places she visited and activities she enjoyed. One note in this diary suggests the extent to which she valued her own physical achievements as well as her opportunities for solitary experience:

> I find myself handling the oars quite like an expert. Oscar took a nap in the afternoon and I took a walk alone. How very far I *did* go. Visited a panorama which showed the Rigi Kulen in all its grandeur—the only audience being myself and *two* soldiers. I wonder what

people thought of me—a young woman strolling about alone. I even took a glass of beer at a friendly little beer garden quite on the edge of the lake. . . .[3]

The enjoyment of such walks about the city remained one of Kate Chopin's deepest pleasures throughout her life. They provided vivid glimpses into the varied lives of the multitudes who filled the streets of New Orleans. In *The Awakening*, Edna Pontellier's assertion to Robert about walking seems an insight into the author's own view: "I always feel so sorry for women who don't like to walk; they miss so much—so many rare little glimpses of life; and we women learn so little of life on the whole." A less pleasant experience, recorded in Kate Chopin's diary, took place during a visit to the university at Bonn. The Chopins' guide was a woman who ostensibly was showing them what was to be seen, but Kate notes:

> We saw nothing remarkably interesting—only a mass of copies from famous pieces of sculpture. The good dame would not take us through the hall in which the students were gathered, "for," she said, "the young gentlemen are not sorry when a young lady passes through their room." I ventured to suggest that my being married might in a manner abate the interest with which they might otherwise regard me; but my argument proved weak and failed utterly.[4]

The young wife had simply come up against one of the usual limitations of being a woman in a man's world, and at a men's university.

Upon their return to America, Kate and Oscar settled in New Orleans, where they were to remain for the next nine years. Here the young wife whose writing career was yet unthought of gave birth to a son, Jean, the first of her six children. Over twenty years later, she set down her vivid recollection of the event:

> This is Jean's birthday . . . I can remember yet that hot southern day on Magazine Street in New Orleans. The noises of the street coming through the open windows; that heaviness with which I dragged myself about; my husband's and mother's solicitude; old Alexandrine the quadroon nurse with her high bandana tignon, her hoop-earrings and placid smile; old Doctor Faget; the

[3]Daniel S. Rankin, *Kate Chopin and Her Creole Stories* (Philadelphia: University of Pennsylvania Press, 1932), p. 72.
[4]Ibid., p. 65.

smell of chloroform, and then waking at 6 in the evening from out of a stupor to see in my mother's arms a
little piece of humanity all dressed in white which they
told me was my little son! The sensation with which I
touched my lips and my finger tips to his soft flesh only
comes once to a mother. It must be pure animal sensation; nothing spiritual could be so real—so poignant.[5]

The years between 1871 and 1880 were filled with the responsibilities of childbearing and the raising of young children. The birth of Jean in 1871 was followed by those of Oscar (1873), George (1874), Frederick (1876), Felix (1878),
and Lelia (1879). Kate, now the mother of six, was not yet
thirty. Oscar pursued his career as a cotton factor and commission merchant. The failure of his business in 1880 because
of poor cotton crops caused him to move his wife and children to a village called Cloutierville in Natchitoches (pronounced Nack-uh-tush) Parish, Louisiana.

Oscar purchased and ran a general store at Cloutierville;
he also managed several of his own small plantations. In this
region Kate absorbed a range of impressions of the rural pop-
ulation of Acadians (Cajuns) and developed her perceptions
of the intimate details of their lives. Since over two thirds of
her tales are set in Louisiana and most of these take place in
Natchitoches Parish—which, as others have noted, functions
in Chopin's fictional world much as Yoknapatawpha County
does in that of William Faulkner—it might be well to distinguish here between her new group of neighbors and the
French Creole society of New Orleans with which Kate was
so familiar.

The somewhat aristocratic and well-to-do descendents of
French emigrants to America (of whom Kate was one on her
mother's side), the Creoles clung to the French tongue and to
French culture from a sense of its superiority. In New Orleans, they clustered in one section of the city, and many
resented the influx of newcomers to the "American" section.
It is interesting to note that as a child, Kate Chopin may well
have spoken French before English, since French was the language used in her family during her childhood.

The Acadians, on the other hand, did not come to America
directly from France. They were the settlers of Acadia, once
a French province in southeastern Canada, now known as
Nova Scotia. Many Acadians left this colony in 1755 rather
than become subjects of the British, to whom the territory

[5]Seyersted, p. 40.

had been ceded. Unlike the modern French spoken by the
Creoles, the French of the Acadians dated from the seventeenth century and was combined with some quaint English
translations. The resulting dialect is captured with great
charm in a number of Mrs. Chopin's tales. According to
Daniel Rankin, Acadians

> slightly chant their phrases in agreeable Southern voices.
> Their Christian names are Evariste, Placide, Muna,
> Alcée, Artemise, Calixta, Fronie, Ozeme, Pelagie, Eu-
> phrasie; their best-known names are quite like Santien,
> St. Denis Godolph, Laballière, Benitou, Bonamour. They
> say "raiderode" for railroad, having settled in Louisiana
> before "chemin de fer" was known. They say of their
> Easter communion every year that it is "to make their
> Easters" because the French is "Faire de Paques."[6]

Indeed, Mrs. Chopin's earliest literary reputation, that of a
local colorist, stems from the fascination of both readers and
critics with the charming and unique Acadians and Creoles
who fill her tales. Unfortunately, her categorization as merely
a talented regional writer long blocked the wider recognition
she deserves.

In 1882, Oscar died of swamp fever. Although Kate remained in Cloutierville for a time, managing her husband's
business interests, she decided to rejoin her mother in St.
Louis. Mrs. O'Flaherty's death in 1885 left Kate a thirty-
four-year-old widow with no close relations other than her
children.

Although Kate Chopin had lived in Cloutierville for fewer
than five years, this rural Louisiana locale seems to have trig-
gered her literary imagination long after she had left. She began her writing career in 1887, a year after a visit to
Natchitoches Parish and at the urging of Dr. Frederick Kol-
benheyer, her family physician and good friend. Impressed by
the highly creative quality of the letters she had written to
him from Louisiana, he recognized the importance writing
might have as an outlet for the observant and energetic
young woman who had experienced such tragic losses. His efforts could not have been better directed.

Once Mrs. Chopin had begun to write, she self-consciously
analyzed the literary techniques of other short story writers
such as Mary E. Wilkins Freeman and Sarah Orne Jewett,

[6]Rankin, p. 137.

but the overwhelming influence on her style and technique was undoubtedly Guy de Maupassant. Some years later, in an essay titled "Confidences" she described the way in which, in about the year 1888,

> there fell accidentally into my hands a volume of Maupassant's tales. These were new to me. I had been in the woods, in the fields, groping around; looking for something big, satisfying, convincing, and finding nothing but—myself; a something neither big nor satisfying, but wholly convincing. It was at this period of my emerging from the vast solitude in which I had been making my own acquaintance, that I stumbled upon Maupassant. I read his stories and marvelled at them. Here was life, not fiction; for where were the plots, the old fashioned mechanism and stage trapping that in a vague, unthinking way I had fancied were essential to the art of story making. Here was a man who had escaped from tradition and authority, who had entered into himself and looked out upon life through his own being and with his own eyes; and who, in a direct and simple way, told us what he saw.

Other sources attest as well to Mrs. Chopin's continued high regard for Maupassant.

Kate Chopin moved very quickly from her early short stories to the writing of her first novel, *At Fault*, published in 1890. By 1894, she had written over forty tales and sketches, achieved acceptance in the prestigious Eastern magazines, and published *Bayou Folk*, a collection of her stories and vignettes.

Five of the tales from that volume are reprinted in this collection. One of these, "Désirée's Baby," is probably her best-known story. Désirée Aubigny is among the Chopin heroines who exist entirely in terms of a traditional patriarchal role. Her traits are carefully catalogued as we are told how the abandoned orphan grew up in her new home "to be beautiful and gentle, affectionate and sincere." Her husband, characterized only briefly—but unpleasantly—rules the slaves of his plantation strictly, and the joy they had once known under his father has gone out of their lives. When he had been reminded before his marriage to Désirée that he had chosen a girl who was "nameless," his response had been that such a detail could not matter "when he could give her one of the

oldest and proudest [names] in Louisiana." His arrogance
and possessiveness toward Désirée call to mind another aristocratic husband, Browning's Duke of Ferrara. The Aubigny
name may not be nine hundred years old, but Armand's
family pride is certainly as great as that of the Duke.

After the birth of their son, Armand's pleasure and general
satisfaction are expressed by his good-natured treatment of
the slaves. Désirée is thrilled that the infant is a boy because
she is convinced that her producing a son has pleased her
husband far better than having a daughter would have.

Désirée's increasing awareness of a threatening atmosphere, which she does not at first understand, and the withdrawal of her husband's love, are sketched by Chopin
with deft economy. The luxurious surroundings of Désirée's
bedroom are a mockery of her bewilderment and isolation.
Armand's angry accusation and Désirée's dependent nature
can lead to only one conclusion. If the denouement of
"Désirée's Baby" is somewhat melodramatic, the story nevertheless delineates very effectively the racial fears and vulnera-
bility of Southern whites as well as the fate of woman as
"damaged property."

"La Belle Zoraïde," another tale from *Bayou Folk* which
deals with race and the bearing of a child, is the deeply sympathetic account of a mulatto servant prevented from marrying the slave she loves and robbed of a child she has
conceived by him. Zoraïde, a slave whose "smooth skin was
the color of *café-au-lait*," has fallen in love with Mézor. She
humbly petitions her mistress (with whom she has grown up
as a companion and friend) that she be allowed to "have
from out of my own race the one whom my heart has
chosen." But Zoraïde's love is a field slave whose body "was
like a column of ebony," whereas Madame Delarivière has
already chosen a husband for the girl—a light mulatto who is
a neighbor's household servant. Because of Ambroise's almost
white appearance and status in the hierarchy of slave society,
the imperious mistress will hear of no other mate for her
beautiful and graceful Zoraïde. Zoraïde, as the tale well
demonstrates, is doubly powerless as a slave and a woman.

Mrs. Chopin uses a framing device in this story, in that
Zoraïde's tragedy is related by a devoted black servant,
Manna-Loulou, to her mistress, Madame Delisle. Each evening, the former slave must soothe Madame by performing
such tasks as bathing her feet and brushing her hair. But
equally important, she must be prepared to tell a true tale in

order to lull her mistress to sleep. The framework provides a Conradian richness, since after mentioning that Zoraïde and Mézor had been forbidden to see one another, Manna-Loulou comments: "But you know how the negroes are, Ma'zélle Titite. ... There is no mistress, no master, no king nor priest who can hinder them from loving when they will." The ironies suggested by the framework are multiplied when we recall that Madame Delisle is the heroine of a slightly earlier tale, "A Lady of Bayou St. John." In that story we learn that she is a widow whose husband, Gustave, was killed during the Civil War. We also know that she has chosen to devote the remainder of her life to the memory of her dead husband, though she was on the verge of running off with another man and was stopped only by the news of Gustave's death. Her overwhelming sympathy for the sorrow and losses of another woman might justifiably be lavished on Madame Delisle's own life.

The two other tales reprinted here from *Bayou Folk*, "Madame Célestin's Divorce" and "At the 'Cadian Ball," deal in very different ways with a variety of courtships. In the first, lawyer Paxton engages in numerous sympathetic discussions with the charming Madame Célestin on the subject of a divorce from her absent and wayward husband. These conversations about her sufferings, as she sweeps her front porch, are transformed into an unusual ritual of courtship for the old bachelor. In "At the 'Cadian Ball," two courtships are resolved simultaneously, but the pairing of the sets of lovers might never have occurred had not Clarisse taken upon herself the role of aggressive "suitor" by following Alcée Laballière to the ball.

The subject of the match made between the aristocratic Alcée with his haughty Clarisse and that of the peasant Bobinôt with his sensual Calixta drew from Chopin a few years later a second treatment of the lives of her young characters. In one of her finest tales, "The Storm" (subtitled "A Sequel to 'At the 'Cadian Ball' "), Calixta and Alcée are thrown together for the first time in more than five years. The passion which they had previously known is rekindled, and their subsequent sexual experience gives to both a quality of sensual pleasure unknown in their marriages. Chopin's description of their sense of fulfillment is remarkably explicit and contemporary in tone:

Her firm, elastic flesh that was knowing for the first time its birthright, was like a creamy lily that the sun invites to contribute its breath and perfume to the undying life of the world.

The generous abundance of her passion, without guile or trickery, was like a white flame which penetrated and found response in depths of his own sensuous nature that had never yet been reached.

When he touched her breasts they gave themselves up in quivering ecstasy, inviting his lips. Her mouth was a fountain of delight. And when he possessed her, they seemed to swoon together at the very borderland of life's mystery.

The story was not published during Chopin's lifetime and, indeed, appeared only recently, when Per Seyersted's edition of Chopin's complete works was printed. The depiction in the story's concluding paragraphs of the general satisfaction of all the characters is marked by a modern sense of irony, as Chopin refrains from any authorial commentary on her characters' actions.

The three stories in this volume reprinted from Kate Chopin's second collection of tales, *A Night in Acadie* (1897)—"Athénaïse," "A Respectable Woman," and "Regret"—make for an interesting glimpse into the feminine experience at three different stages in life. Athénaïse, after two months of marriage to Cazeau, has discovered that she detests being married:

"I hate being Mrs. Cazeau, an' would want to be Athénaïse Miché again. I can't stan' to live with a man; to have him always there; his coats an' pantaloons hanging in my room; his ugly bare feet—washing them in my tub, befo' my very eyes, ugh!"

She returns to her parents' home for a visit and very reluctantly accompanies her husband when he comes to take her home. Cazeau, who is deeply saddened because he is not insensitive to his young wife's feelings, has an unpleasant twinge of memory on their ride back. They pass the old oak tree where as a small boy he stopped briefly with his father on their way home with Black Gabe, a recaptured slave. When Athénaïse leaves him for the second time, Cazeau determines not to search for her:

For the companionship of no woman on earth would he again undergo the humiliating sensation of baseness that had overtaken him in passing the old oak-tree in the fallow meadow. . . .

He knew that he could again compel her return as he had done once before,—compel her to return to the shelter of his roof, compel her cold and unwilling submission to his love and passionate transports; but the loss of self-respect seemed to him too dear a price to pay for a wife.

Cazeau keeps to his resolution, but Athénaïse's month spent hidden in New Orleans demonstrates how confining a routine will be alloted to a young woman alone in the city. She had hoped to find some means of employment, but as Chopin explains, "with the exception of two little girls who had promised to take piano lessons at a price that would be embarrassing to mention, these attempts had been fruitless." She relies heavily on Gouvernail, a fellow lodger at the Dauphine Street house, in order to go about the city. Homesick and isolated, Athénaïse discovers that she is pregnant, and this precipitates her return to her husband and her first passionate response to his embrace.

In "A Respectable Woman," Mrs. Baroda, who has been married a good many years, finds herself overwhelmingly attracted to Gouvernail (who appears in "Athénaïse"), an old friend of her husband's who has come for a visit of a week or two. Her relationship with her husband seems an excellent one, and she is even tempted to discuss her infatuation with him. She does not, however, confide in Gaston, because, as Chopin tells us, "Beside being a respectable woman she was a very sensible one; and she knew there are some battles in life which a human being must fight alone." The tale ends on an effectively ambiguous note, for whatever course of action Mrs. Baroda has decided upon, she merely tells her husband that she is willing that his friend, Gouvernail, should visit them again. On his first visit, she had been somewhat rude and left home for a stay in the city, but now she assures Gaston: "This time I shall be very nice to him."

In the poignant "Regret," the fifty-year-old Aurélie is an independent, self-reliant figure who has never regretted her decision, made thirty years earlier, that she would not marry. A neighbor's emergency trip brings four young children to her household for a two-week stay. Aurélie finds that caring

for the youngsters requires considerable change in her
routine. At bedtime, for example, there are a great many details to be attended to:

> What about the little white nightgowns that had to be
> taken from the pillow-slip in which they were brought
> over, and shaken by some strong hand till they snapped
> like ox-whips? What about the tub of water which had
> to be brought and set in the middle of the floor, in
> which the little tired, dusty, sunbrowned feet had every
> one to be washed sweet and clean? And it made
> Marcéline and Marcélette laugh merrily—the idea that
> Mamzelle Aurélie should for a moment have believed
> that Ti Nomme could fall asleep without being told the
> story of *Croquemitaine* or *Loup-garou*, or both; or that
> Elodie could fall asleep at all without being rocked and
> sung to.

The tasks which begin as unfamiliar work come to give a
great deal of pleasure to the "temporary mother." When the
real mother unexpectedly returns and claims her brood,
Aurélie experiences a wrenching loss. She sobs "like a man."
The experience with Odile's children has brought with it a
crushing knowledge of the softer elements which are lacking
in Aurélie's life. And, of course, the story touches on the
tragic experience of many women, for even those who are
mothers must face a time when the infants who needed them
and gave purpose to their daily routine have grown up and
are ready to leave home.

The breadth of Kate Chopin's vision of life and her understanding of the paradoxes of human existence are suggested if
we compare the theme of "Regret" with that of a somewhat
later tale, "A Pair of Silk Stockings." When Mrs. Sommers
unexpectedly finds herself in possession of fifteen dollars, she
immediately begins to calculate how best to stretch this sum
in outfitting her sons and daughters. She carefully plans to
purchase a gown, shoes, caps, and stockings—all for her children. We are given a glimpse into the life of an impoverished
mother, an existence dominated by stratagems for mending
and scrimping for the sake of others, with no thought of her
own desires or deprivations. Even as she arrives at the store
where she is to shop, she suddenly realizes that "between getting the children fed and the place righted, and preparing

herself for the shopping bout, she had actually forgotten to eat any luncheon at all!"

Mrs. Sommers' temptation comes in the form of a pair of black silk stockings—luxurious, smooth, beautifully made. The esthetic, sensitive self, which has been dormant within her for so long, suddenly springs alive as the spontaneous purchase of the stockings leads Mrs. Sommers to spend more and more of the money on herself. Once she has replaced her old cotton stockings with the new ones, a startling change takes place:

> She was not thinking at all. She seemed for the time to be taking a rest from that laborious and fatiguing function and to have abandoned herself to some mechanical impulse that directed her actions and freed her of responsibility.
>
> How good was the touch of the raw silk to her flesh! She felt like lying back in the cushioned chair and reveling for a while in the luxury of it.

After the purchase of shoes, gloves, and magazines—all for herself—she orders a tasty meal at a fine restaurant and delights in a matinee at a nearby theater. Chopin characterizes Mrs. Sommers throughout these experiences as having an inner delicacy of taste and a quiet distinction about her. Little room exists, however, for these fine discriminations within the financially hard-pressed world of this energetic "mother-woman." Mrs. Sommers, riding home after tasting luxuries only made possible by her forgetting her responsibilities to the children, has "a poignant wish, a powerful longing that the cable car would never stop anywhere, but go on and on with her forever." For Aurélie in "Regret," there has been the discovery of one sort of physical pleasure: that of being close to the small toddler who lies next to her each evening and whose warm breath beats "her cheek like the fanning of a bird's wing." For Mrs. Sommers there is a rediscovery of the exquisite pleasure which luxury makes possible, a pleasure entirely absent from her selfless daily routine. What Kate Chopin knows and writes so well is the truth of both women's experiences. The care of children is a great joy; it is also a great limitation on a woman's freedom.

A third instance of Chopin's concern with the paradoxical nature of human relationships, especially that of the marital bond as experienced by a woman, appears in "The Story of

an Hour." Mrs. Mallard sometimes had loved her husband—
often had not. Upon being told of his death in a railroad accident, she experiences sincere grief, and yet, a few minutes
later, she is overwhelmed by the anticipation of pleasurable
experience to come now that she has been released from marriage.

> She knew that she would weep again when she saw
> the kind, tender hands folded in death; the face that had
> never looked save with love upon her, fixed and gray
> and dead. But she saw beyond that bitter moment a long
> procession of years to come that would belong to her ab-
> solutely. And she opened and spread her arms out to
> them in welcome.
> There would be no one to live for her during those
> coming years; she would live for herself.

One is reminded of the parallel drawn between the slave
Black Gabe and the young wife in "Athénaïse" as Louise
Mallard whispers to herself: " 'Free! Body and soul free!' "
Unlike Athénaïse, however, Mrs. Mallard had probably
never fully verbalized even to herself the sense of oppression
or unhappiness caused by the restrictions of her marriage.
The announcement of Brently Mallard's death brings a rev-
elation to his wife: the desire for a life of self-actualization,
"of self-assertion," is "the strongest impulse of her being!"
Such an existence, however, is not to be hers.

"Charlie," one of Kate Chopin's last stories, was written after the publication of *The Awakening* and never published
during the writer's lifetime. One of only nine pieces produced
after the storm of disapproval caused by the novel, the story
dramatizes the identity crisis of Charlotte Laborde, the seven-
teen-year-old known as "Charlie," who is more comfortable
roaming the woods in her "trouserlets" than sitting in the
classroom with her well-behaved sisters. Much like Huck
Finn in several respects, Charlie is a free spirit, whose lively
imagination, independence, and physical activity are viewed
quite negatively by those around her, who wish that she
would be more demure and ladylike. Chopin treats with a
fine comic sense some of Charlie's attempts to become "feminine" and alluring. The emerging young woman is characterized temporarily by an inordinate love of jewelry and finery,
a series of unsuccessful disfiguring encounters with a curling
iron, and an intense preoccupation with learning to dance
and whitening her hands.

The relationship between Mr. Laborde and his most troublesome daughter is a curious one. In many ways, Charlie plays the role of the son he never had, being the only one of his seven daughters to interest herself in such practical matters as the grooming of a horse. But an unusual note of possessiveness—and even of ardor—appears in Mr. Laborde as he escorts Charlie about New Orleans when he visits her at the school to which she had been sent some months before:

> He did not tell her in so many words how hungry he
> was for her, but he showed it in a hundred ways. He
> was like a school boy on a holiday; it was like a conspiracy; there was a flavor of secrecy about it too. They did
> not go near Aunt Clementine's.

When they meet Mr. Walton, who might be considered a potential suitor of Charlie, and he seems inclined to take the day off from his office and to join them, Mr. Laborde obviously does not want the young man's company and hurriedly departs.

Only after Mr. Laborde loses his arm in an accident and after Julia's engagement to Walton is announced does Charlie find her true self, becoming a capable, strong, and thoughtful young woman. Her ability to manage the plantation and her interest in the livestock—traits which were merely a vexation while Mr. Laborde headed the family—are now necessary to the well-being of all, and especially to her father, who comes to depend upon her totally. The tale seems to suggest that only in a world in which the male authority figure is no longer able to function can Charlie's assertive and active behavior be valued. Per Seyersted has noted that although a major theme of Chopin had always been that of "female self-assertion," until the writing of "Charlie" she had never dealt antagonistically with men in her fiction. He believes that in this story for the first time "she allows herself to disable a man, even a good man, thus subtly hitting back at the males who had labeled her a disgrace and silenced her literary gun because she had represented a woman taking the liberties of a man."[7] Read in this light, "Charlie" provides an interesting glimpse into Chopin's thoughts during the year following the publication of *The Awakening*.

If one turns to that novel which so outraged the sensibilities of Kate Chopin's contemporaries it seems now as though

[7]Seyersted, p. 183.

her subject matter were inevitable. When the creator of such women as Mildred Orme (of "A Shameful Affair"), Athénaïse, Mrs. Baroda, Mrs. Sommers, and Louise Mallard came to write a full-length study of the inner life of a sensitive young woman, her major theme would be the growth of Edna Pontellier's sense of identity and her physical and spiritual awakening to passion and self-knowledge.

A major achievement in American fiction, *The Awakening* successfully weaves together diverse literary themes. From the details of Edna's life as a wife and mother emerges a poignant portrait of a woman oppressed by the roles which are invariably foisted on the female, whether or not she is suited for them. In addition to her sensitive rendering of the feminist themes, Chopin depicts the consequences of the rarely acknowledged sexual drives of a woman, thereby relating the novel thematically to the tradition of naturalistic literature. Further enriching the tapestry of the novel is the dramatization of the larger conflict between an individual and society, a theme central to both the English and American tradition of romantic fiction.

The novel's feminist concerns, which many contemporary readers find refreshingly relevant in tone and subject, have been largely responsible for the recent reevaluation of Chopin's literary achievement. Edna has been married for six years to Léonce Pontellier, who is certainly neither a villain nor a brute, but merely an ordinary husband, a little selfish, a little insensitive, and greatly conventional. The qualities of the relationship between the twenty-eight-year-old Edna and her forty-year-old husband are delineated with consummate skill as Chopin brings the Pontelliers together in an early scene. While Edna is enjoying a mid-day plunge in the Gulf with Robert Lebrun, Léonce, who had gone bathing at daybreak, finds the rest of that Sunday morning seems to drag by, as he reads the previous day's newspaper. The husband's very first words to his wife criticize her arrangement of activities, which differs from his own. He remarks that it is "folly" to go bathing at that hour and in that heat. Léonce's attitude toward Edna is essentially proprietary: " 'You are burnt beyond recognition,' he added, looking at his wife as one looks at a valuable piece of personal property which had suffered some damage." While the husband's annoyance seems incidental here, this exchange functions as a prologue to another, more significant, scene which, again, takes place after Edna has gone bathing.

On that occasion, most of the guests at Madame Lebrun's have trooped down to the beach for a late swim in the moonlight. Edna, who has been attempting to learn to swim all summer long, finally succeeds, in spite of the fearfulness which had characterized her previous attempts:

> ... that night she was like the little tottering, stumbling, clutching child, who of a sudden realizes its powers, and walks for the first time alone, boldly and with over-confidence. She could have shouted for joy. She did shout for joy, as with a sweeping stroke or two she lifted her body to the surface of the water.
>
> A feeling of exultation overtook her, as if some power of significant import had been given her to control the working of her body and her soul.

The ways in which this almost mystical experience of gaining control of the physical responses necessary to conquer the surging water will affect Edna's life are dramatized almost immediately. Returning from the beach with Robert, Edna reclines in a hammock suspended in front of her cottage. Later Léonce returns to the cottage, much surprised to find Edna—now alone—outside. He calls her to come in to bed. When she indicates a desire to remain outside, he paternally asserts his concern for her well-being. He fears that the cold and the mosquitoes will be harmful. But these "reasons" and kind entreaties only thinly mask Léonce's determination that his wife do what he does. Finally, with obvious irritation, Léonce once more refers to his wife's behavior as "folly" and adds: " 'I can't permit you to stay out there all night. You must come in the house instantly.' " In both this instance and the earlier one, there is a strong conviction on the part of the husband that the desires of this married couple ought to be one: namely his.

Edna at this point is thoroughly awake in two senses. Physically, she does not desire to go to bed, but more important, emotionally and spiritually, she is alive to the significance of her husband's tone and to her own strong need to listen instead to her own inner voice.

> She perceived that her will had blazed up, stubborn and resistant. She could not at that moment have done other than denied and resisted. She wondered if her husband had ever spoken to her like that before, and if she had

submitted to his command. Of course she had; she remembered that she had. But she could not realize why or how she should have yielded, feeling as she then did.

She tells him that there is no use in his ordering her to come in and that she does not wish to be spoken to in such a way. Mr. Pontellier's stratagem for not appearing to be dominated by his wife is highly entertaining. He appears on the porch fortified with a glass of wine and a supply of cigars, continuing to smoke these until Edna, now finally tired, enters the house. Even then, he makes a point of staying outside after she has gone in, feigning a desire to finish his cigar. She may have begun the starlight vigil, but he will finish it.

Léonce's behavior throughout the novel is consistent. Later when Edna disobeys his wishes and moves out of their large house into her small "pigeon house" around the corner, he again contrives to save face. This time he sends detailed orders from New York for renovations on his home. Thus, Edna's removal to other quarters will seem a part of his grand plan for the improvement of his house, and society will be satisfied that all goes well with the Pontelliers.

One of Léonce's early complaints about Edna is that she is not sufficiently dedicated to the care of their children, Raoul and Etienne. Certainly Edna recognizes that she is not one of the "mother-women," those creatures at Grand Isle who like Adèle Ratignolle "idolized their children, worshiped their husbands, and esteemed it a holy privilege to efface themselves as individuals and grow wings as ministering angels." She has a vague sense of having drifted into the role of motherhood without any particular talent for it. During the summer months, Adèle, who is a foil for Edna, busily sews little winter garments which will protect her children from threatening drafts and chills. Similarly, her skill at the piano is important merely for the pleasure it provides for her family, and thus she keeps up her music solely for the sake of her children.

Although attracted by Adèle's affectionate and honest nature, Edna never deceives herself into believing that such a lifestyle could be desirable for her. Back in New Orleans, Edna, for the pleasure it gives her, returns to her painting with great absorption and increasingly ignores the claims of housekeeping. She can enjoy a delightful lunch with the Ratignolles, can be touched by the pleasing harmony of their marriage, and can still conclude:

It was not a condition of life which fitted her, and she could see in it but an appalling and hopeless ennui. She was moved by a kind of commiseration for Madame Ratignolle,—a pity for that colorless existence which never uplifted its possessor beyond the region of blind contentment, in which no moment of anguish ever visited her soul, in which she would never have the taste of life's delirium.

Not quite sure of what she means when she thinks of such "delirium," Edna has so far been able to define her new self only in terms of that which she is not.

Her dilemma is not that of a wife who discovers that she loves a man other than her husband. The sensual nature which has been awakened by Robert is independent of his presence. Although she has spent the past months longing for him, just when she has learned that he will soon return to New Orleans, she becomes sexually involved with Alcée Arobin. His kiss "was the first kiss of her life to which her nature had really responded. It was a flaming torch that kindled desire." Her subsequent relations with Alcée (a man for whom she cares little) include "neither shame nor remorse." Instead, "there was a dull pang of regret because it was not the kiss of love which had inflamed her, because it was not love which held this cup of life to her lips." Edna's strongest feeling about her relationship with Arobin is centered in the conviction that she is now truly awake, now truly sees into the heart of the universe. The knowledge she has gained may be both brutal and beautiful, but—most crucial to her—it is inescapable, and without it one lives only in a dream. Essentially, Edna understands and accepts the impersonal erotic drive within her.

When we note that a year after the publication of *The Awakening*, Theodore Dreiser published *Sister Carrie*, which was considered so shocking and immoral that the copies of the novel were never delivered to the bookstores, we can gauge how revolutionary Kate Chopin's depiction of the force of Edna's passionate nature must have been. Dreiser excludes any scene of a sexual nature between Carrie and Drouet as she becomes his mistress. Carrie's actions are symbolized through the nightmares of her sister on that evening: Minnie dreams of watching helplessly as Carrie lowers herself into the pit of a mine; in a second image, she drifts away from Minnie as the waters lap round her. Compared to Dreiser's turn-of-the-century technique of indirection, Chopin's representation of Edna's experience is precisely drawn, unmodified by the literary etiquette of the era. Although never picturing herself as a crusader, Chopin, along with such writers as Dreiser and Crane, attacked the bastion of American prudery in literature. Whereas Carrie often drifts from one situation to another, the newly awakened Edna, never a naturalistic victim of circumstances, is determined to control her life. When Robert finally admits to having had wild hopes that Edna's husband might free her, she bewilders him by declaring, "I am no longer one of Mr. Pontellier's possessions to dispose of or not. I give myself where I choose. If he were to say, 'Here Robert, take her and be happy; she is yours,' I should laugh at you both." Ironically, even as Edna is in the process of asserting her utter freedom from commitment to others, she responds to the summons from the Ratignolles, keeping her promise to go to Adèle when it is time for the birth of the child.

Once again, Chopin focuses on the significance of motherhood as Edna attends Adèle's delivery. In a conversation the two women had once had at Grand Isle, Edna had attempted to define to her friend the difference between them. She had explained:

> "I would give up the unessential; I would give my money, I would give my life for my children; but I wouldn't give myself. I can't make it more clear; it's only something which I am beginning to comprehend, which is revealing itself to me."

Adèle never seems to understand that Edna is unwilling to live her days stifling her own will and identity in order to be the kind of person needed by her children. She has never known the urgent and overpowering emotions experienced by Edna.

After she has lost Robert, Edna unflinchingly faces a vision of her future as it stretches before her: " 'Today it is Arobin; tomorrow it will be some one else. It makes no difference to me, it doesn't matter about Léonce Pontellier—but Raoul and Etienne!' " Prizing her freedom above all else, disdaining to trample on the "little lives" she loves, Edna gives back her life to the waters that had awakened it.

In creating *The Awakening* and her short stories, Chopin, with the same kind of honesty she attributed to Edna, unflinchingly depicted her vision of the paradoxes, complexities, and conflicts of human experience, treating them as no one else had in American fiction. Critics and readers were not yet ready to confront her challenging views. American literature has finally caught up with Kate Chopin, a woman much ahead of her time.

—Barbara H. Solomon
Iona College
New Rochelle, New York

A Note on the Text

THE TEXT of this edition of *The Awakening* is that of the first edition published in 1899 by Herbert S. Stone and Co. of Chicago. Two words have been added to the text: [here] on page 60 and [of] on page 119. Those stories which appeared first in a periodical and later were collected in *Bayou Folk* or *A Night in Acadie* are reprinted from the book version. Stories which appeared only in a newspaper or magazine are reprinted as they appeared in those sources. Two stories, not published during Chopin's life, "The Storm" and "Charlie," are reprinted from *The Complete Works of Kate Chopin*, edited by Per Seyersted, Louisiana State University Press, 1969.

Chronology

1851   Katherine O'Flaherty born St. Louis, February 8.

1855   Father dies in a train wreck.

1860   Kate enrolls as a student at St. Louis Academy of the Sacred Heart.

1863   Deaths of Kate's great-grandmother and half-brother.

1868   Kate graduates from the Academy.

1869   Writes "Emancipation: A Life Fable"; about this time, meets Oscar Chopin.

1870   Kate and Oscar marry and set off for honeymoon in Europe. On their return, they settle in New Orleans.

1871   Birth of son, Jean.

1873   Birth of Oscar.

1874   Birth of George.

1876   Birth of Frederick.

1878   Birth of Felix.

1879   The Chopins move to Cloutierville in Natchitoches Parish, Louisiana. Kate's only daughter, Lelia, born.

1882* Oscar dies of swamp fever; Kate takes up the family business responsibilities.

1884   Kate returns to St. Louis to live with her mother.

1885   Mrs. O'Flaherty dies.

1889   A Chicago magazine, *America*, publishes Kate's poem, "If It Might Be." Two short stories appear: "Wiser Than a God" and "A Point at Issue."

1890   *At Fault*, her first novel, is published.

1891   A second novel, *Young Dr. Gosse*, is completed.

1894   *Bayou Folk* (a collection of stories and sketches) is published by Houghton Mifflin.

1895   *An Embarrassing Position* (a one-act comedy) is published in the *Mirror* in St. Louis.

---

*Although biographers disagree about the date of Oscar's death, a copy of an order for a casket which was made out in 1882 (and which is now at the Bayou Folk Museum in Cloutierville) seems sufficient evidence for accepting that year as the correct date.

1897 *A Night in Acadie,* another collection of stories, is published by Way and Williams.

1899 *The Awakening* is published by Herbert S. Stone and Company.

1904 After a visit to the St. Louis World's Fair on August 30, 1904, she dies of a brain hemorrhage.

Selected Bibliography

OTHER WORKS BY KATE CHOPIN

At Fault. St. Louis: Nixon-Jones Printing Company, 1890.
Bayou Folk. Boston and New York: Houghton-Mifflin, 1894.
A Night in Acadie. Chicago: Way and Williams, 1897.
All of the above, as well as *The Awakening*, are reprinted in *The Complete Works of Kate Chopin*. 2 vols. Edited with an introduction by Per Seyersted. Baton Rouge: Louisiana State University Press, 1969.

BIOGRAPHY AND CRITICISM

Arms, George. "Kate Chopin's *The Awakening* in the Perspective of Her Literary Career." *Essays in American Literature in Honor of Jay B. Hubbell*. Ed. Clarence Gohdes. Durham: University of North Carolina Press, 1967.

Arner, Robert D. "Kate Chopin's Realism: 'At the 'Cadian Ball' and 'The Storm.' " *The Markham Review*, 2 (1970), 1–4.

————. " 'Désirée's Baby.' " *Mississippi Quarterly*, 25 (Spring 1972), 131–140.

Arnavon, Cyrille. "Les Débuts du Roman réaliste américain et l'influence française. *Romanciers Americains Contemporains* (Cahiers des Langues Modernes). Ed Henri Kerst. Paris: Didier, 1946, pp. 9–36.

Bender, Bert. "Kate Chopin's Lyric Short Stories." *Studies in Short Fiction*, 11 (Summer 1974), 257–266.

Cantwell, Robert. "*The Awakening* by Kate Chopin." *Georgia Review*, 10 (Winter 1956), 489–494.

Eble, Kenneth. "A Forgotten Novel: Kate Chopin's *The Awakening*." *Western Humanities Review*, 10 (Summer 1956), 261–269.

Fletcher, Marie. "The Southern Woman in the Fiction of Kate Chopin." *Louisiana History*, 7 (Spring 1966), 117–132.

Gartner, Carol B. "Three Ednas." *The Kate Chopin Newsletter*, 1 (Winter 1975–1976), 11–20.

Gaude, Pamela. " 'The Storm': A Study of Maupassant's Influence." *The Kate Chopin Newsletter*, 1 (Fall 1975), 1–6.

Leary, Lewis. "Kate Chopin's Other Novel." *The Southern Literary Journal*, 1 (Autumn 1968), 60–74.

———. *Southern Excursions: Essays on Mark Twain and Others.* Baton Rouge: Louisiana State University Press, 1971.

May, John R. "Local Color in *The Awakening*." *Southern Review*, 6 (1970), 1031–1040.

Moore, Sue V. "Mrs. Kate Chopin." *St. Louis Life*, 10 (9 June 1894), 11–12.

Pattee, Fred Lewis. *The Development of the American Short Story.* New York: Biblo and Tannen, 1923, pp. 324–327.

Potter, Richard H. "Negroes in the Fiction of Kate Chopin." *Louisiana History*, 12 (Winter 1971), 41–58.

Rankin, Daniel S. *Kate Chopin and Her Creole Stories.* Philadelphia: The University of Pennsylvania Press, 1932.

Ringe, Donald A. "Romantic Imagery in Kate Chopin's *The Awakening*." *American Literature*, 43 (January 1972), 580–588.

Rocks, James E. "Kate Chopin's Ironic Vision." *Revue de Louisiane*, 1 (Winter 1972), 110–120.

Rosen, Kenneth M. "Kate Chopin's *The Awakening*: Ambiguity as Art." *Journal of American Studies*, 5 (August 1971), 197–200.

Seyersted, Per. "Kate Chopin: An Important St. Louis Writer Reconsidered." *Missouri Historical Society Bulletin*, 19 (January 1963), 89–114.

———. *Kate Chopin: A Critical Biography.* Baton Rouge: Louisiana State University Press, 1969.

Skaggs, Merrill M. *The Folk of Southern Fiction.* Athens: University of Georgia Press, 1972, pp. 182–188.

Spangler, George. "Kate Chopin's *The Awakening*: A Partial Dissent." *Novel*, 3 (1970) 249–255.

Sullivan, Ruth, and Stewart Smith. "Narrative Stance in Kate Chopin's *The Awakening*." *Studies in American Fiction*, 1 (September 1973), 62–75.

Toth, Emily. "St. Louis and the Fiction of Kate Chopin." *Missouri Historical Society Bulletin*, 32 (October 1975), 33–50.

———. "Kate Chopin Remembered." *The Kate Chopin Newsletter*, 1 (Winter 1975–1976), 21–27.

Wheeler, Otis B. "The Five Awakenings of Edna Pontellier." *Southern Review*, 11 (January 1975), 118–128.

Wolff, Cynthia Griffin. "Thanatos and Eros: Kate Chopin's *The Awakening*." *American Quarterly*, 25 (October 1973), 449–471.

Ziff, Larzer. *The American 1890s: Life and Times of a Lost Generation.* New York: Viking Press, 1966, pp. 296–305.

Zlotnick, Joan. "A Woman's Will: Kate Chopin on Selfhood, Wifehood and Motherhood." *The Markham Review*, 3 (October 1968) 1–5.

The Awakening

I

A GREEN and yellow parrot, which hung in a cage outside the door, kept repeating over and over:

"Allez vous-en! Allez vous-en! Sapristi![1] That's all right!"

He could speak a little Spanish, and also a language which nobody understood, unless it was the mocking-bird that hung on the other side of the door, whistling his fluty notes out upon the breeze with maddening persistence.

Mr. Pontellier, unable to read his newspaper with any degree of comfort, arose with an expression and an exclamation of disgust. He walked down the gallery and across the narrow "bridges" which connected the Lebrun cottages one with the other. He had been seated before the door of the main house. The parrot and the mocking-bird were the property of Madame Lebrun, and they had the right to make all the noise they wished. Mr. Pontellier had the privilege of quitting their society when they ceased to be entertaining.

He stopped before the door of his own cottage, which was the fourth one from the main building and next to the last. Seating himself in a wicker rocker which was there, he once more applied himself to the task of reading the newspaper. The day was Sunday; the paper was a day old. The Sunday papers had not yet reached Grand Isle. He was already acquainted with the market reports, and he glanced restlessly over the editorials and bits of news which he had not had time to read before quitting New Orleans the day before.

Mr. Pontellier wore eye-glasses. He was a man of forty, of medium height and rather slender build; he stooped a little. His hair was brown and straight, parted on one side. His beard was neatly and closely trimmed.

Once in a while he withdrew his glance from the newspaper and looked about him. There was more noise than ever over at the house. The main building was called "the house," to distinguish it from the cottages. The chattering and whis-

[1]"Get out! Get out! Damnation!"

1

tling birds were still at it. Two young girls, the Farival twins, were playing a duet from "Zampa" upon the piano. Madame Lebrun was bustling in and out, giving orders in a high key to a yard-boy whenever she got inside the house, and directions in an equally high voice to a dining-room servant whenever she got outside. She was a fresh, pretty woman, clad always in white with elbow sleeves. Her starched skirts crinkled as she came and went. Farther down, before one of the cottages, a lady in black was walking demurely up and down, telling her beads. A good many persons of the *pension*[2] had gone over to the *Chênière Caminada*[3] in Beaudelet's lugger to hear mass. Some young people were out under the wateroaks playing croquet. Mr. Pontellier's two children were there—sturdy little fellows of four and five. A quadroon nurse followed them about with a far-away, meditative air.

Mr. Pontellier finally lit a cigar and began to smoke, letting the paper drag idly from his hand. He fixed his gaze upon a white sunshade that was advancing at snail's pace from the beach. He could see it plainly between the gaunt trunks of the water-oaks and across the stretch of yellow camomile. The gulf looked far away, melting hazily into the blue of the horizon. The sunshade continued to approach slowly. Beneath its pink-lined shelter were his wife, Mrs. Pontellier, and young Robert Lebrun. When they reached the cottage, the two seated themselves with some appearance of fatigue upon the upper step of the porch, facing each other, each leaning against a supporting post.

"What folly! to bathe at such an hour in such heat!" exclaimed Mr. Pontellier. He himself had taken a plunge at daylight. That was why the morning seemed long to him.

"You are burnt beyond recognition," he added, looking at his wife as one looks at a valuable piece of personal property which has suffered some damage. She held up her hands, strong, shapely hands, and surveyed them critically, drawing up her lawn sleeves above the wrists. Looking at them reminded her of her rings, which she had given to her husband before leaving for the beach. She silently reached out to him, and he, understanding, took the rings from his vest pocket and dropped them into her open palm. She slipped them upon her fingers; then clasping her knees, she looked across

2Small hotel.
3Like Grand Isle, an island in Jefferson Parish, Louisiana—a resort area for Creole families of New Orleans.

at Robert and began to laugh. The rings sparkled upon her fingers. He sent back an answering smile.

"What is it?" asked Pontellier, looking lazily and amused from one to the other. It was some utter nonsense; some adventure out there in the water, and they both tried to relate it at once. It did not seem half so amusing when told. They realized this, and so did Mr. Pontellier. He yawned and stretched himself. Then he got up, saying he had half a mind to go over to Klein's hotel and play a game of billiards.

"Come go along, Lebrun," he proposed to Robert. But Robert admitted quite frankly that he preferred to stay where he was and talk to Mrs. Pontellier.

"Well, send him about his business when he bores you, Edna," instructed her husband as he prepared to leave.

"Here, take the umbrella," she exclaimed, holding it out to him. He accepted the sunshade, and lifting it over his head descended the steps and walked away.

"Coming back to dinner?" his wife called after him. He halted a moment and shrugged his shoulders. He felt in his vest pocket; there was a ten-dollar bill there. He did not know; perhaps he would return for the early dinner and perhaps he would not. It all depended upon the company which he found over at Klein's and the size of "the game." He did not say this, but she understood it, and laughed, nodding good-by to him.

Both children wanted to follow their father when they saw him starting out. He kissed them and promised to bring them back bonbons and peanuts.

II

Mrs. Pontellier's eyes were quick and bright; they were a yellowish brown, about the color of her hair. She had a way of turning them swiftly upon an object and holding them there as if lost in some inward maze of contemplation or thought.

Her eyebrows were a shade darker than her hair. They were thick and almost horizontal, emphasizing the depth of her eyes. She was rather handsome than beautiful. Her face was captivating by reason of a certain frankness of expression and a contradictory subtle play of features. Her manner was engaging.

Robert rolled a cigarette. He smoked cigarettes because he could not afford cigars, he said. He had a cigar in his pocket

which Mr. Pontellier had presented him with, and he was
saving it for his after-dinner smoke.

This seemed quite proper and natural on his part. In coloring he was not unlike his companion. A clean-shaved face
made the resemblance more pronounced than it would otherwise have been. There rested no shadow of care upon his
open countenance. His eyes gathered in and reflected the light
and languor of the summer day.

Mrs. Pontellier reached over for a palm-leaf fan that lay on
the porch and began to fan herself, while Robert sent between his lips light puffs from his cigarette. They chatted
incessantly: about the things around them; their amusing adventure out in the water—it had again assumed its entertaining aspect; about the wind, the trees, the people who had
gone to the *Chênière;* about the children playing croquet under the oaks, and the Farival twins, who were now performing the overture to "The Poet and the Peasant."

Robert talked a good deal about himself. He was very
young, and did not know any better. Mrs. Pontellier talked a
little about herself for the same reason. Each was interested
in what the other said. Robert spoke of his intention to go to
Mexico in the autumn, where fortune awaited him. He was
always intending to go to Mexico, but some way never got
there. Meanwhile he held on to his modest position in a mer-
cantile house in New Orleans, where an equal familiarity
with English, French and Spanish gave him no small value as
a clerk and correspondent.

He was spending his summer vacation, as he always did,
with his mother at Grand Isle. In former times, before Robert
could remember, "the house" had been a summer luxury of
the Lebruns. Now, flanked by its dozen or more cottages,
which were always filled with exclusive visitors from the
"Quartier Français,"[4] it enabled Madame Lebrun to maintain
the easy and comfortable existence which appeared to be her
birthright.

Mrs. Pontellier talked about her father's Mississippi plantation and her girlhood home in the old Kentucky blue-grass
country. She was an American woman, with a small infusion
of French which seemed to have been lost in dilution. She
read a letter from her sister, who was away in the East, and
who had engaged herself to be married. Robert was interested, and wanted to know what manner of girls the sisters

[4]French Quarter of New Orleans.

were, what the father was like, and how long the mother had been dead.

When Mrs. Pontellier folded the letter it was time for her to dress for the early dinner.

"I see Léonce isn't coming back," she said, with a glance in the direction whence her husband had disappeared. Robert supposed he was not, as there were a good many New Orleans club men over at Klein's.

When Mrs. Pontellier left him to enter her room, the young man descended the steps and strolled over toward the croquet players, where, during the half-hour before dinner, he amused himself with the little Pontellier children, who were very fond of him.

III

It was eleven o'clock that night when Mr. Pontellier returned from Klein's hotel. He was in an excellent humor, in high spirits, and very talkative. His entrance awoke his wife, who was in bed and fast asleep when he came in. He talked to her while he undressed, telling her anecdotes and bits of news and gossip that he had gathered during the day. From his trousers pockets he took a fistful of crumpled bank notes and a good deal of silver coin, which he piled on the bureau indiscriminately with keys, knife, handkerchief, and whatever else happened to be in his pockets. She was overcome with sleep, and answered him with little half utterances.

He thought it very discouraging that his wife, who was the sole object of his existence, evinced so little interest in things which concerned him, and valued so little his conversation.

Mr. Pontellier had forgotten the bonbons and peanuts for the boys. Notwithstanding he loved them very much, and went into the adjoining room where they slept to take a look at them and make sure that they were resting comfortably. The result of his investigation was far from satisfactory. He turned and shifted the youngsters about in bed. One of them began to kick and talk about a basket full of crabs.

Mr. Pontellier returned to his wife with the information that Raoul had a high fever and needed looking after. Then he lit a cigar and went and sat near the open door to smoke it.

Mrs. Pontellier was quite sure Raoul had no fever. He had gone to bed perfectly well, she said, and nothing had ailed him all day. Mr. Pontellier was too well acquainted with fe-

ver symptoms to be mistaken. He assured her the child was
consuming at that moment in the next room.

He reproached his wife with her inattention, her habitual
neglect of the children. If it was not a mother's place to look
after children, whose on earth was it? He himself had his
hands full with his brokerage business. He could not be in
two places at once; making a living for his family on the
street, and staying at home to see that no harm befell them.
He talked in a monotonous, insistent way.

Mrs. Pontellier sprang out of bed and went into the next
room. She soon came back and sat on the edge of the bed,
leaning her head down on the pillow. She said nothing, and
refused to answer her husband when he questioned her.
When his cigar was smoked out he went to bed, and in half a
minute he was fast asleep.

Mrs. Pontellier was by that time thoroughly awake. She began to cry a little, and wiped her eyes on the sleeve of her
peignoir. Blowing out the candle, which her husband had left
burning, she slipped her bare feet into a pair of satin *mules*
at the foot of the bed and went out on the porch, where she
sat down in the wicker chair and began to rock gently to and
fro.

It was then past midnight. The cottages were all dark. A
single faint light gleamed out from the hallway of the house.
There was no sound abroad except the hooting of an old owl
in the top of a water-oak, and the everlasting voice of the
sea, that was not uplifted at that soft hour. It broke like a
mournful lullaby upon the night.

The tears came so fast to Mrs. Pontellier's eyes that the
damp sleeve of her *peignoir* no longer served to dry them.
She was holding the back of her chair with one hand; her
loose sleeve had slipped almost to the shoulder of her uplifted
arm. Turning, she thrust her face, steaming and wet, into the
bend of her arm, and she went on crying there, not caring
any longer to dry her face, her eyes, her arms. She could not
have told why she was crying. Such experiences as the foregoing were not uncommon in her married life. They seemed
never before to have weighed much against the abundance of
her husband's kindness and a uniform devotion which had
come to be tacit and self-understood.

An indescribable oppression, which seemed to generate in
some unfamiliar part of her consciousness, filled her whole
being with a vague anguish. It was like a shadow, like a mist
passing across her soul's summer day. It was strange and un-

familiar; it was a mood. She did not sit there inwardly up-braiding her husband, lamenting at Fate, which had directed her footsteps to the path which they had taken. She was just having a good cry all to herself. The mosquitoes made merry over her, biting her firm, round arms and nipping at her bare insteps.

The little stinging, buzzing imps succeeded in dispelling a mood which might have held her there in the darkness half a night longer.

The following morning Mr. Pontellier was up in good time to take the rockaway[5] which was to convey him to the steamer at the wharf. He was returning to the city to his business, and they would not see him again at the Island till the coming Saturday. He had regained his composure, which seemed to have been somewhat impaired the night before. He was eager to be gone, as he looked forward to a lively week in Carondelet Street.

Mr. Pontellier gave his wife half of the money which he had brought away from Klein's hotel the evening before. She liked money as well as most women, and accepted it with no little satisfaction.

"It will buy a handsome wedding present for Sister Janet!" she exclaimed, smoothing out the bills as she counted them one by one.

"Oh! we'll treat Sister Janet better than that, my dear," he laughed, as he prepared to kiss her good-by.

The boys were tumbling about, clinging to his legs, implor-ing that numerous things be brought back to them. Mr. Pon-tellier was a great favorite, and ladies, men, children, even nurses, were always on hand to say good-by to him. His wife stood smiling and waving, the boys shouting, as he disap-peared in the old rockaway down the sandy road.

A few days later a box arrived for Mrs. Pontellier from New Orleans. It was from her husband. It was filled with *fri-andises*,[6] with luscious and toothsome bits—the finest of fruits, *patés*, a rare bottle or two, delicious syrups, and bon-bons in abundance.

Mrs. Pontellier was always very generous with the contents of such a box; she was quite used to receiving them when away from home. The *patés* and fruit were brought to the dining-room; the bonbons were passed around. And the

[5]A light, horse-drawn carriage.
[6]Goodies.

ladies, selecting with dainty and discriminating fingers and a little greedily, all declared that Mr. Pontellier was the best husband in the world. Mrs. Pontellier was forced to admit that she knew of none better.

IV

It would have been a difficult matter for Mr. Pontellier to define to his own satisfaction or any one else's wherein his wife failed in her duty toward their children. It was something which he felt rather than perceived, and he never voiced the feeling without subsequent regret and ample atonement.

If one of the little Pontellier boys took a tumble whilst at play, he was not apt to rush crying to his mother's arms for comfort; he would more likely pick himself up, wipe the water out of his eyes and the sand out of his mouth, and go on playing. Tots as they were, they pulled together and stood their ground in childish battles with double fists and uplifted voices, which usually prevailed against the other mother-tots. The quadroon nurse was looked upon as a huge encumbrance, only good to button up waists and panties and to brush and part hair; since it seemed to be a law of society that hair must be parted and brushed.

In short, Mrs. Pontellier was not a mother-woman. The mother-women seemed to prevail that summer at Grand Isle. It was easy to know them, fluttering about with extended, protecting wings when any harm, real or imaginary, threatened their precious brood. They were women who idolized their children, worshiped their husbands, and esteemed it a holy privilege to efface themselves as individuals and grow wings as ministering angels.

Many of them were delicious in the rôle; one of them was the embodiment of every womanly grace and charm. If her husband did not adore her, he was a brute, deserving of death by slow torture. Her name was Adèle Ratignolle. There are no words to describe her save the old ones that have served so often to picture the by-gone heroine of romance and the fair lady of our dreams. There was nothing subtle or hidden about her charms; her beauty was all there, flaming and apparent: the spun-gold hair that comb nor confining pin could restrain; the blue eyes that were like nothing but sapphires; two lips that pouted, that were so red one could only think of cherries or some other delicious crimson fruit in looking at them. She was growing a little stout, but it did not seem to detract an iota from the grace of every step, pose, gesture. One would not have wanted her white neck a mite less full or her beautiful arms more slender. Never were hands more exquisite than hers, and it was a joy to look at them when she threaded her needle or adjusted her gold thimble to her taper middle finger as she sewed away on the little night-drawers or fashioned a bodice or a bib.

Madame Ratignolle was very fond of Mrs. Pontellier, and often she took her sewing and went over to sit with her in the afternoons. She was sitting there the afternoon of the day the box arrived from New Orleans. She had possession of the rocker, and she was busily engaged in sewing upon a diminutive pair of night-drawers.

She had brought the pattern of the drawers for Mrs. Pontellier to cut out—a marvel of construction, fashioned to enclose a baby's body so effectually that only two small eyes might look out from the garment, like an Eskimo's. They were designed for winter wear, when treacherous drafts came down chimneys and insidious currents of deadly cold found their way through key-holes.

Mrs. Pontellier's mind was quite at rest concerning the present material needs of her children, and she could not see the use of anticipating and making winter night garments the subject of her summer meditations. But she did not want to appear unamiable and uninterested, so she had brought forth newspapers, which she spread upon the floor of the gallery, and under Madame Ratignolle's directions she had cut a pattern of the impervious garment.

Robert was there, seated as he had been the Sunday before, and Mrs. Pontellier also occupied her former position on the upper step, leaning listlessly against the post. Beside her was a box of bonbons, which she held out at intervals to Madame Ratignolle.

That lady seemed at a loss to make a selection, but finally settled upon a stick of nugat, wondering if it were not too rich; whether it could possibly hurt her. Madame Ratignolle had been married seven years. About every two years she had a baby. At that time she had three babies, and was beginning to think of a fourth one. She was always talking about her "condition." Her "condition" was in no way apparent, and no one would have known a thing about it but for her persistence in making it the subject of conversation.

Robert started to reassure her, asserting that he had known a lady who had subsisted upon nugat during the entire—but seeing the color mount into Mrs. Pontellier's face he checked himself and changed the subject.

Mrs. Pontellier, though she had married a Creole, was not thoroughly at home in the society of Creoles; never before had she been thrown so intimately among them. There were only Creoles that summer at Lebrun's. They all knew each other, and felt like one large family, among whom existed the most amicable relations. A characteristic which distinguished them and which impressed Mrs. Pontellier most forcibly was their entire absence of prudery. Their freedom of expression was at first incomprehensible to her, though she had no difficulty in reconciling it with a lofty chastity which in the Creole woman seems to be inborn and unmistakable.

Never would Edna Pontellier forget the shock with which she heard Madame Ratignolle relating to old Monsieur Farival the harrowing story of one of her *accouchements*,[7] withholding no intimate detail. She was growing accustomed to like shocks, but she could not keep the mounting color back from her cheeks. Oftener than once her coming had interrupted the droll story with which Robert was entertaining some amused group of married women.

A book had gone the rounds of the *pension*. When it came her turn to read it, she did so with profound astonishment. She felt moved to read the book in secret and solitude, though none of the others had done so—to hide it from view at the sound of approaching footsteps. It was openly criticised and freely discussed at table. Mrs. Pontellier gave over being astonished, and concluded that wonders would never cease.

V

They formed a congenial group sitting there that summer afternoon—Madame Ratignolle sewing away, often stopping to relate a story or incident with much expressive gesture of her perfect hands; Robert and Mrs. Pontellier sitting idle, exchanging occasional words, glances or smiles which indicated a certain advanced stage of intimacy and *camaraderie*.

He had lived in her shadow during the past month. No one thought anything of it. Many had predicted that Robert would devote himself to Mrs. Pontellier when he arrived. Since the age of fifteen, which was eleven years before, Robert each summer at Grand Isle had constituted himself

[7] Childbirths.

the devoted attendant of some fair dame or damsel. Sometimes it was a young girl, again a widow; but as often as not it was some interesting married woman.

For two consecutive seasons he lived in the sunlight of Mademoiselle Duvigné's presence. But she died between summers; then Robert posed as an inconsolable, prostrating himself at the feet of Madame Ratignolle for whatever crumbs of sympathy and comfort she might be pleased to vouchsafe.

Mrs. Pontellier liked to sit and gaze at her fair companion as she might look upon a faultless Madonna.

"Could any one fathom the cruelty beneath that fair exterior?" murmured Robert. "She knew that I adored her once, and she let me adore her. It was 'Robert, come; go; stand up; sit down; do this; do that; see if the baby sleeps; my thimble, please, that I left God knows where. Come and read Daudet to me while I sew.' "

"*Par exemple!* I never had to ask. You were always there under my feet, like a troublesome cat."

"You mean like an adoring dog. And just as soon as Ratignolle appeared on the scene, then it *was* like a dog. '*Passez! Adieu! Allez vous-en!*' "[8]

"Perhaps I feared to make Alphonse jealous," she interjoined, with excessive naïveté. That made them all laugh. The right hand jealous of the left! The heart jealous of the soul! But for that matter, the Creole husband is never jealous; with him the gangrene passion is one which has become dwarfed by disuse.

Meanwhile Robert, addressing Mrs. Pontellier, continued to tell of his one time hopeless passion for Madame Ratignolle; of sleepless nights, of consuming flames till the very sea sizzled when he took his daily plunge. While the lady at the needle kept up a little running, contemptuous comment:

"*Blagueur—farceur—gros bête, va!*"[9]

He never assumed this serio-comic tone when alone with Mrs. Pontellier. She never knew precisely what to make of it; at that moment it was impossible for her to guess how much of it was jest and what proportion was earnest. It was understood that he had often spoken words of love to Madame Ratignolle, without any thought of being taken seriously. Mrs. Pontellier was glad he had not assumed a similar rôle toward herself. It would have been unacceptable and annoying.

[8]"Go along! Good-bye! Out you go!"
[9]"Joker—phony—monster!"

Mrs. Pontellier had brought her sketching materials, which she sometimes dabbled with in an unprofessional way. She liked the dabbling. She felt in it satisfaction of a kind which no other employment afforded her.

She had long wished to try herself on Madame Ratignolle. Never had that lady seemed a more tempting subject than at that moment, seated there like some sensuous Madonna, with the gleam of the fading day enriching her splendid color.

Robert crossed over and seated himself upon the step below Mrs. Pontellier, that he might watch her work. She handled her brushes with a certain ease and freedom which came, not from long and close acquaintance with them, but from a natural aptitude. Robert followed her work with close attention, giving forth little ejaculatory expressions of appreciation in French, which he addressed to Madame Ratignolle.

"Mais ce n'est pas mal! Elle s'y connait, elle a de la force, oui."[10]

During his oblivious attention he once quietly rested his head against Mrs. Pontellier's arm. As gently she repulsed him. Once again he repeated the offense. She could not but believe it to be thoughtlessness on his part; yet that was no reason she should submit to it. She did not remonstrate, except again to repulse him quietly but firmly. He offered no apology.

The picture completed bore no resemblance to Madame Ratignolle. She was greatly disappointed to find that it did not look like her. But it was a fair enough piece of work, and in many respects satisfying.

Mrs. Pontellier evidently did not think so. After surveying the sketch critically she drew a broad smudge of paint across its surface, and crumpled the paper between her hands.

The youngsters came tumbling up the steps, the quadroon following at the respectful distance which they required her to observe. Mrs. Pontellier made them carry her paints and things into the house. She sought to detain them for a little talk and some pleasantry. But they were greatly in earnest. They had only come to investigate the contents of the bonbon box. They accepted without murmuring what she chose to give them, each holding out two chubby hands scoop-like, in the vain hope that they might be filled; and then away they went.

The sun was low in the west, and the breeze soft and lan-

---

[10]"It's not bad at all. She knows what she's doing; she has talent, indeed she has."

guorous that came up from the south, charged with the seductive odor of the sea. Children, freshly befurbelowed, were gathering for their games under the oaks. Their voices were high and penetrating.

Madame Ratignolle folded her sewing, placing thimble, scissors and thread all neatly together in the roll, which she pinned securely. She complained of faintness. Mrs. Pontellier flew for the cologne water and a fan. She bathed Madame Ratignolle's face with cologne, while Robert plied the fan with unnecessary vigor.

The spell was soon over, and Mrs. Pontellier could not help wondering if there were not a little imagination responsible for its origin, for the rose tint had never faded from her friend's face.

She stood watching the fair woman walk down the long line of galleries with the grace and majesty which queens are sometimes supposed to possess. Her little ones ran to meet her. Two of them clung about her white skirts, the third she took from its nurse and with a thousand endearments bore it along in her own fond, encircling arms. Though, as everybody well knew, the doctor had forbidden her to lift so much as a pin!

"Are you going bathing?" asked Robert of Mrs. Pontellier. It was not so much a question as a reminder.

"Oh, no," she answered, with a tone of indecision. "I'm tired; I think not." Her glance wandered from his face away toward the Gulf, whose sonorous murmur reached her like a loving but imperative entreaty.

"Oh, come!" he insisted. "You mustn't miss your bath. Come on. The water must be delicious; it will not hurt you. Come."

He reached up for her big, rough straw hat that hung on a peg outside the door, and put it on her head. They descended the steps, and walked away together toward the beach. The sun was low in the west and the breeze was soft and warm.

VI

Edna Pontellier could not have told why, wishing to go to the beach with Robert, she should in the first place have declined, and in the second place have followed in obedience to one of the two contradictory impulses which impelled her.

A certain light was beginning to dawn dimly within her,— the light which, showing the way, forbids it.

At that early period it served but to bewilder her. It moved her to dreams, to thoughtfulness, to the shadowy anguish which had overcome her the midnight when she had abandoned herself to tears.

In short, Mrs. Pontellier was beginning to realize her position in the universe as a human being, and to recognize her relations as an individual to the world within and about her. This may seem like a ponderous weight of wisdom to descend upon the soul of a young woman of twenty-eight—perhaps more wisdom than the Holy Ghost is usually pleased to vouchsafe to any woman.

But the beginning of things, of a world especially, is necessarily vague, tangled, chaotic, and exceedingly disturbing. How few of us ever emerge from such beginning! How many souls perish in its tumult!

The voice of the sea is seductive; never ceasing, whispering, clamoring, murmuring, inviting the soul to wander for a spell in abysses of solitude; to lose itself in mazes of inward contemplation.

The voice of the sea speaks to the soul. The touch of the sea is sensuous, enfolding the body in its soft, close embrace.

VII

Mrs. Pontellier was not a woman given to confidences, a characteristic hitherto contrary to her nature. Even as a child she had lived her own small life all within herself. At a very early period she had apprehended instinctively the dual life—that outward existence which conforms, the inward life which questions.

That summer at Grand Isle she began to loosen a little the mantle of reserve that had always enveloped her. There may have been—there must have been—influences, both subtle and apparent, working in their several ways to induce her to do this; but the most obvious was the influence of Adèle Ratignolle. The excessive physical charm of the Creole had first attracted her, for Edna had a sensuous susceptibility to beauty. Then the candor of the woman's whole existence, which every one might read, and which formed so striking a contrast to her own habitual reserve—this might have furnished a link. Who can tell what metals the gods use in forging the subtle bond which we call sympathy, which we might as well call love.

The two women went away one morning to the beach together, arm in arm, under the huge white sunshade. Edna had prevailed upon Madame Ratignolle to leave the children behind, though she could not induce her to relinquish a diminutive roll of needlework, which Adèle begged to be allowed to slip into the depths of her pocket. In some unaccountable way they had escaped from Robert.

The walk to the beach was no inconsiderable one, consisting as it did of a long, sandy path, upon which a sporadic and tangled growth that bordered it on either side made frequent and unexpected inroads. There were acres of yellow camomile reaching out on either hand. Further away still, vegetable gardens abounded, with frequent small plantations of orange or lemon trees intervening. The dark green clusters glistened from afar in the sun.

The women were both of goodly height, Madame Ratignolle possessing the more feminine and matronly figure. The charm of Edna Pontellier's physique stole insensibly upon you. The lines of her body were long, clean and symmetrical; it was a body which occasionally fell into splendid poses; there was no suggestion of the trim, stereotyped fashion-plate about it. A casual and indiscriminating observer, in passing, might not cast a second glance upon the figure. But with more feeling and discernment he would have recognized the noble beauty of its modeling, and the graceful severity of poise and movement, which made Edna Pontellier different from the crowd.

She wore a cool muslin that morning—white, with a waving vertical line of brown running through it; also a white linen collar and the big straw hat which she had taken from the peg outside the door. The hat rested any way on her yellow-brown hair, that waved a little, was heavy, and clung close to her head.

Madame Ratignolle, more careful of her complexion, had twined a gauze veil about her head. She wore dogskin gloves, with gauntlets that protected her wrists. She was dressed in pure white, with a fluffiness of ruffles that became her. The draperies and fluttering things which she wore suited her rich, luxuriant beauty as a greater severity of line could not have done.

There were a number of bath-houses along the beach, of rough but solid construction, built with small, protecting galleries facing the water. Each house consisted of two compartments, and each family at Lebrun's possessed a compartment for itself, fitted out with all the essential paraphernalia of the bath and whatever other conveniences the owners might desire. The two women had no intention of bathing; they had just strolled down to the beach for a walk and to be alone and near the water. The Pontellier and Ratignolle compartments adjoined one another under the same roof.

Mrs. Pontellier had brought down her key through force of habit. Unlocking the door of her bath-room she went inside, and soon emerged, bringing a rug, which she spread upon the floor of the gallery, and two huge hair pillows covered with crash, which she placed against the front of the building.

The two seated themselves there in the shade of the porch, side by side, with their backs against the pillows and their feet extended. Madame Ratignolle removed her veil, wiped her face with a rather delicate handkerchief, and fanned herself with the fan which she always carried suspended somewhere about her person by a long, narrow ribbon. Edna removed her collar and opened her dress at the throat. She took the fan from Madame Ratignolle and began to fan both herself and her companion. It was very warm, and for a while they did nothing but exchange remarks about the heat, the sun, the glare. But there was a breeze blowing, a choppy, stiff wind that whipped the water into froth. It fluttered the skirts of the two women and kept them for a while engaged in adjusting, readjusting, tucking in, securing hair-pins and hat-pins. A few persons were sporting some distance away in the water. The beach was very still of human sound at that hour. The lady in black was reading her morning devotions on the porch of a neighboring bath-house. Two young lovers were exchanging their hearts' yearnings beneath the children's tent, which they had found unoccupied.

Edna Pontellier, casting her eyes about, had finally kept them at rest upon the sea. The day was clear and carried the gaze out as far as the blue sky went; there were a few white clouds suspended idly over the horizon. A lateen sail was visible in the direction of Cat Island, and others to the south seemed almost motionless in the far distance.

"Of whom—of what are you thinking?" asked Adèle of her companion, whose countenance she had been watching with a little amused attention, arrested by the absorbed expression which seemed to have seized and fixed every feature into a statuesque repose.

"Nothing," returned Mrs. Pontellier, with a start, adding at once: "How stupid! But it seems to me it is the reply we make instinctively to such a question. Let me see," she went on, throwing back her head and narrowing her fine eyes till they shone like two vivid points of light. "Let me see. I was really not conscious of thinking of anything; but perhaps I can retrace my thoughts."

"Oh! never mind!" laughed Madame Ratignolle. "I am not quite so exacting. I will let you off this time. It is really too hot to think, especially to think about thinking."

"But for the fun of it," persisted Edna. "First of all, the sight of the water stretching so far away, those motionless sails against the blue sky, made a delicious picture that I just wanted to sit and look at. The hot wind beating in my face made me think—without any connection that I can trace—of a summer day in Kentucky, of a meadow that seemed as big as the ocean to the very little girl walking through the grass, which was higher than her waist. She threw out her arms as if swimming when she walked, beating the tall grass as one strikes out in the water. Oh, I see the connection now!"

"Where were you going that day in Kentucky, walking through the grass?"

"I don't remember now. I was just walking diagonally across a big field. My sun-bonnet obstructed the view. I could see only the stretch of green before me, and I felt as if I must walk on forever, without coming to the end of it. I don't remember whether I was frightened or pleased. I must have been entertained.

"Likely as not it was Sunday," she laughed; "and I was running away from prayers, from the Presbyterian service, read in a spirit of gloom by my father that chills me yet to think of."

"And have you been running away from prayers ever since, *ma chère?*" asked Madame Ratignolle, amused.

"No! oh, no!" Edna hastened to say. "I was a little unthinking child in those days, just following a misleading impulse without question. On the contrary, during one period of my life religion took a firm hold upon me; after I was twelve and until—until—why, I suppose until now, though I never thought much about it—just driven along by habit. But do you know," she broke off, turning her quick eyes upon Madame Ratignolle and leaning forward a little so as to bring her face quite close to that of her companion, "sometimes I feel this summer as if I were walking through the green meadow again; idly, aimlessly, unthinking and unguided."

Madame Ratignolle laid her hand over that of Mrs. Pontellier, which was near her. Seeing that the hand was not with-

drawn, she clasped it firmly and warmly. She even stroked it
a little, fondly, with the other hand, murmuring in an under-
tone, *"Pauvre chérie."*[11]

The action was at first a little confusing to Edna, but she
soon lent herself readily to the Creole's gentle caress. She was
not accustomed to an outward and spoken expression of affection, either in herself or in others. She and her younger
sister, Janet, had quarreled a good deal through force of unfortunate habit. Her older sister, Margaret, was matronly and
dignified, probably from having assumed matronly and house-
wifely responsibilities too early in life, their mother having
died when they were quite young. Margaret was not effusive;
she was practical. Edna had had an occasional girl friend, but
whether accidentally or not, they seemed to have been all of
one type—the self-contained. She never realized that the
reserve of her own character had much, perhaps everything,
to do with this. Her most intimate friend at school had been
one of rather exceptional intellectual gifts, who wrote fine-
sounding essays, which Edna admired and strove to imitate;
and with her she talked and glowed over the English classics,
and sometimes held religious and political controversies.

Edna often wondered at one propensity which sometimes
had inwardly disturbed her without causing any outward
show or manifestation on her part. At a very early age—perhaps it was when she traversed the ocean of waving grass—
she remembered that she had been passionately enamored of
a dignified and sad-eyed cavalry officer who visited her father
in Kentucky. She could not leave his presence when he was
there, nor remove her eyes from his face, which was something like Napoleon's, with a lock of black hair falling across
the forehead. But the cavalry officer melted imperceptibly out
of her existence.

At another time her affections were deeply engaged by a
young gentleman who visited a lady on a neighboring plantation. It was after they went to Mississippi to live. The young
man was engaged to be married to the young lady, and they
sometimes called upon Margaret, driving over of afternoons
in a buggy. Edna was a little miss, just merging into her
teens; and the realization that she herself was nothing, nothing, nothing to the engaged young man was a bitter affliction
to her. But he, too, went the way of dreams.

She was a grown young woman when she was overtaken

[11]"Poor dear."

by what she supposed to be the climax of her fate. It was when the face and figure of a great tragedian began to haunt her imagination and stir her senses. The persistence of the infatuation lent it an aspect of genuineness. The hopelessness of it colored it with the lofty tones of a great passion.

The picture of the tragedian stood enframed upon her desk. Any one may possess the portrait of a tragedian without exciting suspicion or comment. (This was a sinister reflection which she cherished.) In the presence of others she expressed admiration for his exalted gifts, as she handed the photograph around and dwelt upon the fidelity of the likeness. When alone she sometimes picked it up and kissed the cold glass passionately.

Her marriage to Léonce Pontellier was purely an accident, in this respect resembling many other marriages which masquerade as the decrees of Fate. It was in the midst of her secret great passion that she met him. He fell in love, as men are in the habit of doing, and pressed his suit with an earnestness and an ardor which left nothing to be desired. He pleased her; his absolute devotion flattered her. She fancied there was a sympathy of thought and taste between them, in which fancy she was mistaken. Add to this the violent opposition of her father and her sister Margaret to her marriage with a Catholic, and we need seek no further for the motives which led her to accept Monsieur Pontellier for her husband.

The acme of bliss, which would have been a marriage with the tragedian, was not for her in this world. As the devoted wife of a man who worshiped her, she felt she would take her place with a certain dignity in the world of reality, closing the portals forever behind her upon the realm of romance and dreams.

But it was not long before the tragedian had gone to join the cavalry officer and the engaged young man and a few others; and Edna found herself face to face with the realities. She grew fond of her husband, realizing with some unaccountable satisfaction that no trace of passion or excessive and fictitious warmth colored her affection, thereby threatening its dissolution.

She was fond of her children in an uneven, impulsive way. She would sometimes gather them passionately to her heart; she would sometimes forget them. The year before they had spent part of the summer with their grandmother Pontellier in Iberville. Feeling secure regarding their happiness and welfare, she did not miss them except with an occasional intense longing. Their absence was a sort of relief, though she did not admit this, even to herself. It seemed to free her of a responsibility which she had blindly assumed and for which Fate had not fitted her.

Edna did not reveal so much as all this to Madame Ratignolle that summer day when they sat with faces turned to the sea. But a good part of it escaped her. She had put her head down on Madame Ratignolle's shoulder. She was flushed and felt intoxicated with the sound of her own voice and the unaccustomed taste of candor. It muddled her like wine, or like a first breath of freedom.

There was the sound of approaching voices. It was Robert, surrounded by a troop of children, searching for them. The two little Pontelliers were with him, and he carried Madame Ratignolle's little girl in his arms. There were other children beside, and two nurse-maids followed, looking disagreeable and resigned.

The women at once rose and began to shake out their draperies and relax their muscles. Mrs. Pontellier threw the cushions and rug into the bath-house. The children all scampered off to the awning, and they stood there in a line, gazing upon the intruding lovers, still exchanging their vows and sighs. The lovers got up, with only a silent protest, and walked slowly away somewhere else.

The children possessed themselves of the tent, and Mrs. Pontellier went over to join them.

Madame Ratignolle begged Robert to accompany her to the house; she complained of cramp in her limbs and stiffness of the joints. She leaned draggingly upon his arm as they walked.

VIII

"Do me a favor, Robert," spoke the pretty woman at his side, almost as soon as she and Robert had started on their slow, homeward way. She looked up in his face, leaning on his arm beneath the encircling shadow of the umbrella which he had lifted.

"Granted; as many as you like," he returned, glancing down into her eyes that were full of thoughtfulness and some speculation.

"I only ask for one; let Mrs. Pontellier alone."

"Tiens!" he exclaimed, with a sudden, boyish laugh. *"Voilà que Madame Ratignolle est jalouse!"*[12]

"Nonsense! I'm in earnest; I mean what I say. Let Mrs. Pontellier alone."

"Why?" he asked; himself growing serious at his companion's solicitation.

"She is not one of us; she is not like us. She might make the unfortunate blunder of taking you seriously."

His face flushed with annoyance, and taking off his soft hat he began to beat it impatiently against his leg as he walked. "Why shouldn't she take me seriously?" he demanded sharply. "Am I a comedian, a clown, a jack-in-the-box? Why shouldn't she? You Creoles! I have no patience with you! Am I always to be regarded as a feature of an amusing programme? I hope Mrs. Pontellier does take me seriously. I hope she has discernment enough to find in me something besides the *blagueur*.[13] If I thought there was any doubt——"

"Oh, enough, Robert!" she broke into his heated outburst. "You are not thinking of what you are saying. You speak with about as little reflection as we might expect from one of those children down there playing in the sand. If your attentions to any married woman here were ever offered with any intention of being convincing, you would not be the gentleman we all know you to be, and you would be unfit to associate with the wives and daughters of the people who trust you."

Madame Ratignolle had spoken what she believed to be the law and the gospel. The young man shrugged his shoulders impatiently.

"Oh! well! That isn't it," slamming his hat down vehemently upon his head. "You ought to feel that such things are not flattering to say to a fellow."

"Should our whole intercourse consist of an exchange of compliments? *Ma foi!*"[14]

"It isn't pleasant to have a woman tell you——" he went on, unheedingly, but breaking off suddenly: "Now if I were like Arobin——you remember Alcée Arobin and that story of the consul's wife at Biloxi?" And he related the story of Alcée Arobin and the consul's wife; and another about the tenor of the French Opera, who received letters which should never have been written; and still other stories, grave and gay, till

[12]"There you are; it seems Madame Ratignolle is jealous!"
[13]Clown.
[14]"Really!"

Mrs. Pontellier and her possible propensity for taking young men seriously was apparently forgotten.

Madame Ratignolle, when they had regained her cottage, went in to take the hour's rest which she considered helpful. Before leaving her, Robert begged her pardon for the impatience—he called it rudeness—with which he had received her well-meant caution.

"You made one mistake, Adèle," he said, with a light smile; "there is no earthly possibility of Mrs. Pontellier ever taking me seriously. You should have warned me against taking myself seriously. Your advice might then have carried some weight and given me subject for some reflection. *Au revoir*. But you look tired," he added, solicitously. "Would you like a cup of bouillon? Shall I stir you a toddy? Let me mix you a toddy with a drop of Angostura."

She acceded to the suggestion of bouillon, which was grateful and acceptable. He went himself to the kitchen, which was a building apart from the cottages and lying to the rear of the house. And he himself brought her the golden-brown bouillon, in a dainty Sèvres cup, with a flaky cracker or two on the saucer.

She thrust a bare, white arm from the curtain which shielded her open door, and received the cup from his hands. She told him he was a *bon garçon*, and she meant it. Robert thanked her and turned away toward "the house."

The lovers were just entering the grounds of the *pension*. They were leaning toward each other as the water-oaks bent from the sea. There was not a particle of earth beneath their feet. Their heads might have been turned upside-down, so absolutely did they tread upon blue ether. The lady in black, creeping behind them, looked a trifle paler and more jaded than usual. There was no sign of Mrs. Pontellier and the children. Robert scanned the distance for any such apparition. They would doubtless remain away till the dinner hour. The young man ascended to his mother's room. It was situated at the top of the house, made up of odd angles and a queer sloping ceiling. Two broad dormer windows looked out toward the Gulf, and as far across it as a man's eye might reach. The furnishings of the room were light, cool, and practical.

Madame Lebrun was busily engaged at the sewing-machine. A little black girl sat on the floor, and with her hands worked the treadle of the machine. The Creole woman does not take any chances which may be avoided of imperiling her health.

Robert went over and seated himself on the broad sill of one of the dormer windows. He took a book from his pocket and began energetically to read it, judging by the precision and frequency with which he turned the leaves. The sewing-machine made a resounding clatter in the room; it was of a ponderous, by-gone make. In the lulls, Robert and his mother exchanged bits of desultory conversation.

"Where is Mrs. Pontellier?"

"Down at the beach with the children."

"I promised to lend her the Goncourt. Don't forget to take it down when you go; it's there on the bookshelf over the small table." Clatter, clatter, clatter, bang! for the next five or eight minutes.

"Where is Victor going with the rockaway?"

"The rockaway? Victor?"

"Yes; down there in front. He seems to be getting ready to drive away somewhere."

"Call him." Clatter, clatter!

Robert uttered a shrill, piercing whistle which might have been heard back at the wharf.

"He won't look up."

Madame Lebrun flew to the window. She called "Victor!" She waved a handkerchief and called again. The young fellow below got into the vehicle and started the horse off at a gallop.

Madame Lebrun went back to the machine, crimson with annoyance. Victor was the younger son and brother—a *tête montée*,[15] with a temper which invited violence and a will which no ax could break.

"Whenever you say the word I'm ready to thrash any amount of reason into him that he's able to hold."

"If your father had only lived!" Clatter, clatter, clatter, clatter, bang! It was a fixed belief with Madame Lebrun that the conduct of the universe and all things pertaining thereto would have been manifestly of a more intelligent and higher order had not Monsieur Lebrun been removed to other spheres during the early years of their married life.

"What do you hear from Montel?" Montel was a middle-aged gentleman whose vain ambition and desire for the past twenty years had been to fill the void which Monsieur Le-

[15]Hothead.

brun's taking off had left in the Lebrun household. Clatter, clatter, bang, clatter!

"I have a letter somewhere," looking in the machine drawer and finding the letter in the bottom of the work-basket. "He says to tell you he will be in Vera Cruz the beginning of next month"—clatter, clatter!—"and if you still have the intention of joining him"—bang! clatter, clatter, bang!

"Why didn't you tell me so before, mother? You know I wanted—" Clatter, clatter, clatter!

"Do you see Mrs. Pontellier starting back with the children? She will be in late to luncheon again. She never starts to get ready for luncheon till the last minute." Clatter, clatter! "Where are you going?"

"Where did you say the Goncourt was?"

IX

Every light in the hall was ablaze; every lamp turned as high as it could be without smoking the chimney or threatening explosion. The lamps were fixed at intervals against the wall, encircling the whole room. Some one had gathered orange and lemon branches, and with these fashioned graceful festoons between. The dark green of the branches stood out and glistened against the white muslin curtains which draped the windows, and which puffed, floated, and flapped at the capricious will of a stiff breeze that swept up from the Gulf.

It was Saturday night a few weeks after the intimate conversation held between Robert and Madame Ratignolle on their way from the beach. An unusual number of husbands, fathers, and friends had come down to stay over Sunday; and they were being suitably entertained by their families, with the material help of Madame Lebrun. The dining tables had all been removed to one end of the hall, and the chairs ranged about in rows and in clusters. Each little family group had had its say and exchanged its domestic gossip earlier in the evening. There was now an apparent disposition to relax; to widen the circle of confidences and give a more general tone to the conversation.

Many of the children had been permitted to sit up beyond their usual bedtime. A small band of them were lying on their stomachs on the floor looking at the colored sheets of the comic papers which Mr. Pontellier had brought down.

The little Pontellier boys were permitting them to do so, and making their authority felt.

Music, dancing, and a recitation or two were the entertainments furnished, or rather, offered. But there was nothing systematic about the programme, no appearance of prearrangement nor even premeditation.

At an early hour in the evening the Farival twins were prevailed upon to play the piano. They were girls of fourteen, always clad in the Virgin's colors, blue and white, having been dedicated to the Blessed Virgin at their baptism. They played a duet from "Zampa," and at the earnest solicitation of every one present followed it with the overture to "The Poet and the Peasant."

"*Allez vous-en! Sapristi!*" shrieked the parrot outside the door. He was the only being present who possessed sufficient candor to admit that he was not listening to these gracious performances for the first time that summer. Old Monsieur Farival, grandfather of the twins, grew indignant over the interruption, and insisted upon having the bird removed and consigned to regions of darkness. Victor Lebrun objected; and his decrees were as immutable as those of Fate. The parrot fortunately offered no further interruption to the entertainment, the whole venom of his nature apparently having been cherished up and hurled against the twins in that one impetuous outburst.

Later a young brother and sister gave recitations, which every one present had heard many times at winter evening entertainments in the city.

A little girl performed a skirt dance in the center of the floor. The mother played her accompaniments and at the same time watched her daughter with greedy admiration and nervous apprehension. She need have had no apprehension. The child was mistress of the situation. She had been properly dressed for the occasion in black tulle and black silk tights. Her little neck and arms were bare, and her hair, artificially crimped, stood out like fluffy black plumes over her head. Her poses were full of grace, and her little black-shod toes twinkled as they shot out and upward with a rapidity and suddenness which were bewildering.

But there was no reason why every one should not dance. Madame Ratignolle could not, so it was she who gaily consented to play for the others. She played very well, keeping excellent waltz time and infusing an expression into the strains which was indeed inspiring. She was keeping up her music on account of the children, she said; because she and her husband both considered it a means of brightening the home and making it attractive.

Almost every one danced but the twins, who could not be induced to separate during the brief period when one or the other should be whirling around the room in the arms of a man. They might have danced together, but they did not think of it.

The children were sent to bed. Some went submissively; others with shrieks and protests as they were dragged away. They had been permitted to sit up till after the ice-cream, which naturally marked the limit of human indulgence.

The ice-cream was passed around with cake—gold and silver cake arranged on platters in alternate slices; it had been made and frozen during the afternoon back of the kitchen by two black women, under the supervision of Victor. It was pronounced a great success—excellent if it had only contained a little less vanilla or a little more sugar, if it had been frozen a degree harder, and if the salt might have been kept out of portions of it. Victor was proud of his achievement, and went about recommending it and urging every one to partake of it to excess.

After Mrs. Pontellier had danced twice with her husband, once with Robert, and once with Monsieur Ratignolle, who was thin and tall and swayed like a reed in the wind when he danced, she went out on the gallery and seated herself on the low window-sill, where she commanded a view of all that went on in the hall and could look out toward the Gulf. There was a soft effulgence in the east. The moon was coming up, and its mystic shimmer was casting a million lights across the distant, restless water.

"Would you like to hear Mademoiselle Reisz play?" asked Robert, coming out on the porch where she was. Of course Edna would like to hear Mademoiselle Reisz play; but she feared it would be useless to entreat her.

"I'll ask her," he said. "I'll tell her that you want to hear her. She likes you. She will come." He turned and hurried away to one of the far cottages, where Mademoiselle Reisz was shuffling away. She was dragging a chair in and out of her room, and at intervals objecting to the crying of a baby, which a nurse in the adjoining cottage was endeavoring to put to sleep. She was a disagreeable little woman, no longer young, who had quarreled with almost every one, owing to a temper which was self-assertive and a disposition to trample upon the rights of others. Robert prevailed upon her without any too great difficulty.

She entered the hall with him during a lull in the dance. She made an awkward, imperious little bow as she went in. She was a homely woman, with a small weazened face and body and eyes that glowed. She had absolutely no taste in dress, and wore a batch of rusty black lace with a bunch of artificial violets pinned to the side of her hair.

"Ask Mrs. Pontellier what she would like to hear me play," she requested of Robert. She sat perfectly still before the piano, not touching the keys, while Robert carried her message to Edna at the window. A general air of surprise and genuine satisfaction fell upon every one as they saw the pianist enter. There was a settling down, and a prevailing air of expectancy everywhere. Edna was a trifle embarrassed at being thus signaled out for the imperious little woman's favor. She would not dare to choose, and begged that Mademoiselle Reisz would please herself in her selections.

Edna was what she herself called very fond of music. Musical strains, well rendered, had a way of evoking pictures in her mind. She sometimes liked to sit in the room of mornings when Madame Ratignolle played or practiced. One piece which that lady played Edna had entitled "Solitude." It was a short, plaintive, minor strain. The name of the piece was something else, but she called it "Solitude." When she heard it there came before her imagination the figure of a man standing beside a desolate rock on the seashore. He was naked. His attitude was one of hopeless resignation as he looked toward a distant bird winging its flight away from him.

Another piece called to her mind a dainty young woman clad in an Empire gown, taking mincing dancing steps as she came down a long avenue between tall hedges. Again, another reminded her of children at play, and still another of nothing on earth but a demure lady stroking a cat.

The very first chords which Mademoiselle Reisz struck upon the piano sent a keen tremor down Mrs. Pontellier's spinal column. It was not the first time she had heard an artist at the piano. Perhaps it was the first time she was ready, perhaps the first time her being was tempered to take an impress of the abiding truth.

She waited for the material pictures which she thought would gather and blaze before her imagination. She waited in vain. She saw no pictures of solitude, of hope, of longing, or

of despair. But the very passions themselves were aroused
within her soul, swaying it, lashing it, as the waves daily beat
upon her splendid body. She trembled, she was choking, and
the tears blinded her.

Mademoiselle had finished. She arose, and bowing her stiff,
lofty bow, she went away, stopping for neither thanks nor applause. As she passed along the gallery she patted Edna upon
the shoulder.

"Well, how did you like my music?" she asked. The young
woman was unable to answer; she pressed the hand of the pianist convulsively. Mademoiselle Reisz perceived her agitation and even her tears. She patted her again upon the shoulder as she said:

"You are the only one worth playing for. Those others?
Bah!" and she went shuffling and sidling on down the gallery
toward her room.

But she was mistaken about "those others." Her playing
had aroused a fever of enthusiasm. "What passion!" "What
an artist!" "I have always said no one could play Chopin like
Mademoiselle Reisz!" "That last prelude! Bon Dieu! It shakes
a man!"

It was growing late, and there was a general disposition to
disband. But some one, perhaps it was Robert, thought of a
bath at that mystic hour and under that mystic moon.

X

At all events Robert proposed it, and there was not a dissenting voice. There was not one but was ready to follow
when he led the way. He did not lead the way, however, he
directed the way; and he himself loitered behind with the lovers, who had betrayed a disposition to linger and hold themselves apart. He walked between them, whether with malicious or mischievous intent was not wholly clear, even to
himself.

The Pontelliers and Ratignolles walked ahead; the women
leaning upon the arms of their husbands. Edna could hear
Robert's voice behind them, and could sometimes hear what
he said. She wondered why he did not join them. It was unlike him not to. Of late he had sometimes held away from
her for an entire day, redoubling his devotion upon the next
and the next, as though to make up for hours that had been
lost. She missed him the days when some pretext served to
take him away from her, just as one misses the sun on a

cloudy day without having thought much about the sun when it was shining.

The people walked in little groups toward the beach. They talked and laughed; some of them sang. There was a band playing down at Klein's hotel, and the strains reached them faintly, tempered by the distance. There were strange, rare odors abroad—a tangle of the sea smell and of weeds and damp, new-plowed earth, mingled with the heavy perfume of a field of white blossoms somewhere near. But the night sat lightly upon the sea and the land. There was no weight of darkness; there were no shadows. The white light of the moon had fallen upon the world like the mystery and the softness of sleep.

Most of them walked into the water as though into a native element. The sea was quiet now, and swelled lazily in broad billows that melted into one another and did not break except upon the beach in little foamy crests that coiled back like slow, white serpents.

Edna had attempted all summer to learn to swim. She had received instructions from both the men and women; in some instances from the children. Robert had pursued a system of lessons almost daily; and he was nearly at the point of discouragement in realizing the futility of his efforts. A certain ungovernable dread hung about her when in the water, unless there was a hand near by that might reach out and reassure her.

But that night she was like the little tottering, stumbling, clutching child, who of a sudden realizes its powers, and walks for the first time alone, boldly and with over-confidence. She could have shouted for joy. She did shout for joy, as with a sweeping stroke or two she lifted her body to the surface of the water.

A feeling of exultation overtook her, as if some power of significant import had been given her to control the working of her body and her soul. She grew daring and reckless, overestimating her strength. She wanted to swim far out, where no woman had swum before.

Her unlooked-for achievement was the subject of wonder, applause, and admiration. Each one congratulated himself that his special teachings had accomplished this desired end.

"How easy it is!" she thought. "It is nothing," she said aloud; "why did I not discover before that it was nothing. Think of the time I have lost splashing about like a baby!" She would not join the groups in their sports and bouts, but intoxicated with her newly conquered power, she swam out alone.

She turned her face seaward to gather in an impression of space and solitude, which the vast expanse of water, meeting and melting with the moonlit sky, conveyed to her excited fancy. As she swam, she seemed to be reaching out for the unlimited in which to lose herself.

Once she turned and looked toward the shore, toward the people she had left there. She had not gone any great distance—that is, what would have been a great distance for an experienced swimmer. But to her unaccustomed vision the stretch of water behind her assumed the aspect of a barrier which her unaided strength would never be able to overcome.

A quick vision of death smote her soul, and for a second of time appalled and enfeebled her senses. But by an effort she rallied her staggering faculties and managed to regain the land.

She made no mention of her encounter with death and her flash of terror, except to say to her husband, "I thought I should have perished out there alone."

"You were not so very far, my dear; I was watching you," he told her.

Edna went at once to the bath-house, and she had put on her dry clothes and was ready to return home before the others had left the water. She started to walk away alone. They all called to her and shouted to her. She waved a dissenting hand, and went on, paying no further heed to their renewed cries which sought to detain her.

"Sometimes I am tempted to think that Mrs. Pontellier is capricious," said Madame Lebrun, who was amusing herself immensely and feared that Edna's abrupt departure might put an end to the pleasure.

"I know she is," assented Mr. Pontellier; "sometimes, not often."

Edna had not traversed a quarter of the distance on her way home before she was overtaken by Robert.

"Did you think I was afraid?" she asked him, without a shade of annoyance.

"No; I knew you weren't afraid."

"Then why did you come? Why didn't you stay out there with the others?"

"I never thought of it."

"Thought of what?"

"Of anything. What difference does it make?"

"I'm very tired," she uttered, complainingly.

"I know you are."

"You don't know anything about it. Why should you know? I never was so exhausted in my life. But it isn't unpleasant. A thousand emotions have swept through me tonight. I don't comprehend half of them. Don't mind what I'm saying; I am just thinking aloud. I wonder if I shall ever be stirred again as Mademoiselle Reisz's playing moved me tonight. I wonder if any night on earth will ever again be like this one. It is like a night in a dream. The people about me are like some uncanny, half-human beings. There must be spirits abroad to-night."

"There are," whispered Robert. "Didn't you know this was the twenty-eighth of August?"

"The twenty-eighth of August?"

"Yes. On the twenty-eighth of August, at the hour of midnight, and if the moon is shining—the moon must be shining—a spirit that has haunted these shores for ages rises up from the Gulf. With its own penetrating vision the spirit seeks some one mortal worthy to hold him company, worthy of being exalted for a few hours into realms of the semi-celestials. His search has always hitherto been fruitless, and he has sunk back, disheartened, into the sea. But to-night he found Mrs. Pontellier. Perhaps he will never wholly release her from the spell. Perhaps she will never again suffer a poor, unworthy earthling to walk in the shadow of her divine presence."

"Don't banter me," she said, wounded at what appeared to be his flippancy. He did not mind the entreaty, but the tone with its delicate note of pathos was like a reproach. He could not explain; he could not tell her that he had penetrated her mood and understood. He said nothing except to offer her his arm, for, by her own admission, she was exhausted. She had been walking alone with her arms hanging limp, letting her white skirts trail along the dewy path. She took his arm, but she did not lean upon it. She let her hand lie listlessly, as though her thoughts were elsewhere—somewhere in advance of her body, and she was striving to overtake them.

Robert assisted her into the hammock which swung from the post before her door out to the trunk of a tree.

"Will you stay out here and wait for Mr. Pontellier?" he asked.

"I'll stay out here. Good-night."

"Shall I get you a pillow?"

"There's one here," she said, feeling about, for they were in the shadow.

"It must be soiled; the children have been tumbling it about."

"No matter." And having discovered the pillow, she adjusted it beneath her head. She extended herself in the hammock with a deep breath of relief. She was not a supercilious or an over-dainty woman. She was not much given to reclining in the hammock, and when she did so it was with no cat-like suggestion of voluptuous ease, but with a beneficent repose which seemed to invade her whole body.

"Shall I stay with you till Mr. Pontellier comes?" asked Robert, seating himself on the outer edge of one of the steps and taking hold of the hammock rope which was fastened to the post.

"If you wish. Don't swing the hammock. Will you get my white shawl which I left on the window-sill over at the house?"

"Are you chilly?"

"No; but I shall be presently."

"Presently?" he laughed. "Do you know what time it is? How long are you going to stay out here?"

"I don't know. Will you get the shawl?"

"Of course I will," he said, rising. He went over to the house, walking along the grass. She watched his figure pass in and out of the strips of moonlight. It was past midnight. It was very quiet.

When he returned with the shawl she took it and kept it in her hand. She did not put it around her.

"Did you say I should stay till Mr. Pontellier came back?"

"I said you might if you wished to."

He seated himself again and rolled a cigarette, which he smoked in silence. Neither did Mrs. Pontellier speak. No multitude of words could have been more significant than those moments of silence, or more pregnant with the first-felt throbbings of desire.

When the voices of the bathers were heard approaching, Robert said good-night. She did not answer him. He thought she was asleep. Again she watched his figure pass in and out of the strips of moonlight as he walked away.

XI

"What are you doing out here, Edna? I thought I should find you in bed," said her husband, when he discovered her lying there. He had walked up with Madame Lebrun and left her at the house. His wife did not reply.

"Are you asleep?" he asked, bending down close to look at her.

"No," Her eyes gleamed bright and intense, with no sleepy shadows, as they looked into his.

"Do you know it is past one o'clock? Come on," and he mounted the steps and went into their room.

"Edna!" called Mr. Pontellier from within, after a few moments had gone by.

"Don't wait for me," she answered. He thrust his head through the door.

"You will take cold out there," he said, irritably. "What folly is this? Why don't you come in?"

"It isn't cold; I have my shawl."

"The mosquitoes will devour you."

"There are no mosquitoes."

She heard him moving about the room; every sound indicating impatience and irritation. Another time she would have gone in at his request. She would, through habit, have yielded to his desire; not with any sense of submission or obedience to his compelling wishes, but unthinkingly, as we walk, move, sit, stand, go through the daily treadmill of the life which has been portioned out to us.

"Edna, dear, are you not coming in soon?" he asked again, this time fondly, with a note of entreaty.

"No; I am going to stay out here."

"This is more than folly," he blurted out. "I can't permit you to stay out there all night. You must come in the house instantly."

With a writhing motion she settled herself more securely in the hammock. She perceived that her will had blazed up, stubborn and resistant. She could not at that moment have done other than denied and resisted. She wondered if her husband had ever spoken to her like that before, and if she had submitted to his command. Of course she had; she remembered that she had. But she could not realize why or how she should have yielded, feeling as she then did.

"Léonce, go to bed," she said. "I mean to stay out here. I

don't wish to go in, and I don't intend to. Don't speak to me
like that again; I shall not answer you."

Mr. Pontellier had prepared for bed, but he slipped on an
extra garment. He opened a bottle of wine, of which he kept
a small and select supply in a buffet of his own. He drank a
glass of the wine and went out on the gallery and offered a
glass to his wife. She did not wish any. He drew up the
rocker, hoisted his slippered feet on the rail, and proceeded to
smoke a cigar. He smoked two cigars; then he went inside
and drank another glass of wine. Mrs. Pontellier again declined to accept a glass when it was offered to her. Mr. Pontellier once more seated himself with elevated feet, and after
a reasonable interval of time smoked some more cigars.

Edna began to feel like one who awakens gradually out of
a dream, a delicious, grotesque, impossible dream, to feel
again the realities pressing into her soul. The physical need
for sleep began to overtake her; the exuberance which had
sustained and exalted her spirit left her helpless and yielding
to the conditions which crowded her in.

The stillest hour of the night had come, the hour before
dawn, when the world seems to hold its breath. The moon
hung low, and had turned from silver to copper in the sleeping sky. The old owl no longer hooted, and the water-oaks
had ceased to moan as they bent their heads.

Edna arose, cramped from lying so long and still in the
hammock. She tottered up the steps, clutching feebly at the
post before passing into the house.

"Are you coming in, Léonce?" she asked, turning her face
toward her husband.

"Yes, dear," he answered, with a glance following a misty
puff of smoke. "Just as soon as I have finished my cigar."

XII

She slept but a few hours. They were troubled and feverish
hours, disturbed with dreams that were intangible, that eluded
her, leaving only an impression upon her half-awakened
senses of something unattainable. She was up and dressed in
the cool of the early morning. The air was invigorating and
steadied somewhat her faculties. However, she was not seeking refreshment or help from any source, either external or
from within. She was blindly following whatever impulse
moved her, as if she had placed herself in alien hands for
direction, and freed her soul of responsibility.

Most of the people at that early hour were still in bed and asleep. A few, who intended to go over to the *Chênière* for mass, were moving about. The lovers, who had laid their plans the night before, were already strolling toward the wharf. The lady in black, with her Sunday prayer-book, velvet and gold-clasped, and her Sunday silver beads, was following them at no great distance. Old Monsieur Farival was up, and was more than half inclined to do anything that suggested itself. He put on his big straw hat, and taking his umbrella from the stand in the hall, followed the lady in black, never overtaking her.

The little negro girl who worked Madame Lebrun's sewing-machine was sweeping the galleries with long, absent-minded strokes of the broom. Edna sent her up into the house to awaken Robert.

"Tell him I am going to the *Chênière*. The boat is ready; tell him to hurry."

He had soon joined her. She had never sent for him before. She had never asked for him. She had never seemed to want him before. She did not appear conscious that she had done anything unusual in commanding his presence. He was apparently equally unconscious of anything extraordinary in the situation. But his face was suffused with a quiet glow when he met her.

They went together back to the kitchen to drink coffee. There was no time to wait for any nicety of service. They stood outside the window and the cook passed them their coffee and a roll, which they drank and ate from the window-sill. Edna said it tasted good. She had not thought of coffee nor of anything. He told her he had often noticed that she lacked forethought.

"Wasn't it enough to think of going to the *Chênière* and waking you up?" she laughed. "Do I have to think of everything?—as Léonce says when he's in a bad humor. I don't blame him; he'd never be in a bad humor if it weren't for me."

They took a short cut across the sands. At a distance they could see the curious procession moving toward the wharf—— the lovers, shoulder to shoulder, creeping; the lady in black, gaining steadily upon them; old Monsieur Farival, losing ground inch by inch, and a young barefooted Spanish girl, with a red kerchief on her head and a basket on her arm, bringing up the rear.

Robert knew the girl, and he talked to her a little in the

boat. No one present understood what they said. Her name was Mariequita. She had a round, sly, piquant face and pretty black eyes. Her hands were small, and she kept them folded over the handle of her basket. Her feet were broad and coarse. She did not strive to hide them. Edna looked at her feet, and noticed the sand and slime between her brown toes.

Beaudelet grumbled because Mariequita was there, taking up so much room. In reality he was annoyed at having old Monsieur Farival, who considered himself the better sailor of the two. But he would not quarrel with so old a man as Monsieur Farival, so he quarreled with Mariequita. The girl was deprecatory at one moment, appealing to Robert. She was saucy the next, moving her head up and down, making "eyes" at Robert and making "mouths" at Beaudelet.

The lovers were all alone. They saw nothing, they heard nothing. The lady in black was counting her beads for the third time. Old Monsieur Farival talked incessantly of what he knew about handling a boat, and of what Beaudelet did not know on the same subject.

Edna liked it all. She looked Mariequita up and down, from her ugly brown toes to her pretty black eyes, and back again.

"Why does she look at me like that?" inquired the girl of Robert.

"Maybe she thinks you are pretty. Shall I ask her?"

"No. Is she your sweetheart?"

"She's a married lady, and has two children."

"Oh! well! Francisco ran away with Sylvano's wife, who had four children. They took all his money and one of the children and stole his boat."

"Shut up!"

"Does she understand?"

"Oh, hush!"

"Are those two married over there—leaning on each other?"

"Of course not," laughed Robert.

"Of course not," echoed Mariequita, with a serious, confirmatory bob of the head.

The sun was high up and beginning to bite. The swift breeze seemed to Edna to bury the sting of it into the pores of her face and hands. Robert held his umbrella over her.

As they went cutting sidewise through the water, the sails bellied taut, with the wind filling and overflowing them. Old

Monsieur Farival laughed sardonically at something as he looked at the sails, and Beaudelet swore at the old man under his breath.

Sailing across the bay to the *Chênière Caminada,* Edna felt as if she were being borne away from some anchorage which had held her fast, whose chains had been loosening— had snapped the night before when the mystic spirit was abroad, leaving her free to drift whithersoever she chose to set her sails. Robert spoke to her incessantly; he no longer noticed Mariequita. The girl had shrimps in her bamboo basket. They were covered with Spanish moss. She beat the moss down impatiently, and muttered to herself sullenly.

"Let us go to Grande Terre to-morrow?" said Robert in a low voice.

"What shall we do there?"

"Climb up the hill to the old fort and look at the little wriggling gold snakes, and watch the lizards sun themselves."

She gazed away toward Grande Terre and thought she would like to be alone there with Robert, in the sun, listening to the ocean's roar and watching the slimy lizards writhe in and out among the ruins of the old fort.

"And the next day or the next we can sail to the Bayou Brulow," he went on.

"What shall we do there?"

"Anything—cast bait for fish."

"No; we'll go back to Grande Terre. Let the fish alone."

"We'll go wherever you like," he said. "I'll have Tonie come over and help me patch and trim my boat. We shall not need Beaudelet nor any one. Are you afraid of the pirogue?"

"Oh, no."

"Then I'll take you some night in the pirogue when the moon shines. Maybe your Gulf spirit will whisper to you in which of these islands the treasures are hidden—direct you to the very spot, perhaps."

"And in a day we should be rich!" she laughed. "I'd give it all to you, the pirate gold and every bit of treasure we could dig up. I think you would know how to spend it. Pirate gold isn't a thing to be hoarded or utilized. It is something to squander and throw to the four winds, for the fun of seeing the golden specks fly."

"We'd share it, and scatter it together," he said. His face flushed.

They all went together up to the quaint little Gothic

church of Our Lady of Lourdes, gleaming all brown and yellow with paint in the sun's glare.

Only Beaudelet remained behind, tinkering at his boat, and Mariequita walked away with her basket of shrimps, casting a look of childish ill-humor and reproach at Robert from the corner of her eye.

XIII

A feeling of oppression and drowsiness overcame Edna during the service. Her head began to ache, and the lights on the altar swayed before her eyes. Another time she might have made an effort to regain her composure; but her one thought was to quit the stifling atmosphere of the church and reach the open air. She arose, climbing over Robert's feet with a muttered apology. Old Monsieur Farival, flurried, curious, stood up, but upon seeing that Robert had followed Mrs. Pontellier, he sank back into his seat. He whispered an anxious inquiry of the lady in black, who did not notice him or reply, but kept her eyes fastened upon the pages of her velvet prayer-book.

"I felt giddy and almost overcome," Edna said, lifting her hands instinctively to her head and pushing her straw hat up from her forehead. "I couldn't have stayed through the service." They were outside in the shadow of the church. Robert was full of solicitude.

"It was folly to have thought of going in the first place, let alone staying. Come over to Madame Antoine's; you can rest there." He took her arm and led her away, looking anxiously and continuously down into her face.

How still it was, with only the voice of the sea whispering through the reeds that grew in the salt-water pools! The long line of little gray, weather-beaten houses nestled peacefully among the orange trees. It must always have been God's day on that low, drowsy island, Edna thought. They stopped, leaning over a jagged fence made of sea-drift, to ask for water. A youth, a mild-faced Acadian, was drawing water from the cistern, which was nothing more than a rusty buoy, with an opening on one side, sunk in the ground. The water which the youth handed to them in a tin pail was not cold to taste, but it was cool to her heated face, and it greatly revived and refreshed her.

Madame Antoine's cot was at the far end of the village. She welcomed them with all the native hospitality, as she would have opened her door to let the sunlight in. She was fat, and walked heavily and clumsily across the floor. She could speak no English, but when Robert made her understand that the lady who accompanied him was ill and desired to rest, she was all eagerness to make Edna feel at home and to dispose of her comfortably.

The whole place was immaculately clean, and the big, four-posted bed, snow-white, invited one to repose. It stood in a small side room which looked out across a narrow grass plot toward the shed, where there was a disabled boat lying keel upward.

Madame Antoine had not gone to mass. Her son Tonie had, but she supposed he would soon be back, and she invited Robert to be seated and wait for him. But he went and sat outside the door and smoked. Madame Antoine busied herself in the large front room preparing dinner. She was boiling mullets over a few red coals in the huge fireplace.

Edna, left alone in the little side room, loosened her clothes, removing the greater part of them. She bathed her face, her neck and arms in the basin that stood between the windows. She took off her shoes and stockings and stretched herself in the very center of the high, white bed. How luxurious it felt to rest thus in a strange, quaint bed, with its sweet country odor of laurel lingering about the sheets and mattress! She stretched her strong limbs that ached a little. She ran her fingers through her loosened hair for a while. She looked at her round arms as she held them straight up and rubbed them one after the other, observing closely, as if it were something she saw for the first time, the fine, firm quality and texture of her flesh. She clasped her hands easily above her head, and it was thus she fell asleep.

She slept lightly at first, half awake and drowsily attentive to the things about her. She could hear Madame Antoine's heavy, scraping tread as she walked back and forth on the sanded floor. Some chickens were clucking outside the windows, scratching for bits of gravel in the grass. Later she half heard the voices of Robert and Tonie talking under the shed. She did not stir. Even her eyelids rested numb and heavily over her sleepy eyes. The voices went on—Tonie's slow, Acadian drawl, Robert's quick, soft, smooth French. She understood French imperfectly unless directly addressed, and the voices were only part of the other drowsy, muffled sounds lulling her senses.

When Edna awoke it was with the conviction that she had

slept long and soundly. The voices were hushed under the shed. Madame Antoine's step was no longer to be heard in the adjoining room. Even the chickens had gone elsewhere to scratch and cluck. The mosquito bar was drawn over her; the old woman had come in while she slept and let down the bar. Edna arose quietly from the bed, and looking between the curtains of the window, she saw by the slanting rays of the sun that the afternoon was far advanced. Robert was out there under the shed, reclining in the shade against the sloping keel of the overturned boat. He was reading from a book. Tonie was no longer with him. She wondered what had become of the rest of the party. She peeped out at him two or three times as she stood washing herself in the little basin between the windows.

Madame Antoine had laid some coarse, clean towels upon a chair, and had placed a box of *poudre de riz* within easy reach. Edna dabbed the powder upon her nose and cheeks as she looked at herself closely in the little distorted mirror which hung on the wall above the basin. Her eyes were bright and wide awake and her face glowed.

When she had completed her toilet she walked into the adjoining room. She was very hungry. No one was there. But there was a cloth spread upon the table that stood against the wall, and a cover was laid for one, with a crusty brown loaf and a bottle of wine beside the plate. Edna bit a piece from the brown loaf, tearing it with her strong, white teeth. She poured some of the wine into the glass and drank it down. Then she went softly out of doors, and plucking an orange from the low-hanging bough of a tree, threw it at Robert, who did not know she was awake and up.

An illumination broke over his whole face when he saw her and joined her under the orange tree.

"How many years have I slept?" she inquired. "The whole island seems changed. A new race of beings must have sprung up, leaving only you and me as past relics. How many ages ago did Madame Antoine and Tonie die? and when did our people from Grand Isle disappear from the earth?"

He familiarly adjusted a ruffle upon her shoulder.

"You have slept precisely one hundred years. I was left here to guard your slumbers; and for one hundred years I have been out under the shed reading a book. The only evil I couldn't prevent was to keep a broiled fowl from drying up."

"If it has turned to stone, still will I eat it," said Edna, moving with him into the house. "But really, what has become of Monsieur Farival and the others?"

"Gone hours ago. When they found that you were sleeping they thought it best not to awake you. Any way, I wouldn't have let them. What was I here for?"

"I wonder if Léonce will be uneasy!" she speculated, as she seated herself at table.

"Of course not; he knows you are with me," Robert replied, as he busied himself among sundry pans and covered dishes which had been left standing on the hearth.

"Where are Madame Antoine and her son?" asked Edna.

"Gone to Vespers, and to visit some friends, I believe. I am to take you back in Tonie's boat whenever you are ready to go."

He stirred the smoldering ashes till the broiled fowl began to sizzle afresh. He served her with no mean repast, dripping the coffee anew and sharing it with her. Madame Antoine had cooked little else than the mullets, but while Edna slept Robert had foraged the island. He was childishly gratified to discover her appetite, and to see the relish with which she ate the food which he had procured for her.

"Shall we go right away?" she asked, after draining her glass and brushing together the crumbs of the crusty loaf.

"The sun isn't as low as it will be in two hours," he answered.

"The sun will be gone in two hours."

"Well, let it go; who cares!"

They waited a good while under the orange trees, till Madame Antoine came back, panting, waddling, with a thousand apologies to explain her absence. Tonie did not dare to return. He was shy, and would not willingly face any woman except his mother.

It was very pleasant to stay there under the orange trees, while the sun dipped lower and lower, turning the western sky to flaming copper and gold. The shadows lengthened and crept out like stealthy, grotesque monsters across the grass.

Edna and Robert both sat upon the ground—that is, he lay upon the ground beside her, occasionally picking at the hem of her muslin gown.

Madame Antoine seated her fat body, broad and squat, upon a bench beside the door. She had been talking all the afternoon, and had wound herself up to the story-telling pitch.

And what stories she told them! But twice in her life she

had left the *Chênière Caminada,* and then for the briefest
span. All her years she had squatted and waddled there upon
the island, gathering legends of the Baratarians and the sea.
The night came on, with the moon to lighten it. Edna could
hear the whispering voices of dead men and the click of
muffled gold.

When she and Robert stepped into Tonie's boat, with the
red lateen sail, misty spirit forms were prowling in the
shadows and among the reeds, and upon the water were
phantom ships, speeding to cover.

XIV

The youngest boy, Etienne, had been very naughty,
Madame Ratignolle said, as she delivered him into the hands
of his mother. He had been unwilling to go to bed and had
made a scene; whereupon she had taken charge of him and
pacified him as well as she could. Raoul had been in bed and
asleep for two hours.

The youngster was in his long white nightgown, that kept
tripping him up as Madame Ratignolle led him along by the
hand. With the other chubby fist he rubbed his eyes, which
were heavy with sleep and ill humor. Edna took him in her
arms, and seating herself in the rocker, began to coddle and
caress him, calling him all manner of tender names, soothing
him to sleep.

It was not more than nine o'clock. No one had yet gone to
bed but the children.

Léonce had been very uneasy at first, Madame Ratignolle
said, and had wanted to start at once for the *Chênière.* But
Monsieur Farival had assured him that his wife was only
overcome with sleep and fatigue, that Tonie would bring her
safely back later in the day; and he had thus been dissuaded
from crossing the bay. He had gone over to Klein's, looking
up some cotton broker whom he wished to see in regard to
securities, exchanges, stocks, bonds, or something of the sort,
Madame Ratignolle did not remember what. He said he
would not remain away late. She herself was suffering from
heat and oppression, she said. She carried a bottle of salts
and a large fan. She would not consent to remain with Edna,
for Monsieur Ratignolle was alone, and he detested above all
things to be left alone.

When Etienne had fallen asleep Edna bore him into the
back room, and Robert went and lifted the mosquito bar that

she might lay the child comfortably in his bed. The quadroon had vanished. When they emerged from the cottage Robert bade Edna good-night.

"Do you know we have been together the whole livelong day, Robert—since early this morning?" she said at parting.

"All but the hundred years when you were sleeping. Good-night."

He pressed her hand and went away in the direction of the beach. He did not join any of the others, but walked alone toward the Gulf.

Edna stayed outside, awaiting her husband's return. She had no desire to sleep or to retire; nor did she feel like going over to sit with the Ratignolles, or to join Madame Lebrun and a group whose animated voices reached her as they sat in conversation before the house. She let her mind wander back over her stay at Grand Isle; and she tried to discover wherein this summer had been different from any and every other summer of her life. She could only realize that she herself— her present self—was in some way different from the other self. That she was seeing with different eyes and making the acquaintance of new conditions in herself that colored and changed her environment, she did not yet suspect.

She wondered why Robert had gone away and left her. It did not occur to her to think he might have grown tired of being with her the livelong day. She was not tired, and she felt that he was not. She regretted that he had gone. It was so much more natural to have him stay, when he was not absolutely required to leave her.

As Edna waited for her husband she sang low a little song that Robert had sung as they crossed the bay. It began with "Ah! *Si tu savais,*"[16] and every verse ended with *"si tu savais."*

Robert's voice was not pretentious. It was musical and true. The voice, the notes, the whole refrain haunted her memory.

XV

When Edna entered the dining-room one evening a little late, as was her habit, an unusually animated conversation seemed to be going on. Several persons were talking at once, and Victor's voice was predominating, even over that of his

[16]"If only you knew."

mother. Edna had returned late from her bath, had dressed in some haste, and her face was flushed. Her head, set off by her dainty white gown, suggested a rich, rare blossom. She took her seat at table between old Monsieur Farival and Madame Ratignolle.

As she seated herself and was about to begin to eat her soup, which had been served when she entered the room, several persons informed her simultaneously that Robert was going to Mexico. She laid her spoon down and looked about her bewildered. He had been with her, reading to her all the morning, and had never even mentioned such a place as Mexico. She had not seen him during the afternoon; she had heard some one say he was at the house, upstairs with his mother. This she had thought nothing of, though she was surprised when he did not join her later in the afternoon, when she went down to the beach.

She looked across at him, where he sat beside Madame Lebrun, who presided. Edna's face was a blank picture of bewilderment, which she never thought of disguising. He lifted his eyebrows with the pretext of a smile as he returned her glance. He looked embarrassed and uneasy.

"When is he going?" she asked of everybody in general, as if Robert were not there to answer for himself.

"To-night!" "This very evening!" "Did you ever!" "What possesses him!" were some of the replies she gathered, uttered simultaneously in French and English.

"Impossible!" she exclaimed. "How can a person start off from Grand Isle to Mexico at a moment's notice, as if he were going over to Klein's or to the wharf or down to the beach?"

"I said all along I was going to Mexico; I've been saying so for years!" cried Robert, in an excited and irritable tone, with the air of a man defending himself against a swarm of stinging insects.

Madame Lebrun knocked on the table with her knife handle.

"Please let Robert explain why he is going, and why he is going to-night," she called out. "Really, this table is getting to be more and more like Bedlam every day, with everybody talking at once. Sometimes—I hope God will forgive me—but positively, sometimes I wish Victor would lose the power of speech."

Victor laughed sardonically as he thanked his mother for her holy wish, of which he failed to see the benefit to anybody, except that it might afford her a more ample opportunity and license to talk herself.

Monsieur Farival thought that Victor should have been taken out in mid-ocean in his earliest youth and drowned. Victor thought there would be more logic in thus disposing of old people with an established claim for making themselves universally obnoxious. Madame Lebrun grew a trifle hysterical; Robert called his brother some sharp, hard names.

"There's nothing much to explain, mother," he said; though he explained, nevertheless—looking chiefly at Edna—that he could only meet the gentleman whom he intended to join at Vera Cruz by taking such and such a steamer, which left New Orleans on such a day; that Beaudelet was going out with his lugger-load of vegetables that night, which gave him an opportunity of reaching the city and making his vessel in time.

"But when did you make up your mind to all this?" demanded Monsieur Farival.

"This afternoon," returned Robert, with a shade of annoyance.

"At what time this afternoon?" persisted the old gentleman, with nagging determination, as if he were cross-questioning a criminal in a court of justice.

"At four o'clock this afternoon, Monsieur Farival," Robert replied, in a high voice and with a lofty air, which reminded Edna of some gentleman on the stage.

She had forced herself to eat most of her soup, and now she was picking the flaky bits of a *court bouillon*[17] with her fork.

The lovers were profiting by the general conversation on Mexico to speak in whispers of matters which they rightly considered were interesting to no one but themselves. The lady in black had once received a pair of prayer-beads of curious workmanship from Mexico, with very special indulgence attached to them, but she had never been able to ascertain whether the indulgence extended outside the Mexican border. Father Fochel of the Cathedral had attempted to explain it; but he had not done so to her satisfaction. And she begged that Robert would interest himself, and discover, if possible, whether she was entitled to the indulgence accompanying the remarkably curious Mexican prayer-beads.

Madame Ratignolle hoped that Robert would exercise ex-

[17]Fish stew.

treme caution in dealing with the Mexicans, who, she considered, were a treacherous people, unscrupulous and revengeful. She trusted she did them no injustice in thus condemning them as a race. She had known personally but one Mexican, who made and sold excellent tamales, and whom she would have trusted implicitly, so soft-spoken was he. One day he was arrested for stabbing his wife. She never knew whether he had been hanged or not.

Victor had grown hilarious, and was attempting to tell an anecdote about a Mexican girl who served chocolate one winter in a restaurant in Dauphine Street. No one would listen to him but old Monsieur Farival, who went into convulsions over the droll story.

Edna wondered if they had all gone mad, to be talking and clamoring at that rate. She herself could think of nothing to say about Mexico or the Mexicans.

"At what time do you leave?" she asked Robert.

"At ten," he told her. "Beaudelet wants to wait for the moon."

"Are you all ready to go?"

"Quite ready. I shall only take a hand-bag, and shall pack my trunk in the city."

He turned to answer some question put to him by his mother, and Edna, having finished her black coffee, left the table.

She went directly to her room. The little cottage was close and stuffy after leaving the outer air. But she did not mind; there appeared to be a hundred different things demanding her attention indoors. She began to set the toilet-stand to rights, grumbling at the negligence of the quadroon, who was in the adjoining room putting the children to bed. She gathered together stray garments that were hanging on the backs of chairs, and put each where it belonged in closet or bureau drawer. She changed her gown for a more comfortable and commodious wrapper. She rearranged her hair, combing and brushing it with unusual energy. Then she went in and assisted the quadroon in getting the boys to bed.

They were very playful and inclined to talk—to do anything but lie quiet and go to sleep. Edna sent the quadroon away to her supper and told her she need not return. Then she sat and told the children a story. Instead of soothing it excited them, and added to their wakefulness. She left them in heated argument, speculating about the conclusion of the tale which their mother promised to finish the following night.

The little black girl came in to say that Madame Lebrun would like to have Mrs. Pontellier go and sit with them over at the house till Mr. Robert went away. Edna returned answer that she had already undressed, that she did not feel quite well, but perhaps she would go over to the house later. She started to dress again, and got as far advanced as to remove her *peignoir*. But changing her mind once more she resumed the *peignoir*, and went outside and sat down before her door. She was overheated and irritable, and fanned herself energetically for a while. Madame Ratignolle came down to discover what was the matter.

"All that noise and confusion at the table must have upset me," replied Edna, "and moreover, I hate shocks and surprises. The idea of Robert starting off in such a ridiculously sudden and dramatic way! As if it were a matter of life and death! Never saying a word about it all morning when he was with me."

"Yes," agreed Madame Ratignolle. "I think it was showing us all—you especially—very little consideration. It wouldn't have surprised me in any of the others; those Lebruns are all given to heroics. But I must say I should never have expected such a thing from Robert. Are you not coming down? Come on, dear; it doesn't look friendly."

"No," said Edna, a little sullenly. "I can't go to the trouble of dressing again; I don't feel like it."

"You needn't dress; you look all right; fasten a belt around your waist. Just look at me!"

"No," persisted Edna; "but you go on. Madame Lebrun might be offended if we both stayed away."

Madame Ratignolle kissed Edna good-night, and went away, being in truth rather desirous of joining in the general and animated conversation which was still in progress concerning Mexico and the Mexicans.

Somewhat later Robert came up, carrying his hand-bag.

"Aren't you feeling well?" he asked.

"Oh, well enough. Are you going right away?"

He lit a match and looked at his watch. "In twenty minutes," he said. The sudden and brief flare of the match emphasized the darkness for a while. He sat down upon a stool which the children had left out on the porch.

"Get a chair," said Edna.

"This will do," he replied. He put on his soft hat and nervously took it off again, and wiping his face with his handkerchief, complained of the heat.

"Take the fan," said Edna, offering it to him.

"Oh, no! Thank you. It does no good; you have to stop fanning some time, and feel all the more uncomfortable afterward."

"That's one of the ridiculous things which men always say. I have never known one to speak otherwise of fanning. How long will you be gone?"

"Forever, perhaps. I don't know. It depends upon a good many things."

"Well, in case it shouldn't be forever, how long will it be?"

"I don't know."

"This seems to me perfectly preposterous and uncalled for. I don't like it. I don't understand your motive for silence and mystery, never saying a word to me about it this morning." He remained silent, not offering to defend himself. He only said, after a moment:

"Don't part from me in an ill-humor. I never knew you to be out of patience with me before."

"I don't want to part in any ill-humor," she said. "But can't you understand? I've grown used to seeing you, to having you with me all the time, and your action seems unfriendly, even unkind. You don't even offer an excuse for it. Why, I was planning to be together, thinking of how pleasant it would be to see you in the city next winter."

"So was I," he blurted. "Perhaps that's the—" He stood up suddenly and held out his hand. "Good-by, my dear Mrs. Pontellier; good-by. You won't—I hope you won't completely forget me." She clung to his hand, striving to detain him.

"Write to me when you get there, won't you, Robert?" she entreated.

"I will, thank you. Good-by."

How unlike Robert! The merest acquaintance would have said something more emphatic than "I will, thank you; good-by," to such a request.

He had evidently already taken leave of the people over at the house, for he descended the steps and went to join Beaudelet, who was out there with an oar across his shoulder waiting for Robert. They walked away in the darkness. She could only hear Beaudelet's voice; Robert had apparently not even spoken a word of greeting to his companion.

Edna bit her handkerchief convulsively, striving to hold back and to hide, even from herself as she would have hidden from another, the emotion which was troubling—tearing—her. Her eyes were brimming with tears.

For the first time she recognized anew the symptoms of infatuation which she had felt incipiently as a child, as a girl in her earliest teens, and later as a young woman. The recognition did not lessen the reality, the poignancy of the revelation by any suggestion or promise of instability. The past was nothing to her; offered no lesson which she was willing to heed. The future was a mystery which she never attempted to penetrate. The present alone was significant; was hers, to torture her as it was doing then with the biting conviction that she had lost that which she had held, that she had been denied that which her impassioned, newly awakened being demanded.

XVI

"Do you miss your friend greatly?" asked Mademoiselle Reisz one morning as she came creeping up behind Edna, who had just left her cottage on her way to the beach. She spent much of her time in the water since she had acquired finally the art of swimming. As their stay at Grand Isle drew near its close, she felt that she could not give too much time to a diversion which afforded her the only real pleasurable moments that she knew. When Mademoiselle Reisz came and touched her upon the shoulder and spoke to her, the woman seemed to echo the thought which was ever in Edna's mind; or, better, the feeling which constantly possessed her.

Robert's going had some way taken the brightness, the color, the meaning out of everything. The conditions of her life were in no way changed, but her whole existence was dulled, like a faded garment which seems to be no longer worth wearing. She sought him everywhere—in others whom she induced to talk about him. She went up in the mornings to Madame Lebrun's room, braving the clatter of the old sewing-machine. She sat there and chatted at intervals as Robert had done. She gazed around the room at the pictures and photographs hanging upon the wall, and discovered in some corner an old family album, which she examined with the keenest interest, appealing to Madame Lebrun for enlightenment concerning the many figures and faces which she discovered between its pages.

There was a picture of Madame Lebrun with Robert as a baby, seated in her lap, a round-faced infant with a fist in his mouth. The eyes alone in the baby suggested the man. And that was he also in kilts, at the age of five, wearing long curls and holding a whip in his hand. It made Edna laugh, and she laughed, too, at the portrait in his first long trousers; while another interested her, taken when he left for college, looking thin, long-faced, with eyes full of fire, ambition and great intentions. But there was no recent picture, none which suggested the Robert who had gone away five days ago, leaving a void and wilderness behind him.

"Oh, Robert stopped having his pictures taken when he had to pay for them himself! He found wiser use for his money, he says," explained Madame Lebrun. She had a letter from him, written before he left New Orleans. Edna wished to see the letter, and Madame Lebrun told her to look for it either on the table or the dresser, or perhaps it was on the mantelpiece.

The letter was on the bookshelf. It possessed the greatest interest and attraction for Edna; the envelope, its size and shape, the post-mark, the handwriting. She examined every detail of the outside before opening it. There were only a few lines, setting forth that he would leave the city that afternoon, that he had packed his trunk in good shape, that he was well, and sent her his love and begged to be affectionately remembered to all. There was no special message to Edna except a postscript saying that if Mrs. Pontellier desired to finish the book which he had been reading to her, his mother would find it in his room, among other books there on the table. Edna experienced a pang of jealousy because he had written to his mother rather than to her.

Every one seemed to take for granted that she missed him. Even her husband, when he came down the Saturday following Robert's departure, expressed regret that he had gone.

"How do you get on without him, Edna?" he asked.

"It's very dull without him," she admitted. Mr. Pontellier had seen Robert in the city, and Edna asked him a dozen questions or more. Where had they met? On Carondelet Street, in the morning. They had gone "in" and had a drink and a cigar together. What had they talked about? Chiefly about his prospects in Mexico, which Mr. Pontellier thought were promising. How did he look? How did he seem—grave, or gay, or how? Quite cheerful, and wholly taken up with the idea of his trip, which Mr. Pontellier found altogether natural in a young fellow about to seek fortune and adventure in a strange, queer country.

Edna tapped her foot impatiently, and wondered why the children persisted in playing in the sun when they might be under the trees. She went down and led them out of the sun, scolding the quadroon for not being more attentive.

It did not strike her as in the least grotesque that she should be making of Robert the object of conversation and leading her husband to speak of him. The sentiment which she entertained for Robert in no way resembled that which she felt for her husband, or had ever felt, or ever expected to feel. She had all her life long been accustomed to harbor thoughts and emotions which never voiced themselves. They had never taken the form of struggles. They belonged to her and were her own, and she entertained the conviction that she had a right to them and that they concerned no one but herself. Edna had once told Madame Ratignolle that she would never sacrifice herself for her children, or for any one. Then had followed a rather heated argument; the two women did not appear to understand each other or to be talking the same language. Edna tried to appease her friend, to explain.

"I would give up the unessential; I would give my money, I would give my life for my children; but I wouldn't give myself. I can't make it more clear; it's only something which I am beginning to comprehend, which is revealing itself to me."

"I don't know what you would call the essential, or what you mean by the unessential," said Madame Ratignolle, cheerfully; "but a woman who would give her life for her children could do no more than that—your Bible tells you so. I'm sure I couldn't do more than that."

"Oh, yes you could!" laughed Edna.

She was not surprised at Mademoiselle Reisz's question the morning that lady, following her to the beach, tapped her on the shoulder and asked if she did not greatly miss her young friend.

"Oh, good morning, Mademoiselle; is it you? Why, of course I miss Robert. Are you going down to bathe?"

"Why should I go down to bathe at the very end of the season when I haven't been in the surf all summer," replied the woman, disagreeably.

"I beg your pardon," offered Edna, in some embarrassment, for she should have remembered that Mademoiselle Reisz's avoidance of the water had furnished a theme for much pleasantry. Some among them thought it was on account of her false hair, or the dread of getting the violets wet, while others attributed it to the natural aversion for water sometimes believed to accompany the artistic temperament. Mademoiselle offered Edna some chocolates in a paper bag, which she took from her pocket, by way of showing that she bore no ill feeling. She habitually ate chocolates for their sustaining quality; they contained much nutriment in small compass, she said. They saved her from starvation, as Madame Lebrun's table was utterly impossible; and no one save so impertinent a woman as Madame Lebrun would think of offering such food to people and requiring them to pay for it.

"She must feel very lonely without her son," said Edna, desiring to change the subject. "Her favorite son, too. It must have been quite hard to let him go."

Mademoiselle laughed maliciously.

"Her favorite son! Oh, dear! Who could have been imposing such a tale upon you? Aline Lebrun lives for Victor, and for Victor alone. She has spoiled him into the worthless creature he is. She worships him and the ground he walks on. Robert is very well in a way, to give up all the money he can earn to the family, and keep the barest pittance for himself. Favorite son, indeed! I miss the poor fellow myself, my dear. I liked to see him and to hear him about the place—the only Lebrun who is worth a pinch of salt. He comes to see me often in the city. I like to play to him. That Victor! hanging would be too good for him. It's a wonder Robert hasn't beaten him to death long ago."

"I thought he had great patience with his brother," offered Edna, glad to be talking about Robert, no matter what was said.

"Oh! he thrashed him well enough a year or two ago," said Mademoiselle. "It was about a Spanish girl, whom Victor considered that he had some sort of claim upon. He met Robert one day talking to the girl, or walking with her, or bathing with her, or carrying her basket—I don't remember what;—and he became so insulting and abusive that Robert gave him a thrashing on the spot that has kept him comparatively in order for a good while. It's about time he was getting another."

"Was her name Mariequita?" asked Edna.

"Mariequita—yes, that was it; Mariequita. I had forgotten. Oh, she's a sly one, and a bad one, that Mariequita!"

Edna looked down at Mademoiselle Reisz and wondered how she could have listened to her venom so long. For some reason she felt depressed, almost unhappy. She had not intended to go into the water; but she donned her bathing suit, and left Mademoiselle alone, seated under the shade of the children's tent. The water was growing cooler as the season advanced. Edna plunged and swam about with an abandon that thrilled and invigorated her. She remained a long time in the water, half hoping that Mademoiselle Reisz would not wait for her.

But Mademoiselle waited. She was very amiable during the walk back, and raved much over Edna's appearance in her bathing suit. She talked about music. She hoped that Edna would go to see her in the city, and wrote her address with the stub of a pencil on a piece of card which she found in her pocket.

"When do you leave?" asked Edna.

"Next Monday; and you?"

"The following week," answered Edna, adding, "It has been a pleasant summer, hasn't it, Mademoiselle?"

"Well," agreed Mademoiselle Reisz, with a shrug, "rather pleasant, if it hadn't been for the mosquitoes and the Farival twins."

XVII

The Pontelliers possessed a very charming home on Esplanade Street in New Orleans. It was a large, double cottage, with a broad front veranda, whose round, fluted columns supported the sloping roof. The house was painted a dazzling white; the outside shutters, or jalousies, were green. In the yard, which was kept scrupulously neat, were flowers and plants of every description which flourishes in South Louisiana. Within doors the appointments were perfect after the conventional type. The softest carpets and rugs covered the floors; rich and tasteful draperies hung at doors and windows. There were paintings, selected with judgment and discrimination, upon the walls. The cut glass, the silver, the heavy damask which daily appeared upon the table were the envy of many women whose husbands were less generous than Mr. Pontellier.

Mr. Pontellier was very fond of walking about his house examining its various appointments and details, to see that nothing was amiss. He greatly valued his possessions, chiefly because they were his, and derived genuine pleasure from contemplating a painting, a statuette, a rare lace curtain—no

matter what—after he had bought it and placed it among his
household goods.

On Tuesday afternoons—Tuesday being Mrs. Pontellier's
reception day—there was a constant stream of callers—
women who came in carriages or in the street cars, or walked
when the air was soft and distance permitted. A light-colored
mulatto boy, in dress coat and bearing a diminutive silver
tray for the reception of cards, admitted them. A maid, in
white fluted cap, offered the callers liqueur, coffee, or chocolate, as they might desire. Mrs. Pontellier, attired in a handsome reception gown, remained in the drawing-room the entire afternoon receiving her visitors. Men sometimes called in
the evening with their wives.

This had been the programme which Mrs. Pontellier had
religiously followed since her marriage, six years before. Certain evenings during the week she and her husband attended
the opera or sometimes the play.

Mr. Pontellier left his home in the morning between nine
and ten o'clock, and rarely returned before half-past six or
seven in the evening—dinner being served at half-past seven.

He and his wife seated themselves at table one Tuesday
evening, a few weeks after their return from Grand Isle.
They were alone together. The boys were being put to bed;
the patter of their bare, escaping feet could be heard occasionally, as well as the pursuing voice of the quadroon, lifted
in mild protest and entreaty. Mrs. Pontellier did not wear her
usual Tuesday reception gown; she was in ordinary house
dress. Mr. Pontellier, who was observant about such things,
noticed it, as he served the soup and handed it to the boy in
waiting.

"Tired out, Edna? Whom did you have? Many callers?" he
asked. He tasted his soup and began to season it with pepper,
salt, vinegar, mustard—everything within reach.

"There were a good many," replied Edna, who was eating
her soup with evident satisfaction. "I found their cards when
I got home; I was out."

"Out!" exclaimed her husband, with something like genuine
consternation in his voice as he laid down the vinegar cruet
and looked at her through his glasses. "Why, what could
have taken you out on Tuesday? What did you have to do?"

"Nothing. I simply felt like going out, and I went out."

"Well, I hope you left some suitable excuse," said her husband, somewhat appeased, as he added a dash of cayenne
pepper to the soup.

"No, I left no excuse. I told Joe to say I was out, that was all."

"Why, my dear, I should think you'd understand by this time that people don't do such things; we've got to observe *les convenances*[18] if we ever expect to get on and keep up with the procession. If you felt that you had to leave home this afternoon, you should have left some suitable explanation for your absence.

"This soup is really impossible; it's strange that woman hasn't learned yet to make a decent soup. Any free-lunch stand in town serves a better one. Was Mrs. Belthrop here?"

"Bring the tray with the cards, Joe. I don't remember who was here."

The boy retired and returned after a moment, bringing the tiny silver tray, which was covered with ladies' visiting cards. He handed it to Mrs. Pontellier.

"Give it to Mr. Pontellier," she said.

Joe offered the tray to Mr. Pontellier, and removed the soup.

Mr. Pontellier scanned the names of his wife's callers, reading some of them aloud, with comments as he read.

" 'The Misses Delasidas.' I worked a big deal in futures for their father this morning; nice girls; it's time they were getting married. 'Mrs. Belthrop.' I tell you what it is, Edna; you can't afford to snub Mrs. Belthrop. Why, Belthrop could buy and sell us ten times over. His business is worth a good, round sum to me. You'd better write her a note. 'Mrs. James Highcamp,' Hugh! the less you have to do with Mrs. High-camp, the better. 'Madame Laforcé.' Came all the way from Carrolton, too, poor old soul. 'Miss Wiggs,' 'Mrs. Eleanor Boltons.' " He pushed the cards aside.

"Mercy!" exclaimed Edna, who had been fuming. "Why are you taking the thing so seriously and making such a fuss over it?"

"I'm not making any fuss over it. But it's just such seeming trifles that we've got to take seriously; such things count."

The fish was scorched. Mr. Pontellier would not touch it. Edna said she did not mind a little scorched taste. The roast was in some way not to his fancy, and he did not like the manner in which the vegetables were served.

"It seems to me," he said, "we spend money enough in this house to procure at least one meal a day which a man could eat and retain his self-respect."

18Appearances; society's conventions.

"You used to think the cook was a treasure," returned Edna, indifferently.

"Perhaps she was when she first came; but cooks are only human. They need looking after, like any other class of persons that you employ. Suppose I didn't look after the clerks in my office, just let them run things their own way; they'd soon make a nice mess of me and my business."

"Where are you going?" asked Edna, seeing that her husband arose from table without having eaten a morsel except a taste of the highly-seasoned soup.

"I'm going to get my dinner at the club. Good night." He went into the hall, took his hat and stick from the stand, and left the house.

She was somewhat familiar with such scenes. They had often made her very unhappy. On a few previous occasions she had been completely deprived of any desire to finish her dinner. Sometimes she had gone into the kitchen to administer a tardy rebuke to the cook. Once she went to her room and studied the cookbook during an entire evening, finally writing out a menu for the week, which left her harassed with a feeling that, after all, she had accomplished no good that was worth the name.

But that evening Edna finished her dinner alone, with forced deliberation. Her face was flushed and her eyes flamed with some inward fire that lighted them. After finishing her dinner she went to her room, having instructed the boy to tell any other callers that she was indisposed.

It was a large, beautiful room, rich and picturesque in the soft, dim light which the maid had turned low. She went and stood at an open window and looked out upon the deep tangle of the garden below. All the mystery and witchery of the night seemed to have gathered there amid the perfumes and the dusky and tortuous outlines of flowers and foliage. She was seeking herself and finding herself in just such sweet, half-darkness which met her moods. But the voices were not soothing that came to her from the darkness and the sky above and the stars. They jeered and sounded mournful notes without promise, devoid even of hope. She turned back into the room and began to walk to and fro down its whole length, without stopping, without resting. She carried in her hands a thin handkerchief, which she tore into ribbons, rolled into a ball, and flung from her. Once she stopped, and taking off her wedding ring, flung it upon the carpet. When she saw it lying there, she stamped her heel upon it, striving to crush it. But her small boot heel did not make an indenture, not a mark upon the little glittering circlet.

In a sweeping passion she seized a glass vase from the table and flung it upon the tiles of the hearth. She wanted to destroy something. The crash and clatter were what she wanted to hear.

A maid, alarmed at the din of breaking glass, entered the room to discover what was the matter.

"A vase fell upon the hearth," said Edna. "Never mind; leave it till morning."

"Oh! you might get some of the glass in your feet, ma'am," insisted the young woman, picking up bits of the broken vase that were scattered upon the carpet. "And here's your ring, ma'am, under the chair."

Edna held out her hand, and taking the ring, slipped it upon her finger.

XVIII

The following morning Mr. Pontellier, upon leaving for his office, asked Edna if she would not meet him in town in order to look at some new fixtures for the library.

"I hardly think we need new fixtures, Léonce. Don't let us get anything new; you are too extravagant. I don't believe you ever think of saving or putting by."

"The way to become rich is to make money, my dear Edna, not to save it," he said. He regretted that she did not feel inclined to go with him and select new fixtures. He kissed her good-by, and told her she was not looking well and must take care of herself. She was unusually pale and very quiet.

She stood on the front veranda as he quitted the house, and absently picked a few sprays of jessamine that grew upon a trellis near by. She inhaled the odor of the blossoms and thrust them into the bosom of her white morning gown. The boys were dragging along the banquette a small "express wagon," which they had filled with blocks and sticks. The quadroon was following them with little quick steps, having assumed a fictitious animation and alacrity for the occasion. A fruit vender was crying his wares in the street.

Edna looked straight before her with a self-absorbed expression upon her face. She felt no interest in anything about her. The street, the children, the fruit vender, the flowers growing there under her eyes, were all part and parcel of an alien world which had suddenly become antagonistic.

She went back into the house. She had thought of speaking to the cook concerning her blunders of the previous night; but Mr. Pontellier had saved her that disagreeable mission, for which she was so poorly fitted. Mr. Pontellier's arguments were usually convincing with those whom he employed. He left home feeling quite sure that he and Edna would sit down that evening, and possibly a few subsequent evenings, to a dinner deserving of the name.

Edna spent an hour or two in looking over some of her old sketches. She could see their shortcomings and defects, which were glaring in her eyes. She tried to work a little, but found she was not in the humor. Finally she gathered together a few of the sketches—those which she considered the least discreditable; and she carried them with her when, a little later, she dressed and left the house. She looked handsome and distinguished in her street gown. The tan of the seashore had left her face, and her forehead was smooth, white, and polished beneath her heavy, yellow-brown hair. There were a few freckles on her face, and a small, dark mole near the under lip and one on the temple, half-hidden in her hair.

As Edna walked along the street she was thinking of Robert. She was still under the spell of her infatuation. She had tried to forget him, realizing the inutility of remembering. But the thought of him was like an obsession, ever pressing itself upon her. It was not that she dwelt upon details of their acquaintance, or recalled in any special or peculiar way his personality; it was his being, his existence, which dominated her thought, fading sometimes as if it would melt into the mist of the forgotten, reviving again with an intensity which filled her with an incomprehensible longing.

Edna was on her way to Madame Ratignolle's. Their intimacy, begun at Grand Isle, had not declined, and they had seen each other with some frequency since their return to the city. The Ratignolles lived at no great distance from Edna's home, on the corner of a side street, where Monsieur Ratignolle owned and conducted a drug store which enjoyed a steady and prosperous trade. His father had been in the business before him, and Monsieur Ratignolle stood well in the community and bore an enviable reputation for integrity and clearheadedness. His family lived in commodious apartments over the store, having an entrance on the side within the *porte cochère.*[19] There was something which Edna

[19]Carriage entrance.

thought very French, very foreign, about their whole manner of living. In the large and pleasant salon which extended across the width of the house, the Ratignolles entertained their friends once a fortnight with a *soirée musicale*,[20] sometimes diversified by card-playing. There was a friend who played upon the 'cello. One brought his flute and another his violin, while there were some who sang and a number who performed upon the piano with various degrees of taste and agility. The Ratignolles' *soirées musicales* were widely known, and it was considered a privilege to be invited to them.

Edna found her friend engaged in assorting the clothes which had returned that morning from the laundry. She at once abandoned her occupation upon seeing Edna, who had been ushered without ceremony into her presence.

" 'Cité can do it as well as I; it is really her business," she explained to Edna, who apologized for interrupting her. And she summoned a young black woman, whom she instructed, in French, to be very careful in checking off the list which she handed her. She told her to notice particularly if a fine linen handkerchief of Monsieur Ratignolle's, which was missing last week, had been returned; and to be sure to set to one side such pieces as required mending and darning.

Then placing an arm around Edna's waist, she led her to the front of the house, to the salon, where it was cool and sweet with the odor of great roses that stood upon the hearth in jars.

Madame Ratignolle looked more beautiful than ever there at home in a negligé which left her arms almost wholly bare and exposed the rich, melting curves of her white throat.

"Perhaps I shall be able to paint your picture some day," said Edna with a smile when they were seated. She produced the roll of sketches and started to unfold them. "I believe I ought to work again. I feel as if I wanted to be doing something. What do you think of them? Do you think it worth while to take it up again and study some more? I might study for a while with Laidpore."

She knew that Madame Ratignolle's opinion in such a matter would be next to valueless, that she herself had not alone decided, but determined; but she sought the words of praise and encouragement that would help her to put heart into her venture.

"Your talent is immense, dear!"

[20]An evening's entertainment of music.

"Nonsense!" protested Edna, well pleased.

"Immense, I tell you," persisted Madame Ratignolle, surveying the sketches one by one, at close range, then holding them at arm's length, narrowing her eyes, and dropping her head on one side. "Surely, this Bavarian peasant is worthy of framing; and this basket of apples! never have I seen anything more lifelike. One might almost be tempted to reach out a hand and take one."

Edna could not control a feeling which bordered upon complacency at her friend's praise, even realizing, as she did, its true worth. She retained a few of the sketches, and gave all the rest to Madame Ratignolle, who appreciated the gift far beyond its value and proudly exhibited the pictures to her husband when he came up from the store a little later for his midday dinner.

Mr. Ratignolle was one of those men who are called the salt of the earth. His cheerfulness was unbounded, and it was matched by his goodness of heart, his broad charity, and common sense. He and his wife spoke English with an accent which was only discernible through its un-English emphasis and a certain carefulness and deliberation. Edna's husband spoke English with no accent whatever. The Ratignolles understood each other perfectly. If ever the fusion of two human beings into one has been accomplished on this sphere it was surely in their union.

As Edna seated herself at table with them she thought, "Better a dinner of herbs," though it did not take her long to discover that [here] was no dinner of herbs, but a delicious repast, simple, choice, and in every way satisfying.

Monsieur Ratignolle was delighted to see her, though he found her looking not so well as at Grand Isle, and he advised a tonic. He talked a good deal on various topics, a little politics, some city news and neighborhood gossip. He spoke with an animation and earnestness that gave an exaggerated importance to every syllable he uttered. His wife was keenly interested in everything he said, laying down her fork the better to listen, chiming in, taking the words out of his mouth.

Edna felt depressed rather than soothed after leaving them. The little glimpse of domestic harmony which had been offered her, gave her no regret, no longing. It was not a condition of life which fitted her, and she could see in it but an appalling and hopeless ennui. She was moved by a kind of commiseration for Madame Ratignolle,—a pity for that colorless existence which never uplifted its possessor beyond the region of blind contentment, in which no moment of anguish ever visited her soul, in which she would never have the taste of life's delirium. Edna vaguely wondered what she meant by "life's delirium." It had crossed her thought like some unsought, extraneous impression.

XIX

Edna could not help but think that it was very foolish, very childish, to have stamped upon her wedding ring and smashed the crystal vase upon the tiles. She was visited by no more outbursts, moving her to such futile expedients. She began to do as she liked and to feel as she liked. She completely abandoned her Tuesdays at home, and did not return the visits of those who had called upon her. She made no ineffectual efforts to conduct her household *en bonne ménagère,*[21] going and coming as it suited her fancy, and, so far as she was able, lending herself to any passing caprice.

Mr. Pontellier had been a rather courteous husband so long as he met a certain tacit submissiveness in his wife. But her new and unexpected line of conduct completely bewildered him. It shocked him. Then her absolute disregard for her duties as a wife angered him. When Mr. Pontellier became rude, Edna grew insolent. She had resolved never to take another step backward.

"It seems to me the utmost folly for a woman at the head of a household, and the mother of children, to spend in an atelier days which would be better employed contriving for the comfort of her family."

"I feel like painting," answered Edna. "Perhaps I shan't always feel like it."

"Then in God's name paint! but don't let the family go to the devil. There's Madame Ratignolle; because she keeps up her music, she doesn't let everything else go to chaos. And she's more of a musician than you are a painter."

"She isn't a musician, and I'm not a painter. It isn't on account of painting that I let things go."

"On account of what, then?"

"Oh! I don't know. Let me alone; you bother me."

It sometimes entered Mr. Pontellier's mind to wonder if his wife were not growing a little unbalanced mentally. He could see plainly that she was not herself. That is, he could not see

[21]As a good housewife.

that she was becoming herself and daily casting aside that fictitious self which we assume like a garment with which to appear before the world.

Her husband let her alone as she requested, and went away
to his office. Edna went up to her atelier—a bright room in
the top of the house. She was working with great energy and
interest, without accomplishing anything, however, which satisfied her even in the smallest degree. For a time she had the
whole household enrolled in the service of art. The boys
posed for her. They thought it amusing at first, but the occupation soon lost its attractiveness when they discovered that it
was not a game arranged especially for their entertainment.
The quadroon sat for hours before Edna's palette, patient as
a savage, while the house-maid took charge of the children,
and the drawing-room went undusted. But the house-maid,
too, served her term as model when Edna perceived that the
young woman's back and shoulders were molded on classic
lines, and that her hair, loosened from its confining cap, became an inspiration. While Edna worked she sometimes sang
low the little air *"Ah! si tu savais!"*

It moved her with recollections. She could hear again the
ripple of the water, the flapping sail. She could see the glint
of the moon upon the bay, and could feel the soft, gusty
beating of the hot south wind. A subtle current of desire
passed through her body, weakening her hold upon the
brushes and making her eyes burn.

There were days when she was very happy without knowing why. She was happy to be alive and breathing, when her
whole being seemed to be one with the sunlight, the color,
the odors, the luxuriant warmth of some perfect Southern
day. She liked then to wander alone into strange and unfamiliar places. She discovered many a sunny, sleepy corner,
fashioned to dream in. And she found it good to dream and be
alone and unmolested.

There were days when she was unhappy, she did not know
why,—when it did not seem worth while to be glad or sorry,
to be alive or dead; when life appeared to her like a grotesque pandemonium and humanity like worms struggling
blindly toward inevitable annihilation. She could not work on
such a day, nor weave fancies to stir her pulses and warm her
blood.

XX

It was during such a mood that Edna hunted up Mademoiselle Reisz. She had not forgotten the rather disagreeable impression left upon her by their last interview; but she nevertheless felt a desire to see her—above all, to listen while she played upon the piano. Quite early in the afternoon she started upon her quest for the pianist. Unfortunately she had mislaid or lost Mademoiselle Reisz's card, and looking up her address in the city directory, she found that the woman lived on Bienville Street, some distance away. The directory which fell into her hands was a year or more old, however, and upon reaching the number indicated, Edna discovered that the house was occupied by a respectable family of mulattoes who had *chambres garnies*[22] to let. They had been living there for six months, and knew absolutely nothing of a Mademoiselle Reisz. In fact, they knew nothing of any of their neighbors; their lodgers were all people of the highest distinction, they assured Edna. She did not linger to discuss class distinctions with Madame Pouponne, but hastened to a neighboring grocery store, feeling sure that Mademoiselle would have left her address with the proprietor.

He knew Mademoiselle Reisz a good deal better than he wanted to know her, he informed his questioner. In truth, he did not want to know her at all, or anything concerning her—the most disagreeable and unpopular woman who ever lived in Bienville Street. He thanked heaven she had left the neighborhood, and was equally thankful that he did not know where she had gone.

Edna's desire to see Mademoiselle Reisz had increased tenfold since these unlooked-for obstacles had arisen to thwart it. She was wondering who could give her the information she sought, when it suddenly occurred to her that Madame Lebrun would be the one most likely to do so. She knew it was useless to ask Madame Ratignolle, who was on the most distant terms with the musician, and preferred to know nothing concerning her. She had once been almost as emphatic in expressing herself upon the subject as the corner grocer.

Edna knew that Madame Lebrun had returned to the city, for it was the middle of November. And she also knew where the Lebruns lived, on Chartres Street.

[22]Furnished rooms.

Their home from the outside looked like a prison, with iron bars before the door and lower windows. The iron bars were a relic of the old *régime*, and no one had ever thought of dislodging them. At the side was a high fence enclosing the garden. A gate or door opening upon the street was locked. Edna rang the bell at this side garden gate, and stood upon the banquette, waiting to be admitted.

It was Victor who opened the gate for her. A black woman, wiping her hands upon her apron, was close at his heels. Before she saw them Edna could hear them in altercation, the woman—plainly an anomaly—claiming the right to be allowed to perform her duties, one of which was to answer the bell.

Victor was surprised and delighted to see Mrs. Pontellier, and he made no attempt to conceal either his astonishment or his delight. He was a dark-browed, good-looking youngster of nineteen, greatly resembling his mother, but with ten times her impetuosity. He instructed the black woman to go at once and inform Madame Lebrun that Mrs. Pontellier desired to see her. The woman grumbled a refusal to do part of her duty when she had not been permitted to do it all, and started back to her interrupted task of weeding the garden. Whereupon Victor administered a rebuke in the form of a volley of abuse, which, owing to its rapidity and incoherence, was all but incomprehensible to Edna. Whatever it was, the rebuke was convincing, for the woman dropped her hoe and went mumbling into the house.

Edna did not wish to enter. It was very pleasant there on the side porch, where there were chairs, a wicker lounge, and a small table. She seated herself, for she was tired from her long tramp; and she began to rock gently and smooth out the folds of her silk parasol. Victor drew up his chair beside her. He at once explained that the black woman's offensive conduct was all due to imperfect training, as he was not there to take her in hand. He had only come up from the island the morning before, and expected to return next day. He stayed all winter at the island; he lived there, and kept the place in order and got things ready for the summer visitors.

But a man needed occasional relaxation, he informed Mrs. Pontellier, and every now and again he drummed up a pretext to bring him to the city. My! but he had had a time of it the evening before! He wouldn't want his mother to know, and he began to talk in a whisper. He was scintillant with recollections. Of course, he couldn't think of telling Mrs.

Pontellier all about it, she being a woman and not comprehending such things. But it all began with a girl peeping and smiling at him through the shutters as he passed by. Oh! but she was a beauty! Certainly he smiled back, and went up and talked to her. Mrs. Pontellier did not know him if she supposed he was one to let an opportunity like that escape him. Despite herself, the youngster amused her. She must have betrayed in her look some degree of interest or entertainment. The boy grew more daring, and Mrs. Pontellier might have found herself, in a little while, listening to a highly colored story but for the timely appearance of Madame Lebrun.

That lady was still clad in white, according to her custom of the summer. Her eyes beamed an effusive welcome. Would not Mrs. Pontellier go inside? Would she partake of some refreshment? Why had she not been there before? How was that dear Mr. Pontellier and how were those sweet children? Had Mrs. Pontellier ever known such a warm November?

Victor went and reclined on the wicker lounge behind his mother's chair, where he commanded a view of Edna's face. He had taken her parasol from her hands while he spoke to her, and he now lifted it and twirled it above him as he lay on his back. When Madame Lebrun complained that it was *so* dull coming back to the city; that she saw *so* few people now; that even Victor, when he came up from the island for a day or two, had *so* much to occupy him and engage his time; then it was that the youth went into contortions on the lounge and winked mischievously at Edna. She somehow felt like a confederate in crime, and tried to look severe and disapproving.

There had been but two letters from Robert, with little in them, they told her. Victor said it was really not worth while to go inside for the letters, when his mother entreated him to go in search of them. He remembered the contents, which in truth he rattled off very glibly when put to the test.

One letter was written from Vera Cruz and the other from the City of Mexico. He had met Montel, who was doing everything toward his advancement. So far, the financial situation was no improvement over the one he had left in New Orleans, but of course the prospects were vastly better. He wrote of the City of Mexico, the buildings, the people and their habits, the conditions of life which he found there. He sent his love to the family. He inclosed a check to his mother, and hoped she would affectionately remember him to all his friends. That was about the substance of the two letters. Edna felt that if there had been a message for her, she would have received it. The despondent frame of mind in which she had left home began again to overtake her, and she remembered that she wished to find Mademoiselle Reisz.

Madame Lebrun knew where Mademoiselle Reisz lived. She gave Edna the address, regretting that she would not consent to stay and spend the remainder of the afternoon, and pay a visit to Mademoiselle Reisz some other day. The afternoon was already well advanced.

Victor escorted her out upon the banquette, lifted her parasol, and held it over her while he walked to the car with her. He entreated her to bear in mind that the disclosures of the afternoon were strictly confidential. She laughed and bantered him a little, remembering too late that she should have been dignified and reserved.

"How handsome Mrs. Pontellier looked!" said Madame Lebrun to her son.

"Ravishing!" he admitted. "The city atmosphere has improved her. Some way she doesn't seem like the same woman."

XXI

Some people contended that the reason Mademoiselle Reisz always chose apartments up under the roof was to discourage the approach of beggars, peddlars and callers. There were plenty of windows in her little front room. They were for the most part dingy, but as they were nearly always open it did not make so much difference. They often admitted into the room a good deal of smoke and soot; but at the same time all the light and air that there was came through them. From her windows could be seen the crescent of the river, the masts of ships and the big chimneys of the Mississippi steamers. A magnificent piano crowded the apartment. In the next room she slept, and in the third and last she harbored a gasoline stove on which she cooked her meals when disinclined to descend to the neighboring restaurant. It was there also that she ate, keeping her belongings in a rare old buffet, dingy and battered from a hundred years of use.

When Edna knocked at Mademoiselle Reisz's front room door and entered, she discovered that person standing beside the window, engaged in mending or patching an old prunella gaiter. The little musician laughed all over when she saw Edna. Her laugh consisted of a contortion of the face and all the muscles of the body. She seemed strikingly homely, standing there in the afternoon light. She still wore the shabby lace and the artificial bunch of violets on the side of her head.

"So you remembered me at last," said Mademoiselle. "I had said to myself, 'Ah, bah! she will never come.'"

"Did you want me to come?" asked Edna with a smile.

"I had not thought much about it," answered Mademoiselle. The two had seated themselves on a little bumpy sofa which stood against the wall. "I am glad, however, that you came. I have the water boiling back there, and was just about to make some coffee. You will drink a cup with me. And how is *la belle dame*? Always handsome! always healthy! always contented!" She took Edna's hand between her strong wiry fingers, holding it loosely without warmth, and executing a sort of double theme upon the back and palm.

"Yes," she went on; "I sometimes thought: 'She will never come. She promised as those women in society always do, without meaning it. She will not come.' For I really don't believe you like me, Mrs. Pontellier."

"I don't know whether I like you or not," replied Edna, gazing down at the little woman with a quizzical look.

The candor of Mrs. Pontellier's admission greatly pleased Mademoiselle Reisz. She expressed her gratification by repairing forthwith to the region of the gasoline stove and rewarding her guest with the promised cup of coffee. The coffee and the biscuit accompanying it proved very acceptable to Edna, who had declined refreshment at Madame Lebrun's and was now beginning to feel hungry. Mademoiselle set the tray which she brought in upon a small table near at hand, and seated herself once again on the lumpy sofa.

"I have had a letter from your friend," she remarked, as she poured a little cream into Edna's cup and handed it to her.

"My friend?"

"Yes, your friend Robert. He wrote to me from the City of Mexico."

"Wrote to *you*?" repeated Edna in amazement, stirring her coffee absently.

"Yes, to me. Why not? Don't stir all the warmth out of your coffee; drink it. Though the letter might as well have been sent to you; it was nothing but Mrs. Pontellier from beginning to end."

"Let me see it," requested the young woman, entreatingly.

"No; a letter concerns no one but the person who writes it and the one to whom it is written."

"Haven't you just said it concerned me from beginning to end?"

"It was written about you, not to you. 'Have you seen Mrs. Pontellier? How is she looking?' he asks. 'As Mrs. Pontellier says,' or 'as Mrs. Pontellier once said.' 'If Mrs. Pontellier should call upon you, play for her that Impromptu of Chopin's, my favorite. I heard it here a day or two ago, but not as you play it. I should like to know how it affects her,' and so on, as if he supposed we were constantly in each other's society."

"Let me see the letter."

"Oh, no."

"Have you answered it?"

"No."

"Let me see the letter."

"No, and again, no."

"Then play the Impromptu for me."

"It is growing late; what time do you have to be home?"

"Time doesn't concern me. Your question seems a little rude. Play the Impromptu."

"But you have told me nothing of yourself. What are you doing?"

"Painting!" laughed Edna. "I am becoming an artist. Think of it!"

"Ah! an artist! You have pretensions, Madame."

"Why pretensions? Do you think I could not become an artist?"

"I do not know you well enough to say. I do not know your talent or your temperament. To be an artist includes much; one must possess many gifts—absolute gifts—which have not been acquired by one's own effort. And, moreover, to succeed, the artist must possess the courageous soul."

"What do you mean by the courageous soul?"

"Courageous, *ma foi!* The brave soul. The soul that dares and defies."

"Show me the letter and play for me the Impromptu. You see that I have persistence. Does that quality count for anything in art?"

"It counts with a foolish old woman whom you have captivated," replied Mademoiselle, with her wriggling laugh.

The letter was right there at hand in the drawer of the little table upon which Edna had just placed her coffee cup.

Mademoiselle opened the drawer and drew forth the letter, the topmost one. She placed it in Edna's hands, and without further comment arose and went to the piano.

Mademoiselle played a soft interlude. It was an improvisation. She sat low at the instrument, and the lines of her body settled into ungraceful curves and angles that gave it an appearance of deformity. Gradually and imperceptibly the interlude melted into the soft opening minor chords of the Chopin Impromptu.

Edna did not know when the Impromptu began or ended. She sat in the sofa corner reading Robert's letter by the fading light. Mademoiselle had glided from the Chopin into the quivering love-notes of Isolde's song, and back again to the Impromptu with its soulful and poignant longing.

The shadows deepened in the little room. The music grew strange and fantastic—turbulent, insistent, plaintive and soft with entreaty. The shadows grew deeper. The music filled the room. It floated out upon the night, over the housetops, the crescent of the river, losing itself in the silence of the upper air.

Edna was sobbing, just as she had wept one midnight at Grand Isle when strange, new voices awoke in her. She arose in some agitation to take her departure. "May I come again, Mademoiselle?" she asked at the threshold.

"Come whenever you feel like it. Be careful; the stairs and landings are dark; don't stumble."

Mademoiselle reëntered and lit a candle. Robert's letter was on the floor. She stooped and picked it up. It was crumpled and damp with tears. Mademoiselle smoothed the letter out, restored it to the envelope, and replaced it in the table drawer.

XXII

One morning on his way into town Mr. Pontellier stopped at the house of his old friend and family physician, Doctor Mandelet. The Doctor was a semi-retired physician, resting, as the saying is, upon his laurels. He bore a reputation for wisdom rather than skill—leaving the active practice of medicine to his assistants and younger contemporaries—and was much sought for in matters of consultation. A few families, united to him by bonds of friendship, he still attended when they required the services of a physician. The Pontelliers were among these.

Mr. Pontellier found the Doctor reading at the open window of his study. His house stood rather far back from the street, in the center of a delightful garden, so that it was quiet and peaceful at the old gentleman's study window. He was a great reader. He stared up disapprovingly over his eyeglasses as Mr. Pontellier entered, wondering who had the temerity to disturb him at that hour of the morning.

"Ah, Pontellier! Not sick, I hope. Come and have a seat. What news do you bring this morning?" He was quite portly, with a profusion of gray hair, and small blue eyes which age had robbed of much of their brightness but none of their penetration.

"Oh! I'm never sick, Doctor. You know that I come of tough fiber—of that old Creole race of Pontelliers that dry up and finally blow away. I came to consult—no, not precisely to consult—to talk to you about Edna. I don't know what ails her."

"Madame Pontellier not well?" marveled the Doctor. "Why, I saw her—I think it was a week ago—walking along Canal Street, the picture of health, it seemed to me."

"Yes, yes; she seems quite well," said Mr. Pontellier, leaning forward and whirling his stick between his two hands; "but she doesn't act well. She's odd, she's not like herself. I can't make her out, and I thought perhaps you'd help me."

"How does she act?" inquired the doctor.

"Well, it isn't easy to explain," said Mr. Pontellier, throwing himself back in his chair. "She lets the housekeeping go to the dickens."

"Well, well; women are not all alike, my dear Pontellier. We've got to consider—"

"I know that; I told you I couldn't explain. Her whole attitude—toward me and everybody and everything—has changed. You know I have a quick temper, but I don't want to quarrel or be rude to a woman, especially my wife; yet I'm driven to it, and feel like ten thousand devils after I've made a fool of myself. She's making it devilishly uncomfortable for me," he went on nervously. "She's got some sort of notion in her head concerning the eternal rights of women; and—you understand—we meet in the morning at the breakfast table."

The old gentleman lifted his shaggy eyebrows, protruded his thick nether lip, and tapped the arms of his chair with his cushioned finger-tips.

"What have you been doing to her, Pontellier?"

"Doing! *Parbleu!*"

"Has she," asked the Doctor, with a smile, "has she been associating of late with a circle of pseudo-intellectual women—super-spiritual superior beings? My wife has been telling me about them."

"That's the trouble," broke in Mr. Pontellier, "she hasn't been associating with any one. She has abandoned her Tuesdays at home, has thrown over all her acquaintances, and goes tramping about by herself, moping in the street-cars, getting in after dark. I tell you she's peculiar. I don't like it; I feel a little worried over it."

This was a new aspect for the Doctor. "Nothing hereditary?" he asked, seriously. "Nothing peculiar about her family antecedents, is there?"

"Oh, no, indeed! She comes of sound old Presbyterian Kentucky stock. The old gentleman, her father, I have heard, used to atone for his week-day sins with his Sunday devotions. I know for a fact, that his race horses literally ran away with the prettiest bit of Kentucky farming land I ever laid eyes upon. Margaret—you know Margaret—she has all the Presbyterianism undiluted. And the youngest is something of a vixen. By the way, she gets married in a couple of weeks from now."

"Send your wife up to the wedding," exclaimed the Doctor, foreseeing a happy solution. "Let her stay among her own people for a while; it will do her good."

"That's what I want her to do. She won't go to the marriage. She says a wedding is one of the most lamentable spectacles on earth. Nice thing for a woman to say to her husband!" exclaimed Mr. Pontellier, fuming anew at the recollection.

"Pontellier," said the Doctor, after a moment's reflection, "let your wife alone for a while. Don't bother her, and don't let her bother you. Woman, my dear friend, is a very peculiar and delicate organism—a sensitive and highly organized woman, such as I know Mrs. Pontellier to be, is especially peculiar. It would require an inspired psychologist to deal successfully with them. And when ordinary fellows like you and me attempt to cope with their idiosyncrasies the result is bungling. Most women are moody and whimsical. This is some passing whim of your wife, due to some cause or causes which you and I needn't try to fathom. But it will pass happily over, especially if you let her alone. Send her around to see me."

"Oh! I couldn't do that; there'd be no reason for it," objected Mr. Pontellier.

"Then I'll go around and see her," said the Doctor. "I'll drop in to dinner some evening *en bon ami*."[23]

"Do! by all means," urged Mr. Pontellier. "What evening will you come? Say Thursday. Will you come Thursday?" he asked, rising to take his leave.

"Very well; Thursday. My wife may possibly have some engagement for me Thursday. In case she has, I shall let you know. Otherwise, you may expect me."

Mr. Pontellier turned before leaving to say:

"I am going to New York on business very soon. I have a big scheme on hand, and want to be on the field proper to pull the ropes and handle the ribbons. We'll let you in on the inside if you say so, Doctor," he laughed.

"No, I thank you, my dear sir," returned the Doctor. "I leave such ventures to you younger men with the fever of life still in your blood."

"What I wanted to say," continued Mr. Pontellier, with his hand on the knob; "I may have to be absent a good while. Would you advise me to take Edna along?"

"By all means, if she wishes to go. If not, leave her here. Don't contradict her. The mood will pass, I assure you. It may take a month, two, three months—possibly longer, but it will pass; have patience."

"Well, good-by, *à jeudi*,"[24] said Mr. Pontellier, as he let himself out.

The Doctor would have liked during the course of conversation to ask, "Is there any man in the case?" but he knew his Creole too well to make such a blunder as that.

He did not resume his book immediately, but sat for a while meditatively looking out into the garden.

XXIII

Edna's father was in the city, and had been with them several days. She was not very warmly or deeply attached to him, but they had certain tastes in common, and when together they were companionable. His coming was in the nature of a welcome disturbance; it seemed to furnish a new direction for her emotions.

[23]Casually; as a good friend.
[24]See you on Thursday.

He had come to purchase a wedding gift for his daughter, Janet, and an outfit for himself in which he might make a creditable appearance at her marriage. Mr. Pontellier had selected the bridal gift, as every one immediately connected with him always deferred to his taste in such matters. And his suggestions on the question of dress—which too often assumes the nature of a problem—were of inestimable value to his father-in-law. But for the past few days the old gentleman had been upon Edna's hands, and in his society she was becoming acquainted with a new set of sensations. He had been a colonel in the Confederate army, and still maintained, with the title, the military bearing which had always accompanied it. His hair and mustache were white and silky, emphasizing the rugged bronze of his face. He was tall and thin, and wore his coats padded, which gave a fictitious breadth and depth to his shoulders and chest. Edna and her father looked very distinguished together, and excited a good deal of notice during their perambulations. Upon his arrival she began by introducing him to her atelier and making a sketch of him. He took the whole matter very seriously. If her talent had been tenfold greater than it was, it would not have surprised him, convinced as he was that he had bequeathed to all of his daughters the germs of a masterful capability, which only depended upon their own efforts to be directed toward successful achievement.

Before her pencil he sat rigid and unflinching, as he had faced the cannon's mouth in days gone by. He resented the intrusion of the children, who gaped with wondering eyes at him, sitting so stiff up there in their mother's bright atelier. When they drew near he motioned them away with an expressive action of the foot, loath to disturb the fixed lines of his countenance, his arms, or his rigid shoulders.

Edna, anxious to entertain him, invited Mademoiselle Reisz to meet him, having promised him a treat in her piano playing; but Mademoiselle declined the invitation. So together they attended a *soirée musicale* at the Ratignolle's. Monsieur and Madame Ratignolle made much of the Colonel, installing him as the guest of honor and engaging him at once to dine with them the following Sunday, or any day which he might select. Madame coquetted with him in the most captivating and naïve manner, with eyes, gestures, and a profusion of compliments, till the Colonel's old head felt thirty years younger on his padded shoulders. Edna marveled, not comprehending. She herself was almost devoid of coquetry.

There were one or two men whom she observed at the *soirée musicale;* but she would never have felt moved to any kittenish display to attract their notice—to any feline or feminine wiles to express herself toward them. Their personality attracted her in an agreeable way. Her fancy selected them, and she was glad when a lull in the music gave them an opportunity to meet her and talk with her. Often on the street the glance of strange eyes had lingered in her memory, and sometimes had disturbed her.

Mr. Pontellier did not attend these *soirées musicales.* He considered them *bourgeois,* and found more diversion at the club. To Madame Ratignolle he said the music dispensed at her *soirées* was too "heavy," too far beyond his untrained comprehension. His excuse flattered her. But she disapproved of Mr. Pontellier's club and she was frank enough to tell Edna so.

"It's a pity Mr. Pontellier doesn't stay home more in the evenings. I think you would be more—well, if you don't mind my saying it—more united, if he did."

"Oh! dear no!" said Edna, with a blank look in her eyes. "What should I do if he stayed home? We wouldn't have anything to say to each other."

She had not much of anything to say to her father, for that matter; but he did not antagonize her. She discovered that he interested her, though she realized that he might not interest her long; and for the first time in her life she felt as if she were thoroughly acquainted with him. He kept her busy serving him and ministering to his wants. It amused her to do so. She would not permit a servant or one of the children to do anything for him which she might do herself. Her husband noticed, and thought it was the expression of a deep filial attachment which he had never suspected.

The Colonel drank numerous "toddies" during the course of the day, which left him, however, imperturbed. He was an expert at concocting strong drinks. He had even invented some, to which he had given fantastic names, and for whose manufacture he required diverse ingredients that it devolved upon Edna to procure for him.

When Doctor Mandelet dined with the Pontelliers on Thursday he could discern in Mrs. Pontellier no trace of that morbid condition which her husband had reported to him. She was excited and in a manner radiant. She and her father had been to the race course, and their thoughts when they seated themselves at table were still occupied with the events of the afternoon, and their talk was still of the track. The Doctor had not kept pace with turf affairs. He had certain recollections of racing in what he called "the good old times" when the Lecompte stables flourished, and he drew upon this fund of memories so that he might not be left out and seem wholly devoid of the modern spirit. But he failed to impose upon the Colonel, and was even far from impressing him with this trumped-up knowledge of bygone days. Edna had staked her father on his last venture, with the most gratifying results to both of them. Besides, they had met some very charming people, according to the Colonel's impressions. Mrs. Mortimer Merriman and Mrs. James Highcamp, who were there with Alcée Arobin, had joined them and had enlivened the hours in a fashion that warmed him to think of.

Mr. Pontellier himself had no particular leaning toward horse-racing, and was even rather inclined to discourage it as a pastime, especially when he considered the fate of that blue-grass farm in Kentucky. He endeavored, in a general way, to express a particular disapproval, and only succeeded in arousing the ire and opposition of his father-in-law. A pretty dispute followed, in which Edna warmly espoused her father's cause and the Doctor remained neutral.

He observed his hostess attentively from under his shaggy brows, and noted a subtle change which had transformed her from the listless woman he had known into a being who, for the moment, seemed palpitant with the forces of life. Her speech was warm and energetic. There was no repression in her glance or gesture. She reminded him of some beautiful, sleek animal waking up in the sun.

The dinner was excellent. The claret was warm and the champagne was cold, and under their beneficent influence the threatened unpleasantness melted and vanished with the fumes of the wine.

Mr. Pontellier warmed up and grew reminiscent. He told some amusing plantation experiences, recollections of old Iberville and his youth, when he hunted 'possum in company with some friendly darky; thrashed the pecan trees, shot the grosbec, and roamed the woods and fields in mischievous idleness.

The Colonel, with little sense of humor and of the fitness of things, related a somber episode of those dark and bitter days, in which he had acted a conspicuous part and always formed a central figure. Nor was the Doctor happier in his selection, when he told the old, ever new and curious story of the waning of a woman's love, seeking strange, new channels, only to return to its legitimate source after days of fierce unrest. It was one of the many little human documents which had been unfolded to him during his long career as a physician. The story did not seem especially to impress Edna. She had one of her own to tell, of a woman who paddled away with her lover one night in a pirogue and never came back. They were lost amid the Baratarian Islands, and no one ever heard of them or found trace of them from that day to this. It was a pure invention. She said that Madame Antoine had related it to her. That, also, was an invention. Perhaps it was a dream she had had. But every glowing word seemed real to those who listened. They could feel the hot breath of the Southern night; they could hear the long sweep of the pirogue through the glistening moonlit water, the beating of birds' wings, rising startled from among the reeds in the salt-water pools; they could see the faces of the lovers, pale, close together, rapt in oblivious forgetfulness, drifting into the unknown.

The champagne was cold, and its subtle fumes played fantastic tricks with Edna's memory that night.

Outside, away from the glow of the fire and the soft lamplight, the night was chill and murky. The Doctor doubled his old-fashioned cloak across his breast as he strode home through the darkness. He knew his fellow-creatures better than most men; knew that inner life which so seldom unfolds itself to unanointed eyes. He was sorry he had accepted Pontellier's invitation. He was growing old, and beginning to need rest and an imperturbed spirit. He did not want the secrets of other lives thrust upon him.

"I hope it isn't Arobin," he muttered to himself as he walked. "I hope to heaven it isn't Alcée Arobin."

XXIV

Edna and her father had a warm, and almost violent dispute upon the subject of her refusal to attend her sister's wedding. Mr. Pontellier declined to interfere, to interpose either his influence or his authority. He was following Doctor Mandelet's advice, and letting her do as she liked. The Colonel reproached his daughter for her lack of filial kindness and respect, her want of sisterly affection and womanly consideration. His arguments were labored and unconvincing. He doubted if Janet would accept any excuse—forgetting that Edna had offered none. He doubted if Janet would ever speak to her again, and he was sure Margaret would not.

Edna was glad to be rid of her father when he finally took himself off with his wedding garments and his bridal gifts, with his padded shoulders, his Bible reading, his "toddies" and ponderous oaths.

Mr. Pontellier followed him closely. He meant to stop at the wedding on his way to New York and endeavor by every means which money and love could devise to atone somewhat for Edna's incomprehensible action.

"You are too lenient, too lenient by far, Léonce," asserted the Colonel. "Authority, coercion are what is needed. Put your foot down good and hard; the only way to manage a wife. Take my word for it."

The Colonel was perhaps unaware that he had coerced his own wife into her grave. Mr. Pontellier had a vague suspicion of it which he thought it needless to mention at that late day.

Edna was not so consciously gratified at her husband's leaving home as she had been over the departure of her father. As the day approached when he was to leave her for a comparatively long stay, she grew melting and affectionate, remembering his many acts of consideration and his repeated expressions of an ardent attachment. She was solicitous about his health and his welfare. She bustled around, looking after his clothing, thinking about heavy underwear, quite as Madame Ratignolle would have done under similar circumstances. She cried when he went away, calling him her dear, good friend, and she was quite certain she would grow lonely before long and go to join him in New York.

But after all, a radiant peace settled upon her when she at last found herself alone. Even the children were gone. Old Madame Pontellier had come herself and carried them off to Iberville with their quadroon. The old madame did not venture to say she was afraid they would be neglected during Léonce's absence; she hardly ventured to think so. She was hungry for them—even a little fierce in her attachment. She did not want them to be wholly "children of the pavement," she always said when begging to have them for a space. She wished them to know the country, with its streams, its fields, its woods, its freedom, so delicious to the young. She wished them to taste something of the life their father had lived and known and loved when he, too, was a little child.

When Edna was at last alone, she breathed a big, genuine

sigh of relief. A feeling that was unfamiliar but very delicious came over her. She walked all through the house, from one room to another, as if inspecting it for the first time. She tried the various chairs and lounges, as if she had never sat and reclined upon them before. And she perambulated around the outside of the house, investigating, looking to see if windows and shutters were secure and in order. The flowers were like new acquaintances; she approached them in a familiar spirit, and made herself at home among them. The garden walks were damp, and Edna called to the maid to bring out her rubber sandals. And there she stayed, and stooped, digging around the plants, trimming, picking dead, dry leaves. The children's little dog came out, interfering, getting in her way. She scolded him, laughed at him, played with him. The garden smelled so good and looked so pretty in the afternoon sunlight. Edna plucked all the bright flowers she could find, and went into the house with them, she and the little dog.

Even the kitchen assumed a sudden interesting character which she had never before perceived. She went in to give directions to the cook, to say that the butcher would have to bring much less meat, that they would require only half their usual quantity of bread, of milk and groceries. She told the cook that she herself would be greatly occupied during Mr. Pontellier's absence, and she begged her to take all thought and responsibility of the larder upon her own shoulders.

That night Edna dined alone. The candelabra, with a few candles in the center of the table, gave all the light she needed. Outside the circle of light in which she sat, the large dining-room looked solemn and shadowy. The cook, placed upon her mettle, served a delicious repast—a luscious tenderloin broiled à point.[25] The wine tasted good; the marron glacé[26] seemed to be just what she wanted. It was so pleasant, too, to dine in a comfortable peignoir.

She thought a little sentimentally about Léonce and the children, and wondered what they were doing. As she gave a dainty scrap or two to the doggie, she talked intimately to him about Etienne and Raoul. He was beside himself with astonishment and delight over these companionable advances,

[25]Medium.
[26]Glazed chestnut.

and showed his appreciation by his little quick, snappy barks and a lively agitation.

Then Edna sat in the library after dinner and read Emerson until she grew sleepy. She realized that she had neglected her reading, and determined to start anew upon a course of improving studies, now that her time was completely her own to do with as she liked.

After a refreshing bath, Edna went to bed. And as she snuggled comfortably beneath the eiderdown a sense of restfulness invaded her, such as she had not known before.

XXV

When the weather was dark and cloudy Edna could not work. She needed the sun to mellow and temper her mood to the sticking point. She had reached a stage when she seemed to be no longer feeling her way, working, when in the humor, with sureness and ease. And being devoid of ambition, and striving not toward accomplishment, she drew satisfaction from the work in itself.

On rainy or melancholy days Edna went out and sought the society of the friends she had made at Grand Isle. Or else she stayed indoors and nursed a mood with which she was becoming too familiar for her own comfort and peace of mind. It was not despair; but it seemed to her as if life were passing by, leaving its promise broken and unfulfilled. Yet there were other days when she listened, was led on and deceived by fresh promises which her youth held out to her.

She went again to the races, and again. Alcée Arobin and Mrs. Highcamp called for her one bright afternoon in Arobin's drag. Mrs. Highcamp was a worldly but unaffected, intelligent, slim, tall blonde woman in the forties, with an indifferent manner and blue eyes that stared. She had a daughter who served her as a pretext for cultivating the society of young men of fashion. Alcée Arobin was one of them. He was a familiar figure at the race course, the opera, the fashionable clubs. There was a perpetual smile in his eyes, which seldom failed to awaken a corresponding cheerfulness in any one who looked into them and listened to his good-humored voice. His manner was quiet, and at times a little insolent. He possessed a good figure, a pleasing face, not overburdened with depth of thought or feeling; and his dress was that of the conventional man of fashion.

He admired Edna extravagantly, after meeting her at the

races with her father. He had met her before on other occasions, but she had seemed to him unapproachable until that day. It was at his instigation that Mrs. Highcamp called to ask her to go with them to the Jockey Club to witness the turf event of the season.

There were possibly a few track men out there who knew the race horse as well as Edna, but there was certainly none who knew it better. She sat between her two companions as one having authority to speak. She laughed at Arobin's pretensions, and deplored Mrs. Highcamp's ignorance. The race horse was a friend and intimate associate of her childhood. The atmosphere of the stables and the breath of the blue grass paddock revived in her memory and lingered in her nostrils. She did not perceive that she was talking like her father as the sleek geldings ambled in review before them. She played for very high stakes, and fortune favored her. The fever of the game flamed in her cheeks and eyes, and it got into her blood and into her brain like an intoxicant. People turned their heads to look at her, and more than one lent an attentive ear to her utterances, hoping thereby to secure the elusive but ever-desired "tip." Arobin caught the contagion of excitement which drew him to Edna like a magnet. Mrs. Highcamp remained, as usual, unmoved, with her indifferent stare and uplifted eyebrows.

Edna stayed and dined with Mrs. Highcamp upon being urged to do so. Arobin also remained and sent away his drag.

The dinner was quiet and uninteresting, save for the cheerful efforts of Arobin to enliven things. Mrs. Highcamp deplored the absence of her daughter from the races, and tried to convey to her what she had missed by going to the "Dante reading" instead of joining them. The girl held a geranium leaf up to her nose and said nothing, but looked knowing and noncommittal. Mr. Highcamp was a plain, bald-headed man, who only talked under compulsion. He was unresponsive. Mrs. Highcamp was full of delicate courtesy and consideration toward her husband. She addressed most of her conversation to him at table. They sat in the library after dinner and read the evening papers together under the drop-light; while the younger people went into the drawing-room near by and talked. Miss Highcamp played some selections from Grieg upon the piano. She seemed to have apprehended all of the composer's coldness and none of his poetry. While Edna listened she could not help wondering if she had lost her taste for music.

When the time came for her to go home, Mr. Highcamp grunted a lame offer to escort her, looking down at his slippered feet with tactless concern. It was Arobin who took her home. The car ride was long, and it was late when they reached Esplanade Street. Arobin asked permission to enter for a second to light his cigarette—his match safe was empty. He filled his match safe, but did not light his cigarette until he left her, after she had expressed her willingness to go to the races with him again.

Edna was neither tired nor sleepy. She was hungry again, for the Highcamp dinner, though of excellent quality, had lacked abundance. She rummaged in the larder and brought forth a slice of "Gruyère" and some crackers. She opened a bottle of beer which she found in the ice-box. Edna felt extremely restless and excited. She vacantly hummed a fantastic tune as she poked at the wood embers on the hearth and munched a cracker.

She wanted something to happen—something, anything; she did not know what. She regretted that she had not made Arobin stay a half hour to talk over the horses with her. She counted the money she had won. But there was nothing else to do, so she went to bed, and tossed there for hours in a sort of monotonous agitation.

In the middle of the night she remembered that she had forgotten to write her regular letter to her husband; and she decided to do so next day and tell him about her afternoon at the Jockey Club. She lay wide awake composing a letter which was nothing like the one which she wrote next day. When the maid awoke her in the morning Edna was dreaming of Mr. Highcamp playing on the piano at the entrance of a music store on Canal Street, while his wife was saying to Alcée Arobin, as they boarded an Esplanade Street car:

"What a pity that so much talent has been neglected! but I must go."

When, a few days later, Alcée Arobin again called for Edna in his drag, Mrs. Highcamp was not with him. He said they would pick her up. But as that lady had not been apprised of his intention of picking her up, she was not at home. The daughter was just leaving the house to attend the meeting of a branch Folk Lore Society, and regretted that she could not accompany them. Arobin appeared nonplused, and asked Edna if there were any one else she cared to ask.

She did not deem it worth while to go in search of any of the fashionable acquaintances from whom she had withdrawn herself. She thought of Madame Ratignolle, but knew that her fair friend did not leave the house, except to take a languid walk around the block with her husband after nightfall. Mademoiselle Reisz would have laughed at such a request from Edna. Madame Lebrun might have enjoyed the outing, but for some reason Edna did not want her. So they went alone, she and Arobin.

The afternoon was intensely interesting to her. The excitement came back upon her like a remittent fever. Her talk grew familiar and confidential. It was no labor to become intimate with Arobin. His manner invited easy confidence. The preliminary stage of becoming acquainted was one which he always endeavored to ignore when a pretty and engaging woman was concerned.

He stayed and dined with Edna. He stayed and sat beside the wood fire. They laughed and talked; and before it was time to go he was telling her how different life might have been if he had known her years before. With ingenuous frankness he spoke of what a wicked, ill-disciplined boy he had been, and impulsively drew up his cuff to exhibit upon his wrist the scar from a saber cut which he had received in a duel outside of Paris when he was nineteen. She touched his hand as she scanned the red cicatrice on the inside of his white wrist. A quick impulse that was somewhat spasmodic impelled her fingers to close in a sort of clutch upon his hand. He felt the pressure of her pointed nails in the flesh of his palm.

She arose hastily and walked toward the mantel.

"The sight of a wound or scar always agitates and sickens me," she said. "I shouldn't have looked at it."

"I beg your pardon," he entreated, following her; "it never occurred to me that it might be repulsive."

He stood close to her, and the effrontery in his eyes repelled the old, vanishing self in her, yet drew all her awakening sensuousness. He saw enough in her face to impel him to take her hand and hold it while he said his lingering good night.

"Will you go to the races again?" he asked.

"No," she said. "I've had enough of the races. I don't want to lose all the money I've won, and I've got to work when the weather is bright, instead of—"

"Yes; work; to be sure. You promised to show me your work. What morning may I come up to your atelier? To-morrow?"

"No!"

"Day after?"

"No, no."

"Oh, please don't refuse me! I know something of such things. I might help you with a stray suggestion or two."

"No. Good night. Why don't you go after you have said good night? I don't like you," she went on in a high, excited pitch. attempting to draw away her hand. She felt that her words lacked dignity and sincerity, and she knew that he felt it.

"I'm sorry you don't like me. I'm sorry I offended you. How have I offended you? What have I done? Can't you forgive me?" And he bent and pressed his lips upon her hand as if he wished never more to withdraw them.

"Mr. Arobin," she complained, "I'm greatly upset by the excitement of the afternoon; I'm not myself. My manner must have misled you in some way. I wish you to go, please." She spoke in a monotonous, dull tone. He took his hat from the table, and stood with eyes turned from her, looking into the dying fire. For a moment or two he kept an impressive silence.

"Your manner has not misled me, Mrs. Pontellier," he said finally. "My own emotions have done that. I couldn't help it. When I'm hear you, how could I help it? Don't think anything of it, don't bother, please. You see, I go when you command me. If you wish me to stay away, I shall do so. If you let me come back, I—oh! you will let me come back?"

He cast one appealing glance at her, to which she made no response. Alcée Arobin's manner was so genuine that it often deceived even himself.

Edna did not care or think whether it were genuine or not. When she was alone she looked mechanically at the back of her hand which he had kissed so warmly. Then she leaned her head down on the mantelpiece. She felt somewhat like a woman who in a moment of passion is betrayed into an act of infidelity, and realizes the significance of the act without being wholly awakened from its glamour. The thought was passing vaguely through her mind, "What would he think?"

She did not mean her husband; she was thinking of Robert Lebrun. Her husband seemed to her now like a person whom she had married without love as an excuse.

She lit a candle and went up to her room. Alcée Arobin was absolutely nothing to her. Yet his presence, his manners, the warmth of his glances, and above all the touch of his lips upon her hand had acted like a narcotic upon her.

She slept a languorous sleep, interwoven with vanishing dreams.

XXVI

Alcée Arobin wrote Edna an elaborate note of apology, palpitant with sincerity. It embarrassed her; for in a cooler, quieter moment it appeared to her absurd that she should have taken his action so seriously, so dramatically. She felt sure that the significance of the whole occurrence had lain in her own self-consciousness. If she ignored his note it would give undue importance to a trivial affair. If she replied to it in a serious spirit it would still leave in his mind the impression that she had in a susceptible moment yielded to his influence. After all, it was no great matter to have one's hand kissed. She was provoked at his having written the apology. She answered in as light and bantering a spirit as she fancied it deserved, and said she would be glad to have him look in upon her at work whenever he felt the inclination and his business gave him the opportunity.

He responded at once by presenting himself at her home with all his disarming naïveté. And then there was scarcely a day which followed that she did not see him or was not reminded of him. He was prolific in pretexts. His attitude became one of good-humored subservience and tacit adoration. He was ready at all times to submit to her moods, which were as often kind as they were cold. She grew accustomed to him. They became intimate and friendly by imperceptible degrees, and then by leaps. He sometimes talked in a way that astonished her at first and brought the crimson into her face; in a way that pleased her at last, appealing to the animalism that stirred impatiently within her.

There was nothing which so quieted the turmoil of Edna's senses as a visit to Mademoiselle Reisz. It was then, in the presence of that personality which was offensive to her, that the woman, by her divine art, seemed to reach Edna's spirit and set it free.

It was misty, with heavy, lowering atmosphere, one afternoon, when Edna climbed the stairs to the pianist's apartments under the roof. Her clothes were dripping with moisture. She felt chilled and pinched as she entered the room. Mademoiselle was poking at a rusty stove that smoked a little and warmed the room indifferently. She was endeavoring to heat a pot of chocolate on the stove. The room looked cheerless and dingy to Edna as she entered. A bust of Beethoven, covered with a hood of dust, scowled at her from the mantelpiece.

"Ah! here comes the sunlight!" exclaimed Mademoiselle, rising from her knees before the stove. "Now it will be warm and bright enough; I can let the fire alone."

She closed the stove door with a bang, and approaching, assisted in removing Edna's dripping mackintosh.

"You are cold; you look miserable. The chocolate will soon be hot. But would you rather have a taste of brandy? I have scarcely touched the bottle which you brought me for my cold." A piece of red flannel was wrapped around Mademoiselle's throat; a stiff neck compelled her to hold her head on one side.

"I will take some brandy," said Edna, shivering as she removed her gloves and overshoes. She drank the liquor from the glass as a man would have done. Then flinging herself upon the uncomfortable sofa she said, "Mademoiselle, I am going to move away from my house on Esplanade Street."

"Ah!" ejaculated the musician, neither surprised nor especially interested. Nothing ever seemed to astonish her very much. She was endeavoring to adjust the bunch of violets which had become loose from its fastening in her hair. Edna drew her down upon the sofa, and taking a pin from her own hair, secured the shabby artificial flowers in their accustomed place.

"Aren't you astonished?"

"Passably. Where are you going? to New York? to Iberville? to your father in Mississippi? where?"

"Just two steps away," laughed Edna, "in a little four-room house around the corner. It looks so cozy, so inviting and restful, whenever I pass by; and it's for rent. I'm tired looking after that big house. It never seemed like mine, anyway—like home. It's too much trouble. I have to keep too many servants. I am tired bothering with them."

"That is not your true reason, *ma belle*. There is no use in telling me lies. I don't know your reason, but you have not told me the truth." Edna did not protest or endeavor to justify herself.

"The house, the money that provides for it, are not mine. Isn't that enough reason?"

"They are your husband's," returned Mademoiselle, with a shrug and a malicious elevation of the eyebrows.

"Oh! I see there is no deceiving you. Then let me tell you:

It is a caprice. I have a little money of my own from my mother's estate, which my father sends me by driblets. I won a large sum this winter on the races, and I am beginning to sell my sketches. Laidpore is more and more pleased with my work; he says it grows in force and individuality. I cannot judge of that myself, but I feel that I have gained in ease and confidence. However, as I said, I have sold a good many through Laidpore. I can live in the tiny house for little or nothing, with one servant. Old Celestine, who works occasionally for me, says she will come stay with me and do my work. I know I shall like it, like the feeling of freedom and independence."

"What does your husband say?"

"I have not told him yet. I only thought of it this morning. He will think I am demented, no doubt. Perhaps you think so."

Mademoiselle shook her head slowly. "Your reason is not yet clear to me," she said.

Neither was it quite clear to Edna herself; but it unfolded itself as she sat for a while in silence. Instinct had prompted her to put away her husband's bounty in casting off her allegiance. She did not know how it would be when he returned. There would have to be an understanding, an explanation. Conditions would some way adjust themselves, she felt; but whatever came, she had resolved never again to belong to another than herself.

"I shall give a grand dinner before I leave the old house!" Edna exclaimed. "You will have to come to it, Mademoiselle. I will give you everything that you like to eat and to drink. We shall sing and laugh and be merry for once." And she uttered a sigh that came from the very depths of her being.

If Mademoiselle happened to have received a letter from Robert during the interval of Edna's visits, she would give her the letter unsolicited. And she would seat herself at the piano and play as her humor prompted her while the young woman read the letter.

The little stove was roaring; it was red-hot, and the chocolate in the tin sizzled and sputtered. Edna went forward and opened the stove door, and Mademoiselle rising, took a letter from under the bust of Beethoven and handed it to Edna.

"Another! so soon!" she exclaimed, her eyes filled with delight. "Tell me, Mademoiselle, does he know that I see his letters?"

"Never in the world! He would be angry and would never

write to me again if he thought so. Does he write to you?
Never a line. Does he send you a message? Never a word. It
is because he loves you, poor fool, and is trying to forget
you, since you are not free to listen to him or to belong to
him."

"Why do you show me his letters, then?"

"Haven't you begged for them? Can I refuse you anything?
Oh! you cannot deceive me," and Mademoiselle approached
her beloved instrument and began to play. Edna did not at
once read the letter. She sat holding it in her hand, while the
music penetrated her whole being like an effulgence, warming
and brightening the dark places of her soul. It prepared her
for joy and exultation.

"Oh!" she exclaimed, letting the letter fall to the floor.
"Why did you not tell me?" She went and grasped Made-
moiselle's hands up from the keys. "Oh! unkind! malicious!
Why did you not tell me?"

"That he was coming back? No great news, *ma foi*. I wonder he did not come long ago."

"But when, when?" cried Edna, impatiently. "He does not
say when."

"He says 'very soon.' You know as much about it as I do;
it is all in the letter."

"But why? Why is he coming? Oh, if I thought—" and she
snatched the letter from the floor and turned the pages this
way and that way, looking for the reason, which was left untold.

"If I were young and in love with a man," said Mademoiselle, turning on the stool and pressing her wiry hands between her knees as she looked down at Edna, who sat on the
floor holding the letter, "it seems to me he would have to be
some *grand esprit;* a man with lofty aims and ability to reach
them; one who stood high enough to attract the notice of his
fellow-men. It seems to me if I were young and in love I
should never deem a man of ordinary caliber worthy of my
devotion."

"Now it is you who are telling lies and seeking to deceive
me, Mademoiselle; or else you have never been in love, and
know nothing about it. Why," went on Edna, clasping her
knees and looking up into Mademoiselle's twisted face, "do
you suppose a woman knows why she loves? Does she select?
Does she say to herself: 'Go to! Here is a distinguished
statesman with presidential possibilities; I shall proceed to fall
in love with him.' Or, 'I shall set my heart upon this musi-

cian, whose fame is on every tongue?' Or, 'This financier, who controls the world's money markets?' "

"You are purposely misunderstanding me, *ma reine*. Are you in love with Robert?"

"Yes," said Edna. It was the first time she had admitted it, and a glow overspread her face, blotching it with red spots.

"Why?" asked her companion. "Why do you love him when you ought not to?"

Edna, with a motion or two, dragged herself on her knees before Mademoiselle Reisz, who took the glowing face between her two hands.

"Why? Because his hair is brown and grows away from his temples; because he opens and shuts his eyes, and his nose is a little out of drawing; because he has two lips and a square chin, and a little finger which he can't straighten from having played baseball too energetically in his youth. Because—"

"Because you do, in short," laughed Mademoiselle. "What will you do when he comes back?" she asked.

"Do? Nothing, except feel glad and happy to be alive."

She was already glad and happy to be alive at the mere thought of his return. The murky, lowering sky, which had depressed her a few hours before, seemed bracing and invigorating as she splashed through the streets on her way home.

She stopped at a confectioner's and ordered a huge box of bonbons for the children in Iberville. She slipped a card in the box, on which she scribbled a tender message and sent an abundance of kisses.

Before dinner in the evening Edna wrote a charming letter to her husband, telling him of her intention to move for a while into the little house around the block, and to give a farewell dinner before leaving, regretting that he was not there to share it, to help her out with the menu and assist her in entertaining the guests. Her letter was brilliant and brimming with cheerfulness.

XXVII

"What is the matter with you?" asked Arobin that evening. "I never found you in such a happy mood." Edna was tired by that time, and was reclining on the lounge before the fire.

"Don't you know the weather prophet has told us we shall see the sun pretty soon?"

"Well, that ought to be reason enough," he acquiesced. "You wouldn't give me another if I sat here all night imploring you." He sat close to her on a low tabouret, and as he spoke his fingers lightly touched the hair that fell a little over her forehead. She liked the touch of his fingers through her hair, and closed her eyes sensitively.

"One of these days," she said, "I'm going to pull myself together for a while and think—try to determine what character of a woman I am; for, candidly, I don't know. By all the codes which I am acquainted with, I am a devilishly wicked specimen of the sex. But some way I can't convince myself that I am. I must think about it."

"Don't. What's the use? Why should you bother thinking about it when I can tell you what manner of woman you are." His fingers strayed occasionally down to her warm, smooth cheeks and firm chin, which was growing a little full and double.

"Oh, yes! You will tell me that I am adorable; everything that is captivating. Spare yourself the effort."

"No; I shan't tell you anything of the sort, though I shouldn't be lying if I did."

"Do you know Mademoiselle Reisz?" she asked irrelevantly.

"The pianist? I know her by sight. I've heard her play."

"She says queer things sometimes in a bantering way that you don't notice at the time and you find yourself thinking about afterward."

"For instance?"

"Well, for instance, when I left her today, she put her arms around me and felt my shoulder blades, to see if my wings were strong, she said. 'The bird that would soar above the level plain of tradition and prejudice must have strong wings. It is a sad spectacle to see the weaklings bruised, exhausted, fluttering back to earth.' "

"Whither would you soar?"

"I'm not thinking of any extraordinary flights. I only half comprehend her."

"I've heard she's partially demented," said Arobin.

"She seems to me wonderfully sane," Edna replied.

"I'm told she's extremely disagreeable and unpleasant. Why have you introduced her at a moment when I desired to talk of you?"

"Oh! talk of me if you like," cried Edna, clasping her hands beneath her head; "but let me think of something else while you do."

"I'm jealous of your thoughts to-night. They're making you

a little kinder than usual; but some way I feel as if they were wandering, as if they were not here with me." She only looked at him and smiled. His eyes were very near. He leaned upon the lounge with an arm extended across her while the other hand still rested upon her hair. They continued silently to look into each other's eyes. When he leaned forward and kissed her, she clasped his head, holding his lips to hers.

It was the first kiss of her life to which her nature had really responded. It was a flaming torch that kindled desire.

XXVIII

Edna cried a little that night after Arobin left her. It was only one phase of the multitudinous emotions which had assailed her. There was with her an overwhelming feeling of irresponsibility. There was the shock of the unexpected and the unaccustomed. There was her husband's reproach looking at her from the external things around her which he had provided for her external existence. There was Robert's reproach making itself felt by a quicker, fiercer, more overpowering love, which had awakened within her toward him. Above all, there was understanding. She felt as if a mist had been lifted from her eyes, enabling her to look upon and comprehend the significance of life, that monster made up of beauty and brutality. But among the conflicting sensations which assailed her, there was neither shame nor remorse. There was a dull pang of regret because it was not the kiss of love which had inflamed her, because it was not love which had held this cup of life to her lips.

XXIX

Without even waiting for an answer from her husband regarding his opinion or wishes in the matter, Edna hastened her preparations for quitting her home on Esplanade Street and moving into the little house around the block. A feverish anxiety attended her every action in that direction. There was no moment of deliberation, no interval of repose between the thought and its fulfillment. Early upon the morning following those hours passed in Arobin's society, Edna set about securing her new abode and hurrying her arrangements for occupying it. Within the precincts of her home she felt like one who has entered and lingered within the portals of some forbidden temple in which a thousand muffled voices bade her begone.

Whatever was her own in the house, everything which she had acquired aside from her husband's bounty, she caused to be transported to the other house, supplying simple and meager deficiencies from her own resources.

Arobin found her with rolled sleeves, working in company with the house-maid when he looked in during the afternoon. She was splendid and robust, and had never appeared handsomer than in the old blue gown, with a red silk handkerchief knotted at random around her head to protect her hair from the dust. She was mounted upon a high step-ladder, unhooking a picture from the wall when he entered. He had found the front door open, and had followed his ring by walking in unceremoniously.

"Come down!" he said. "Do you want to kill yourself?" She greeted him with affected carelessness, and appeared absorbed in her occupation.

If he had expected to find her languishing, reproachful, or indulging in sentimental tears, he must have been greatly surprised.

He was no doubt prepared for any emergency, ready for any one of the foregoing attitudes, just as he bent himself easily and naturally to the situation which confronted him.

"Please come down," he insisted, holding the ladder and looking up at her.

"No," she answered; "Ellen is afraid to mount the ladder. Joe is working over at the 'pigeon house'—that's the name Ellen gives it, because it's so small and looks like a pigeon house—and some one has to do this."

Arobin pulled off his coat, and expressed himself ready and willing to tempt fate in her place. Ellen brought him one of her dust-caps, and went into contortions of mirth, which she found it impossible to control, when she saw him put it on before the mirror as grotesquely as he could. Edna herself could not refrain from smiling when she fastened it at his request. So it was he who in turn mounted the ladder, unhooking pictures and curtains, and dislodging ornaments as Edna directed. When he had finished he took off his dust-cap and went out to wash his hands.

Edna was sitting on the tabouret, idly brushing the tips of a feather duster along the carpet when he came in again.

"Is there anything more you will let me do?" he asked.

"That is all," she answered. "Ellen can manage the rest."

She kept the young woman occupied in the drawing-room, unwilling to be left alone with Arobin.

"What about the dinner?" he asked; "the grand event, the *coup d'état?*"

"It will be day after to-morrow. Why do you call it the '*coup d'état?*' Oh! it will be very fine; all my best of everything—crystal, silver and gold, Sèvres, flowers, music, and champagne to swim in. I'll let Léonce pay the bills. I wonder what he'll say when he sees the bills."

"And you ask me why I call it a *coup d'état?*" Arobin had put on his coat, and he stood before her and asked if his cravat was plumb. She told him it was, looking no higher than the tip of his collar.

"When do you go to the 'pigeon house?'—with all due acknowledgment to Ellen."

"Day after to-morrow, after the dinner. I shall sleep there."

"Ellen, will you very kindly get me a glass of water?" asked Arobin. "The dust in the curtains, if you will pardon me for hinting such a thing, has parched my throat to a crisp."

"While Ellen gets the water," said Edna, rising, "I will say good-by and let you go. I must get rid of this grime, and I have a million things to do and think of."

"When shall I see you?" asked Arobin, seeking to detain her, the maid having left the room.

"At the dinner, of course. You are invited."

"Not before?—not to-night or to-morrow morning or to-morrow noon or night? or the day after morning or noon? Can't you see yourself, without my telling you, what an eternity it is?"

He had followed her into the hall and to the foot of the stairway, looking up at her as she mounted with her face half turned to him.

"Not an instant sooner," she said. But she laughed and looked at him with eyes that at once gave him courage to wait and made it torture to wait.

XXX

Though Edna had spoken of the dinner as a very grand affair, it was in truth a very small affair and very select, in so much as the guests invited were few and were selected with discrimination. She had counted upon an even dozen seating themselves at her round mahogany board, forgetting for the moment that Madame Ratignolle was to the last degree *souffrante*[27] and unpresentable, and not foreseeing that Madame Lebrun would send a thousand regrets at the last moment. So there were only ten, after all, which made a cozy, comfortable number.

There were Mr. and Mrs. Merriman, a pretty, vivacious little woman in the thirties; her husband, a jovial fellow, something of a shallow-pate, who laughed a good deal at other people's witticisms, and had thereby made himself extremely popular. Mrs. Highcamp had accompanied them. Of course, there was Alcée Arobin; and Mademoiselle Reisz had consented to come. Edna had sent her a fresh bunch of violets with black lace trimmings for her hair. Monsieur Ratignolle brought himself and his wife's excuses. Victor Lebrun, who happened to be in the city, bent upon relaxation, had accepted with alacrity. There was a Miss Mayblunt, no longer in her teens, who looked at the world through lorgnettes and with the keenest interest. It was thought and said that she was intellectual; it was suspected of her that she wrote under a *nom de guerre*.[28] She had come with a gentleman by the name of Gouvernail, connected with one of the daily papers, of whom nothing special could be said, except that he was observant and seemed quiet and inoffensive. Edna herself made the tenth, and at half-past eight they seated themselves at table, Arobin and Monsieur Ratignolle on either side of their hostess.

Mrs. Highcamp sat between Arobin and Victor Lebrun. Then came Mrs. Merriman, Mr. Gouvernail, Miss Mayblunt, Mr. Merriman, and Mademoiselle Reisz next to Monsieur Ratignolle.

There was something extremely gorgeous about the appearance of the table, an effect of splendor conveyed by a cover of pale yellow satin under strips of lace-work. There were wax candles in massive brass candelabra, burning softly under yellow silk shades; full, fragrant roses, yellow and red, abounded. There were silver and gold, as she had said there would be, and crystal which glittered like the gems which the women wore.

The ordinary stiff dining chairs had been discarded for the occasion and replaced by the most commodious and luxurious which could be collected throughout the house. Made-

---

[27]Feeling very poorly in her pregnancy.
[28]Assumed name.

moiselle Reisz, being exceedingly diminutive, was elevated upon cushions, as small children are sometimes hoisted at table upon bulky volumes.

"Something new, Edna?" exclaimed Miss Mayblunt, with lorgnette directed toward a magnificent cluster of diamonds that sparkled, that almost sputtered, in Edna's hair, just over the center of her forehead.

"Quite new; 'brand' new, in fact; a present from my husband. It arrived this morning from New York. I may as well admit that this is my birthday, and that I am twenty-nine. In good time I expect you to drink to my health. Meanwhile, I shall ask you to begin with this cocktail, composed—would you say 'composed?'" with an appeal to Miss Mayblunt—"composed by my father in honor of Sister Janet's wedding."

Before each guest stood a tiny glass that looked and sparkled like a garnet gem.

"Then, all things considered," spoke Arobin, "it might not be amiss to start out by drinking the Colonel's health in the cocktail which he composed, on the birthday of the most charming of women—the daughter whom he invented."

Mr. Merriman's laugh at this sally was such a genuine outburst and so contagious that it started the dinner with an agreeable swing that never slackened.

Miss Mayblunt begged to be allowed to keep her cocktail untouched before her, just to look at. The color was marvelous! She could compare it to nothing she had ever seen, and the garnet lights which it emitted were unspeakably rare. She pronounced the Colonel an artist, and stuck to it.

Monsieur Ratignolle was prepared to take things seriously: the *mets*, the *entre-mets*,[29] the service, the decorations, even the people. He looked up from his pompono and inquired of Arobin if he were related to the gentleman of that name who formed one of the firm of Laitner and Arobin, lawyers. The young man admitted that Laitner was a warm personal friend, who permitted Arobin's name to decorate the firm's letter-heads and to appear upon a shingle that graced Perdido Street.

"There are so many inquisitive people and institutions abounding," said Arobin, "that one is really forced as a matter of convenience these days to assume the virtue of an occupation if he has it not."

Monsieur Ratignolle stared a little, and turned to ask

[29]Main dishes and side dishes.

Mademoiselle Reisz if she considered the symphony concerts up to the standard which had been set the previous winter. Mademoiselle Reisz answered Monsieur Ratignolle in French, which Edna thought a little rude, under the circumstances, but characteristic. Mademoiselle had only disagreeable things to say of the symphony concerts, and insulting remarks to make of all the musicians of New Orleans, singly and collectively. All her interest seemed to be centered upon the delicacies placed before her.

Mr. Merriman said that Mr. Arobin's remark about inquisitive people reminded him of a man from Waco the other day at the St. Charles Hotel—but as Mr. Merriman's stories were always lame and lacking point, his wife seldom permitted him to complete them. She interrupted him to ask if he remembered the name of the author whose book she had bought the week before to send to a friend in Geneva. She was talking "books" with Mr. Gouvernail and trying to draw from him his opinion upon current literary topics. Her husband told the story of the Waco man privately to Miss Mayblunt, who pretended to be greatly amused and to think it extremely clever.

Mrs. Highcamp hung with languid but unaffected interest upon the warm and impetuous volubility of her left-hand neighbor, Victor Lebrun. Her attention was never for a moment withdrawn from him after seating herself at table; and when he turned to Mrs. Merriman, who was prettier and more vivacious than Mrs. Highcamp, she waited with easy indifference for an opportunity to reclaim his attention. There was the occasional sound of music, of mandolins, sufficiently removed to be an agreeable accompaniment rather than an interruption to the conversation. Outside the soft, monotonous splash of a fountain could be heard; the sound penetrated into the room with the heavy odor of jessamine that came through the open windows.

The golden shimmer of Edna's satin gown spread in rich folds on either side of her. There was a soft fall of lace encircling her shoulders. It was the color of her skin, without the glow, the myriad living tints that one may sometimes discover in vibrant flesh. There was something in her attitude, in her whole appearance when she leaned her head against the high-backed chair and spread her arms, which suggested the regal woman, the one who rules, who looks on, who stands alone.

But as she sat there amid her guests, she felt the old ennui overtaking her; the hopelessness which so often assailed her, which came upon her like an obsession, like something extraneous, independent of volition. It was something which announced itself; a chill breath that seemed to issue from some vast cavern wherein discords wailed. There came over her the acute longing which always summoned into her spiritual vision the presence of the beloved one, overpowering her at once with a sense of the unattainable.

The moments glided on, while a feeling of good fellowship passed around the circle like a mystic cord, holding and binding these people together with jest and laughter. Monsieur Ratignolle was the first to break the pleasant charm. At ten o'clock he excused himself. Madame Ratignolle was waiting for him at home. She was *bien souffrante,* and she was filled with vague dread, which only her husband's presence could allay.

Mademoiselle Reisz arose with Monsieur Ratignolle, who offered to escort her to the car. She had eaten well; she had tasted the good, rich wines, and they must have turned her head, for she bowed pleasantly to all as she withdrew from the table. She kissed Edna upon the shoulder, and whispered: *"Bonne nuit, ma reine; soyez sage."*[30] She had been a little bewildered upon rising, or rather, descending from her cushions, and Monsieur Ratignolle gallantly took her arm and led her away.

Mrs. Highcamp was weaving a garland of roses, yellow and red. When she had finished the garland, she laid it lightly upon Victor's black curls. He was reclining far back in the luxurious chair, holding a glass of champagne to the light.

As if a magician's wand had touched him, the garland of roses transformed him into a vision of Oriental beauty. His cheeks were the color of crushed grapes, and his dusky eyes glowed with a languishing fire.

"Sapristi!" exclaimed Arobin.

But Mrs. Highcamp had one more touch to add to the picture. She took from the back of her chair a white silken scarf, with which she had covered her shoulders in the early part of the evening. She draped it across the boy in graceful folds, and in a way to conceal his black, conventional evening dress. He did not seem to mind what she did to him, only smiled, showing a faint gleam of white teeth, while he

[30]"Goodnight, dear one; behave yourself."

continued to gaze with narrowing eyes at the light through his glass of champagne.

"Oh! to be able to paint in color rather than in words!" exclaimed Miss Mayblunt, losing herself in a rhapsodic dream as she looked at him.

" 'There was a graven image of Desire
    Painted with red blood on a ground of gold.' "

murmured Gouvernail, under his breath.

The effect of the wine upon Victor was, to change his accustomed volubility into silence. He seemed to have abandoned himself to reverie, and to be seeing pleasing visions in the amber bead.

"Sing," entreated Mrs. Highcamp. "Won't you sing to us?"

"Let him alone," said Arobin.

"He's posing," offered Mr. Merriman; "let him have it out."

"I believe he's paralyzed," laughed Mrs. Merriman. And leaning over the youth's chair, she took the glass from his hand and held it to his lips. He sipped the wine slowly, and when he had drained the glass she laid it upon the table and wiped his lips with her little filmy handkerchief.

"Yes, I'll sing for you," he said, turning in his chair toward Mrs. Highcamp. He clasped his hands behind his head, and looking up at the ceiling began to hum a little, trying his voice like a musician tuning an instrument. Then, looking at Edna, he began to sing:

"Ah! si tu savais!"

"Stop!" she cried, "don't sing that. I don't want you to sing it," and she laid her glass so impetuously and blindly upon the table as to shatter it against a caraffe. The wine spilled over Arobin's legs and some of it trickled down upon Mrs. Highcamp's black gauze gown. Victor had lost all idea of courtesy, or else he thought his hostess was not in earnest, for he laughed and went on:

"Ah! si tu savais
    Ce que tes yeux me disent"—[81]

[81]"Ah! if only you knew
    What your eyes tell me"—

"Oh! you mustn't! you mustn't," exclaimed Edna, and pushing back her chair she got up, and going behind him placed her hand over his mouth. He kissed the soft palm that pressed upon his lips.

"No, no, I won't, Mrs. Pontellier. I didn't know you meant it," looking up at her with caressing eyes. The touch of his lips was like a pleasing sting to her hand. She lifted the garland of roses from his head and flung it across the room.

"Come, Victor; you've posed long enough. Give Mrs. Highcamp her scarf."

Mrs. Highcamp undraped the scarf from about him with her own hands. Miss Mayblunt and Mr. Gouvernail suddenly conceived the notion that it was time to say good night. And Mr. and Mrs. Merriman wondered how it could be so late.

Before parting from Victor, Mrs. Highcamp invited him to call upon her daughter, who she knew would be charmed to meet him and talk French and sing French songs with him. Victor expressed his desire and intention to call upon Miss Highcamp at the first opportunity which presented itself. He asked if Arobin were going his way. Arobin was not.

The mandolin players had long since stolen away. A profound stillness had fallen upon the broad, beautiful street. The voices of Edna's disbanding guests jarred like a discordant note upon the quiet harmony of the night.

XXXI

"Well?" questioned Arobin, who had remained with Edna after the others had departed.

"Well," she reiterated, and stood up, stretching her arms, and feeling the need to relax her muscles after having been so long seated.

"What next?" he asked.

"The servants are all gone. They left when the musicians did. I have dismissed them. The house has to be closed and locked, and I shall trot around to the pigeon house, and shall send Celestine over in the morning to straighten things up."

He looked around, and began to turn out some of the lights.

"What about upstairs?" he inquired.

"I think it is all right; but there may be a window or two unlatched. We had better look; you might take a candle and see. And bring me my wrap and hat on the foot of the bed in the middle room."

He went up with the light, and Edna began closing doors and windows. She hated to shut in the smoke and the fumes of the wine. Arobin found her cape and hat, which he brought down and helped her to put on.

When everything was secured and the lights put out, they left through the front door, Arobin locking it and taking the key, which he carried for Edna. He helped her down the steps.

"Will you have a spray of jessamine?" he asked, breaking off a few blossoms as he passed.

"No; I don't want anything."

She seemed disheartened, and had nothing to say. She took his arm, which he offered her, holding up the weight of her satin train with the other hand. She looked down, noticing the black line of his leg moving in and out so close to her against the yellow shimmer of her gown. There was the whistle of a railway train somewhere in the distance, and the midnight bells were ringing. They met no one in their short walk.

The "pigeon-house" stood behind a locked gate, and a shallow *parterre*[32] that had been somewhat neglected. There was a small front porch, upon which a long window and the front door opened. The door opened directly into the parlor; there was no side entry. Back in the yard was a room for servants, in which old Celestine had been ensconced.

Edna had left a lamp burning low upon the table. She had succeeded in making the room look habitable and homelike. There were some books on the table and a lounge near at hand. On the floor was a fresh matting, covered with a rug or two; and on the walls hung a few tasteful pictures. But the room was filled with flowers. These were a surprise to her. Arobin had sent them, and had had Celestine distribute them during Edna's absence. Her bedroom was adjoining, and across a small passage were the dining-room and kitchen.

Edna seated herself with every appearance of discomfort.

"Are you tired?" he asked.

"Yes, and chilled, and miserable. I feel as if I had been wound up to a certain pitch—too tight—and something inside of me had snapped." She rested her head against the table upon her bare arm.

"You want to rest," he said, "and to be quiet. I'll go; I'll leave you and let you rest."

[32]Flower bed.

"Yes," she replied.

He stood up beside her and smoothed her hair with his soft, magnetic hand. His touch conveyed to her a certain physical comfort. She could have fallen quietly asleep there if he had continued to pass his hand over her hair. He brushed the hair upward from the nape of her neck.

"I hope you will feel better and happier in the morning," he said. "You have tried to do too much in the past few days. The dinner was the last straw; you might have dispensed with it."

"Yes," she admitted; "it was stupid."

"No, it was delightful; but it has worn you out." His hand had strayed to her beautiful shoulders, and he could feel the response of her flesh to his touch. He seated himself beside her and kissed her lightly upon the shoulder.

"I thought you were going away," she said, in an uneven voice.

"I am, after I have said good night."

"Good night," she murmured.

He did not answer, except to continue to caress her. He did not say good night until she had become supple to his gentle, seductive entreaties.

XXXII

When Mr. Pontellier learned of his wife's intention to abandon her home and take up her residence elsewhere, he immediately wrote her a letter of unqualified disapproval and remonstrance. She had given reasons which he was unwilling to acknowledge as adequate. He hoped she had not acted upon her rash impulse; and he begged her to consider first, foremost, and above all else, what people would say. He was not dreaming of scandal when he uttered this warning; that was a thing which would never have entered into his mind to consider in connection with his wife's name or his own. He was simply thinking of his financial integrity. It might get noised about that the Pontelliers had met with reverses, and were forced to conduct their *ménage* on a humbler scale than heretofore. It might do incalculable mischief to his business prospects.

But remembering Edna's whimsical turn of mind of late, and foreseeing that she had immediately acted upon her impetuous determination, he grasped the situation with his usual promptness and handled it with his well-known business tact and cleverness.

The same mail which brought to Edna his letter of disapproval carried instructions—the most minute instructions—to a well-known architect concerning the remodeling of his home, changes which he had long contemplated, and which he desired carried forward during his temporary absence.

Expert and reliable packers and movers were engaged to convey the furniture, carpets, pictures—everything movable, in short—to places of security. And in an incredibly short time the Pontellier house was turned over to the artisans. There was to be an addition—a small snuggery; there was to be frescoing, and hardwood flooring was to be put into such rooms as had not yet been subjected to this improvement.

Furthermore, in one of the daily papers appeared a brief notice to the effect that Mr. and Mrs. Pontellier were contemplating a summer sojourn abroad, and that their handsome residence on Esplanade Street was undergoing sumptuous alterations, and would not be ready for occupancy until their return. Mr. Pontellier had saved appearances!

Edna admired the skill of his maneuver, and avoided any occasion to balk his intentions. When the situation as set forth by Mr. Pontellier was accepted and taken for granted, she was apparently satisfied that it should be so.

The pigeon-house pleased her. It at once assumed the intimate character of a home, while she herself invested it with a charm which it reflected like a warm glow. There was with her a feeling of having descended in the social scale, with a corresponding sense of having risen in the spiritual. Every step which she took toward relieving herself from obligations added to her strength and expansion as an individual. She began to look with her own eyes; to see and to apprehend the deeper undercurrents of life. No longer was she content to "feed upon opinion" when her own soul had invited her.

After a little while, a few days, in fact, Edna went up and spent a week with her children in Iberville. They were delicious February days, with all the summer's promise hovering in the air.

How glad she was to see the children! She wept for very pleasure when she felt their little arms clasping her; their hard, ruddy cheeks pressed against her own glowing cheeks. She looked into their faces with hungry eyes that could not be satisfied with looking. And what stories they had to tell their mother! About the pigs, the cows, the mules! About rid-

ing to the mill behind Gluglu; fishing back in the lake with
their Uncle Jasper; picking pecans with Lidie's little black
brood, and hauling chips in their express wagon. It was a
thousand times more fun to haul real chips for old lame
Susie's real fire than to drag painted blocks along the banquette on Esplanade Street!

She went with them herself to see the pigs and the cows, to
look at the darkies laying the cane, to thrash the pecan trees,
and catch fish in the back lake. She lived with them a whole
week long, giving them all of herself, and gathering and filling herself with their young existence. They listened,
breathless, when she told them the house in Esplanade Street
was crowded with workmen, hammering, nailing, sawing, and
filling the place with clatter. They wanted to know where
their bed was; what had been done with their rocking-horse;
and where did Joe sleep, and where had Ellen gone, and the
cook? But, above all, they were fired with a desire to see the
little house around the block. Was there any place to play?
Were there any boys next door? Raoul, with pessimistic fore-
boding, was convinced that there were only girls next door.
Where would they sleep, and where would papa sleep? She
told them the fairies would fix it all right.

The old Madame was charmed with Edna's visit, and
showered all manner of delicate attentions upon her. She was
delighted to know that the Esplanade Street house was in a
dismantled condition. It gave her the promise and pretext to
keep the children indefinitely.

It was with a wrench and a pang that Edna left her children. She carried away with her the sound of their voices and
the touch of their cheeks. All along the journey homeward
their presence lingered with her like the memory of a delicious song. But by the time she had regained the city the
song no longer echoed in her soul. She was again alone.

XXXIII

It happened sometimes when Edna went to see Mademoiselle Reisz that the little musician was absent, giving a lesson
or making some small necessary household purchase. The key
was always left in a secret hiding-place in the entry, which
Edna knew. If Mademoiselle happened to be away, Edna
would usually enter and wait for her return.

When she knocked at Mademoiselle Reisz's door one afternoon there was no response; so unlocking the door, as usual,

she entered and found the apartment deserted, as she had expected. Her day had been quite filled up, and it was for a rest, for a refuge, and to talk about Robert, that she sought out her friend.

She had worked at her canvas—a young Italian character study—all the morning, completing the work without the model; but there had been many interruptions, some incident to her modest housekeeping, and others of a social nature.

Madame Ratignolle had dragged herself over, avoiding the too public thoroughfares, she said. She complained that Edna had neglected her much of late. Besides, she was consumed with curiosity to see the little house and the manner in which it was conducted. She wanted to hear all about the dinner party; Monsieur Ratignolle had left *so* early. What had happened after he left? The champagne and grapes which Edna sent over were *too* delicious. She had so little appetite; they had refreshed and toned her stomach. Where on earth was she going to put Mr. Pontellier in that little house, and the boys? And then she made Edna promise to go to her when her hour of trial overtook her.

"At any time—any time of the day or night, dear," Edna assured her.

Before leaving Madame Ratignolle said:

"In some way you seem to me like a child, Edna. You seem to act without a certain amount of reflection which is necessary in this life. That is the reason I want to say you mustn't mind if I advise you to be a little careful while you are living here alone. Why don't you have some one come and stay with you? Wouldn't Mademoiselle Reisz come?"

"No; she wouldn't wish to come, and I shouldn't want her always with me."

"Well, the reason—you know how evil-minded the world is—some one was talking of Alcée Arobin visiting you. Of course, it wouldn't matter if Mr. Arobin had not such a dreadful reputation. Monsieur Ratignolle was telling me that his attentions alone are considered enough to ruin a woman's name."

"Does he boast of his successes?" asked Edna, indifferently, squinting at her picture.

"No, I think not. I believe he is a decent fellow as far as that goes. But his character is so well known among the men. I shan't be able to come back and see you; it was very, very imprudent to-day."

"Mind the step!" cried Edna.

"Don't neglect me," entreated Madame Ratignolle; "and don't mind what I said about Arobin, or having some one to stay with you."

"Of course not," Edna laughed. "You may say anything you like to me." They kissed each other good-by. Madame Ratignolle had not far to go, and Edna stood on the porch a while watching her walk down the street.

Then in the afternoon Mrs. Merriman and Mrs. Highcamp had made their "party call." Edna felt that they might have dispensed with the formality. They had also come to invite her to play *vingt-et-un*[33] one evening at Mrs. Merriman's. She was asked to go early, to dinner, and Mr. Merriman or Mr. Arobin would take her home. Edna accepted in a half-hearted way. She sometimes felt very tired of Mrs. Highcamp and Mrs. Merriman.

Late in the afternoon she sought refuge with Mademoiselle Reisz, and stayed there alone, waiting for her, feeling a kind of repose invade her with the very atmosphere of the shabby, unpretentious little room.

Edna sat at the window, which looked out over the house-tops and across the river. The window frame was filled with pots of flowers, and she sat and picked the dry leaves from a rose geranium. The day was warm, and the breeze which blew from the river was very pleasant. She removed her hat and laid it on the piano. She went on picking the leaves and digging around the plants with her hat pin. Once she thought she heard Mademoiselle Reisz approaching. But it was a young black girl, who came in, bringing a small bundle of laundry, which she deposited in the adjoining room, and went away.

Edna seated herself at the piano, and softly picked out with one hand the bars of a piece of music which lay open before her. A half-hour went by. There was the occasional sound of people going and coming in the lower hall. She was growing interested in her occupation of picking out the aria, when there was a second rap at the door. She vaguely wondered what these people did when they found Mademoiselle's door locked.

"Come in," she called, turning her face toward the door. And this time it was Robert Lebrun who presented himself. She attempted to rise; she could not have done so without betraying the agitation which mastered her at sight of him, so

[33]Twenty-one.

she fell back upon the stool, only exclaiming, "Why, Robert!"

He came and clasped her hand, seemingly without knowing what he was saying or doing.

"Mrs. Pontellier! How do you happen—oh! how well you look! Is Mademoiselle Reisz not here? I never expected to see you."

"When did you come back?" asked Edna in an unsteady voice, wiping her face with her handkerchief. She seemed ill at ease on the piano stool, and he begged her to take the chair by the window. She did so, mechanically, while he seated himself on the stool.

"I returned day before yesterday," he answered, while he leaned his arm on the keys, bringing forth a crash of discordant sound.

"Day before yesterday!" she repeated, aloud; and went on thinking to herself, "day before yesterday," in a sort of an uncomprehending way. She had pictured him seeking her at the very first hour, and he had lived under the same sky since day before yesterday; while only by accident had he stumbled upon her. Mademoiselle must have lied when she said, "Poor fool, he loves you."

"Day before yesterday," she repeated, breaking off a spray of Mademoiselle's geranium; "then if you had not met me here to-day you wouldn't—when—that is, didn't you mean to come and see me?"

"Of course, I should have gone to see you. There have been so many things—" he turned the leaves of Mademoiselle's music nervously. "I started in at once yesterday with the old firm. After all there is as much chance for me here as there was there—that is, I might find it profitable some day. The Mexicans were not very congenial."

So he had come back because the Mexicans were not congenial; because business was as profitable here as there; because of any reason, and not because he cared to be near her. She remembered the day she sat on the floor, turning the pages of his letter, seeking the reason which was left untold.

She had not noticed how he looked—only feeling his presence; but she turned deliberately and observed him. After all, he had been absent but a few months, and was not changed. His hair—the color of hers—waved back from his temples in the same way as before. His skin was not more burned than it had been at Grand Isle. She found in his eyes, when he looked at her for one silent moment, the same tender caress, with an added warmth and entreaty which had not been there before—the same glance which had penetrated to the sleeping places of her soul and awakened them.

A hundred times Edna had pictured Robert's return, and imagined their first meeting. It was usually at her home, whither he had sought her out at once. She always fancied him expressing or betraying in some way his love for her. And here, the reality was that they sat ten feet apart, she at the window, crushing geranium leaves in her hand and smelling them, he twirling around on the piano stool, saying:

"I was very much surprised to hear of Mr. Pontellier's absence; it's a wonder Mademoiselle Reisz did not tell me; and your moving—mother told me yesterday. I should think you would have gone to New York with him, or to Iberville with the children, rather than be bothered here with housekeeping. And you are going abroad, too, I hear. We shan't have you at Grand Isle next summer; it won't seem—do you see much of Mademoiselle Reisz? She often spoke of you in the few letters she wrote."

"Do you remember that you promised to write to me when you went away?" A flush overspread his whole face.

"I couldn't believe that my letters would be of any interest to you."

"That is an excuse; it isn't the truth." Edna reached for her hat on the piano. She adjusted it, sticking the hat pin through the heavy coil of hair with some deliberation.

"Are you not going to wait for Mademoiselle Reisz?" asked Robert.

"No; I have found when she is absent this long, she is liable not to come back till late." She drew on her gloves, and Robert picked up his hat.

"Won't you wait for her?" asked Edna.

"Not if you think she will not be back till late," adding, as if suddenly aware of some discourtesy in his speech, "and I should miss the pleasure of walking home with you." Edna locked the door and put the key back in its hiding-place.

They went together, picking their way across muddy streets and sidewalks encumbered with the cheap display of small tradesmen. Part of the distance they rode in the car, and after disembarking, passed the Pontellier mansion, which looked broken and half torn asunder. Robert had never known the house, and looked at it with interest.

"I never knew you in your home," he remarked.

"I am glad you did not."

"Why?" She did not answer. They went on around the corner, and it seemed as if her dreams were coming true after all, when he followed her into the little house.

"You must stay and dine with me, Robert. You see I am all alone, and it is so long since I have seen you. There is so much I want to ask you."

She took off her hat and gloves. He stood irresolute, making some excuse about his mother who expected him; he even muttered something about an engagement. She struck a match and lit the lamp on the table; it was growing dusk. When he saw her face in the lamp-light, looking pained, with all the soft lines gone out of it, he threw his hat aside and seated himself.

"Oh! you know I want to stay if you will let me!" he exclaimed. All the softness came back. She laughed, and went and put her hand on his shoulder.

"This is the first moment you have seemed like the old Robert. I'll go tell Celestine." She hurried away to tell Celestine to set an extra place. She even sent her off in search of some added delicacy which she had not thought of for herself. And she recommended great care in dripping the coffee and having the omelet done to a proper turn.

When she reëntered, Robert was turning over magazines, sketches, and things that lay upon the table in great disorder. He picked up a photograph, and exclaimed:

"Alcée Arobin! What on earth is his picture doing here?"

"I tried to make a sketch of his head one day," answered Edna, "and he thought the photograph might help me. It was at the other house. I thought it had been left there. I must have packed it up with my drawing materials."

"I should think you would give it back to him if you have finished with it."

"Oh! I have a great many such photographs. I never think of returning them. They don't amount to anything." Robert kept on looking at the picture.

"It seems to me—do you think his head worth drawing? Is he a friend of Mr. Pontellier's? You never said you knew him."

"He isn't a friend of Mr. Pontellier's; he's a friend of mine. I always knew him—that is, it is only of late that I know him pretty well. But I'd rather talk about you, and know what you have been seeing and doing and feeling out there in Mexico." Robert threw aside the picture.

"I've been seeing the waves and the white beach of Grand Isle; the quiet, grassy street of the *Chênière*; the old fort at

Grande Terre. I've been working like a machine, and feeling like a lost soul. There was nothing interesting."

She leaned her head upon her hand to shade her eyes from the light.

"And what have you been seeing and doing and feeling all these days?" he asked.

"I've been seeing the waves and the white beach of Grand Isle; the quiet, grassy street of the *Chênière Caminada;* the old sunny fort at Grande Terre. I've been working with a little more comprehension than a machine, and still feeling like a lost soul. There was nothing interesting."

"Mrs. Pontellier, you are cruel," he said, with feeling, closing his eyes and resting his head back in his chair. They remained in silence till old Celestine announced dinner.

XXXIV

THE dining-room was very small. Edna's round mahogany would have almost filled it. As it was there was but a step or two from the little table to the kitchen, to the mantel, the small buffet, and the side door that opened out on the narrow brick-paved yard.

A certain degree of ceremony settled upon them with the announcement of dinner. There was no return to personalities. Robert related incidents of his sojourn in Mexico, and Edna talked of events likely to interest him, which had occurred during his absence. The dinner was of ordinary quality, except for the few delicacies, which she had sent out to purchase. Old Celestine, with a bandana *tignon*[34] twisted about her head, hobbled in and out, taking a personal interest in everything; and she lingered occasionally to talk patois with Robert, whom she had known as a boy.

He went out to a neighboring cigar stand to purchase cigarette papers, and when he came back he found that Celestine had served the black coffee in the parlor.

"Perhaps I shouldn't have come back," he said. "When you are tired of me, tell me to go."

"You never tire me. You must have forgotten the hours and hours at Grand Isle in which we grew accustomed to each other and used to being together."

"I have forgotten nothing at Grand Isle." he said, not looking at her, but rolling a cigarette. His tobacco pouch, which

[34]Chignon.

he laid upon the table, was a fantastic embroidered silk affair, evidently the handiwork of a woman.

"You used to carry your tobacco in a rubber pouch," said Edna, picking up the pouch and examining the needlework.

"Yes; it was lost."

"Where did you buy this one? In Mexico?"

"It was given to me by a Vera Cruz girl; they are very generous," he replied, striking a match and lighting his cigarette.

"They are very handsome, I suppose, those Mexican women; very picturesque, with their black eyes and their lace scarfs."

"Some are; others are hideous. Just as you find women everywhere."

"What was she like—the one who gave you the pouch? You must have known her very well."

"She was very ordinary. She wasn't of the slightest importance. I knew her well enough."

"Did you visit at her house? Was it interesting? I should like to know and hear about the people you met, and the impressions they made on you."

"There are some people who leave impressions not so lasting as the imprint of an oar upon the water."

"Was she such a one?"

"It would be ungenerous for me to admit that she was of that order and kind." He thrust the pouch back in his pocket, as if to put away the subject with the trifle which had brought it up.

Arobin dropped in with a message from Mrs. Merriman, to say that the card party was postponed on account of the illness of one of her children.

"How do you do, Arobin?" said Robert, rising from the obscurity.

"Oh! Lebrun. To be sure! I heard yesterday you were back. How did they treat you down in Mexique?"

"Fairly well."

"But not well enough to keep you there. Stunning girls, though, in Mexico. I thought I should never get away from Vera Cruz when I was down there a couple of years ago."

"Did they embroider slippers and tobacco pouches and hat-bands and things for you?" asked Edna.

"Oh! my! no! I didn't get so deep in their regard. I fear they made more impression on me than I made on them."

"You were less fortunate than Robert, then."

"I am always less fortunate than Robert. Has he been imparting tender confidences?"

"I've been imposing myself long enough," said Robert, rising, and shaking hands with Edna. "Please convey my regards to Mr. Pontellier when you write."

He shook hands with Arobin and went away.

"Fine fellow, that Lebrun," said Arobin when Robert had gone. "I never heard you speak of him."

"I knew him last summer at Grand Isle," she replied. "Here is that photograph of yours. Don't you want it?"

"What do I want with it? Throw it away." She threw it back on the table.

"I'm not going to Mrs. Merriman's," she said. "If you see her, tell her so. But perhaps I had better write. I think I shall write now, and say that I am sorry her child is sick, and tell her not to count on me."

"It would be a good scheme," acquiesced Arobin. "I don't blame you; stupid lot!"

Edna opened the blotter, and having procured paper and pen, began to write the note. Arobin lit a cigar and read the evening paper, which he had in his pocket.

"What is the date?" she asked. He told her.

"Will you mail this for me when you go out?"

"Certainly." He read to her little bits out of the newspaper, while she straightened things on the table.

"What do you want to do?" he asked, throwing aside the paper. "Do you want to go out for a walk or a drive or anything? It would be a fine night to drive."

"No; I don't want to do anything but just be quiet. You go away and amuse yourself. Don't stay."

"I'll go away if I must; but I shan't amuse myself. You know that I only live when I am near you."

He stood up to bid her good night.

"Is that one of the things you always say to women?"

"I have said it before, but I don't think I ever came so near meaning it," he answered with a smile. There were no warm lights in her eyes; only a dreamy, absent look.

"Good night. I adore you. Sleep well," he said, and he kissed her hand and went away.

She stayed alone in a kind of reverie—a sort of stupor. Step by step she lived over every instant of the time she had been with Robert after he had entered Mademoiselle Reisz's door. She recalled his words, his looks. How few and meager they had been for her hungry heart! A vision—a transcendently seductive vision of a Mexican girl arose before her. She writhed with a jealous pang. She wondered when he would come back. He had not said he would come back. She had been with him, had heard his voice and touched his hand. But some way he had seemed nearer to her off there in Mexico.

XXXV

The morning was full of sunlight and hope. Edna could see before her no denial—only the promise of excessive joy. She lay in bed awake, with bright eyes full of speculation. "He loves you, poor fool." If she could but get that conviction firmly fixed in her mind, what mattered about the rest? She felt she had been childish and unwise the night before in giving herself over to despondency. She recapitulated the motives which no doubt explained Robert's reserve. They were not insurmountable; they would not hold if he really loved her; they could not hold against her own passion, which he must come to realize in time. She pictured him going to his business that morning. She even saw how he was dressed; how he walked down one street, and turned the corner of another; saw him bending over his desk, talking to people who entered the office, going to his lunch, and perhaps watching for her on the street. He would come to her in the afternoon or evening, sit and roll his cigarette, talk a little, and go away as he had done the night before. But how delicious it would be to have him there with her! She would have no regrets, nor seek to penetrate his reserve if he still chose to wear it.

Edna ate her breakfast only half dressed. The maid brought her a delicious printed scrawl from Raoul, expressing his love, asking her to send him some bonbons, and telling her they had found that morning ten tiny white pigs all lying in a row beside Lidie's big white pig.

A letter also came from her husband, saying he hoped to be back early in March, and then they would get ready for that journey abroad which he had promised her so long, which he felt now fully able to afford; he felt able to travel as people should, without any thought of small economies— thanks to his recent speculations in Wall Street.

Much to her surprise she received a note from Arobin, written at midnight from the club. It was to say good morning to her, to hope that she had slept well, to assure her of his devotion, which he trusted she in some faintest manner returned.

All these letters were pleasing to her. She answered the children in a cheerful frame of mind, promising them bon-bons, and congratulating them upon their happy find of the little pigs.

She answered her husband with friendly evasiveness,—not with any fixed design to mislead him, only because all sense of reality had gone out of her life; she had abandoned herself to Fate, and awaited the consequences with indifference.

To Arobin's note she made no reply. She put it under Celestine's stove-lid.

Edna worked several hours with much spirit. She saw no one but a picture dealer, who asked her if it were true that she was going abroad to study in Paris.

She said possibly she might, and he negotiated with her for some Parisian studies to reach him in time for the holiday trade in December.

Robert did not come that day. She was keenly disappointed. He did not come the following day, nor the next. Each morning she awoke with hope, and each night she was a prey to despondency. She was tempted to seek him out. But far from yielding to the impulse, she avoided any occasion which might throw her in his way. She did not go to Mademoiselle Reisz's nor pass by Madame Lebrun's, as she might have done if he had still been in Mexico.

When Arobin, one night, urged her to drive with him, she went—out to the lake, on the Shell Road. His horses were full of mettle, and even a little unmanageable. She liked the rapid gait at which they spun along, and the quick, sharp sound of the horses' hoofs on the hard road. They did not stop anywhere to eat or to drink. Arobin was not needlessly imprudent. But they ate and they drank when they regained Edna's little dining-room—which was comparatively early in the evening.

It was late when he left her. It was getting to be more than a passing whim with Arobin to see her and be with her. He had detected the latent sensuality, which unfolded under his delicate sense of her nature's requirements like a torpid, torrid, sensitive blossom.

There was no despondency when she fell asleep that night; nor was there hope when she awoke in the morning.

XXXVI

There was a garden out in the suburbs; a small, leafy corner, with a few green tables under the orange trees. An old cat slept all day on the stone step in the sun, and an old *mulatresse* slept her idle hours away in her chair at the open window, till some one happened to knock on one of the green tables. She had milk and cream cheese to sell, and bread and butter. There was no one who could make such excellent coffee or fry a chicken so golden brown as she.

The place was too modest to attract the attention of people of fashion, and so quiet as to have escaped the notice of those in search of pleasure and dissipation. Edna had discovered it accidentally one day when the high-board gate stood ajar. She caught sight of a little green table, blotched with the checkered sunlight that filtered through the quivering leaves overhead. Within she had found the slumbering *mulatresse,* the drowsy cat, and a glass of milk which reminded her of the milk she had tasted in Iberville.

She often stopped there during her perambulations; sometimes taking a book with her, and sitting an hour or two under the trees when she found the place deserted. Once or twice she took a quiet dinner there alone, having instructed Celestine beforehand to prepare no dinner at home. It was the last place in the city where she would have expected to meet any one she knew.

Still she was not astonished when, as she was partaking of a modest dinner late in the afternoon, looking into an open book, stroking the cat, which had made friends with her—she was not greatly astonished to see Robert come in at the tall garden gate.

"I am destined to see you only by accident," she said, shoving the cat off the chair beside her. He was surprised, ill at ease, almost embarrassed at meeting her thus so unexpectedly.

"Do you come here often?" he asked.

"I almost live here," she said.

"I used to drop in very often for a cup of Catiche's good coffee. This is the first time since I came back."

"She'll bring you a plate, and you will share my dinner. There's always enough for two—even three." Edna had intended to be indifferent and as reserved as he when she met him; she had reached the determination by a laborious train of reasoning, incident to one of her despondent moods. But her resolve melted when she saw him before her, seated there beside her in the little garden, as if a designing Providence had led him into her path.

"Why have you kept away from me, Robert?" she asked, closing the book that lay open upon the table.

"Why are you so personal, Mrs. Pontellier? Why do you force me to idiotic subterfuges?" he exclaimed with sudden warmth. "I suppose there's no use telling you I've been very busy, or that I've been sick, or that I've been to see you and not found you at home. Please let me off with any one of these excuses."

"You are the embodiment of selfishness," she said. "You save yourself something—I don't know what—but there is some selfish motive, and in sparing yourself you never consider for a moment what I think, or how I feel your neglect and indifference. I suppose this is what you would call unwomanly; but I have got into a habit of expressing myself. It doesn't matter to me, and you may think me unwomanly if you like."

"No; I only think you cruel, as I said the other day. Maybe not intentionally cruel; but you seem to be forcing me into disclosures which can result in nothing; as if you would have me bare a wound for the pleasure of looking at it, without the intention or power of healing it."

"I'm spoiling your dinner, Robert; never mind what I say. You haven't eaten a morsel."

"I only came in for a cup of coffee." His sensitive face was all disfigured with excitement.

"Isn't this a delightful place?" she remarked. "I am so glad it has never actually been discovered. It is so quiet, so sweet, here. Do you notice there is scarcely a sound to be heard? It's so out of the way; and a good walk from the car. However, I don't mind walking. I always feel so sorry for women who don't like to walk; they miss so much—so many rare little glimpses of life; and we women learn so little of life on the whole.

"Catiche's coffee is always hot. I don't know how she manages it, here in the open air. Celestine's coffee gets cold bringing it from the kitchen to the dining-room. Three lumps! How can you drink it so sweet? Take some of the cress with your chop; it's so biting and crisp. Then there's the advantage of being able to smoke with your coffee out here. Now, in the city—aren't you going to smoke?"

"After a while," he said, laying a cigar on the table.

"Who gave it to you?" she laughed.

"I bought it. I suppose I'm getting reckless; I bought a whole box." She was determined not to be personal again and make him uncomfortable.

The cat made friends with him, and climbed into his lap when he smoked his cigar. He stroked her silky fur, and talked a little about her. He looked at Edna's book, which he had read; and he told her the end, to save her the trouble of wading through it, he said.

Again he accompanied her back to her home; and it was after dusk when they reached the little "pigeon-house." She did not ask him to remain, which he was grateful for, as it permitted him to stay without the discomfort of blundering through an excuse which he had no intention of considering. He helped her to light the lamp; then she went into her room to take off her hat and to bathe her face and hands.

When she came back Robert was not examining the pictures and magazines as before; he sat off in the shadow, leaning his head back on the chair as if in a reverie. Edna lingered a moment beside the table, arranging the books there. Then she went across the room to where he sat. She bent over the arm of his chair and called his name.

"Robert," she said, "are you asleep?"

"No," he answered, looking up at her.

She leaned over and kissed him—a soft, cool, delicate kiss, whose voluptuous sting penetrated his whole being—then she moved away from him. He followed, and took her in his arms, just holding her close to him. She put her hand up to his face and pressed his cheek against her own. The action was full of love and tenderness. He sought her lips again. Then he drew her down upon the sofa beside him and held her hand in both of his.

"Now you know," he said, "now you know what I have been fighting against since last summer at Grand Isle; what drove me away and drove me back again."

"Why have you been fighting against it?" she asked. Her face glowed with soft lights.

"Why? Because you were not free; you were Léonce Pontellier's wife. I couldn't help loving you if you were ten times his wife; but so long as I went away from you and kept away

I could help telling you so." She put her free hand up to his shoulder, and then against his cheek, rubbing it softly. He kissed her again. His face was warm and flushed.

"There in Mexico I was thinking of you all the time, and longing for you."

"But not writing to me," she interrupted.

"Something put into my head that you cared for me; and I lost my senses. I forgot everything but a wild dream of your some way becoming my wife."

"Your wife!"

"Religion, loyalty, everything would give way if only you cared."

"Then you must have forgotten that I was Léonce Pontellier's wife."

"Oh! I was demented, dreaming of wild, impossible things, recalling men who had set their wives free, we have heard of such things."

"Yes, we have heard of such things."

"I came back full of vague, mad intentions. And when I got here—"

"When you got here you never came near me!" She was still caressing his cheek.

"I realized what a cur I was to dream of such a thing, even if you had been willing."

She took his face between her hands and looked into it as if she would never withdraw her eyes more. She kissed him on the forehead, the eyes, the cheeks, and the lips.

"You have been a very, very foolish boy, wasting your time dreaming of impossible things when you speak of Mr. Pontellier setting me free! I am no longer one of Mr. Pontellier's possessions to dispose of or not. I give myself where I choose. If he were to say, 'Here, Robert, take her and be happy; she is yours,' I should laugh at you both."

His face grew a little white. "What do you mean?" he asked.

There was a knock at the door. Old Celestine came in to say that Madame Ratignolle's servant had come around the back way with a message that Madame had been taken sick and begged Mrs. Pontellier to go to her immediately.

"Yes, yes," said Edna, rising; "I promised. Tell her yes—to wait for me. I'll go back with her."

"Let me walk over with you," offered Robert.

"No," she said; "I will go with the servant." She went into her room to put on her hat, and when she came in again she sat once more upon the sofa beside him. He had not stirred. She put her arms about his neck.

"Good-by, my sweet Robert. Tell me good-by." He kissed her with a degree of passion which had not before entered into his caress, and strained her to him.

"I love you," she whispered, "only you; no one but you. It was you who awoke me last summer out of a life-long, stupid dream. Oh! you have made me so unhappy with your indifference. Oh! I have suffered, suffered! Now you are here we shall love each other, my Robert. We shall be everything to each other. Nothing else in the world is of any consequence. I must go to my friend; but you will wait for me? No matter how late; you will wait for me, Robert?"

"Don't go; don't go! Oh! Edna, stay with me," he pleaded. "Why should you go? Stay with me, stay with me."

"I shall come back as soon as I can; I shall find you here." She buried her face in his neck, and said good-by again. Her seductive voice, together with his great love for her, had enthralled his senses, had deprived him of every impulse but the longing to hold her and keep her.

XXXVII

Edna looked in at the drug store. Monsieur Ratignolle was putting up a mixture himself, very carefully, dropping a red liquid into a tiny glass. He was grateful to Edna for having come; her presence would be a comfort to his wife. Madame Ratignolle's sister, who had always been with her at such trying times, had not been able to come up from the plantation, and Adèle had been inconsolable until Mrs. Pontellier so kindly promised to come to her. The nurse had been with them at night for the past week, as she lived a great distance away. And Dr. Mandelet had been coming and going all the afternoon. They were then looking for him any moment.

Edna hastened upstairs by a private stairway that led from the rear of the store to the apartments above. The children were all sleeping in a back room. Madame Ratignolle was in the salon, whither she had strayed in her suffering impatience. She sat on the sofa, clad in an ample white *peignoir*, holding a handkerchief tight in her hand with a nervous clutch. Her face was drawn and pinched, her sweet blue eyes haggard and unnatural. All her beautiful hair had been drawn back and plaited. It lay in a long braid on the sofa pillow, coiled like a golden serpent. The nurse, a comfortable looking *Griffe*[35] woman in white apron and cap, was urging her to return to her bedroom.

"There is no use, there is no use," she said at once to Edna. "We must get rid of Mandelet; he is getting too old and careless. He said he would be here at half-past seven; now it must be eight. See what time it is, Joséphine."

The woman was possessed of a cheerful nature, and refused to take any situation too seriously, especially a situation with which she was so familiar. She urged Madame to have courage and patience. But Madame only set her teeth hard into her under lip, and Edna saw the sweat gather in beads on her white forehead. After a moment or two she uttered a profound sigh and wiped her face with the handkerchief rolled in a ball. She appeared exhausted. The nurse gave her a fresh handkerchief, sprinkled with cologne water.

"This is too much!" she cried. "Mandelet ought to be killed! Where is Alphonse? Is it possible I am to be abandoned like this—neglected by every one?"

"Neglected, indeed!" exclaimed the nurse. Wasn't she there? And here was Mrs. Pontellier leaving, no doubt, a pleasant evening at home to devote to her? And wasn't Monsieur Ratignolle coming that very instant through the hall? And Joséphine was quite sure she had heard Doctor Mandelet's coupé. Yes, there it was, down at the door.

Adèle consented to go back to her room. She sat on the edge of a little low couch next to her bed.

Doctor Mandelet paid no attention to Madame Ratignolle's upbraidings. He was accustomed to them at such times, and was too well convinced of her loyalty to doubt it.

He was glad to see Edna, and wanted her to go with him into the salon and entertain him. But Madame Ratignolle would not consent that Edna should leave her for an instant. Between agonizing moments, she chatted a little, and said it took her mind off her sufferings.

Edna began to feel uneasy. She was seized with a vague dread. Her own like experiences seemed far away, unreal, and only half remembered. She recalled faintly an ecstasy of pain, the heavy odor of chloroform, a stupor which had deadened sensation, and an awakening to find a little new life

---

[35]Offspring of a black and a mulatto.

to which she had given being, added to the great unnumbered multitude of souls that come and go.

She began to wish she had not come; her presence was not necessary. She might have invented a pretext for staying away; she might even invent a pretext now for going. But Edna did not go. With an inward agony, with a flaming, outspoken revolt against the ways of Nature, she witnessed the scene [of] torture.

She was still stunned and speechless with emotion when later she leaned over her friend to kiss her and softly say good-by. Adèle, pressing her cheek, whispered in an exhausted voice: "Think of the children, Edna. Oh think of the children! Remember them!"

XXXVIII

Edna still felt dazed when she got outside in the open air. The Doctor's coupé had returned for him and stood before the *porte cochère*. She did not wish to enter the coupé, and told Doctor Mandelet she would walk; she was not afraid, and would go alone. He directed his carriage to meet him at Mrs. Pontellier's, and he started to walk home with her.

Up—away up, over the narrow street between the tall houses, the stars were blazing. The air was mild and caressing, but cool with the breath of spring and the night. They walked slowly, the Doctor with a heavy, measured tread and his hands behind him; Edna, in an absent-minded way, as she had walked one night at Grand Isle, as if her thoughts had gone ahead of her and she was striving to overtake them.

"You shouldn't have been there, Mrs. Pontellier," he said. "That was no place for you. Adèle is full of whims at such times. There were a dozen women she might have had with her, unimpressionable women. I felt that it was cruel, cruel. You shouldn't have gone."

"Oh, well!" she answered, indifferently. "I don't know that it matters after all. One has to think of the children some time or other; the sooner the better."

"When is Léonce coming back?"

"Quite soon. Some time in March."

"And you are going abroad?"

"Perhaps—no, I am not going. I'm not going to be forced into doing things. I don't want to go abroad. I want to be let alone. Nobody has any right—except children, perhaps—and even then, it seems to me—or it did seem—" She felt that her speech was voicing the incoherency of her thoughts, and stopped abruptly.

"The trouble is," sighed the Doctor, grasping her meaning intuitively, "that youth is given up to illusions. It seems to be a provision of Nature; a decoy to secure mothers for the race. And Nature takes no account of moral consequences, of arbitrary conditions which we create, and which we feel obliged to maintain at any cost."

"Yes," she said. "The years that are gone seem like dreams—if one might go on sleeping and dreaming—but to wake up and find—oh! well! perhaps it is better to wake up after all, even to suffer, rather than to remain a dupe to illusions all one's life."

"It seems to me, my dear child," said the Doctor at parting, holding her hand, "you seem to me to be in trouble. I am not going to ask for your confidence. I will only say that if ever you feel moved to give it to me, perhaps I might help you. I know I would understand, and I tell you there are not many who would—not many, my dear."

"Some way I don't feel moved to speak of things that trouble me. Don't think I am ungrateful or that I don't appreciate your sympathy. There are periods of despondency and suffering which take possession of me. But I don't want anything but my own way. That is wanting a good deal, of course, when you have to trample upon the lives, the hearts, the prejudices of others—but no matter—still, I shouldn't want to trample upon the little lives. Oh! I don't know what I'm saying, Doctor. Good night. Don't blame me for anything."

"Yes, I will blame you if you don't come and see me soon. We will talk of things you never have dreamt of talking about before. It will do us both good. I don't want you to blame yourself, whatever comes. Good night, my child."

She let herself in at the gate, but instead of entering she sat upon the step of the porch. The night was quiet and soothing. All the tearing emotion of the last few hours seemed to fall away from her like a somber, uncomfortable garment, which she had but to loosen to be rid of. She went back to that hour before Adèle had sent for her; and her senses kindled afresh in thinking of Robert's words, the pressure of his arms, and the feeling of his lips upon her own. She could picture at that moment no greater bliss on earth than possession of the beloved one. His expression of love had already given him to her in part. When she thought that he was there at hand, waiting for her, she grew numb with the intoxication of expectancy. It was so late; he would be asleep perhaps. She would awaken him with a kiss. She hoped he would be asleep that she might arouse him with her caresses.

Still, she remembered Adèle's voice whispering, "Think of the children; think of them." She meant to think of them; that determination had driven into her soul like a death wound—but not to-night. To-morrow would be time to think of everything.

Robert was not waiting for her in the little parlor. He was nowhere at hand. The house was empty. But he had scrawled on a piece of paper that lay in the lamplight:

"I love you. Good-by—because I love you."

Edna grew faint when she read the words. She went and sat on the sofa. Then she stretched herself out there, never uttering a sound. She did not sleep. She did not go to bed. The lamp sputtered and went out. She was still awake in the morning, when Celestine unlocked the kitchen door and came in to light the fire.

XXXIX

Victor, with hammer and nails and scraps of scantling, was patching a corner of one of the galleries. Mariequita sat near by, dangling her legs, watching him work, and handing him nails from the tool-box. The sun was beating down upon them. The girl had covered her head with her apron folded into a square pad. They had been talking for an hour or more. She was never tired of hearing Victor describe the dinner at Mrs. Pontellier's. He exaggerated every detail, making it appear a veritable Lucillean feast. The flowers were in tubs, he said. The champagne was quaffed from huge golden goblets. Venus rising from the foam could have presented no more entrancing a spectacle than Mrs. Pontellier, blazing with beauty and diamonds at the head of the board, while the other women were all of them youthful houris, possessed of incomparable charms.

She got it into her head that Victor was in love with Mrs. Pontellier, and he gave her evasive answers, framed so as to confirm her belief. She grew sullen and cried a little, threatening to go off and leave him to his fine ladies. There were a dozen men crazy about her at the *Chênière;* and since it was the fashion to be in love with married people, why, she could run away any time she liked to New Orleans with Célina's husband.

Célina's husband was a fool, a coward, and a pig, and to prove it to her, Victor intended to hammer his head into a jelly the next time he encountered him. This assurance was very consoling to Mariequita. She dried her eyes, and grew cheerful at the prospect.

They were still talking of the dinner and the allurements of city life when Mrs. Pontellier herself slipped around the corner of the house. The two youngsters stayed dumb with amazement before what they considered to be an apparition. But it was really she in flesh and blood, looking tired and a little travel-stained.

"I walked up from the wharf," she said, "and heard the hammering. I supposed it was you, mending the porch. It's a good thing. I was always tripping over those loose planks last summer. How dreary and deserted everything looks!"

It took Victor some little time to comprehend that she had come in Beaudelet's lugger, that she had come alone, and for no purpose but to rest.

"There's nothing fixed up yet, you see. I'll give you my room; it's the only place."

"Any corner will do," she assured him.

"And if you can stand Philomel's cooking," he went on, "though I might try to get her mother while you are here. Do you think she would come?" turning to Mariequita.

Mariequita thought that perhaps Philomel's mother might come for a few days, and money enough.

Beholding Mrs. Pontellier make her appearance, the girl had at once suspected a lovers' rendezvous. But Victor's astonishment was so genuine, and Mrs. Pontellier's indifference so apparent, that the disturbing notion did not lodge long in her brain. She contemplated with the greatest interest this woman who gave the most sumptuous dinners in America, and who had all the men in New Orleans at her feet.

"What time will you have dinner?" asked Edna. "I'm very hungry; but don't get anything extra."

"I'll have it ready in little or no time," he said, bustling and packing away his tools. "You may go to my room to brush up and rest yourself. Mariequita will show you."

"Thank you," said Edna. "But, do you know, I have a no-

tion to go down to the beach and take a good wash and even
a little swim, before dinner?"

"The water is too cold!" they both exclaimed. "Don't think
of it."

"Well, I might go down and try—dip my toes in. Why, it
seems to me the sun is hot enough to have warmed the very
depths of the ocean. Could you get me a couple of towels?
I'd better go right away, so as to be back in time. It would be
a little too chilly if I waited till this afternoon."

Mariequita ran over to Victor's room, and returned with
some towels, which she gave to Edna.

"I hope you have fish for dinner," said Edna, as she started
to walk away; "but don't do anything extra if you haven't."

"Run and find Philomel's mother," Victor instructed the
girl. "I'll go to the kitchen and see what I can do. By Gim-
miny! Women have no consideration! She might have sent me
word."

Edna walked on down to the beach rather mechanically,
not noticing anything special except that the sun was hot. She
was not dwelling upon any particular train of thought. She
had done all the thinking which was necessary after Robert
went away, when she lay awake upon the sofa till morning.

She had said over and over to herself: "To-day it is Arobin; to-morrow it will be some one else. It makes no difference to me, it doesn't matter about Léonce Pontellier—but
Raoul and Etienne!" She understood now clearly what she
had meant long ago when she said to Adèle Ratignolle that
she would give up the unessential, but she would never sacrifice herself for her children.

Despondency had come upon her there in the wakeful
night, and had never lifted. There was no one thing in the
world that she desired. There was no human being whom she
wanted near her except Robert; and she even realized that
the day would come when he, too, and the thought of him
would melt out of her existence, leaving her alone. The children appeared before her like antagonists who had overcome
her; who had overpowered and sought to drag her into the
soul's slavery for the rest of her days. But she knew a way to
elude them. She was not thinking of these things when she
walked down to the beach.

The water of the Gulf stretched out before her, gleaming
with the million lights of the sun. The voice of the sea is

seductive, never ceasing, whispering, clamoring, murmuring, inviting the soul to wander in abysses of solitude. All along the white beach, up and down, there was no living thing in sight. A bird with a broken wing was beating the air above, reeling, fluttering, circling disabled down, down to the water.

Edna had found her old bathing suit still hanging, faded, upon its accustomed peg.

She put it on, leaving her clothing in the bath-house. But when she was there beside the sea, absolutely alone, she cast the unpleasant, pricking garments from her, and for the first time in her life she stood naked in the open air, at the mercy of the sun, the breeze that beat upon her, and the waves that invited her.

How strange and awful it seemed to stand naked under the sky! how delicious! She felt like some new-born creature, opening its eyes in a familiar world that it had never known.

The foamy wavelets curled up to her white feet, and coiled like serpents about her ankles. She walked out. The water was chill, but she walked on. The water was deep, but she lifted her white body and reached out with a long, sweeping stroke. The touch of the sea is sensuous, enfolding the body in its soft, close embrace.

She went on and on. She remembered the night she swam far out, and recalled the terror that seized her at the fear of being unable to regain the shore. She did not look back now, but went on and on, thinking of the blue-grass meadow that she had traversed when a little child, believing that it had no beginning and no end.

Her arms and legs were growing tired.

She thought of Léonce and the children. They were a part of her life. But they need not have thought that they could possess her, body and soul. How Mademoiselle Reisz would have laughed, perhaps sneered, if she knew! "And you call yourself an artist! What pretensions, Madame! The artist must possess the courageous soul that dares and defies."

Exhaustion was pressing upon and over-powering her.

"Good-by—because I love you." He did not know; he did not understand. He would never understand. Perhaps Doctor Mandelet would have understood if she had seen him—but it was too late; the shore was far behind her, and her strength was gone.

She looked into the distance, and the old terror flamed up for an instant, then sank again. Edna heard her father's voice and her sister Margaret's. She heard the barking of an old dog that was chained to the sycamore tree. The spurs of the cavalry officer clanged as he walked across the porch. There was the hum of bees, and the musky odor of pinks filled the air.

Wiser Than a God

"To love and be wise
is scarcely granted even to a god."
—*Latin Proverb.*

I

"YOU MIGHT at least show some distaste for the task, Paula,"
said Mrs. Von Stoltz, in her querulous invalid voice, to her
daughter who stood before the glass bestowing a few final
touches of embellishment upon an otherwise plain toilet.

"And to what purpose, Mutterchen? The task is not entirely to my liking, I'll admit; but there can be no question as
to its results, which you even must concede are gratifying."

"Well, it's not the career your poor father had in view for
you. How often he has told me when I complained that you
were kept too closely at work, 'I want that Paula shall be at
the head,' " with appealing look through the window and up
into the gray, November sky into that far "somewhere,"
which might be the abode of her departed husband.

"It isn't a career at all, mamma; it's only a make-shift," answered the girl, noting the happy effect of an amber pin that
she had thrust through the coils of her lustrous yellow hair.
"The pot must be kept boiling at all hazards, pending the appearance of that hoped for career. And you forget that an occasion like this gives me the very opportunities I want."

"I can't see the advantages of bringing your talent down to
such banale servitude. Who are those people, anyway?"

The mother's question ended in a cough which shook her
into speechless exhaustion.

"Ah! I have let you sit too long by the window, mother,"
said Paula, hastening to wheel the invalid's chair nearer the
grate fire that was throwing genial light and warmth into the
room, turning its plainness to beauty as by a touch of en-
chantment. "By the way," she added, having arranged her
mother as comfortably as might be, "I haven't yet qualified
for that 'banale servitude,' as you call it." And approaching
126

the piano which stood in a distant alcove of the room, she took up a roll of music that lay curled up on the instrument, straightened it out before her. Then, seeming to remember the question which her mother had asked, turned on the stool to answer it. "Don't you know? The Brainards, very swell people, and awfully rich. The daughter is that girl whom I once told you about, having gone to the Conservatory to cultivate her voice and old Engfelder told her in his brusque way to go back home, that his system was not equal to overcoming impossibilities."

"Oh, those people."

"Yes; this little party is given in honor of the son's return from Yale or Harvard, or some place or other." And turning to the piano she softly ran over the dances, whilst the mother gazed into the fire with unresigned sadness, which the bright music seemed to deepen.

"Well, there'll be no trouble about *that*." said Paula, with comfortable assurance, having ended the last waltz. "There's nothing here to tempt me into flights of originality; there'll be no difficulty in keeping to the hand-organ effect."

"Don't leave me with those dreadful impressions, Paula; my poor nerves are on edge."

"You are too hard on the dances, mamma. There are certain strains here and there that I thought not bad."

"It's your youth that finds it so; I have outlived such illusions."

"What an inconsistent little mother it is!" the girl exclaimed, laughing. "You told me only yesterday it was my youth that was so impatient with the commonplace happenings of everyday life. That age, needing to seek its delights, finds them often in unsuspected places, wasn't that it?"

"Don't chatter, Paula; some music, some music!"

"What shall it be?" asked Paula, touching a succession of harmonious chords. "It must be short."

"The 'Berceuse,' then; Chopin's. But soft, soft and a little slowly as your dear father used to play it."

Mrs. Von Stoltz leaned her head back amongst the cushions, and with eyes closed, drank in the wonderful strains that came like an ethereal voice out of the past, lulling her spirit into the quiet of sweet memories.

When the last soft notes had melted into silence, Paula approached her mother and looking into the pale face saw that tears stood beneath the closed eyelids. "Ah! mamma, I have made you unhappy," she cried, in distress.

"No, my child; you have given me a joy that you don't dream of. I have no more pain. Your music has done for me what Faranelli's singing did for poor King Philip of Spain; it has cured me."

There was a glow of pleasure on the warm face and the eyes with almost the brightness of health. "Whilst I listened to you, Paula, my soul went out from me and lived again through an evening long ago. We were in our pretty room at Leipsic. The soft air and the moonlight came through the open-curtained window, making a quivering fret-work along the gleaming waxed floor. You lay in my arms and I felt again the pressure of your warm, plump little body against me. Your father was at the piano playing the 'Berceuse,' and all at once you drew my head down and whispered, 'Ist es nicht wonderschen, mama?' When it ended, you were sleeping and your father took you from my arms and laid you gently in bed."

Paula knelt beside her mother, holding the frail hands which she kissed tenderly.

"Now you must go, liebchen. Ring for Berta, she will do all that is needed. I feel very strong to-night. But do not come back too late."

"I shall be home as early as possible; likely in the last car, I couldn't stay longer or I should have to walk. You know the house in case there should be need to send for me?"

"Yes, yes; but there will be no need."

Paula kissed her mother lovingly and went out into the drear November night with the roll of dances under her arm.

II

THE DOOR of the stately mansion at which Paula rang, was opened by a footman, who invited her to "kindly walk up-stairs."

"Show the young lady into the music room, James," called from some upper region a voice, doubtless the same whose impossibilities had been so summarily dealt with by Herr Engfelder, and Paula was led through a suite of handsome apartments, the warmth and mellow light of which were very grateful, after the chill out-door air.

Once in the music room, she removed her wraps and seated herself comfortably to await developments. Before her stood the magnificent "Steinway," on which her eyes rested with greedy admiration, and her fingers twitched with a desire to awaken its inviting possibilities. The odor of flowers impregnated the air like a subtle intoxicant and over every-thing hung a quiet smile of expectancy, disturbed by an occasional feminine flutter above stairs, or muffled suggestions of distant household sounds.

Presently, a young man entered the drawing-room,—no doubt, the college student, for he looked critically and with an air of proprietorship at the festive arrangements, venturing the bestowal of a few improving touches. Then, gazing with pardonable complacency at his own handsome, athletic figure in the mirror, he saw reflected Paula looking at him, with a demure smile lighting her blue eyes.

"By Jove!" was his startled exclamation. Then, approaching, "I beg pardon, Miss—Miss—"

"Von Stoltz."

"Miss Von Stoltz," drawing the right conclusion from her simple toilet and the roll of music. "I hadn't seen you when I came in. Have you been here long? and sitting all alone, too? That's certainly rough."

"Oh, I've been here but a few moments, and was very well entertained."

"I dare say," with a glance full of prognostic complimentary utterances, which a further acquaintance might develop.

As he was lighting the gas of a side bracket that she might better see to read her music, Mrs. Brainard and her daughter came into the room, radiantly attired and both approached Paula with sweet and polite greeting.

"George, in mercy!" exclaimed his mother, "put out that gas, you are killing the effect of the candle light."

"But Miss Von Stoltz can't read her music without it, mother."

"I've no doubt Miss Von Stoltz knows her pieces by heart," Mrs. Brainard replied, seeking corroboration from Paula's glance.

"No, madam; I'm not accustomed to playing dance music, and this is quite new to me," the girl rejoined, touching the loose sheets that George had conveniently straightened out and placed on the rack.

"Oh, dear! 'not accustomed'?" said Miss Brainard. "And Mr. Sohmeir told us he knew you would give satisfaction."

Paula hastened to re-assure the thoroughly alarmed young lady on the point of her ability to give perfect satisfaction.

The door bell now began to ring incessantly. Up the stairs, tripped fleeting opera-cloaked figures, followed by their black robed attendants. The rooms commenced to fill with the pretty hub-bub that a bevy of girls can make when inspired by a close masculine proximity; and Paula, not waiting to be asked, struck the opening bars of an inspiring waltz.

Some hours later, during a lull in the dancing, when the men were making vigorous applications of fans and handkerchiefs; and the girls beginning to throw themselves into attitudes of picturesque exhaustion—save for the always indefatigable few—a proposition was ventured, backed by clamorous entreaties, which induced George to bring forth his banjo. And an agreeable moment followed, in which that young man's skill met with a truly deserving applause. Never had his audience beheld such proficiency as he displayed in the handling of his instrument, which was now behind him, now over-head, and again swinging in mid-air like the pendulum of a clock and sending forth the sounds of stirring melody. Sounds so inspiring that a pretty little black-eyed fairy, an acknowledged votary of Terpsichore, and George's particular admiration, was moved to contribute a few passes of a Virginia break-down, as she had studied it from life on a Southern plantation. The act closing amid a spontaneous babel of hand clapping and admiring bravos.

It must be admitted that this little episode, however graceful, was hardly a fitting prelude to the magnificent "Jewel Song from 'Faust,'" with which Miss Brainard next consented to regale the company. That Miss Brainard possessed a voice, was a fact that had existed as matter of tradition in the family as far back almost as the days of that young lady's baby utterances, in which loving ears had already detected the promise which time had so recklessly fulfilled.

True genius is not to be held in abeyance, though a host of Engfelders would rise to quell it with their mundane protests!

Miss Brainard's rendition was a triumphant achievement of sound, and with the proud flush of success moving her to kind condescension, she asked Miss Von Stoltz to "please play something."

Paula amiably consented, choosing a selection from the Modern Classic. How little did her auditors appreciate in the performance the results of a life study, of a drilling that had made her amongst the knowing an acknowledged mistress of technique. But to her skill she added the touch and interpretation of the artist; and in hearing her, even Ignorance paid to her genius the tribute of a silent emotion.

When she arose there was a moment of quiet, which was

broken by the black-eyed fairy, always ready to cast herself into a breach, observing, flippantly, "How pretty!" "Just lovely!" from another; and "What wouldn't I give to play like that." Each inane compliment falling like a dash of cold water on Paula's ardor.

She then became solicitous about the hour, with reference to her car, and George who stood near looked at his watch and informed her that the last car had gone by a full half hour before.

"But," he added, "if you are not expecting any one to call for you, I will gladly see you home."

"I expect no one, for the car that passes here would have set me down at my door," and in this avowal of difficulties, she tacitly accepted George's offer.

The situation was new. It gave her a feeling of elation to be walking through the quiet night with this handsome young fellow. He talked so freely and so pleasantly. She felt such a comfort in his strong protective nearness. In clinging to him against the buffets of the staggering wind she could feel the muscles of his arms, like steel.

He was so unlike any man of her acquaintance. Strictly unlike Poldorf, the pianist, the short rotundity of whose person could have been less objectionable, if she had not known its cause to lie in an inordinate consumption of beer. Old Engfelder, with his long hair, his spectacles and his loose, disjointed figure, was hors de combat[1] in comparison. And of Max Kuntzler, the talented composer, her teacher of harmony, she could at that moment think of no positive point of objection against him, save the vague, general, serious one of his unlikeness to George.

Her new-awakened admiration, though, was not deaf to a little inexplicable wish that he had not been so proficient with the banjo.

On they went chatting gaily, until turning the corner of the street in which she lived, Paula saw that before the door stood Dr. Sinn's buggy.

Brainard could feel the quiver of surprised distress that shook her frame, as she said, hurrying along, "Oh! mamma must be ill—worse; they have called the doctor."

Reaching the house, she threw open wide the door that was unlocked, and he stood hesitatingly back. The gas in the small hall burned at its full, and showed Berta at the top of

[1] Out of it all.

the stairs, speechless, with terrified eyes, looking down at her. And coming to meet her, was a neighbor, who strove with well-meaning solicitude to keep her back, to hold her yet a moment in ignorance of the cruel blow that fate had dealt her whilst she had in happy unconsciousness played her music for the dance.

III

SEVERAL MONTHS had passed since the dreadful night when death had deprived Paula for the second time of a loved parent.

After the first shock of grief was over, the girl had thrown all her energies into work, with the view of attaining that position in the musical world which her father and mother had dreamed might be hers.

She had remained in the small home occupying now but the half of it; and here she kept house with the faithful Berta's aid.

Friends were both kind and attentive to the stricken girl. But there had been two, whose constant devotion spoke of an interest deeper than mere friendly solicitude.

Max Kuntzler's love for Paula was something that had taken hold of his sober middle age with an enduring strength which was not to be lessened or shaken, by her rejection of it. He had asked leave to remain her friend, and while holding the tender, watchful privileges which that comprehensive title may imply, had refrained from further thrusting a warmer feeling on her acceptance.

Paula one evening was seated in her small sitting-room, working over some musical transpositions, when a ring at the bell was followed by a footstep in the hall which made her hand and heart tremble.

George Brainard entered the room, and before she could rise to greet him, had seated himself in the vacant chair beside her.

"What an untiring worker you are," he said, glancing down at the scores before her. "I always feel that my presence interrupts you; and yet I don't know that a judicious interruption isn't the wholesomest thing for you sometimes."

"You forget," she said, smiling into his face, "that I was trained to it. I must keep myself fitted to my calling. Rest would mean deterioration."

"Would you not be willing to follow some other calling?"

he asked, looking at her with unusual earnestness in his dark, handsome eyes.

"Oh, never!"

"Not if it were a calling that asked only for the labor of loving?"

She made no answer, but kept her eyes fixed on the idle traceries that she drew with her pencil on the sheets before her.

He arose and made a few impatient turns about the room, then coming again to her side, said abruptly:

"Paula, I love you. It isn't telling you something that you don't know, unless you have been without bodily perceptions. To-day there is something driving me to speak it out in words. Since I have known you," he continued, striving to look into her face that bent low over the work before her, "I have been mounting into higher and always higher circles of Paradise, under a blessed illusion that you—cared for me. But to-day, a feeling of dread has been forcing itself upon me—dread that with a word you might throw me back into a gulf that would now be one of everlasting misery. Say if you love me, Paula. I believe you do, and yet I wait with indefinable doubts for your answer."

He took her hand which she did not withdraw from his.

"Why are you speechless? Why don't you say something to me!" he asked desperately.

"I am speechless with joy and misery," she answered. "To know that you love me, gives me happiness enough to brighten a lifetime. And I am miserable, feeling that you have spoken the signal that must part us."

"You love me, and speak of parting. Never! You will be my wife. From this moment we belong to each other. Oh, my Paula," he said, drawing her to his side, "my whole existence will be devoted to your happiness."

"I can't marry you," she said shortly, disengaging his hand from her waist.

"Why?" he asked abruptly. They stood looking into each other's eyes.

"Because it doesn't enter into the purpose of my life."

"I don't ask you to give up anything in your life. I only beg you to let me share it with you."

George had known Paula only as the daughter of the unde-monstrative American woman. He had never before seen her with the father's emotional nature aroused in her. The color mounted into her cheeks, and her blue eyes were almost black with intensity of feeling.

"Hush," she said; "don't tempt me further." And she cast herself on her knees before the table near which they stood, gathering the music that lay upon it into an armful, and resting her hot cheek upon it.

"What do you know of my life," she exclaimed passionately. "What can you guess of it? Is music anything more to you than the pleasing distraction of an idle moment? Can't you feel that with me, it courses with the blood through my veins? That it's something dearer than life, than riches, even than love?" with a quiver of pain.

"Paula listen to me; don't speak like a mad woman."

She sprang up and held out an arm to ward away his nearer approach.

"Would you go into a convent, and ask to be your wife a nun who has vowed herself to the service of God?"

"Yes, if that nun loved me; she would owe to herself, to me and to God to be my wife."

Paula seated herself on the sofa, all emotion seeming suddenly to have left her; and he came and sat beside her.

"Say only that you love me, Paula." he urged persistently.

"I love you," she answered low and with pale lips.

He took her in his arms, holding her in silent rapture against his heart and kissing the white lips back into red life.

"You will be my wife?"

"You must wait. Come back in a week and I will answer you." He was forced to be content with the delay.

The days of probation being over, George went for his answer, which was given him by the old lady who occupied the upper story.

"Ach Gott! Fräulein Von Stoltz ist schon im Leipsic gegangen!"—[2] All that has not been many years ago. George Brainard is as handsome as ever, though growing a little stout in the quiet routine of domestic life. He has quite lost a pretty taste for music that formerly distinguished him as a skilful banjoist. This loss his little black-eyed wife deplores; though she has herself made concessions to the advancing years, and abandoned Virginia break-downs as incompatible with the serious offices of wifehood and matrimony.

You may have seen in the morning paper, that the

[2]"Miss Von Stoltz has gone to Leipsic!"

renowned pianist, Fräulein Paula Von Stoltz, is resting in Leipsic, after an extended and remunerative concert tour.

Professor Max Kuntzler is also in Leipsic—with the ever persistent will—the dogged patience that so often wins in the end.

Written and published, 1889

˙A Point at Issue!

MARRIED—
On Tuesday, May 11,
Eleanor Gail to Charles Faraday.

NOTHING BEARING the shape of a wedding announcement
could have been less obtrusive than the foregoing hidden in a
remote corner of the Plymdale *Promulgator*, clothed in the
palest and smallest of type, and modestly wedged in between
the big, black-lettered offer of the *Promulgator* to mail itself
free of extra charge to subscribers leaving home for the summer months, and an equally somber-clad notice (doubtless as-
tray as to place and application) that Hammersmith & Co.
were carrying a large and varied assortment of marble and
granite monuments!

Yet notwithstanding its sandwiched condition, that little
marriage announcement seemed to Eleanor to parade the
whole street.

Whichever way she turned her eyes, it glowered at her with
scornful reproach.

She felt it to be an indelicate thrusting of herself upon the
public notice; and at the sight she was plunged in regret at
having made to the proprieties the concession of permitting it.

She hoped now that the period for making concessions was
ended. She had endured long and patiently the trials that
beset her path when she chose to diverge from the beaten
walks of female Plymdaledom. Had stood stoically enough
the questionable distinction of being relegated to a place
amid that large and ill-assorted family of "cranks," feeling
the discomfit and attending opprobrium to be far outbalanced
by the satisfying consciousness of roaming the heights of free
thought, and tasting the sweets of a spiritual emancipation.

The closing act of Eleanor's young ladyhood, when she
chose to be married without pre-announcement, without the
paraphernalia of accessories so dear to a curious public—had
been in keeping with previous methods distinguishing her

career. The disappointed public cheated of its entertainment, was forced to seek such compensation for the loss as was offered in reflections that while condemning her present, were unsparing of her past, and full with damning prognostic of her future.

Charles Faraday, who added to his unembellished title that of Professor of Mathematics of the Plymdale University, had found in Eleanor Gail his ideal woman.

Indeed, she rather surpassed that ideal, which had of necessity been but an adorned picture of woman as he had known her. A mild emphasizing of her merits, a soft toning down of her defects had served to offer to his fancy a prototype of that bequoted creature.

"Not too good for human nature's daily food," yet so good that he had cherished no hope of beholding such a one in the flesh. Until Eleanor had come, supplanting his idea, and making of that fanciful creation a very simpleton by contrast. In the beginning he had found her extremely good to look at, with her combination of graceful womanly charms, unmarred by self-conscious mannerisms that was as rare as it was engaging. Talking with her, he had caught a look from her eyes into his that he recognized at once as a free masonry of intellect. And the longer he knew her, the greater grew his wonder at the beautiful revelations of her mind that unfurled itself to his, like the curling petals of some hardy blossom that opens to the inviting warmth of the sun. It was not that Eleanor knew many things. According to her own modest estimate of herself, she knew nothing. There were school girls in Plymdale who surpassed her in the amount of their positive knowledge. But she was possessed of a clear intellect: sharp in its reasoning, strong and unprejudiced in its outlook. She was that *rara avis,*[1] a logical woman—something which Faraday had not encountered in his life before. True, he was not hoary with age. At 30 the types of women he had met with were not legion; but he felt safe in doubting that the hedges of the future would grow logical women for him, more than they had borne such prodigies in the past.

He found Eleanor ready to take broad views of life and humanity; able to grasp a question and anticipate conclusions by a quick intuition which he himself reached by the slower, consecutive steps of reason.

[1]Strange creature.

During the months that shaped themselves into the cycle of a year these two dwelt together in the harmony of a united purpose.

Together they went looking for the good things of life, knocking at the closed doors of philosophy; venturing into the open fields of science, she, with uncertain steps, made steady by his help.

Whithersoever he led she followed, oftentimes in her eagerness taking the lead into unfamiliar ways in which he, weighted with a lingering conservatism, had hesitated to venture.

So did they grow in their oneness of thought to belong each so absolutely to the other that the idea seemed not to have come to them that this union might be made faster by marriage. Until one day it broke upon Faraday, like a revelation from the unknown, the possibility of making her his wife.

When he spoke, eager with the new awakened impulse, she laughingly replied:

"Why not?" She had thought of it long ago.

In entering upon their new life they decided to be governed by no precedential methods. Marriage was to be a form, that while fixing legally their relation to each other, was in no wise to touch the individuality of either; that was to be preserved intact. Each was to remain a free integral of humanity, responsible to no dominating exactions of so-called marriage laws. And the element that was to make possible such a union was trust in each other's love, honor, courtesy, tempered by the reserving clause of readiness to meet the consequences of reciprocal liberty.

Faraday appreciated the need of offering to his wife advantages for culture which had been of impossible attainment during her girlhood.

Marriage, which marks too often the closing period of a woman's intellectual existence, was to be in her case the open portal through which she might seek the embellishments that her strong, graceful mentality deserved.

An urgent desire with Eleanor was to acquire a thorough speaking knowledge of the French language. They agreed that a lengthy sojourn in Paris could be the only practical and reliable means of accomplishing such an end.

Faraday's three months of vacation were to be spent by them in the idle happiness of a loitering honeymoon through the continent of Europe, then he would leave his wife in the

French capital for a stay that might extend indefinitely—two, three years—as long as should be found needful, he returning to join her with the advent of each summer, to renew their love in a fresh and re-strengthened union.

And so, in May, they were married, and in September we find Eleanor established in the pension of the old couple Clairegobeau and comfortably ensconced in her pretty room that opened on to the Rue Rivoli, her heart full of sweet memories that were to cheer her coming solitude.

On the wall, looking always down at her with his quiet, kind glance, hung the portrait of her husband. Beneath it stood the fanciful little desk at which she hoped to spend many happy hours.

Books were everywhere, giving character to the graceful furnishings which their united taste had evolved from the paucity of the Clairegobeau germ, and out of the window was Paris!

Eleanor was supremely satisfied amid her new and attractive surroundings. The pang of parting from her husband seeming to lend sharp zest to a situation that offered the fulfillment of a cherished purpose.

Faraday, with the stronger man-nature, felt more keenly the discomfit of giving up a companionship that in its brief duration had been replete with the duality of accomplished delight and growing promise.

But to him also was the situation made acceptable by its involving a principle which he felt it incumbent upon him to uphold. He returned to Plymdale and to his duties at the university, and resumed his bachelor existence as quietly as though it had been interrupted but by the interval of a day.

The small public with which he had acquaintance, and which had forgotten his existence during the past few months, was fired anew with indignant astonishment at the effrontery of the situation which his singular coming back offered to their contemplation.

That two young people should presume to introduce such innovations into matrimony!

It was uncalled for!

It was improper!

It was indecent!

He must have already tired of her idiosyncrasies, since he had left her in Paris.

And in Paris, of all places, to leave a young woman alone! Why not at once in Hades?

She had been left in Paris forsooth to learn French. And since when was Mme. Belaire's French, as it had been taught to select generations of Plymdalions, considered insufficient for the practical needs of existence as related by that foreign tongue?

But Faraday's life was full with occupation and his brief moments of leisure were too precious to give to heeding the idle gossip that floated to his hearing and away again without holding his thoughts an instant.

He lived uninterruptedly a certain existence with his wife through the medium of letters. True, an inadequate substitute for her actual presence, but there was much satisfaction in this constant communion of thought between them.

They told such details of their daily lives as they thought worth the telling.

Their readings were discussed. Opinions exchanged. Newspaper cuttings sent back and forth, bearing upon questions that interested them. And what did not interest them?

Nothing was so large that they dared not look at it. Happenings, small in themselves, but big in their psychological comprehensiveness, held them with strange fascination. Her earnestness and intensity in such matters were extreme; but happily, Faraday brought to this union humorous instincts, and an optimism that saved it from a too monotonous sombreness.

The young man had his friends in Plymdale. Certainly none that ever remotely approached the position which Eleanor held in that regard. She stood pre-eminent. She was himself.

But his nature was genial. He invited companionship from his fellow beings, who, however short that companionship might be, carried always away a gratifying consciousness of having made their personalities felt.

The society in Plymdale which he most frequented was that of the Beatons.

Beaton père was a fellow professor, many years older than Faraday, but one of those men with whom time, after putting its customary stamp upon his outward being, took no further care.

The spirit of his youth had remained untouched, and formed the nucleus around which the family gathered, drawing the light of their own cheerfulness.

Mrs. Beaton was a woman whose aspirations went not further than the desire for her family's good, and her bearing announced in its every feature, the satisfaction of completed hopes.

Of the daughters, Margaret, the eldest, was looked upon as slightly erratic, owing to a timid leaning in the direction of Woman's Suffrage.

Her activity in that regard, taking the form of a desultory correspondence with members of a certain society of protest; the fashioning and donning of garments of mysterious shape, which, while stamping their wearer with the distinction of a quasi-emancipation, defeated the ultimate purpose of their construction by inflicting a personal discomfort that extended beyond the powers of long endurance. Miss Kitty Beaton, the youngest daughter, and just returned from boarding-school, while clamoring for no privileges doubtful of attainment and of remote and questionable benefit, with a Napoleonic grip, possessed herself of such rights as were at hand and exercised them in keeping the household under her capricious command.

She was at that age of blissful illusion when a girl is in love with her own youth and beauty and happiness. That age which heeds no purpose in the scope of creation further than may touch her majesty's enjoyment. Who would not smilingly endure with that charming selfishness of youth, knowing that the rough hand of experience is inevitably descending to disturb the short-lived dream?

They were all clever people, bright and interesting, and in this family circle Faraday found an acceptable relaxation from work and enforced solitude.

If they ever doubted the wisdom or expediency of his domestic relations, courtesy withheld the expression of any such doubts. Their welcome was always complete in its friendliness, and the interest which they evinced in the absent Eleanor proved that she was held in the highest esteem.

With Beaton Faraday enjoyed that pleasant intercourse which may exist between men whose ways, while not too divergent, are yet divided by an appreciable interval.

But it remained for Kitty to touch him with her girlish charms in a way, which, though not too usual with Faraday, meant so little to the man that he did not take the trouble to resent it.

Her laughter and song, the restless motions of her bubbling happiness, he watched with the casual pleasure that one follows the playful gambols of a graceful kitten.

He liked the soft shining light of her eyes. When she was

near him the velvet smoothness of her pink cheeks stirred him with a feeling that could have found satisfying expression in a kiss.

It is idle to suppose that even the most exemplary men go through life with their eyes closed to woman's beauty and their senses steeled against its charm.

Faraday thought little of this feeling (and so should we if it were not outspoken).

In writing one day to his wife, with the cold-blooded impartiality of choosing a subject which he thought of neither more nor less prominence than the next, he descanted at some length upon the interesting emotions which Miss Kitty's pretty femininity aroused in him.

If he had given serious thought to the expediency of touching upon such a theme with one's wife, he still would not have been deterred. Was not Eleanor's large comprehensiveness far above the littleness of ordinary women?

Did it not enter into the scheme of their lives, to keep free from prejudices that hold their sway over the masses?

But he thought not of that, for, after all, his interest in Kitty and his interest in his university class bore about an equal reference to Eleanor and his love for her.

His letter was sent, and he gave no second thought to the matter of its contents.

The months went by for Faraday with few distinctive features to mark them outside the enduring desire for his wife's presence.

There had been a visit of sharp disturbance once when her customary letter failed him, and the tardy missive coming, carried an inexplicable coldness that dealt him a pain which, however, did not long survive a little judicious reflection and a very deluge of letters from Paris that shook him with their unusual ardor.

May had come again, and at its approach Faraday with the impatience of a hundred lovers hastened across the seas to join his Eleanor.

It was evening and Eleanor paced to and fro in her room, making the last of a series of efforts that she had been putting forth all day to fight down a misery of the heart, against which her reason was in armed rebellion. She had tried the strategy of simply ignoring its presence, but the attempt had failed utterly. During her daily walk it had embodied itself in every object that her eyes rested upon. It had enveloped her like a smoke mist, through which Paris looked more dull than the desolation of Sahara.

She had thought to displace it with work, but, like the disturbing element in the chemist's crucible, it rose again and again overspreading the surface of her labor.

Alone in her room, the hour had come when she meant to succeed by the unaided force of reason—proceeding first to make herself bodily comfortable in the folds of a majestic flowing gown, in which she looked a distressed goddess.

Her hair hung heavy and free about her shoulders, for those reasoning powers were to be spurred by a plunging of white fingers into the golden mass.

In this dishevelled state Eleanor's presence seemed too large for the room and its delicate furnishings. The place fitted well an Eleanor in repose but not an Eleanor who swept the narrow confines like an incipient cyclone.

Reason did good work and stood its ground bravely, but against it were the too great odds of a woman's heart, backed by the soft prejudices of a far-reaching heredity.

She finally sank into a chair before her pretty writing desk. The golden head fell upon the outspread arms waiting to receive it, and she burst into a storm of sobs and tears. It was the signal of surrender.

It is a gratifying privilege to be permitted to ignore the reason of such unusual disturbance in a woman of Eleanor's high qualifications. The cause of that abandonment of grief will never be learned unless she chooses to disclose it herself.

When Faraday first folded his wife in his arms he saw but the Eleanor of his constant dreams. But he soon began to perceive how more beautiful she had grown; with a richness of coloring and fullness of health that Plymdale had never been able to bestow. And the object of her stay in Paris was gaining fast to accomplishment, for she had already acquired a knowledge of French that would not require much longer to perfect.

They sat together in her room discussing plans for the summer, when a timid knock at the door caused Eleanor to look up, to see the little housemaid eyeing her with the glance of a fellow conspirator and holding in her hand a card that she suffered to be but partly visible.

Eleanor hastily approached her, and reading the name upon the card thrust it into her pocket, exchanging some whispered words with the girl, among which were audible, "excuse me," "engaged," "another time." She came back to her husband looking a little flustered, to resume the conversation where it had been interrupted and he offered no inquiries about her mysterious caller.

Entering the salon not many days later he found that in doing so he interrupted a conversation between his wife and a very striking looking gentleman who seemed on the point of taking his leave.

They were both disconcerted; she especially, in bowing, almost thrusting him out, had the appearance of wanting to run away; to do any thing but meet her husband's glance.

He asked with assumed indifference who her friend might be.

"Oh, no one special," with a hopeless attempt at brazenness.

He accepted the situation without protest, only indulging the reflection that Eleanor was losing something of her frankness.

But when his wife asked him on another occasion to dispense with her company for a whole afternoon, saying that she had an urgent call upon her time, he began to wonder if there might not be modifications to this marital liberty of which he was so staunch an advocate.

She left him with a hundred little endearments that she seemed to have acquired with her French.

He forced himself to the writing of a few urgent letters, but his restlessness did not permit him to do more.

It drove him to ugly thoughts, then to the means of dispelling them.

He gazed out of the window, wondered why he was remaining indoors, and followed up the reflection by seizing his hat and plunging out into the street.

The Paris boulevards of a day in early summer are calculated to dispel almost any ache but one of that nature, which was making itself incipiently felt with Faraday.

It was at that stage when it moves a man to take exception at the inadequacy of every thing that is offered to his contemplation or entertainment.

The sun was too hot.

The shop windows were vulgar; lacking artistic detail in their make-up.

How could he ever have found the Paris women attractive? They had lost their chic. Most of them were scrawny—not worth looking at.

He thought to go and stroll through the galleries of art. He knew Eleanor would wish to be with him; then he was tempted to go alone.

Finally, more tired from inward than outward restlessness, he took refuge at one of the small tables of a café, called for a "Mazarin," and, so seated for an unheeded time, let the panorama of Paris pass before his indifferent eyes.

When suddenly one of the scenes in this shifting show struck him with stunning effect.

It was the sight of his wife riding in a fiacre with her caller of a few days back, both conversing and in high spirits.

He remained for a moment enervated, then the blood came tingling back into his veins like fire, making his finger ends twitch with a desire (full worthy of any one of the "prejudiced masses") to tear the scoundrel from his seat and paint the boulevard red with his villainous blood.

A rush of wild intentions crowded into his brain.

Should he follow and demand an explanation? Leave Paris without ever looking into her face again? and more not worthy of the man.

It is right to say that his better self and better senses came quickly back to him.

That first revolt was like the unwilling protest of the flesh against the surgeon's knife before a man has steeled himself to its endurance.

Every thing came back to him from their short, common past—their dreams, their large intentions for the shaping of their lives. Here was the first test, and should he be the one to cry out, "I cannot endure it."

When he returned to the pension, Eleanor was impatiently waiting for him in the entry, radiant with gladness at his coming.

She was under a suppressed excitement that prevented her noting his disturbed appearance.

She took his listless hand and led him into the small drawing-room that adjoined their sleeping chamber.

There stood her companion of the fiacre, smiling as was she at the pleasure of introducing him to another Eleanor disposed on the wall in the best possible light to display the gorgeous radiance of her wonderful beauty and the skill of the man who had portrayed it.

The most sanguine hopes of Eleanor and her artist could not have anticipated anything like the rapture with which Faraday received this surprise.

"Monsieur l'Artiste" went away with his belief in the undemonstrativeness of the American very much shaken; and in his pocket substantial evidence of American appreciation of art.

Then the story was told how the portrait was intended as a surprise for his arrival. How there had been delay in its completion. The artist had required one more sitting, which she gave him that day, and the two had brought the picture home in the fiacre, he to give it the final advantages of a judicious light; to witness its effect upon Mons. Faraday and finally the excusable wish to be presented to the husband of the lady who had captivated his deepest admiration and esteem.

"You shall take it home with you," said Eleanor.

Both were looking at the lovely creation by the soft light of a reckless expenditure of bougie.[2]

"Yes, dearest," he answered, with feeble elation at the prospect of returning home with that exquisite piece of inanimation.

"Have you engaged your return passage?" she asked.

She sat at his knee, arrayed in the gown that had one evening clothed such a goddess in distress.

"Oh, no. There's plenty time for that," was his answer. "Why do you ask?"

"I'm sure I don't know," and after a while:

"Charlie, I think—I mean, don't you think—I have made wonderful progress in French?"

"You've done marvels, Nellie. I find no difference between your French and Mme. Clairegobeau's, except that yours is far prettier."

"Yes?" she rejoined, with a little squeeze of the hand.

"I mayn't be right and I want you to give me your candid opinion. I believe Mme. Belaire—now that I have gone so far—don't you think—hadn't you better engage passage for two?"

His answer took the form of a pantomimic rapture of assenting gratefulness, during which each gave speechless assurance of a love that could never more take a second place.

"Nellie," he asked, looking into the face that nestled in close reach of his warm kisses, "I have often wanted to know, though you needn't tell it if it doesn't suit you," he added, laughing, "why you once failed to write to me, and then sent a letter whose coldness gave me a week's heart trouble?"

She flushed, and hesitated, but finally answered him

[2]Candles.

bravely, "It was when—when you cared so much for that Kitty Beaton."

Astonishment for a moment deprived him of speech.

"But Eleanor! In the name of reason! It isn't possible!"

"I know all you would say," she replied, "I have been over the whole ground myself, over and over, but it is useless. I have found that there are certain things which a woman can't philosophize about, any more than she can about death when it touches that which is near to her."

"But you don't think—"

"Hush! don't speak of it ever again. I think nothing!" closing her eyes, and with a little shudder drawing closer to him.

As he kissed his wife with passionate fondness, Faraday thought, "I love her none the less for it, but my Nellie is only a woman, after all."

With man's usual inconsistency, he had quite forgotten the episode of the portrait.

Written and published, 1889

A Shameful Affair

I

MILDRED ORME, seated in the snuggest corner of the big front porch of the Kraummer farmhouse, was as content as a girl need hope to be.

This was no such farm as one reads about in humorous fiction. Here were swelling acres where the undulating wheat gleamed in the sun like a golden sea. For silver there was the Meramec—or, better, it was pure crystal, for here and there one might look clean through it down to where the pebbles lay like green and yellow gems. Along the river's edge trees were growing to the very water, and in it, sweeping it when they were willows.

The house itself was big and broad, as country houses should be. The master was big and broad, too. The mistress was small and thin, and it was always she who went out at noon to pull the great clanging bell that called the farmhands in to dinner.

From her agreeable corner where she lounged with her Browning or her Ibsen, Mildred watched the woman do this every day. Yet when the clumsy farmhands all came tramping up the steps and crossed the porch in going to their meal that was served within, she never looked at them. Why should she? Farmhands are not so very nice to look at, and she was nothing of an anthropologist. But once when the half dozen men came along, a paper which she had laid carelessly upon the railing was blown across their path. One of them picked it up, and when he had mounted the steps restored it to her. He was young, and brown, of course, as the sun had made him. He had nice blue eyes. His fair hair was dishevelled. His shoulders were broad and square and his limbs strong and clean. A not unpicturesque figure in the rough attire that bared his throat to view and gave perfect freedom to his every motion.

Mildred did not make these several observations in the half

second that she looked at him in courteous acknowledgment. It took her as many days to note them all. For she signaled him out each time that he passed her, meaning to give him a condescending little smile, as she knew how. But he never looked at her. To be sure, clever young women of twenty, who are handsome, besides, who have refused their half dozen offers and are settling down to the conviction that life is a tedious affair, are not going to care a straw whether farmhands look at them or not. And Mildred did not care, and the thing would not have occupied her a moment if Satan had not intervened, in offering the employment which natural conditions had failed to supply. It was summer time; she was idle; she was piqued, and that was the beginning of the shameful affair.

"Who are these men, Mrs. Kraummer, that work for you? Where do you pick them up?"

"Oh, ve picks 'em up everyvere. Some is neighbors, some is tramps, and so."

"And that broad-shouldered young fellow—is he a neighbor? The one who handed me my paper the other day—you remember?"

"Gott, no! You might yust as well say he vas a tramp. Aber he vorks like a steam ingine."

"Well, he's an extremely disagreeable-looking man. I should think you'd be afraid to have him about, not knowing him."

"Vat you vant to be 'fraid for?" laughed the little woman. "He don't talk no more un ven he vas deef und dumb. I didn't t'ought you vas sooch a baby."

"But, Mrs. Kraummer, I don't want you to think I'm a baby, as you say—a coward, as you mean. Ask the man if he will drive me to church to-morrow. You see, I'm not so very much afraid of him," she added with a smile.

The answer which this unmannerly farmhand returned to Mildred's request was simply a refusal. He could not drive her to church because he was going fishing.

"Aber," offered good Mrs. Kraummer, "Hans Platzfeldt will drive you to church, odor vereever you vants. He vas a goot boy vat you can trust, dat Hans."

"Oh, thank him very much. But I find I have so many letters to write to-morrow, and it promises to be hot, too. I shan't care to go to church after all."

She could have cried for vexation. Snubbed by a farmhand! a tramp, perhaps. She, Mildred Orme, who ought really to have been with the rest of the family at Narragansett—who had come to seek in this retired spot the repose that would enable her to follow exalted lines of thought. She marvelled at the problematic nature of farmhands.

After sending her the uncivil message already recorded, and as he passed beneath the porch where she sat, he did look at her finally, in a way to make her positively gasp at the sudden effrontery of the man.

But the inexplicable look stayed with her. She could not banish it.

II

It was not so very hot after all, the next day, when Mildred walked down the long narrow footpath that led through the bending wheat to the river. High above her waist reached the yellow grain. Mildred's brown eyes filled with a reflected golden light as they caught the glint of it, as she heard the trill that it answered to the gentle breeze. Anyone who has walked through the wheat in midsummer-time knows that sound.

In the woods it was sweet and solemn and cool. And there beside the river was the wretch who had annoyed her, first, with his indifference, then with the sudden boldness of his glance.

"Are you fishing?" she asked politely and with kindly dignity, which she supposed would define her position toward him. The inquiry lacked not pertinence, seeing that he sat motionless, with a pole in his hand and his eyes fixed on a cork that bobbed aimlessly on the water.

"Yes, madam," was his brief reply.

"It won't disturb you if I stand here a moment, to see what success you will have?"

"No, madam."

She stood very still, holding tight to the book she had brought with her. Her straw hat had slipped disreputably to one side, over the wavy bronze-brown bang that half covered her forehead. Her cheeks were ripe with color that the sun had coaxed there; so were her lips.

All the other farmhands had gone forth in Sunday attire. Perhaps this one had none better than these working clothes that he wore. A feminine commiseration swept her at the thought. He spoke never a word. She wondered how many hours he could sit there, so patiently waiting for fish to come to his hook. For her part, the situation began to pall, and she wanted to change it at last.

"Let me try a moment, please? I have an idea—"

"Yes, madam."

"The man is surely an idiot, with his monosyllables," she commented inwardly. But she remembered that monosyllables belong to a boor's equipment.

She laid her book carefully down and took the pole gingerly that he came to place in her hands. Then it was his turn to stand back and look respectfully and silently on at the absorbing performance.

"Oh!" cried the girl, suddenly, seized with excitement upon seeing the line dragged deep in the water.

"Wait, wait! Not yet."

He sprang to her side. With his eyes eagerly fastened on the tense line, he grasped the pole to prevent her drawing it, as her intention seemed to be. That is, he meant to grasp the pole, but instead, his brown hand came down upon Mildred's white one.

He started violently at finding himself so close to a bronze-brown tangle that almost swept his chin—to a hot cheek only a few inches away from his shoulder, to a pair of young, dark eyes that gleamed for an instant unconscious things into his own.

Then, why ever it happened, or how ever it happened, his arms were holding Mildred and he kissed her lips. She did not know if it was ten times or only once.

She looked around—her face milk-white—to see him disappear with rapid strides through the path that had brought her there. Then she was alone.

Only the birds had seen, and she could count on their discretion. She was not wildly indignant, as many would have been. Shame stunned her. But through it she gropingly wondered if she should tell the Kraummers that her chaste lips had been rifled of their innocence. Publish her own confusion? No! Once in her room she would give calm thought to the situation, and determine then how to act. The secret must remain her own: a hateful burden to bear alone until she could forget it.

III

And because she feared not to forget it, Mildred wept that night. All day long a hideous truth had been thrusting itself upon her that made her ask herself if she could be mad. She feared it. Else why was that kiss the most delicious thing she had known in her twenty years of life? The sting of it had never left her lips since it was pressed into them. The sweet trouble of it banished sleep from her pillow.

But Mildred would not bend the outward conditions of her life to serve any shameful whim that chanced to visit her soul, like an ugly dream. She would avoid nothing. She would go and come as always.

In the morning she found in her chair upon the porch the book she had left by the river. A fresh indignity! But she came and went as she intended to, and sat as usual upon the porch amid her familiar surroundings. When the Offender passed her by she knew it, though her eyes were never lifted. Are there only sight and sound to tell such things? She discerned it by a wave that swept her with confusion and she knew not what besides.

She watched him furtively, one day, when he talked with Farmer Kraummer out in the open. When he walked away she remained like one who has drunk much wine. Then unhesitatingly she turned and began her preparations to leave the Kraummer farmhouse.

When the afternoon was far spent they brought letters to her. One of them read like this:

"My Mildred, deary! I am only now at Narragansett, and so broke up not to find you. So you are down at that Kraummer farm, on the Iron Mountain. Well! What do you think of that delicious crank, Fred Evelyn? For a man must be a crank who does such things. Only fancy! Last year he chose to drive an engine back and forth across the plains. This year he tills the soil with laborers. Next year it will be something else as insane—because he likes to live more lives than one kind, and other Quixotic reasons. We are great chums. He writes me he's grown as strong as an ox. But he hasn't mentioned that you are there. I know you don't get on with him, for he isn't a bit intellectual—detests Ibsen and abuses Tolstoi. He doesn't read 'in books'—says they are spectacles for the short-sighted to look at life through. Don't snub him, dear, or be too hard on him; he has a heart of gold, if he is the first crank in America."

Mildred tried to think—to feel that the intelligence which this letter brought to her would take somewhat of the sting from the shame that tortured her. But it did not. She knew that it could not.

In the gathering twilight she walked again through the wheat that was heavy and fragrant with dew. The path was very long and very narrow. When she was midway she saw the Offender coming toward her. What could she do? Turn and run, as a little child might? Spring into the wheat, as some frightened four-footed creature would? There was nothing but to pass him with the dignity which the occasion clearly demanded.

But he did not let her pass. He stood squarely in the pathway before her, hat in hand, a perturbed look upon his face.

"Miss Orme," he said, "I have wanted to say to you, every hour of the past week, that I am the most consummate hound that walks the earth."

She made no protest. Her whole bearing seemed to indicate that her opinion coincided with his own.

"If you have a father, or brother, or any one, in short, to whom you may say such things—"

"I think you aggravate the offense, sir, by speaking of it. I shall ask you never to mention it again. I want to forget that it ever happened. Will you kindly let me by."

"Oh," he ventured eagerly, "you want to forget it! Then, maybe, since you are willing to forget, you will be generous enough to forgive the offender some day?"

"Some day," she repeated, almost inaudibly, looking seemingly through him, but not at him—"some day—perhaps; when I shall have forgiven myself."

He stood motionless, watching her slim, straight figure lessening by degrees as she walked slowly away from him. He was wondering what she meant. Then a sudden, quick wave came beating into his brown throat and staining it crimson. when he guessed what it might be.

Written, 1891; published, 1893

Miss McEnders

I

WHEN Miss Georgie McEnders had finished an elaborately simple toilet of gray and black, she divested herself completely of rings, bangles, brooches—everything to suggest that she stood in friendly relations with fortune. For Georgie was going to read a paper upon "The Dignity of Labor" before the Woman's Reform Club; and if she was blessed with an abundance of wealth, she possessed a no less amount of good taste.

Before entering the neat victoria that stood at her father's too-sumptuous door—and that was her special property—she turned to give certain directions to the coachman. First upon the list from which she read was inscribed: "Look up Mademoiselle Salambre."

"James," said Georgie, flushing a pretty pink, as she always did with the slightest effort of speech, "we want to look up a person named Mademoiselle Salambre, in the southern part of town, on Arsenal street," indicating a certain number and locality. Then she seated herself in the carriage, and as it drove away proceeded to study her engagement list further and to knit her pretty brows in deep and complex thought.

"Two o'clock—look up M. Salambre," said the list. "Three-thirty—read paper before Woman's Ref. Club. Four-thirty—" and here followed cabalistic abbreviations which meant: "Join committee of ladies to investigate moral condition of St. Louis factory-girls. Six o'clock—dine with papa. Eight o'clock—hear Henry George's lecture on Single Tax."

So far, Mademoiselle Salambre was only a name to Georgie McEnders, one of several submitted to her at her own request by her furnishers, Push and Prodem, an enterprising firm charged with the construction of Miss McEnders' very elaborate trousseau. Georgie liked to know the people who worked for her, as far as she could.

154

She was a charming young woman of twenty-five, though almost too white-souled for a creature of flesh and blood. She possessed ample wealth and time to squander, and a burning desire to do good—to elevate the human race, and start the world over again on a comfortable footing for everybody.

When Georgie had pushed open the very high gate of a very small yard she stood confronting a robust German woman, who, with dress tucked carefully between her knees, was in the act of noisily "redding" the bricks.

"Does M'selle Salambre live here?" Georgie's tall, slim figure was very erect. Her face suggested a sweet peach blossom, and she held a severely simple lorgnon up to her short-sighted blue eyes.

"Ya! ya! aber oop stairs!" cried the woman brusquely and impatiently. But Georgie did not mind. She was used to greetings that lacked the ring of cordiality.

When she had ascended the stairs that led to an upper porch she knocked at the first door that presented itself, and was told to enter by Mlle. Salambre herself.

The woman sat at an opposite window, bending over a bundle of misty white goods that lay in a fluffy heap in her lap. She was not young. She might have been thirty, or she might have been forty. There were lines about her round, piquante face that denoted close acquaintance with struggles, hardships and all manner of unkind experiences.

Georgie had heard a whisper here and there touching the private character of Mlle. Salambre which had determined her to go in person and make the acquaintance of the woman and her surroundings; which latter were poor and simple enough, and not too neat. There was a little child at play upon the floor.

Mlle. Salambre had not expected so unlooked-for an apparition as Miss McEnders, and seeing the girl standing there in the door she removed the eye-glasses that had assisted her in the delicate work, and stood up also.

"Mlle. Salambre, I suppose?" said Georgie, with a courteous inclination.

"Ah! Mees McEndairs! What an agree'ble surprise! Will you be so kind to take a chair." Mademoiselle had lived many years in the city, in various capacities, which brought her in touch with the fashionable set. There were few people in polite society whom Mademoiselle did not know—by sight, at least; and their private histories were as familiar to her as her own.

"You 'ave come to see your the work?" the woman went on with a smile that quite brightened her face. "It is a pleasure to handle such fine, such delicate quality of goods, Mees," and she went and laid several pieces of her handiwork upon the table beside Georgie, at the same time indicating such details as she hoped would call forth her visitor's approval.

There was something about the woman and her surroundings, and the atmosphere of the place, that affected the girl unpleasantly. She shrank instinctively, drawing her invisible mantle of chastity closely about her. Mademoiselle saw that her visitor's attention was divided between the lingerie and the child upon the floor, who was engaged in battering a doll's unyielding head against the unyielding floor.

"The child of my neighbor down-stairs," said Mademoiselle, with a wave of the hand which expressed volumes of unutterable ennui. But at that instant the little one, with instinctive mistrust, and in seeming defiance of the repudiation, climbed to her feet and went rolling and toddling towards her mother, clasping the woman about the knees, and calling her by the endearing title which was her own small right.

A spasm of annoyance passed over Mademoiselle's face, but still she called the child *"Chene,"* as she grasped its arm to keep it from falling. Miss McEnders turned every shade of carmine.

"Why did you tell me an untruth?" she asked, looking indignantly into the woman's lowered face. "Why do you call yourself 'Mademoiselle' if this child is yours?"

"For the reason that it is more easy to obtain employment. For reasons that you would not understand," she continued, with a shrug of the shoulders that expressed some defiance and a sudden disregard for consequences. "Life is not all *couleur de rose,* Mees McEndairs; you do not know what life is, you!" And drawing a handkerchief from an apron pocket she mopped an imaginary tear from the corner of her eye, and blew her nose till it glowed again.

Georgie could hardly recall the words or actions with which she quitted Mademoiselle's presence. As much as she wanted to, it had been impossible to stand and read the woman a moral lecture. She had simply thrown what disapproval she could into her hasty leave-taking, and that was all for the moment. But as she drove away, a more practical form of rebuke suggested itself to her not too nimble intelligence—one that she promised herself to act upon as soon as her home was reached.

When she was alone in her room, during an interval between her many engagements, she then attended to the affair of Mlle. Salambre.

Georgie believed in discipline. She hated unrighteousness. When it pleased God to place the lash in her hand she did not hesitate to apply it. Here was this Mlle. Salambre living in her sin. Not as one who is young and blinded by the glamour of pleasure, but with cool and deliberate intention. Since she chose to transgress, she ought to suffer, and be made to feel that her ways were iniquitous and invited rebuke. It lay in Georgie's power to mete out a small dose of that chastisement which the woman deserved, and she was glad that the opportunity was hers.

She seated herself forthwith at her writing table, and penned the following note to her furnishers:

"Messrs. Push & Prodem.

"*Gentlemen*—Please withdraw from Mademoiselle Salambre all work of mine, and return same to me at once—finished or unfinished.

Yours truly,
Georgie McEnders."

II

On the second day following this summary proceeding, Georgie sat at her writing-table, looking prettier and pinker than ever, in a luxurious and soft-toned robe de chambre that suited her own delicate coloring, and fitted the pale amber tints of her room decorations.

There were books, pamphlets, and writing material set neatly upon the table before her. In the midst of them were two framed photographs, which she polished one after another with a silken scarf that was near.

One of these was a picture of her father, who looked like an Englishman, with his clean-shaved mouth and chin, and closely-cropped side-whiskers, just turning gray. A good-humored shrewdness shone in his eyes. From the set of his thin, firm lips one might guess that he was in the foremost rank in the interesting game of "push" that occupies mankind. One might further guess that his cleverness in using opportunities had brought him there, and that a dexterous management of elbows had served him no less. The other picture was that of Georgie's fiancé, Mr. Meredith Holt, approaching more closely then he liked to his forty-fifth year and an unbecoming corpulence. Only one who knew beforehand that he was a *viveur*[1] could have detected evidence of such in his face, which told little more than that he was a good-looking and amiable man of the world, who might be counted on to do the gentlemanly thing always. Georgie was going to marry him because his personality pleased her; because his easy knowledge of life—such as she apprehended it—commended itself to her approval; because he was likely to interfere in no way with her "work." Yet she might not have given any of these reasons if asked for one. Mr. Meredith Holt was simply an eligible man, whom almost any girl in her set would have accepted for a husband.

Georgie had just discovered that she had yet an hour to spare before starting out with the committee of four to further investigate the moral condition of the factory-girl, when a maid appeared with the announcement that a person was below who wished to see her.

"A person? Surely not a visitor at this hour?"

"I left her in the hall, miss, and she says her name is Mademoiselle Sal-Sal—"

"Oh, yes! Ask her to kindly walk up to my room, and show her the way, please, Hannah."

Mademoiselle Salambre came in with a sweep of skirts that bristled defiance, and a poise of the head that was aggressive in its backward tilt. She seated herself, and with an air of challenge waited to be questioned or addressed.

Georgie felt at ease amid her own familiar surroundings. While she made some idle tracings with a pencil upon a discarded envelope, she half turned to say:

"This visit of yours if very surprising, madam, and wholly useless. I suppose you guess my motive in recalling my work, as I have done."

"Maybe I do, and maybe I do not, Mees McEndairs," replied the woman, with an impertinent uplifting of the eyebrows.

Georgie felt the same shrinking which had overtaken her

[1]Rake.

before in the woman's presence. But she knew her duty, and from that there was no shrinking.

"You must be made to understand, madam, that there is a right way to live, and that there is a wrong way," said Georgie with more condescension than she knew. "We cannot defy God's laws with impunity, and without incurring His displeasure. But in His infinite justice and mercy He offers forgiveness, love and protection to those who turn away from evil and repent. It is for each of us to follow the divine way as well as may be. And I am only humbly striving to do His will."

"A most charming sermon, Mees McEndairs!" mademoiselle interrupted with a nervous laugh; "it seems a great pity to waste it upon so small an audience. And it grieves me, I cannot express, that I have not the time to remain and listen to its close."

She arose and began to talk volubly, swiftly, in a jumble of French and English, and with a wealth of expression and gesture which Georgie could hardly believe was natural, and not something acquired and rehearsed.

She had come to inform Miss McEnders that she did not want her work; that she would not touch it with the tips of her fingers. And her little, gloved hands recoiled from an imaginary pile of lingerie with unspeakable disgust. Her eyes had traveled nimbly over the room, and had been arrested by the two photographs on the table. Very small, indeed, were her worldly possessions, she informed the young lady; but as Heaven was her witness—not a mouthful of bread that she had not earned. And her parents over yonder in France! As honest as the sunlight! Poor, ah! for that—poor as rats. God only knew how poor; and God only knew how honest. Her eyes remained fixed upon the picture of Horace McEnders. Some people might like fine houses, and servants, and horses, and all the luxury which dishonest wealth brings. Some people might enjoy such surroundings. As for her!—and she drew up her skirts ever so carefully and daintily, as though she feared contamination to her petticoats from the touch of the rich rug upon which she stood.

Georgie's blue eyes were filled with astonishment as they followed the woman's gestures. Her face showed aversion and perplexity.

"Please let this interview come to an end at once," spoke the girl. She would not deign to ask an explanation of the mysterious allusions to ill-gotten wealth. But mademoiselle had not yet said all that she had come there to say.

"If it was only me to say so," she went on, still looking at the likeness, "but, *cher maître!* Go, yourself, Mees Mc-Endairs, and stand for a while on the street and ask the people passing by how your dear papa has made his money, and see what they will say."

Then shifting her glance to the photograph of Meredith Holt, she stood in an attitude of amused contemplation, with a smile of commiseration playing about her lips.

"Mr. Meredith Holt!" she pronounced with quiet, suppressed emphasis—"ah! *c'est un propre, celui la!*[2] You know him very well, no doubt, Mees McEndairs. You would not care to have my opinion of Mr. Meredith Holt. It would make no difference to you, Mees McEndairs, to know that he is not fit to be the husband of a self-respecting bar-maid. Oh! you know a good deal, my dear young lady. You can preach sermons in *merveille!*"[3]

When Georgie was finally alone, there came to her, through all her disgust and indignation, an indefinable uneasiness. There was no misunderstanding the intention of the woman's utterances in regard to the girl's fiancé and her father. A sudden, wild, defiant desire came to her to test the suggestion which Mademoiselle Salambre had let fall.

Yes, she would go stand there on the corner and ask the passers-by how Horace McEnders made his money. She could not yet collect her thoughts for calm reflection; and the house stifled her. It was fully time for her to join her committee of four, but she would meddle no further with morals till her own were adjusted, she thought. Then she quitted the house, very pale, even to her lips that were tightly set.

Georgie stationed herself on the opposite side of the street, on the corner, and waited there as though she had appointed to meet some one.

The first to approach her was a kind-looking old gentleman, very much muffled for the pleasant spring day. Georgie did not hesitate an instant to accost him:

"I beg pardon, sir. Will you kindly tell me whose house that is?" pointing to her own domicile across the way.

[2]"He's really something, he is."
[3]Marvellously.

"That is Mr. Horace McEnders' residence, Madame," replied the old gentleman, lifting his hat politely.

"Could you tell me how he made the money with which to build so magnificent a home?"

"You should not ask indiscreet questions, my dear young lady," answered the mystified old gentleman, as he bowed and walked away.

The girl let one or two persons pass her. Then she stopped a plumber, who was going cheerily along with his bag of tools on his shoulder.

"I beg pardon," began Georgie again; "but may I ask whose residence that is across the street?"

"Yes'um. That's the McEnderses."

"Thank you; and can you tell me how Mr. McEnders made such an immense fortune?"

"Oh, that ain't my business; but they say he made the biggest pile of it in the Whisky Ring."

So the truth would come to her somehow! These were the people from whom to seek it—who had not learned to veil their thoughts and opinions in polite subterfuge.

When a careless little news-boy came strolling along, she stopped him with the apparent intention of buying a paper from him.

"Do you know whose house that is?" she asked him, handing him a piece of money and nodding over the way.

"W'y, dats ole MicAndrus' house."

"I wonder where he got the money to build such a fine house."

"He stole it. dats w'ere he got it. Thank you," pocketing the change which Georgie declined to take, and he whistled a popular air as he disappeared around the corner.

Georgie had heard enough. Her heart was beating violently now, and her cheeks were flaming. So everybody knew it; even to the street gamins! The men and women who visited her and broke bread at her father's table, knew it. Her co-workers, who strove with her in Christian endeavor, knew. The very servants who waited upon her doubtless knew this, and had their jests about it.

She shrank within herself as she climbed the stairway to her room.

Upon the table there she found a box of exquisite white spring blossoms that a messenger had brought from Meredith

Holt, during her absence. Without an instant's hesitation, Georgie cast the spotless things into the wide, sooty, fireplace. Then she sank into a chair and wept bitterly.

Written, 1892; published, 1897

At the 'Cadian Ball

BOBINÔT, that big, brown, good-natured Bobinôt, had no intention of going to the ball, even though he knew Calixta would be there. For what came of those balls but heartache, and a sickening disinclination for work the whole week through, till Saturday night came again and his tortures began afresh? Why could he not love Ozéina, who would marry him to-morrow; or Fronie, or any one of a dozen others, rather than that little Spanish vixen? Calixta's slender foot had never touched Cuban soil; but her mother's had, and the Spanish was in her blood all the same. For that reason the prairie people forgave her much that they would not have overlooked in their own daughters or sisters.

Her eyes,—Bobinôt thought of her eyes, and weakened,—the bluest, the drowsiest, most tantalizing that ever looked into a man's; he thought of her flaxen hair that kinked worse than a mulatto's close to her head; that broad, smiling mouth and tiptilted nose, that full figure; that voice like a rich contralto song, with cadences in it that must have been taught by Satan, for there was no one else to teach her tricks on that 'Cadian prairie. Bobinôt thought of them all as he plowed his rows of cane.

There had even been a breath of scandal whispered about her a year ago, when she went to Assumption,—but why talk of it? No one did now. "C'est Espagnol, ça,"[1] most of them said with lenient shoulder-shrugs. "Bon chien tient de race,"[2] the old men mumbled over their pipes, stirred by recollections. Nothing was made of it, except that Fronie threw it up to Calixta when the two quarreled and fought on the church steps after mass one Sunday, about a lover. Calixta swore roundly in fine 'Cadian French and with true Spanish spirit, and slapped Fronie's face. Fronie had slapped her back;

[1] "It's the Spanish in her."
[2] "Blood will tell."

"Tiens, cocotte, va!"[3] "Espèce de lionèse; prends ça, et ça!"[4]
till the curé himself was obliged to hasten and make peace
between them. Bobinôt thought of it all, and would not go to
the ball.

But in the afternoon, over at Friedheimer's store, where he
was buying a trace-chain, he heard some one say that Alcée
Laballière would be there. Then wild horses could not have
kept him away. He knew how it would be—or rather he did
not know how it would be—if the handsome young planter
came over to the ball as he sometimes did. If Alcée happened
to be in a serious mood, he might only go to the card-room
and play a round or two; or he might stand out on the galleries talking crops and politics with the old people. But there
was no telling. A drink or two could put the devil in his
head,—that was what Bobinôt said to himself, as he wiped
the sweat from his brow with his red bandanna; a gleam
from Calixta's eyes, a flash of her ankle, a twirl of her skirts
could do the same. Yes, Bobinôt would go to the ball.

That was the year Alcée Laballière put nine hundred acres
in rice. It was putting a good deal of money into the ground,
but the returns promised to be glorious. Old Madame Laballière, sailing about the spacious galleries in her white volante, figured it all out in her head. Clarisse, her goddaughter,
helped her a little, and together they built more air-castles
than enough. Alcée worked like a mule that time; and if he
did not kill himself, it was because his constitution was an
iron one. It was an every-day affair for him to come in from
the field well-nigh exhausted, and wet to the waist. He did
not mind if there were visitors; he left them to his mother
and Clarisse. There were often guests: young men and
women who came up from the city, which was but a few
hours away, to visit his beautiful kinswoman. She was worth
going a good deal farther than that to see. Dainty as a lily;
hardy as a sunflower; slim, tall, graceful, like one of the reeds
that grew in the marsh. Cold and kind and cruel by turn, and
everything that was aggravating to Alcée.

He would have liked to sweep the place of those visitors,
often. Of the men, above all, with their ways and their manners; their swaying of fans like women, and dandling about
hammocks. He could have pitched them over the levee into

---

[3]"What a whore you are!"
[4]"You alley cat; take that, and that!"

the river, if it hadn't meant murder. That was Alcée. But he must have been crazy the day he came in from the rice-field, and, toil-stained as he was, clasped Clarisse by the arms and panted a volley of hot, blistering love-words into her face. No man had ever spoken love to her like that.

"Monsieur!" she exclaimed, looking him full in the eyes, without a quiver. Alcée's hands dropped and his glance wavered before the chill of her calm, clear eyes.

"*Par exemple!*" she muttered disdainfully, as she turned from him, deftly adjusting the careful toilet that he had so brutally disarranged.

That happened a day or two before the cyclone came that cut into the rice like fine steel. It was an awful thing, coming so swiftly, without a moment's warning in which to light a holy candle or set a piece of blessed palm burning. Old madame wept openly and said her beads, just as her son Didier, the New Orleans one, would have done. If such a thing had happened to Alphonse, the Laballière planting cotton up in Natchitoches, he would have raved and stormed like a second cyclone, and made his surroundings unbearable for a day or two. But Alcée took the misfortune differently. He looked ill and gray after it, and said nothing. His speechlessness was frightful. Clarisse's heart melted with tenderness; but when she offered her soft, purring words of condolence, he accepted them with mute indifference. Then she and her nénaine[5] wept afresh in each other's arms.

A night or two later, when Clarisse went to her window to kneel there in the moonlight and say her prayers before retiring, she saw that Bruce, Alcée's negro servant, had led his master's saddle-horse noiselessly along the edge of the sward that bordered the gravel-path, and stood holding him near by. Presently, she heard Alcée quit his room, which was beneath her own, and traverse the lower portico. As he emerged from the shadow and crossed the strip of moonlight, she perceived that he carried a pair of well-filled saddle-bags which he at once flung across the animal's back. He then lost no time in mounting, and after a brief exchange of words with Bruce, went cantering away, taking no precaution to avoid the noisy gravel as the negro had done.

Clarisse had never suspected that it might be Alcée's custom to sally forth from the plantation secretly, and at such an hour; for it was nearly midnight. And had it not been for

[5]Godmother.

the telltale saddle-bags, she would only have crept to bed, to wonder, to fret and dream unpleasant dreams. But her impatience and anxiety would not be held in check. Hastily unbolting the shutters of her door that opened upon the gallery, she stepped outside and called softly to the old negro.

"Gre't Peter! Miss Clarisse. I was n' sho it was a ghos' o' w'at, stan'in' up dah, plumb in de night, dataway."

He mounted halfway up the long, broad flight of stairs. She was standing at the top.

"Bruce, w'ere has Monsieur Alcée gone?" she asked.

"W'y, he gone 'bout he business, I reckin," replied Bruce, striving to be non-committal at the outset.

"W'ere has Monsieur Alcée gone?" she reiterated, stamping her bare foot. "I won't stan' any nonsense or any lies; mine, Bruce."

"I don' ric'lic ez I eva tole you lie *yit*, Miss Clarisse. Mista Alcée, he all broke up, sho."

"W'ere—has—he gone? Ah, Sainte Vierge! faut de la patience! butor, va!"

"W'en I was in he room, a-breshin' off he clo'es to-day," the darkey began, settling himself against the stair-rail, "he look dat speechless an' down, I say, 'You 'pear to me like some pussun w'at gwine have a spell o' sickness, Mista Alcée.' He say, 'You reckin?' 'I dat he git up, go look hisse'f stiddy in de glass. Den he go to de chimbly an' jerk up de quinine bottle an' po' a gre't hoss-dose on to he han'. An' he swalla dat mess in a wink, an' wash hit down wid a big dram o' w'iskey w'at he keep in he room, aginst he come all soppin' wet outen de fiel'.

"He 'lows, 'No, I ain' gwine be sick, Bruce.' Den he square off. He say, 'I kin mak out to stan' up an' gi' an' take wid any man I knows, lessen hit 's John L. Sulvun. But w'en God A'mighty an' a 'oman jines fo'ces agin me, dat's one too many fur me.' I tell 'im, 'Jis so,' whils' I 'se makin' out to bresh a spot off w'at ain' dah, on he coat colla. I tell 'im, 'You wants li'le res', suh.' He say, 'No, I wants li'le fling; dat w'at I wants; an' I gwine git it. Pitch me a fis'ful o' clo'es in dem 'ar saddle-bags.' Dat w'at he say. Don't you bodda, missy. He jis' gone a-caperin' yonda to de Cajun ball. Uh—uh—de skeeters is fair' a-swarmin' like bees roun' yo' foots!"

The mosquitoes were indeed attacking Clarisse's white feet savagely. She had unconsciously been alternately rubbing one foot over the other during the darkey's recital.

"The 'Cadian ball," she repeated contemptuously.

"Humph! *Par exemple! Nice* conduc' for a Laballière. An' he needs a saddle-bag, fill' with clothes, to go to the 'Cadian ball!"

"Oh, Miss Clarisse; you go on to bed, chile; git yo' soun' sleep. He 'low he come back in couple weeks o' so. I kiarn be repeatin' lot o' truck w'at young mans say, out heah face o' young gal."

Clarisse said no more, but turned and abruptly reëntered the house.

"You done talk too much wid yo' mouf a'ready, you ole fool nigga, you," muttered Bruce to himself as he walked away.

Alcée reached the ball very late, of course—too late for the chicken gumbo which had been served at midnight.

The big, low-ceiled room—they called it a hall—was packed with men and women dancing to the music of three fiddles. There were broad galleries all around it. There was a room at one side where sober-faced men were playing cards. Another, in which babies were sleeping, was called *le parc aux petits.* Any one who is white may go to a 'Cadian ball, but he must pay for his lemonade, his coffee and chicken gumbo. And he must behave himself like a 'Cadian. Grosbœuf was giving this ball. He had been giving them since he was a young man, and he was a middle-aged one, now. In that time he could recall but one disturbance, and that was caused by American railroaders, who were not in touch with their surroundings and had no business there. "Ces maudits gens du raiderode,"[6] Grosbœuf called them.

Alcée Laballière's presence at the ball caused a flutter even among the men, who could not but admire his "nerve" after such misfortune befalling him. To be sure, they knew the Laballières were rich—that there were resources East, and more again in the city. But they felt it took a *brave homme* to stand a blow like that philosophically. One old gentleman, who was in the habit of reading a Paris newspaper and knew things, chuckled gleefully to everybody that Alcée's conduct was altogether *chic, mais chic.* That he had more *panache* than Boulanger. Well, perhaps he had.

But what he did not show outwardly was that he was in a mood for ugly things to-night. Poor Bobinôt alone felt it vaguely. He discerned a gleam of it in Alcée's handsome eyes, as the young planter stood in the doorway, looking with

[6]"These damned railroad people."

rather feverish glance upon the assembly, while he laughed and talked with a 'Cadian farmer who was beside him.

Bobinôt himself was dull-looking and clumsy. Most of the men were. But the young women were very beautiful. The eyes that glanced into Alcée's as they passed him were big, dark, soft as those of the young heifers standing out in the cool prairie grass.

But the belle was Calixta. Her white dress was not nearly so handsome or well made as Fronie's (she and Fronie had quite forgotten the battle on the church steps, and were friends again), nor were her slippers so stylish as those of Ozéina; and she fanned herself with a handkerchief, since she had broken her red fan at the last ball, and her aunts and uncles were not willing to give her another. But all the men agreed she was at her best to-night. Such animation! and abandon! such flashes of wit!

"Hé, Bobinôt! *Mais* w'at 's the matta? W'at you standin' *planté là*[7] like ole Ma'ame Tina's cow in the bog, you?"

That was good. That was an excellent thrust at Bobinôt, who had forgotten the figure of the dance with his mind bent on other things, and it started a clamor of laughter at his expense. He joined good-naturedly. It was better to receive even such notice as that from Calixta than none at all. But Madame Suzonne, sitting in a corner, whispered to her neighbor that if Ozéina were to conduct herself in a like manner, she should immediately be taken out to the mule-cart and driven home. The women did not always approve of Calixta.

Now and then were short lulls in the dance, when couples flocked out upon the galleries for a brief respite and fresh air. The moon had gone down pale in the west, and in the east was yet no promise of day. After such an interval, when the dancers again assembled to resume the interrupted quadrille, Calixta was not among them.

She was sitting upon a bench out in the shadow, with Alcée beside her. They were acting like fools. He had attempted to take a little gold ring from her finger; just for the fun of it, for there was nothing he could have done with the ring but replace it again. But she clinched her hand tight. He pretended that it was a very difficult matter to open it. Then he kept the hand in his. They seemed to forget about it. He played with her earring, a thin crescent of gold hanging from

[7]Stuck there.

her small brown ear. He caught a wisp of the kinky hair that had escaped its fastening, and rubbed the ends of it against his shaven cheek.

"You know, last year in Assumption, Calixta?" They belonged to the younger generation, so preferred to speak English.

"Don't come say Assumption to me, M'sieur Alcée. I done yeard Assumption till I'm plumb sick."

"Yes, I know. The idiots! Because you were in Assumption, and I happened to go to Assumption, they must have it that we went together. But it was nice—*hein*, Calixta?—in Assumption?"

They saw Bobinôt emerge from the hall and stand a moment outside the lighted doorway, peering uneasily and searchingly into the darkness. He did not see them, and went slowly back.

"There is Bobinôt looking for you. You are going to set poor Bobinôt crazy. You'll marry him some day; *hein*, Calixta?"

"I don't say no, me," she replied, striving to withdraw her hand, which he held more firmly for the attempt.

"But come, Calixta; you know you said you would go back to Assumption, just to spite them."

"No, I neva said that, me. You mus' dreamt that."

"Oh, I thought you did. You know I'm going down to the city."

"W'en?"

"To-night."

"Betta make has'e, then; it 's mos' day."

"Well, to-morrow 'll do."

"W'at you goin' do, yonda?"

"I don't know. Drown myself in the lake, maybe; unless you go down there to visit your uncle."

Calixta's senses were reeling; and they well-nigh left her when she felt Alcée's lips brush her ear like the touch of a rose.

"Mista Alcée! Is dat Mista Alcée?" the thick voice of a negro was asking; he stood on the ground, holding to the banister-rails near which the couple sat.

"W'at do you want now?" cried Alcée impatiently. "Can't I have a moment of peace?"

"I ben huntin' you high an' low, suh," answered the man. "Dey—dey some one in de road, onda de mulbare-tree, want see you a minute."

"I wouldn't go out to the road to see the Angel Gabriel. And if you come back here with any more talk, I'll have to break your neck." The negro turned mumbling away.

Alcée and Calixta laughed softly about it. Her boisterousness was all gone. They talked low, and laughed softly, as lovers do.

"Alcée! Alcée Laballière!"

It was not the negro's voice this time; but one that went through Alcée's body like an electric shock, bringing him to his feet.

Clarisse was standing there in her riding-habit, where the negro had stood. For an instant confusion reigned in Alcée's thoughts, as with one who awakes suddenly from a dream. But he felt that something of serious import had brought his cousin to the ball in the dead of night.

"W'at does this mean, Clarisse?" he asked.

"It means something has happen' at home. You mus' come."

"Happened to maman?" he questioned, in alarm.

"No; nénaine is well, and asleep. It is something else. Not to frighten you. But you mus' come. Come with me, Alcée."

There was no need for the imploring note. He would have followed the voice anywhere.

She had now recognized the girl sitting back on the bench.

"Ah, c'est vous, Calixta? Comment ça va, mon enfant?"[8]

"Tcha va b'en; et vous, mam'zélle?"[9]

Alcée swung himself over the low rail and started to follow Clarisse, without a word, without a glance back at the girl. He had forgotten he was leaving her there. But Clarisse whispered something to him, and he turned back to say "Goodnight, Calixta," and offer his hand to press through the railing. She pretended not to see it.

"How come that? You settin' yere by yo'se'f, Calixta?" It was Bobinôt who had found her there alone. The dancers had not yet come out. She looked ghastly in the faint, gray light struggling out of the east.

"Yes, that's me. Go yonda in the *parc aux petits* an' ask Aunt Olisse fu' my hat. She knows w'ere 't is. I want to go home, me."

"How you came?"

[8]"Is that you, Calixta? How are things going, my dear?"
[9]"I'm fine; and how are you, miss?"

"I come afoot, with the Cateaus. But I'm goin' now. I ent goin' wait fu' 'em. I'm plumb wo' out, me."

"Kin I go with you, Calixta?"

"I don' care."

They went together across the open prairie and along the edge of the fields, stumbling in the uncertain light. He told her to lift her dress that was getting wet and bedraggled; for she was pulling at the weeds and grasses with her hands.

"I don' care; it 's got to go in the tub, anyway. You been sayin' all along you want to marry me, Bobinôt. Well, if you want, yet, I don' care, me."

The glow of a sudden and overwhelming happiness shone out in the brown, rugged face of the young Acadian. He could not speak, for very joy. It choked him.

"Oh well, if you don' want," snapped Calixta, flippantly, pretending to be piqued at his silence.

"*Bon Dieu!* You know that makes me crazy, w'at you sayin'. You mean that, Calixta? You ent goin' turn roun' agin?"

"I neva tole you that much *yet*, Bobinôt. I mean that. *Tiens*," and she held out her hand in the business-like manner of a man who clinches a bargain with a hand-clasp. Bobinôt grew bold with happiness and asked Calixta to kiss him. She turned her face, that was almost ugly after the night's dissipation, and looked steadily into his.

"I don' want to kiss you, Bobinôt," she said, turning away again, "not to-day. Some other time. *Bonté divine!* ent you satisfy, *yet!*"

"Oh, I'm satisfy, Calixta," he said.

Riding through a patch of wood, Clarisse's saddle became ungirted, and she and Alcée dismounted to readjust it.

For the twentieth time he asked her what had happened at home.

"But, Clarisse, w'at is it? Is it a misfortune?"

"Ah, Dieu sait![10] It 's only something that happen' to me."

"To you!"

"I saw you go away las' night, Alcée, with those saddle-bags," she said, haltingly, striving to arrange something about the saddle, "an' I made Bruce tell me. He said you had gone to the ball, an' wouldn' be home for weeks an' weeks. I

[10]God knows!

thought, Alcée—maybe you were going to—to Assumption. I got wild. An' then I knew if you did n't come back, *now*, to-night. I couldn't stan' it,—again."

She had her face hidden in her arm that she was resting against the saddle when she said that.

He began to wonder if this meant love. But she had to tell him so, before he believed it. And when she told him, he thought the face of the Universe was changed—just like Bobinôt. Was it last week the cyclone had well-nigh ruined him? The cyclone seemed a huge joke, now. It was he, then, who, an hour ago was kissing little Calixta's ear and whispering nonsense into it. Calixta was like a myth, now. The one, only, great reality in the world was Clarisse standing before him, telling him that she loved him.

In the distance they heard the rapid discharge of pistol-shots; but it did not disturb them. They knew it was only the negro musicians who had gone into the yard to fire their pistols into the air, as the custom is, and to announce *"le bal est fini."*[11]

Written and published, 1892

[11]The dance is over.

Désirée's Baby

As THE day was pleasant, Madame Valmondé drove over to L'Abri to see Désirée and the baby.

It made her laugh to think of Désirée with a baby. Why, it seemed but yesterday that Désirée was little more than a baby herself; when Monsieur in riding through the gateway of Valmondé had found her lying asleep in the shadow of the big stone pillar.

The little one awoke in his arms and began to cry for "Dada." That was as much as she could do or say. Some people thought she might have strayed there of her own accord, for she was of the toddling age. The prevailing belief was that she had been purposely left by a party of Texans, whose canvas-covered wagon, late in the day, had crossed the ferry that Coton Maïs kept, just below the plantation. In time Madame Valmondé abandoned every speculation but the one that Désirée had been sent to her by a beneficent Providence to be the child of her affection, seeing that she was without child of the flesh. For the girl grew to be beautiful and gentle, affectionate and sincere,—the idol of Valmondé.

It was no wonder, when she stood one day against the stone pillar in whose shadow she had lain asleep, eighteen years before, that Armand Aubigny riding by and seeing her there, had fallen in love with her. That was the way all the Aubignys fell in love, as if struck by a pistol shot. The wonder was that he had not loved her before; for he had known her since his father brought him home from Paris, a boy of eight, after his mother died there. The passion that awoke in him that day, when he saw her at the gate, swept along like an avalanche, or like a prairie fire, or like anything that drives headlong over all obstacles.

Monsieur Valmondé grew practical and wanted things well considered: that is, the girl's obscure origin. Armand looked into her eyes and did not care. He was reminded that she was nameless. What did it matter about a name when he could give her one of the oldest and proudest in Louisiana? He ordered the *corbeille*[1] from Paris, and contained himself with what patience he could until it arrived; then they were married.

Madame Valmondé had not seen Désirée and the baby for four weeks. When she reached L'Abri she shuddered at the first sight of it, as she always did. It was a sad looking place, which for many years had not known the gentle presence of a mistress, old Monsieur Aubigny having married and buried his wife in France, and she having loved her own land too well ever to leave it. The roof came down steep and black like a cowl, reaching out beyond the wide galleries that encircled the yellow stuccoed house. Big, solemn oaks grew close to it, and their thick-leaved, far-reaching branches shadowed it like a pall. Young Aubigny's rule was a strict one, too, and under it his negroes had forgotten how to be gay, as they had been during the old master's easy-going and indulgent lifetime.

The young mother was recovering slowly, and lay full length, in her soft white muslins and laces, upon a couch. The baby was beside her, upon her arm, where he had fallen asleep, at her breast. The yellow nurse woman sat beside a window fanning herself.

Madame Valmondé bent her portly figure over Désirée and kissed her, holding her an instant tenderly in her arms. Then she turned to the child.

"This is not the baby!" she exclaimed, in startled tones. French was the language spoken at Valmondé in those days.

"I knew you would be astonished," laughed Désirée, "at the way he has grown. The little *cochon de lait!*[2] Look at his legs, mamma, and his hands and fingernails,—real fingernails. Zandrine had to cut them this morning. Isn't it true, Zandrine?"

The woman bowed her turbaned head majestically, "Mais si, Madame."

"And the way he cries," went on Désirée, "is deafening. Armand heard him the other day as far away as La Blanche's cabin."

Madame Valmondé had never removed her eyes from the child. She lifted it and walked with it over to the window that was lightest. She scanned the baby narrowly, then looked as

[1] Trousseau.
[2] Milk-drinking piggy.

searchingly at Zandrine, whose face was turned to gaze across the fields.

"Yes, the child has grown, has changed," said Madame Valmondé, slowly, as she replaced it beside its mother. "What does Armand say?"

Désirée's face became suffused with a glow that was happiness itself.

"Oh, Armand is the proudest father in the parish, I believe, chiefly because it is a boy, to bear his name; though he says not,—that he would have loved a girl as well. But I know it isn't true. I know he says that to please me. And mamma," she added, drawing Madame Valmondé's head down to her, and speaking in a whisper, "he hasn't punished one of them—not one of them—since baby is born. Even Négrillon, who pretended to have burnt his leg that he might rest from work—he only laughed, and said Négrillon was a great scamp. Oh, mamma, I'm so happy; it frightens me."

What Deésirée said was true. Marriage, and later the birth of his son had softened Armand Aubigny's imperious and exacting nature greatly. This was what made the gentle Désirée so happy, for she loved him desperately. When he frowned she trembled, but loved him. When he smiled, she asked no greater blessing of God. But Armand's dark, handsome face had not often been disfigured by frowns since the day he fell in love with her.

When the baby was about three months old, Désirée awoke one day to the conviction that there was something in the air menacing her peace. It was at first too subtle to grasp. It had only been a disquieting suggestion; an air of mystery among the blacks; unexpected visits from far-off neighbors who could hardly account for their coming. Then a strange, an awful change in her husband's manner, which she dared not ask him to explain. When he spoke to her, it was with averted eyes, from which the old love-light seemed to have gone out. He absented himself from home; and when there, avoided her presence and that of her child, without excuse. And the very spirit of Satan seemed suddenly to take hold of him in his dealings with the slaves. Désirée was miserable enough to die.

She sat in her room, one hot afternoon, in her *peignoir*, listlessly drawing through her fingers the strands of her long, silky brown hair that hung about her shoulders. The baby, half naked, lay asleep upon her own great mahogany bed, that was like a sumptuous throne, with its satin-lined half-canopy. One of La Blanche's little quadroon boys—half naked too—stood fanning the child slowly with a fan of peacock feathers. Désirée's eyes had been fixed absently and sadly upon the baby, while she was striving to penetrate the threatening mist that she felt closing about her. She looked from her child to the boy who stood beside him, and back again; over and over. "Ah!" It was a cry that she could not help; which she was not conscious of having uttered. The blood turned like ice in her veins, and a clammy moisture gathered upon her face.

She tried to speak to the little quadroon boy; but no sound would come, at first. When he heard his name uttered, he looked up, and his mistress was pointing to the door. He laid aside the great, soft fan, and obediently stole away, over the polished floor, on his bare tiptoes.

She stayed motionless, with gaze riveted upon her child, and her face the picture of fright.

Presently her husband entered the room, and without noticing her, went to a table and began to search among some papers which covered it.

"Armand," she called to him, in a voice which must have stabbed him, if he was human. But he did not notice. "Armand," she said again. Then she rose and tottered towards him. "Armand," she panted once more, clutching his arm, "look at our child. What does it mean? tell me."

He coldly but gently loosened her fingers from about his arm and thrust the hand away from him. "Tell me what it means!" she cried despairingly.

"It means," he answered lightly, "that the child is not white; it means that you are not white."

A quick conception of all that this accusation meant for her nerved her with unwonted courage to deny it. "It is a lie; it is not true, I am white! Look at my hair, it is brown; and my eyes are gray, Armand, you know they are gray. And my skin is fair," seizing his wrist. "Look at my hand; whiter than yours, Armand," she laughed hysterically.

"As white as La Blanche's," he returned cruelly; and went away leaving her alone with their child.

When she could hold a pen in her hand, she sent a despairing letter to Madame Valmondé.

"My mother, they tell me I am not white. Armand has told me I am not white. For God's sake tell them it is not true. You must know it is not true. I shall die. I must die. I cannot be so unhappy, and live."

The answer that came was as brief:

"My own Désirée: Come home to Valmondé; back to your mother who loves you. Come with your child."

When the letter reached Désirée she went with it to her husband's study, and laid it open upon the desk before which he sat. She was like a stone image: silent, white, motionless after she placed it there.

In silence he ran his cold eyes over the written words. He said nothing. "Shall I go, Armand?" she asked in tones sharp with agonized suspense.

"Yes, go."

"Do you want me to go?"

"Yes, I want you to go."

He thought Almighty God had dealt cruelly and unjustly with him; and felt, somehow, that he was paying Him back in kind when he stabbed thus into his wife's soul. Moreover he no longer loved her, because of the unconscious injury she had brought upon his home and his name.

She turned away like one stunned by a blow, and walked slowly towards the door, hoping he would call her back.

"Good-by, Armand," she moaned.

He did not answer her. That was his last blow at fate.

Désirée went in search of her child. Zandrine was pacing the sombre gallery with it. She took the little one from the nurse's arms with no word of explanation, and descending the steps, walked away, under the live-oak branches.

It was an October afternoon; the sun was just sinking. Out in the still fields the negroes were picking cotton.

Désirée had not changed the thin white garment nor the slippers which she wore. Her hair was uncovered and the sun's rays brought a golden gleam from its brown meshes. She did not take the broad, beaten road which led to the far-off plantation of Valmondé. She walked across a deserted field, where the stubble bruised her tender feet, so delicately shod, and tore her thin gown to shreds.

She disappeared among the reeds and willows that grew thick along the banks of the deep, sluggish bayou; and she did not come back again.

Some weeks later there was a curious scene enacted at L'Abri. In the centre of the smoothly swept back yard was a great bonfire. Armand Aubigny sat in the wide hallway that commanded a view of the spectacle; and it was he who dealt out to a half dozen negroes the material which kept this fire ablaze.

A graceful cradle of willow, with all its dainty furbishings, was laid upon the pyre, which had already been fed with the richness of a priceless *layette*. Then there were silk gowns, and velvet and satin ones added to these; laces, too, and embroideries; bonnets and gloves; for the *corbeille* had been of rare quality.

The last thing to go was a tiny bundle of letters; innocent little scribblings that Désirée had sent to him during the days of their espousal. There was the remnant of one back in the drawer from which he took them. But it was not Désirée's; it was part of an old letter from his mother to his father. He read it. She was thanking God for the blessing of her husband's love:—

"But, above all," she wrote, "night and day, I thank the good God for having so arranged our lives that our dear Armand will never know that his mother, who adores him, belongs to the race that is cursed with the brand of slavery."

Written, 1892; published, 1893

Madame Célestin's Divorce

MADAME CÉLESTIN always wore a neat and snugly fitting calico wrapper when she went out in the morning to sweep her small gallery. Lawyer Paxton thought she looked very pretty in the gray one that was made with a graceful Watteau fold at the back: and with which she invariably wore a bow of pink ribbon at the throat. She was always sweeping her gallery when lawyer Paxton passed by in the morning on his way to his office in St. Denis Street.

Sometimes he stopped and leaned over the fence to say good-morning at his ease; to criticise or admire her rose-bushes; or, when he had time enough, to hear what she had to say. Madame Célestin usually had a good deal to say. She would gather up the train of her calico wrapper in one hand, and balancing the broom gracefully in the other, would go tripping down to where the lawyer leaned, as comfortably as he could, over her picket fence.

Of course, she had talked to him of her troubles. Every one knew Madame Célestin's troubles.

"Really, madame." he told her once, in his deliberate, calculating, lawyer-tone, "it's more than human nature—woman's nature—should be called upon to endure. Here you are, working your fingers off"—she glanced down at two rosy finger-tips that showed through the rents in her baggy doeskin gloves—"taking in sewing; giving music lessons; doing God knows what in the way of manual labor to support yourself and those two little ones"—Madame Célestin's pretty face beamed with satisfaction at this enumeration of her trials.

"You right, Judge. Not a picayune, not one, not one, have I lay my eyes on in the pas' fo' months that I can say Célestin give it to me or sen' it to me."

"The scoundrel!" muttered lawyer Paxton in his beard.

"An' *pourtant*,"[1] she resumed, "they say he's making money down roun' Alexandria w'en he wants to work."

[1] Yet.

"I dare say you haven't seen him for months?" suggested the lawyer.

"It's good six month' since I see a sight of Célestin," she admitted.

"That's it, that's what I say; he has practically deserted you; fails to support you. It wouldn't surprise me a bit to learn that he has ill treated you."

"Well, you know, Judge," with an evasive cough, "a man that drinks—w'at can you expec'? An' if you would know the promises he has made me! Ah, If I had as many dolla' as I had promise from Célestin, I wouldn' have to work, *je vous garantis.*"[2]

"And in my opinion, Madame, you would be a foolish woman to endure it longer, when the divorce court is there to offer you redress."

"You spoke about that befo', Judge: I'm goin' think about that divo'ce. I believe you right."

Madame Célestin thought about the divorce and talked about it, too; and lawyer Paxton grew deeply interested in the theme.

"You know, about that divo'ce, Judge," Madame Célestin was waiting for him that morning, "I been talking to my family an' my frien's, an' it's me that tells you, they all plumb agains' that divo'ce."

"Certainly, to be sure; that's to be expected, Madame, in this community of Creoles. I warned you that you would meet with opposition, and would have to face it and brave it."

"Oh, don't fear, I'm going to face it! Maman says it's a disgrace like it's neva been in the family. But it's good for Maman to talk, her. W'at trouble she ever had? She says I mus' go by all means consult with Père Duchéron—it's my confessor, you undastan'—Well, I'll go, Judge, to please Maman. But all the confessor' in the worl' ent goin' make me put up with that conduc' of Célestin any longa."

A day or two later, she was there waiting for him again. "You know, Judge, about that divo'ce."

"Yes, yes," responded the lawyer, well pleased to trace a new determination in her brown eyes and in the curves of her pretty mouth. "I suppose you saw Père Duchéron and had to brave it out with him, too."

"Oh, fo' that, a perfec' sermon, I assho you. A talk of giv-

[2]I assure you.

ing scandal an' bad example that I thought would neva en'! He says, fo' him, he wash' his hands; I mus' go see the bishop."

"You won't let the bishop dissuade you, I trust," stammered the lawyer more anxiously than he could well understand.

"You don't know me yet, Judge," laughed Madame Célestin with a turn of the head and a flirt of the broom which indicated that the interview was at an end.

"Well, Madame Célestin! And the bishop!" Lawyer Paxton was standing there holding to a couple of the shaky pickets. She had not seen him. "Oh, it's you, Judge?" and she hastened towards him with an *empressement*[3] that could not but have been flattering.

"Yes, I saw Monseigneur," she began. The lawyer had already gathered from her expressive countenance that she had not wavered in her determination. "Ah, he's a eloquent man. It's not a mo' eloquent man in Natchitoches parish. I was fo'ced to cry, the way he talked to me about my troubles; how he undastan's them, an' feels for me. It would move even you, Judge, to hear how he talk' about that step I want to take; its danga, its temptation. How it is the duty of a Catholic to stan' everything till the las' extreme. An' that life of retirement an' self-denial I would have to lead,—he tole me all that."

"But he has n't turned you from your resolve, I see," laughed the lawyer complacently.

"For that, no," she returned emphatically. "The bishop don't know w'at it is to be married to a man like Célestin, an' have to endu' that conduc' like I have to endu' it. The Pope himse'f can't make me stan' that any longer, if you say I got the right in the law to sen' Célestin sailing."

A noticeable change had come over lawyer Paxton. He discarded his work-day coat and began to wear his Sunday one to the office. He grew solicitous as to the shine of his boots, his collar, and the set of his tie. He brushed and trimmed his whiskers with a care that had not before been apparent. Then he fell into a stupid habit of dreaming as he walked the streets of the old town. It would be very good to take unto himself a wife, he dreamed. And he could dream of no other than pretty Madame Célestin filling that sweet and sacred office as she filled his thoughts, now. Old Natchitoches would

[3]Eagerness.

not hold them comfortably, perhaps; but the world was surely
wide enough to live in, outside of Natchitoches town.

His heart beat in a strangely irregular manner as he neared
Madame Célestin's house one morning, and discovered her
behind the rosebushes, as usual plying her broom. She had
finished the gallery and steps and was sweeping the little
brick walk along the edge of the violet border.

"Good-morning, Madame Célestin."

"Ah, it's you, Judge? Good-morning." He waited. She
seemed to be doing the same. Then she ventured, with some
hesitancy, "You know, Judge, about that divo'ce. I been
thinking,—I reckon you betta neva mine about that divo'ce."
She was making deep rings in the palm of her gloved hand
with the end of the broomhandle, and looking at them critically. Her face seemed to the lawyer to be unusually rosy;
but maybe it was only the reflection of the pink bow at the
throat. "Yes, I reckon you need n' mine. You see, Judge,
Célestin came home las' night. An' he's promise me on his
word an' honor he's going to turn ova a new leaf."

Written 1893, published, 1894

A Lady of Bayou St. John

THE DAYS and the nights were very lonely for Madame Delisle. Gustave, her husband, was away yonder in Virginia somewhere, with Beauregard, and she was here in the old house on Bayou St. John, alone with her slaves.

Madame was very beautiful. So beautiful, that she found much diversion in sitting for hours before the mirror, contemplating her own loveliness; admiring the brilliancy of her golden hair, the sweet languor of her blue eyes, the graceful contours of her figure, and the peach-like bloom of her flesh. She was very young. So young that she romped with the dogs, teased the parrot, and could not fall asleep at night unless old black Manna-Loulou sat beside her bed and told her stories.

In short, she was a child, not able to realize the significance of the tragedy whose unfolding kept the civilized world in suspense. It was only the immediate effect of the awful drama that moved her: the gloom that, spreading on all sides, penetrated her own existence and deprived it of joyousness.

Sépincourt found her looking very lonely and disconsolate one day when he stopped to talk with her. She was pale, and her blue eyes were dim with unwept tears. He was a Frenchman who lived near by. He shrugged his shoulders over this strife between brothers, this quarrel which was none of his; and he resented it chiefly upon the ground that it made life uncomfortable; yet he was young enough to have had quicker and hotter blood in his veins.

When he left Madame Delisle that day, her eyes were no longer dim, and a something of the dreariness that weighted her had been lifted away. That mysterious, that treacherous bond called sympathy, had revealed them to each other.

He came to her very often that summer, clad always in cool, white duck, with a flower in his buttonhole. His pleasant brown eyes sought hers with warm, friendly glances that comforted her as a caress might comfort a disconsolate child. She took to watching for his slim figure, a little bent, walking lazily up the avenue between the double line of magnolias.

They would sit sometimes during whole afternoons in the vine-sheltered corner of the gallery, sipping the black coffee that Manna-Loulou brought to them at intervals; and talking, talking incessantly during the first days when they were unconsciously unfolding themselves to each other. Then a time came—it came very quickly—when they seemed to have nothing more to say to one another.

He brought her news of the war; and they talked about it listlessly, between long intervals of silence, of which neither took account. An occasional letter came by round-about ways from Gustave—guarded and saddening in its tone. They would read it and sigh over it together.

Once they stood before his portrait that hung in the drawing-room and that looked out at them with kind, indulgent eyes. Madame wiped the picture with her gossamer handkerchief and impulsively pressed a tender kiss upon the painted canvas. For months past the living image of her husband had been receding further and further into a mist which she could penetrate with no faculty or power that she possessed.

One day at sunset, when she and Sépincourt stood silently side by side, looking across the *marais*,[1] aflame with the western light, he said to her: *"M'amie, let us go away from this country that is so triste.[2] Let us go to Paris, you and me."*

She thought that he was jesting, and she laughed nervously. "Yes, Paris would surely be gayer than Bayou St. John," she answered. But he was not jesting. She saw it at once in the glance that penetrated her own; in the quiver of his sensitive lip and the quick beating of a swollen vein in his brown throat.

"Paris, or anywhere—with you—ah, *bon Dieu!*"[3] he whispered, seizing her hands. But she withdrew from him, frightened, and hurried away into the house, leaving him alone.

That night, for the first time, Madame did not want to hear Manna-Loulou's stories, and she blew out the wax

[1] Swamp.
[2] Sad.
[3] Good God.

candle that till now had burned nightly in her sleeping-room, under its tall, crystal globe. She had suddenly become a woman capable of love or sacrifice. She would not hear Manna-Loulou's stories. She wanted to be alone, to tremble and to weep.

In the morning her eyes were dry, but she would not see Sépincourt when he came. Then he wrote her a letter.

"I have offended you and I would rather die!" it ran. "Do not banish me from your presence that is life to me. Let me lie at your feet, if only for a moment, in which to hear you say that you forgive me."

Men have written just such letters before, but Madame did not know it. To her it was a voice from the unknown, like music, awaking in her a delicious tumult that seized and held possession of her whole being.

When they met, he had but to look into her face to know that he need not lie at her feet craving forgiveness. She was waiting for him beneath the spreading branches of a live-oak that guarded the gate of her home like a sentinel.

For a brief moment he held her hands, which trembled. Then he folded her in his arms and kissed her many times. "You will go with me, *m'amie?* I love you—oh, I love you! Will you not go with me, *m'amie?*"

"Anywhere, anywhere," she told him in a fainting voice that he could scarcely hear.

But she did not go with him. Chance willed it otherwise. That night a courier brought her a message from Beauregard, telling her that Gustave, her husband, was dead.

When the new year was still young, Sépincourt decided that, all things considered, he might, without any appearance of indecent haste, speak again of his love to Madame Delisle. That love was quite as acute as ever; perhaps a little sharper, from the long period of silence and waiting to which he had subjected it. He found her, as he had expected, clad in deepest mourning. She greeted him precisely as she had welcomed the curé, when the kind old priest had brought to her the consolations of religion—clasping his two hands warmly, and calling him *"cher ami."*[4] Her whole attitude and bearing brought to Sépincourt the poignant, the bewildering conviction that he held no place in her thoughts.

They sat in the drawing-room before the portrait of Gustave, which was draped with his scarf. Above the picture

4Dear friend.

hung his sword, and beneath it was an embankment of flowers. Sépincourt felt an almost irresistible impulse to bend his knee before this altar, upon which he saw foreshadowed the immolation of his hopes.

There was a soft air blowing gently over the *marais*. It came to them through the open window, laden with a hundred subtle sounds and scents of the springtime. It seemed to remind Madame of something far, far away, for she gazed dreamily out into the blue firmament. It fretted Sépincourt with impulses to speech and action which he found it impossible to control.

"You must know what has brought me," he began impulsively, drawing his chair nearer to hers. "Through all these months I have never ceased to love you and to long for you. Night and day the sound of your dear voice has been with me; your eyes"—

She held out her hand deprecatingly. He took it and held it. She let it lie unresponsive in his.

"You cannot have forgotten that you loved me not long ago," he went on eagerly, "that you were ready to follow me anywhere,—anywhere; do you remember? I have come now to ask you to fulfill that promise; to ask you to be my wife, my companion, the dear treasure of my life."

She heard his warm and pleading tones as though listening to a strange language, imperfectly understood.

She withdrew her hand from his, and leaned her brow thoughtfully upon it.

"Can you not feel—can you not understand, *mon ami*," she said calmly, "that now such a thing—such a thought, is impossible to me?"

"Impossible?"

"Yes, impossible. Can you not see that now my heart, my soul, my thought—my very life, must belong to another? It could not be different."

"Would you have me believe that you can wed your young existence to the dead?" he exclaimed with something like horror. Her glance was sunk deep in the embankment of flowers before her.

"My husband has never been so living to me as he is now," she replied with a faint smile of commiseration for Sépincourt's fatuity. "Every object that surrounds me speaks to me of him. I look yonder across the *marais*, and I see him coming toward me, tired and toil-stained from the hunt. I see him again sitting in this chair or in that one. I hear his familiar voice, his footsteps upon the galleries. We walk once more together beneath the magnolias; and at night in dreams I feel that he is there, there, near me. How could it be different! Ah! I have memories, memories to crowd and fill my life, if I live a hundred years!"

Sépincourt was wondering why she did not take the sword from her altar and thrust it through his body here and there. The effect would have been infinitely more agreeable than her words, penetrating his soul like fire. He arose confused, enraged with pain.

"Then, Madame," he stammered, "there is nothing left for me but to take my leave. I bid you adieu."

"Do not be offended, *mon ami*," she said kindly, holding out her hand. "You are going to Paris, I suppose?"

"What does it matter," he exclaimed desperately, "where I go?"

"Oh, I only wanted to wish you *bon voyage*," she assured him amiably.

Many days after that Sépincourt spent in the fruitless mental effort of trying to comprehend that psychological enigma, a woman's heart.

Madame still lives on Bayou St. John. She is rather an old lady now, a very pretty old lady, against whose long years of widowhood there has never been a breath of reproach. The memory of Gustave still fills and satisfies her days. She has never failed, once a year, to have a solemn high mass said for the repose of his soul.

Written and published, 1893

La Belle Zoraïde

THE SUMMER night was hot and still; not a ripple of air
swept over the *marais*.[1] Yonder, across Bayou St. John, lights
twinkled here and there in the darkness, and in the dark sky
above a few stars were blinking. A lugger that had come out
of the lake was moving with slow, lazy motion down the
bayou. A man in the boat was singing a song.

The notes of the song came faintly to the ears of old
Manna-Loulou, herself as black as the night, who had gone
out upon the gallery to open the shutters wide.

Something in the refrain reminded the woman of an old,
half-forgotten Creole romance, and she began to sing it low
to herself while she threw the shutters open:—

> "Lisett' to kité la plaine,
> Mo perdi bonhair à moué;
> Ziés à moué semblé fontaine,
> Dépi mo pa miré toué."

And then this old song, a lover's lament for the loss of his
mistress, floating into her memory, brought with it the story
she would tell to Madame, who lay in her sumptuous mahogany bed, waiting to be fanned and put to sleep to the
sound of one of Manna-Loulou's stories. The old negress had
already bathed her mistress's pretty white feet and kissed
them lovingly, one, then the other. She had brushed her
mistress's beautiful hair, that was as soft and shining as satin,
and was the color of Madame's wedding-ring. Now, when she
reëntered the room, she moved softly toward the bed, and
seating herself there began gently to fan Madame Delisle.

Manna-Loulou was not always ready with her story, for
Madame would hear none but those which were true. But to-
night the story was all there in Manna-Loulou's head—the

[1]Swamp.

188

story of la belle Zoraïde—and she told it to her mistress in the soft Creole patois, whose music and charm no English words can convey.

"La belle Zoraïde had eyes that were so dusky, so beautiful, that any man who gazed too long into their depths was sure to lose his head, and even his heart sometimes. Her soft, smooth skin was the color of *café-au-lait*. As for her elegant manners, her *svelte* and graceful figure, they were the envy of half the ladies who visited her mistress, Madame Delarivière.

"No wonder Zoraïde was as charming and as dainty as the finest lady of la rue Royale: from a toddling thing she had been brought up at her mistress's side; her fingers had never done rougher work than sewing a fine muslin seam; and she even had her own little black servant to wait upon her. Madame, who was her godmother as well as her mistress, would often say to her:—

" 'Remember, Zoraïde, when you are ready to marry, it must be in a way to do honor to your bringing up. It will be at the Cathedral. Your wedding gown, your *corbeille*,[2] all will be of the best; I shall see to that myself. You know, M'sieur Ambroise is ready whenever you say the word; and his master is willing to do as much for him as I shall do for you. It is a union that will please me in every way.'

"M'sieur Ambroise was then the body servant of Doctor Langlé. La belle Zoraïde detested the little mulatto, with his shining whiskers like a white man's, and his small eyes, that were cruel and false as a snake's. She would cast down her own mischievous eyes, and say:—

" 'Ah, nénaine,[3] I am so happy, so contented here at your side just as I am. I don't want to marry now; next year, perhaps, or the next.' And Madame would smile indulgently and remind Zoraïde that a woman's charms are not everlasting.

"But the truth of the matter was, Zoraïde had seen le beau Mézor dance the Bamboula in Congo Square. That was a sight to hold one rooted to the ground. Mézor was as straight as a cypress-tree and as proud looking as a king. His body, bare to the waist, was like a column of ebony and it glistened like oil.

"Poor Zoraïde's heart grew sick in her bosom with love for le beau Mézor from the moment she saw the fierce gleam of his eye, lighted by the inspiring strains of the Bamboula, and

[2]Trousseau.
[3]Dear Godmother.

beheld the stately movements of his splendid body swaying and quivering through the figures of the dance.

"But when she knew him later, and he came near her to speak with her, all the fierceness was gone out of his eyes, and she saw only kindness in them and heard only gentleness in his voice; for love had taken possession of him also, and Zoraïde was more distracted than ever. When Mézor was not dancing Bamboula in Congo Square, he was hoeing sugarcane, barefooted and half naked, in his master's field outside of the city. Doctor Langlé was his master as well as M'sieur Ambroise's.

"One day, when Zoraïde knelt before her mistress, drawing on Madame's silken stockings, that were of the finest, she said:

" 'Nénaine, you have spoken to me often of marrying. Now, at last, I have chosen a husband, but it is not M'sieur Ambroise; it is le beau Mézor that I want and no other.' And Zoraïde hid her face in her hands when she had said that, for she guessed, rightly enough, that her mistress would be very angry. And, indeed, Madame Delarivière was at first speechless with rage. When she finally spoke it was only to gasp out, exasperated:—

" 'That negro! that negro! Bon Dieu Seigneur,[4] but this is too much!'

" 'Am I white, nénaine?' pleaded Zoraïde.

" 'You white! Malheureuse![5] You deserve to have the lash laid upon you like any other slave; you have proven yourself no better than the worst.'

" 'I am not white,' persisted Zoraïde, respectfully and gently. 'Doctor Langlé gives me his slave to marry, but he would not give me his son. Then, since I am not white, let me have from out of my own race the one whom my heart has chosen.'

"However, you may well believe that Madame would not hear to that. Zoraïde was forbidden to speak to Mézor, and Mézor was cautioned against seeing Zoraïde again. But you know how the negroes are, Ma'zélle Titite," added Manna-Loulou, smiling a little sadly. "There is no mistress, no master, no king nor priest who can hinder them from loving when they will. And these two found ways and means.

"When months had passed by, Zoraïde, who had grown

[4]Good Lord God.
[5]Unhappy woman.

unlike herself,—sober and preoccupied,—said again to her mistress:—

" 'Nénaine, you would not let me have Mézor for my husband; but I have disobeyed you, I have sinned. Kill me if you wish, nénaine: forgive me if you will; but when I heard le beau Mézor say to me, "Zoraïde, mo l'aime toi,"[6] I could have died, but I could not have helped loving him.'

"This time Madame Delarivière was so actually pained, so wounded at hearing Zoraïde's confession, that there was no place left in her heart for anger. She could utter only confused reproaches. But she was a woman of action rather than of words, and she acted promptly. Her first step was to induce Doctor Langlé to sell Mézor. Doctor Langlé, who was a widower, had long wanted to marry Madame Delarivière, and he would willingly have walked on all fours at noon through the Place d'Armes if she wanted him to. Naturally he lost no time in disposing of le beau Mézor, who was sold away into Georgia, or the Carolinas, or one of those distant countries far away, where he would no longer hear his Creole tongue spoken, nor dance Calinda, nor hold la belle Zoraïde in his arms.

"The poor thing was heartbroken when Mézor was sent away from her, but she took comfort and hope in the thought of her baby that she would soon be able to clasp to her breast.

"La belle Zoraïde's sorrows had now begun in earnest. Not only sorrows but sufferings, and with the anguish of maternity came the shadow of death. But there is no agony that a mother will not forget when she holds her first-born to her heart, and presses her lips upon the baby flesh that is her own, yet far more precious than her own.

"So, instinctively, when Zoraïde came out of the awful shadow she gazed questioningly about her and felt with her trembling hands upon either side of her. 'Où, li, mo piti a moin? (Where is my little one?)' she asked imploringly. Madame who was there and the nurse who was there both told her in turn, 'To piti à toi, li mouri' ('Your little one is dead'), which was a wicked falsehood that must have caused the angels in heaven to weep. For the baby was living and well and strong. It had at once been removed from its mother's side, to be sent away to Madame's plantation, far up

[6] "I love you."

the coast. Zoraïde could only moan in reply, 'Li mouri, li mouri,'[7] and she turned her face to the wall.

"Madame had hoped, in thus depriving Zoraïde of her child, to have her young waiting-maid again at her side free, happy, and beautiful as of old. But there was a more powerful will than Madame's at work—the will of the good God, who had already designed that Zoraïde should grieve with a sorrow that was never more to be lifted in this world. La belle Zoraïde was no more. In her stead was a sad-eyed woman who mourned night and day for her baby. 'Li mouri, li mouri,' she would sigh over and over again to those about her, and to herself when others grew weary of her complaint.

"Yet, in spite of all, M'sieur Ambroise was still in the notion to marry her. A sad wife or a merry one was all the same to him so long as that wife was Zoraïde. And she seemed to consent, or rather submit, to the approaching marriage as though nothing mattered any longer in this world.

"One day, a black servant entered a little noisily the room in which Zoraïde sat sewing. With a look of strange and vacuous happiness upon her face, Zoraïde arose hastily, 'Hush, hush,' she whispered, lifting a warning finger, 'my little one is asleep; you must not awaken her.'

"Upon the bed was a senseless bundle of rags shaped like an infant in swaddling clothes. Over this dummy the woman had drawn the mosquito bar, and she was sitting contentedly beside it. In short, from that day Zoraïde was demented. Night nor day did she lose sight of the doll that lay in her bed or in her arms.

"And now was Madame stung with sorrow and remorse at seeing this terrible affliction that had befallen her dear Zoraïde. Consulting with Doctor Langlé, they decided to bring back to the mother the real baby of flesh and blood that was now toddling about, and kicking its heels in the dust yonder upon the plantation.

"It was Madame herself who led the pretty, tiny little 'griffe'[8] girl to her mother. Zoraïde was sitting upon a stone bench in the courtyard, listening to the soft splashing of the fountain, and watching the fitful shadows of the palm leaves upon the broad, white flagging.

" 'Here,' said Madame, approaching, 'here, my poor dear

[7]"He's dead, he's dead."
[8]Offspring of a Negro and a mulatto.

Zoraïde, is your own little child. Keep her; she is yours. No one will ever take her from you again.'

"Zoraïde looked with sullen suspicion upon her mistress and the child before her. Reaching out a hand she thrust the little one mistrustfully away from her. With the other hand she clasped the rag bundle fiercely to her breast; for she suspected a plot to deprive her of it.

"Nor could she ever be induced to let her own child approach her; and finally the little one was sent back to the plantation, where she was never to know the love of mother or father.

"And now this is the end of Zoraïde's story. She was never known again as la belle Zoraïde, but ever after as Zoraïde la folle, whom no one ever wanted to marry—not even M'sieur Ambroise. She lived to be an old woman, whom some people pitied and others laughed at—always clasping her bundle of rags—her 'piti.'

"Are you asleep, Ma'zélle Titite?"

"No, I am not asleep; I was thinking. Ah, the poor little one, Man Loulou, the poor little one! better had she died!"

But this is the way Madame Delisle and Manna-Loulou really talked to each other:—

"Vou pré droumi, Ma'zélle Titite?"

"Non, pa pré droumi; mo yapré zongler. Ah, la pauv' piti, Man Loulou. La pauv' piti! Mieux li mouri!"

Written, 1893; published, 1894

A Respectable Woman

MRS. BARODA was a little provoked to learn that her husband expected his friend, Gouvernail, up to spend a week or two on the plantation.

They had entertained a good deal during the winter; much of the time had also been passed in New Orleans in various forms of mild dissipation. She was looking forward to a period of unbroken rest, now, and undisturbed tête-à-tête with her husband, when he informed her that Gouvernail was coming up to stay a week or two.

This was a man she had heard much of but never seen. He had been her husband's college friend; was now a journalist, and in no sense a society man or "a man about town," which were, perhaps, some of the reasons she had never met him. But she had unconsciously formed an image of him in her mind. She pictured him tall, slim, cynical; with eye-glasses, and his hands in his pockets; and she did not like him. Gouvernail was slim enough, but he wasn't very tall nor very cynical; neither did he wear eye-glasses nor carry his hands in his pockets. And she rather liked him when he first presented himself.

But why she liked him she could not explain satisfactorily to herself when she partly attempted to do so. She could discover in him none of those brilliant and promising traits which Gaston, her husband, had often assured her that he possessed. On the contrary, he sat rather mute and receptive before her chatty eagerness to make him feel at home and in face of Gaston's frank and wordy hospitality. His manner was as courteous toward her as the most exacting woman could require; but he made no direct appeal to her approval or even esteem.

Once settled at the plantation he seemed to like to sit upon the wide portico in the shade of one of the big Corinthian pillars, smoking his cigar lazily and listening attentively to Gaston's experience as a sugar planter.

"This is what I call living," he would utter with deep satisfaction, as the air that swept across the sugar field caressed him with its warm and scented velvety touch. It pleased him also to get on familiar terms with the big dogs that came about him, rubbing themselves sociably against his legs. He did not care to fish, and displayed no eagerness to go out and kill grosbecs when Gaston proposed doing so.

Gouvernail's personality puzzled Mrs. Baroda, but she liked him. Indeed, he was a lovable, inoffensive fellow. After a few days, when she could understand him no better than at first, she gave over being puzzled and remained piqued. In this mood she left her husband and her guest, for the most part, alone together. Then finding that Gouvernail took no manner of exception to her action, she imposed her society upon him, accompanying him in his idle strolls to the mill and walks along the batture. She persistently sought to penetrate the reserve in which he had unconsciously enveloped himself.

"When is he going—your friend?" she one day asked her husband. "For my part, he tires me frightfully."

"Not for a week yet, dear. I can't understand; he gives you no trouble."

"No. I should like him better if he did; if he were more like others, and I had to plan somewhat for his comfort and enjoyment."

Gaston took his wife's pretty face between his hands and looked tenderly and laughingly into her troubled eyes. They were making a bit of toilet sociably together in Mrs. Baroda's dressing-room.

"You are full of surprises, ma belle," he said to her. "Even I can never count upon how you are going to act under given conditions." He kissed her and turned to fasten his cravat before the mirror.

"Here you are," he went on, "taking poor Gouvernail seriously and making a commotion over him, the last thing he would desire or expect."

"Commotion!" she hotly resented. "Nonsense! How can you say such a thing? Commotion, indeed! But, you know, you said he was clever."

"So he is. But the poor fellow is run down by overwork now. That's why I asked him here to take a rest."

"You used to say he was a man of ideas." she retorted, unconciliated. "I expected him to be interesting, at least. I'm going to the city in the morning to have my spring gowns

fitted. Let me know when Mr. Gouvernail is gone; I shall be
at my Aunt Octavie's."

That night she went and sat alone upon a bench that stood
beneath a live oak tree at the edge of the gravel walk.

She had never known her thoughts or her intentions to be
so confused. She could gather nothing from them but the
feeling of a distinct necessity to quit her home in the morning.

Mrs. Baroda heard footsteps crunching the gravel; but
could discern in the darkness only the approaching red point
of a lighted cigar. She knew it was Gouvernail, for her husband did not smoke. She hoped to remain unnoticed, but her
white gown revealed her to him. He threw away his cigar and
seated himself upon the bench beside her; without a suspicion
that she might object to his presence.

"Your husband told me to bring this to you, Mrs. Baroda,"
he said, handing her a filmy, white scarf with which she
sometimes enveloped her head and shoulders. She accepted
the scarf from him with a murmur of thanks, and let it lie in
her lap.

He made some commonplace observation upon the baneful
effect of the night air at that season. Then as his gaze reached
out into the darkness, he murmured, half to himself:

> " 'Night of south winds—night of the large few stars!
>   Still nodding night—' "

She made no reply to this apostrophe to the night, which
indeed, was not addressed to her.

Gouvernail was in no sense a diffident man, for he was not
a self-conscious one. His periods of reserve were not constitutional, but the result of moods. Sitting there beside Mrs.
Baroda, his silence melted for the time.

He talked freely and intimately in a low, hesitating drawl
that was not unpleasant to hear. He talked of the old college
days when he and Gaston had been a good deal to each
other; of the days of keen and blind ambitions and large intentions. Now there was left with him, at least, a philosophic
acquiescence to the existing order—only a desire to be permitted to exist, with now and then a little whiff of genuine
life, such as he was breathing now.

Her mind only vaguely grasped what he was saying. Her
physical being was for the moment predominant. She was not
thinking of his words, only drinking in the tones of his voice.

She wanted to reach out her hand in the darkness and touch him with the sensitive tips of her fingers upon the face or the lips. She wanted to draw close to him and whisper against his cheek—she did not care what—as she might have done if she had not been a respectable woman.

The stronger the impulse grew to bring herself near him, the further, in fact, did she draw away from him. As soon as she could so do without an appearance of too great rudeness, she rose and left him there alone.

Before she reached the house, Gouvernail had lighted a fresh cigar and ended his apostrophe to the night.

Mrs. Baroda was greatly tempted that night to tell her husband—who was also her friend—of this folly that had seized her. But she did not yield to the temptation. Beside being a respectable woman she was a very sensible one; and she knew there are some battles in life which a human being must fight alone.

When Gaston arose in the morning, his wife had already departed. She had taken an early morning train to the city. She did not return till Gouvernail was gone from under her roof.

There was some talk of having him back during the summer that followed. That is, Gaston greatly desired it; but this desire yielded to his wife's strenuous opposition.

However, before the year ended, she proposed, wholly from herself, to have Gouvernail visit them again. Her husband was surprised and delighted with the suggestion coming from her.

"I am glad, chère amie,[1] to know that you have finally overcome your dislike for him; truly he did not deserve it."

"Oh," she told him, laughingly, after pressing a long, tender kiss upon his lips, "I have overcome everything! you will see. This time I shall be very nice to him."

Written and published, 1894

[1]Dear one.

The Story of an Hour

KNOWING THAT Mrs. Mallard was afflicted with a heart trouble, great care was taken to break to her as gently as possible the news of her husband's death.

It was her sister Josephine who told her, in broken sentences; veiled hints that revealed in half concealing. Her husband's friend Richards was there, too, near her. It was he who had been in the newspaper office when intelligence of the railroad disaster was received, with Brently Mallard's name leading the list of "killed." He had only taken the time to assure himself of its truth by a second telegram, and had hastened to forestall any less careful, less tender friend in bearing the sad message.

She did not hear the story as many women have heard the same, with a paralyzed inability to accept its significance. She wept at once, with sudden, wild abandonment, in her sister's arms. When the storm of grief had spent itself she went away to her room alone. She would have no one follow her.

There stood, facing the open window, a comfortable, roomy armchair. Into this she sank, pressed down by a physical exhaustion that haunted her body and seemed to reach into her soul.

She could see in the open square before her house the tops of trees that were all aquiver with the new spring life. The delicious breath of rain was in the air. In the street below a peddler was crying his wares. The notes of a distant song which some one was singing reached her faintly, and countless sparrows were twittering in the eaves.

There were patches of blue sky showing here and there through the clouds that had met and piled one above the other in the west facing her window.

She sat with her head thrown back upon the cushion of the chair, quite motionless, except when a sob came up into her throat and shook her, as a child who has cried itself to sleep continues to sob in its dreams.

She was young, with a fair, calm face, whose lines bespoke repression and even a certain strength. But now there was a dull stare in her eyes, whose gaze was fixed away off yonder on one of those patches of blue sky. It was not a glance of reflection, but rather indicated a suspension of intelligent thought.

There was something coming to her and she was waiting for it, fearfully. What was it? She did not know; it was too subtle and elusive to name. But she felt it, creeping out of the sky, reaching toward her through the sounds, the scents, the color that filled the air.

Now her bosom rose and fell tumultuously. She was beginning to recognize this thing that was approaching to possess her, and she was striving to beat it back with her will—as powerless as her two white slender hands would have been.

When she abandoned herself a little whispered word escaped her slightly parted lips. She said it over and over under her breath: "free, free, free!" The vacant stare and the look of terror that had followed it went from her eyes. They stayed keen and bright. Her pulses beat fast, and the coursing blood warmed and relaxed every inch of her body.

She did not stop to ask if it were or were not a monstrous joy that held her. A clear and exalted perception enabled her to dismiss the suggestion as trivial.

She knew that she would weep again when she saw the kind, tender hands folded in death; the face that had never looked save with love upon her, fixed and gray and dead. But she saw beyond that bitter moment a long procession of years to come that would belong to her absolutely. And she opened and spread her arms out to them in welcome.

There would be no one to live for her during those coming years; she would live for herself. There would be no powerful will bending hers in that blind persistence with which men and women believe they have a right to impose a private will upon a fellow-creature. A kind intention or a cruel intention made the act seem no less a crime as she looked upon it in that brief moment of illumination.

And yet she had loved him—sometimes. Often she had not. What did it matter! What could love, the unsolved mystery, count for in face of this possession of self-assertion which she suddenly recognized as the strongest impulse of her being!

"Free! Body and soul free!" she kept whispering.

Josephine was kneeling before the closed door with her lips

to the keyhole, imploring for admission. "Louise, open the door! I beg; open the door—you will make yourself ill. What are you doing, Louise? For heaven's sake open the door."

"Go away. I am not making myself ill." No; she was drinking in a very elixir of life through that open window.

Her fancy was running riot along those days ahead of her. Spring days, and summer days, and all sorts of days that would be her own. She breathed a quick prayer that life might be long. It was only yesterday she had thought with a shudder that life might be long.

She arose at length and opened the door to her sister's importunities. There was a feverish triumph in her eyes, and she carried herself unwittingly like a goddess of Victory. She clasped her sister's waist, and together they descended the stairs. Richards stood waiting for them at the bottom.

Some one was opening the front door with a latchkey. It was Brently Mallard who entered, a little travel-stained, composedly carrying his grip-sack and umbrella. He had been far from the scene of accident, and did not even know there had been one. He stood amazed at Josephine's piercing cry; at Richards' quick motion to screen him from the view of his wife.

But Richards was too late.

When the doctors came they said she had died of heart disease—of joy that kills.

Written and published, 1894

Regret

MAMZELLE AURÉLIE possessed a good strong figure, ruddy cheeks, hair that was changing from brown to gray, and a determined eye. She wore a man's hat about the farm, and an old blue army overcoat when it was cold, and sometimes topboots.

Mamzelle Aurélie had never thought of marrying. She had never been in love. At the age of twenty she had received a proposal, which she had promptly declined, and at the age of fifty she had not yet lived to regret it.

So she was quite alone in the world, except for her dog Ponto, and the negroes who lived in her cabins and worked her crops, and the fowls, a few cows, a couple of mules, her gun (with which she shot chicken-hawks), and her religion.

One morning Mamzelle Aurélie stood upon her gallery, contemplating, with arms akimbo, a small band of very small children who, to all intents and purposes, might have fallen from the clouds, so unexpected and bewildering was their coming, and so unwelcome. They were the children of her nearest neighbor, Odile, who was not such a near neighbor, after all.

The young woman had appeared but five minutes before, accompanied by these four children. In her arms she carried little Elodie; she dragged Ti Nomme by an unwilling hand; while Marcéline and Marcélette followed with irresolute steps.

Her face was red and disfigured from tears and excitement. She had been summoned to a neighboring parish by the dangerous illness of her mother; her husband was away in Texas—it seemed to her a million miles away; and Valsin was waiting with the mule-cart to drive her to the station.

"It's no question, Mamzelle Aurélie; you jus' got to keep those youngsters fo' me tell I come back. Dieu sait,[1] I wouldn' botha you with 'em if it was any otha way to do! Make 'em mine you, Mamzelle Aurélie; don' spare 'em. Me, there, I'm half crazy between the chil'ren, an' Léon not

---

[1] God knows.

201

home, an' maybe not even to fine po' maman alive
encore!"—a harrowing possibility which drove Odile to take a
final hasty and convulsive leave of her disconsolate family.

She left them crowded into the narrow strip of shade on
the porch of the long, low house; the white sunlight was
beating in on the white old boards; some chickens were
scratching in the grass at the foot of the steps, and one had
boldly mounted, and was stepping heavily, solemnly, and
aimlessly across the gallery. There was a pleasant odor of
pinks in the air, and the sound of negroes' laughter was coming across the flowering cotton-field.

Mamzelle Aurélie stood contemplating the children. She
looked with a critical eye upon Marcéline, who had been left
staggering beneath the weight of the chubby Elodie. She surveyed with the same calculating air Marcélette mingling her
silent tears with the audible grief and rebellion of Ti Nomme.
During those few contemplative moments she was collecting
herself, determining upon a line of action which should be
identical with a line of duty. She began by feeding them.

If Mamzelle Aurélie's responsibilities might have begun
and ended there, they could easily have been dismissed; for
her larder was amply provided against an emergency of this
nature. But little children are not little pigs; they require and
demand attentions which were wholly unexpected by
Mamzelle Aurélie, and which she was ill prepared to give.

She was, indeed, very inapt in her management of Odile's
children during the first few days. How could she know that
Marcélette always wept when spoken to in a loud and commanding tone of voice? It was a peculiarity of Marcélette's.
She became acquainted with Ti Nomme's passion for flowers
only when he had plucked all the choicest gardenias and
pinks for the apparent purpose of critically studying their
botanical construction.

" 'Tain't enough to tell 'im, Mamzelle Aurélie," Marcéline
instructed her; "you got to tie 'im in a chair. It's w'at maman
all time do w'en he's bad: she tie 'im in a chair." The chair
in which Mamzelle Aurélie tied Ti Nomme was roomy and
comfortable, and he seized the opportunity to take a nap in
it, the afternoon being warm.

At night, when she ordered them one and all to bed as she
would have shooed the chickens into the hen-house, they
stayed uncomprehending before her. What about the little
white nightgowns that had to be taken from the pillow-slip in
which they were brought over, and shaken by some strong

hand till they snapped like ox-whips? What about the tub of water which had to be brought and set in the middle of the floor, in which the little tired, dusty, sunbrowned feet had every one to be washed sweet and clean? And it made Marcéline and Marcélette laugh merrily—the idea that Mamzelle Aurélie should for a moment have believed that Ti Nomme could fall asleep without being told the story of *Croquemitaine*[2] or *Loup-garou*,[3] or both; or that Elodie could fall asleep at all without being rocked and sung to.

"I tell you, Aunt Ruby," Mamzelle Aurélie informed her cook in confidence; "me, I'd rather manage a dozen plantation' than fo' chil'ren. It's terrassent! Bonté![4] Don't talk to me about chil'ren!"

" 'Tain' ispected sich as you would know airy thing 'bout 'em, Mamzelle Aurélie. I see dat plainly yistiddy w'en I spy dat li'le chile playin' wid yo' baskit o' keys. You don' know dat makes chillun grow up hard-headed, to play wid keys? Des like it make 'em teeth hard to look in a lookin'-glass. Them's the things you got to know in the raisin' an' manigement o' chillun."

Mamzelle Aurélie certainly did not pretend or aspire to such subtle and far-reaching knowledge on the subject as Aunt Ruby possessed, who had "raised five an' bared (buried) six" in her day. She was glad enough to learn a few little mother-tricks to serve the moment's need.

Ti Nomme's sticky fingers compelled her to unearth white aprons that she had not worn for years, and she had to accustom herself to his moist kisses—the expressions of an affectionate and exuberant nature. She got down her sewing-basket, which she seldom used, from the top shelf of the armoire, and placed it within the ready and easy reach which torn slips and buttonless waists demanded. It took her some days to become accustomed to the laughing, the crying, the chattering that echoed through the house and around it all day long. And it was not the first or the second night that she could sleep comfortably with little Elodie's hot, plump body pressed close against her, and the little one's warm breath beating her cheek like the fanning of a bird's wing.

But at the end of two weeks Mamzelle Aurélie had grown quite used to these things, and she no longer complained.

[2]The "Bogeyman."
[3]The "Werewolf."
[4]"It's exhausting! Goodness."

It was also at the end of two weeks that Mamzelle Aurélie, one evening, looking away toward the crib where the cattle were being fed, saw Valsin's blue cart turning the bend of the road. Odile sat beside the mulatto, upright and alert. As they drew near, the young woman's beaming face indicated that her homecoming was a happy one.

But this coming, unannounced and unexpected, threw Mamzelle Aurélie into a flutter that was almost agitation. The children had to be gathered. Where was Ti Nomme? Yonder in the shed, putting an edge on his knife at the grindstone. And Marcéline and Marcélette? Cutting and fashioning doll-rags in the corner of the gallery. As for Elodie, she was safe enough in Mamzelle Aurélie's arms; and she had screamed with delight at sight of the familiar blue cart which was bringing her mother back to her.

The excitement was all over, and they were gone. How still it was when they were gone! Mamzelle Aurélie stood upon the gallery, looking and listening. She could no longer see the cart; the red sunset and the blue-gray twilight had together flung a purple mist across the fields and road that hid it from her view. She could no longer hear the wheezing and creaking of its wheels. But she could still faintly hear the shrill, glad voices of the children.

She turned into the house. There was much work awaiting her, for the children had left a sad disorder behind them; but she did not at once set about the task of righting it. Mamzelle Aurélie seated herself beside the table. She gave one slow glance through the room, into which the evening shadows were creeping and deepening around her solitary figure. She let her head fall down upon her bended arm, and began to cry. Oh, but she cried! Not softly, as women often do. She cried like a man, with sobs that seemed to tear her very soul. She did not notice Ponto licking her hand.

Written and published, 1894

The Kiss

IT WAS still quite light out of doors, but inside with the curtains drawn and the smouldering fire sending out a dim, uncertain glow, the room was full of deep shadows.

Brantain sat in one of these shadows; it had overtaken him and he did not mind. The obscurity lent him courage to keep his eyes fastened as ardently as he liked upon the girl who sat in the firelight.

She was very handsome, with a certain fine, rich coloring that belongs to the healthy brune type. She was quite composed, as she idly stroked the satiny coat of the cat that lay curled in her lap, and she occasionally sent a slow glance into the shadow where her companion sat. They were talking low, of indifferent things which plainly were not the things that occupied their thoughts. She knew that he loved her—a frank, blustering fellow without guile enough to conceal his feelings, and no desire to do so. For two weeks past he had sought her society eagerly and persistently. She was confidently waiting for him to declare himself and she meant to accept him. The rather insignificant and unattractive Brantain was enormously rich; and she liked and required the entourage which wealth could give her.

During one of the pauses between their talk of the last tea and the next reception the door opened and a young man entered whom Brantain knew quite well. The girl turned her face toward him. A stride or two brought him to her side, and bending over her chair—before she could suspect his intention, for she did not realize that he had not seen her visitor—he pressed an ardent, lingering kiss upon her lips.

Brantain slowly arose; so did the girl arise, but quickly, and the newcomer stood between them, a little amusement and some defiance struggling with the confusion in his face.

"I believe," stammered Brantain, "I see that I have stayed too long. I—I had no idea—that is, I must wish you goodby." He was clutching his hat with both hands, and probably did not perceive that she was extending her hand to him, her presence of mind had not completely deserted her; but she could not have trusted herself to speak.

"Hang me if I saw him sitting there, Nattie! I know it's deuced awkward for you. But I hope you'll forgive me this once—this very first break. Why, what's the matter?"

"Don't touch me; don't come near me," she returned angrily. "What do you mean by entering the house without ringing?"

"I came in with your brother, as I often do," he answered coldly, in self-justification. "We came in the side way. He went upstairs and I came in here hoping to find you. The explanation is simple enough and ought to satisfy you that the misadventure was unavoidable. But do say that you forgive me, Nathalie," he entreated, softening.

"Forgive you! You don't know what you are talking about. Let me pass. It depends upon—a good deal whether I ever forgive you."

At that next reception which she and Brantain had been talking about she approached the young man with a delicious frankness of manner when she saw him there.

"Will you let me speak to you a moment or two, Mr. Brantain?" she asked with an engaging but perturbed smile. He seemed extremely unhappy; but when she took his arm and walked away with him, seeking a retired corner, a ray of hope mingled with the almost comical misery of his expression. She was apparently very outspoken.

"Perhaps I should not have sought this interview, Mr. Brantain; but—but, oh, I have been very uncomfortable, almost miserable since that little encounter the other afternoon. When I thought how you might have misinterpreted it, and believed things"—hope was plainly gaining the ascendancy over misery in Brantain's round, guileless face—"of course, I know it is nothing to you, but for my own sake I do want you to understand that Mr. Harvy is an intimate friend of long standing. Why, we have always been like cousins—like brother and sister, I may say. He is my brother's most intimate associate and often fancies that he is entitled to the same privileges as the family. Oh, I know it is absurd, uncalled for, to tell you this; undignified even," she was almost weeping, "but it makes so much difference to me what you think of—of me." Her voice had grown very low and agitated. The misery had all disappeared from Brantain's face.

"Then you do really care what I think, Miss Nathalie?

May I call you Miss Nathalie?" They turned into a long, dim corridor that was lined on either side with tall, graceful plants. They walked slowly to the very end of it. When they turned to retrace their steps Brantain's face was radiant and hers was triumphant.

Harvy was among the guests at the wedding; and he sought her out in a rare moment when she stood alone.

"Your husband," he said, smiling, "has sent me over to kiss you."

A quick blush suffused her face and round polished throat. "I suppose it's natural for a man to feel and act generously on an occasion of this kind. He tells me he doesn't want his marriage to interrupt wholly that pleasant intimacy which has existed between you and me. I don't know what you've been telling him," with an insolent smile, "but he has sent me here to kiss you."

She felt like a chess player who, by the clever handling of his pieces, sees the game taking the course intended. Her eyes were bright and tender with a smile as they glanced up into his; and her lips looked hungry for the kiss which they invited.

"But, you know," he went on quietly, "I didn't tell him so, it would have seemed ungrateful, but I can tell you. I've stopped kissing women; it's dangerous."

Well, she had Brantain and his million left. A person can't have everything in this world; and it was a little unreasonable of her to expect it.

Written, 1894; published, 1895

Athénaïse

I

ATHÉNAÏSE went away in the morning to make a visit to her
parents, ten miles back on rigolet de Bon Dieu. She did not
return in the evening, and Cazeau, her husband, fretted not
a little. He did not worry much about Athénaïse, who, he suspected, was resting only too content in the bosom of her
family; his chief solicitude was manifestly for the pony she
had ridden. He felt sure those "lazy pigs," her brothers, were
capable of neglecting it seriously. This misgiving Cazeau
communicated to his servant, old Félicité, who waited upon
him at supper.

His voice was low pitched, and even softer than Félicité's.
He was tall, sinewy, swarthy, and altogether severe looking.
His thick black hair waved, and it gleamed like the breast of
a crow. The sweep of his mustache, which was not so black,
outlined the broad contour of the mouth. Beneath the under
lip grew a small tuft which he was much given to twisting,
and which he permitted to grow, apparently for no other purpose. Cazeau's eyes were dark blue, narrow and over-
shadowed. His hands were coarse and stiff from close acquaintance with farming tools and implements, and he
handled his fork and knife clumsily. But he was distinguished
looking, and succeeded in commanding a good deal of respect, and even fear sometimes.

He ate his supper alone, by the light of a single coal-oil
lamp that but faintly illuminated the big room, with its bare
floor and huge rafters, and its heavy pieces of furniture that
loomed dimly in the gloom of the apartment. Félicité, ministering to his wants, hovered about the table like a little, bent,
restless shadow.

She served him with a dish of sunfish fried crisp and
brown. There was nothing else set before him beside the
bread and butter and the bottle of red wine which she locked

carefully in the buffet after he had poured his second glass. She was occupied with her mistress's absence, and kept reverting to it after he had expressed his solicitude about the pony.

"Dat beat me! on'y marry two mont', an' got de head turn' a'ready to go 'broad. C'est pas Chrétien, tenez!"[1]

Cazeau shrugged his shoulders for answer, after he had drained his glass and pushed aside his plate. Félicité's opinion of the unchristianlike behavior of his wife in leaving him thus alone after two months of marriage weighed little with him. He was used to solitude, and did not mind a day or a night or two of it. He had lived alone ten years, since his first wife died, and Félicité might have known better than to suppose that he cared. He told her she was a fool. It sounded like a compliment in his modulated, caressing voice. She grumbled to herself as she set about clearing the table, and Cazeau arose and walked outside on the gallery; his spur, which he had not removed upon entering the house, jangled at every step.

The night was beginning to deepen, and to gather black about the clusters of trees and shrubs that were grouped in the yard. In the beam of light from the open kitchen door a black boy stood feeding a brace of snarling, hungry dogs; further away, on the steps of a cabin, some one was playing the accordion; and in still another direction a little negro baby was crying lustily. Cazeau walked around to the front of the house, which was square, squat and one-story.

A belated wagon was driving in at the gate, and the impatient driver was swearing hoarsely at his jaded oxen. Félicité stepped out on the gallery, glass and polishing towel in hand, to investigate, and to wonder, too, who could be singing out on the river. It was a party of young people paddling around, waiting for the moon to rise, and they were singing Juanita, their voices coming tempered and melodious through the distance and the night.

Cazeau's horse was waiting, saddled, ready to be mounted, for Cazeau had many things to attend to before bed-time; so many things that there was not left to him a moment in which to think of Athénaïse. He felt her absence, though, like a dull, insistent pain.

However, before he slept that night he was visited by the thought of her, and by a vision of her fair young face with its drooping lips and sullen and averted eyes. The marriage had

[1] "It's not Christian, you know."

been a blunder; he had only to look into her eyes to feel that,
to discover her growing aversion. But it was a thing not by
any possibility to be undone. He was quite prepared to make
the best of it, and expected no less than a like effort on her
part. The less she revisited the rigolet, the better. He would
find means to keep her at home hereafter.

These unpleasant reflections kept Cazeau awake far into
the night, notwithstanding the craving of his whole body for
rest and sleep. The moon was shining, and its pale effulgence
reached dimly into the room, and with it a touch of the cool
breath of the spring night. There was an unusual stillness
abroad; no sound to be heard save the distant, tireless, plaintive notes of the accordion.

II

Athénaïse did not return the following day, even though
her husband sent her word to do so by her brother,
Montéclin, who passed on his way to the village early in the
morning.

On the third day Cazeau saddled his horse and went himself in search of her. She had sent no word, no message, ex-
plaining her absence, and he felt that he had good cause to
be offended. It was rather awkward to have to leave his work,
even though late in the afternoon,—Cazeau had always so
much to do; but among the many urgent calls upon him, the
task of bringing his wife back to a sense of her duty seemed
to him for the moment paramount.

The Michés, Athénaïse's parents, lived on the old Gotrain
place. It did not belong to them; they were "running" it for a
merchant in Alexandria. The house was far too big for their
use. One of the lower rooms served for the storing of wood
and tools; the person "occupying" the place before Miché
having pulled up the flooring in despair of being able to
patch it. Upstairs, the rooms were so large, so bare, that they
offered a constant temptation to lovers of the dance, whose
importunities Madame Miché was accustomed to meet with
amiable indulgence. A dance at Miché's and a plate of
Madame Miché's gumbo filé at midnight were pleasures not
to be neglected or despised, unless by such serious souls as
Cazeau.

Long before Cazeau reached the house his approach had
been observed, for there was nothing to obstruct the view of
the outer road; vegetation was not yet abundantly advanced,

and there was but a patchy, straggling stand of cotton and corn in Miché's field.

Madame Miché, who had been seated on the gallery in a rocking-chair, stood up to greet him as he drew near. She was short and fat, and wore a black skirt and loose muslin sack fastened at the throat with a hair brooch. Her own hair, brown and glossy, showed but a few threads of silver. Her round pink face was cheery, and her eyes were bright and good humored. But she was plainly perturbed and ill at ease as Cazeau advanced.

Montéclin, who was there too, was not ill at ease, and made no attempt to disguise the dislike with which his brother-in-law inspired him. He was a slim, wiry fellow of twenty-five, short of stature like his mother, and resembling her in feature. He was in shirt-sleeves, half leaning, half sitting, on the insecure railing of the gallery, and fanning himself with his broad-rimmed felt hat.

"Cochon!" he muttered under his breath as Cazeau mounted the stairs,—"sacré cochon!"[2]

"Cochon" had sufficiently characterized the man who had once on a time declined to lend Montéclin money. But when this same man had had the presumption to propose marriage to his well-beloved sister, Athénaïse, and the honor to be accepted by her, Montéclin felt that a qualifying epithet was needed fully to express his estimate of Cazeau.

Miché and his oldest son were absent. They both esteemed Cazeau highly, and talked much of his qualities of head and heart, and thought much of his excellent standing with city merchants.

Athénaïse had shut herself up in her room. Cazeau had seen her rise and enter the house at perceiving him. He was a good deal mystified, but no one could have guessed it when he shook hands with Madame Miché. He had only nodded to Montéclin, with a muttered "Comment ça va?"[3]

"Tiens! something tole me you were coming to-day!" exclaimed Madame Miché, with a little blustering appearance of being cordial and at ease, as she offered Cazeau a chair.

He ventured a short laugh as he seated himself.

"You know, nothing would do," she went on, with much gesture of her small, plump hands, "nothing would do but

[2]"Pig . . . damn pig!"
[3]"How are things?"

Athénaïse mus' stay las' night fo' a li'le dance. The boys wouldn' year to their sister leaving."

Cazeau shrugged his shoulders significantly, telling as plainly as words that he knew nothing about it.

"Comment! Montéclin didn' tell you we were going to keep Athénaïse?" Montéclin had evidently told nothing.

"An' how about the night befo'," questioned Cazeau, "an' las' night? It isn't possible you dance every night out yere on the Bon Dieu!"

Madame Miché laughed, with amiable appreciation of the sarcasm; and turning to her son, "Montéclin, my boy, go tell yo' sister that Monsieur Cazeau is yere."

Montéclin did not stir except to shift his position and settle himself more securely on the railing.

"Did you year me, Montéclin?"

"Oh yes, I yeard you plain enough," responded her son, "but you know as well as me it's no use to tell 'Thénaïse anything. You been talkin' to her yo'se'f since Monday; an' pa's preached himse'f hoa'se on the subject; an' you even had uncle Achille down yere yesterday to reason with her. W'en 'Thénaïse said she wasn' goin' to set her foot back in Cazeau's house, she meant it."

This speech, which Montéclin delivered with thorough unconcern, threw his mother into a condition of painful but dumb embarrassment. It brought two fiery red spots to Cazeau's cheeks, and for the space of a moment he looked wicked.

What Montéclin had spoken was quite true, though his taste in the manner and choice of time and place in saying it were not of the best. Athénaïse, upon the first day of her arrival, had announced that she came to stay, having no intention of returning under Cazeau's roof. The announcement had scattered consternation, as she knew it would. She had been implored, scolded, entreated, stormed at, until she felt herself like a dragging sail that all the winds of heaven had beaten upon. Why in the name of God had she married Cazeau? Her father had lashed her with the question a dozen times. Why indeed? It was difficult now for her to understand why, unless because she supposed it was customary for girls to marry when the right opportunity came. Cazeau, she knew, would make life more comfortable for her; and again, she had liked him, and had even been rather flustered when he pressed her hands and kissed them, and kissed her lips and cheeks and eyes, when she accepted him.

Montéclin himself had taken her aside to talk the thing over. The turn of affairs was delighting him.

"Come, now, 'Thénaïse, you mus' explain to me all about it, so we can settle on a good cause, an' secu' a separation fo' you. Has he been mistreating an' abusing you, the sacré cochon?" They were alone together in her room, whither she had taken refuge from the angry domestic elements.

"You please to reserve yo' disgusting expressions, Montéclin. No, he has not abused me in any way that I can think."

"Does he drink? Come 'Thénaïse, think well over it. Does he ever get drunk?"

"Drunk! Oh, mercy, no,—Cazeau never gets drunk."

"I see; it's jus' simply you feel like me; you hate him."

"No, I don't hate him," she returned reflectively; adding with a sudden impulse, "It's jus' being married that I detes' an' despise. I hate being Mrs. Cazeau, an' would want to be Athénaïse Miché again. I can't stan' to live with a man; to have him always there; his coats an' pantaloons hanging in my room; his ugly bare feet—washing them in my tub, befo' my very eyes, ugh!" She shuddered with recollections, and resumed, with a sigh that was almost a sob: "Mon Dieu, mon Dieu! Sister Marie Angélique knew w'at she was saying; she knew me better than myse'f w'en she said God had sent me a vocation an' I was turning deaf ears. W'en I think of a blessed life in the convent, at peace! Oh, w'at was I dreaming of!" and then the tears came.

Montéclin felt disconcerted and greatly disappointed at having obtained evidence that would carry no weight with a court of justice. The day had not come when a young woman might ask the court's permission to return to her mamma on the sweeping ground of a constitutional disinclination for marriage. But if there was no way of untying this Gordian knot of marriage, there was surely a way of cutting it.

"Well, 'Thénaïse, I'm mighty durn sorry you got no better groun's 'an w'at you say. But you can count on me to stan' by you w'atever you do. God knows I don' blame you fo' not wantin' to live with Cazeau."

And now there was Cazeau himself, with the red spots flaming in his swarthy cheeks, looking and feeling as if he wanted to thrash Montéclin into some semblance of decency. He arose abruptly, and approaching the room which he had seen his wife enter, thrust open the door after a hasty preliminary knock. Athénaïse, who was standing erect at a far window, turned at his entrance.

She appeared neither angry nor frightened, but thoroughly unhappy, with an appeal in her soft dark eyes and a tremor on her lips that seemed to him expressions of unjust reproach, that wounded and maddened him at once. But whatever he might feel, Cazeau knew only one way to act toward a woman.

"Athénaïse, you are not ready?" he asked in his quiet tones. "It's getting late; we havn' any time to lose."

She knew that Montéclin had spoken out, and she had hoped for a wordy interview, a stormy scene, in which she might have held her own as she had held it for the past three days against her family, with Montéclin's aid. But she had no weapon with which to combat subtlety. Her husband's looks, his tones, his mere presence, brought to her a sudden sense of hopelessness, an instinctive realization of the futility of rebellion against a social and sacred institution.

Cazeau said nothing further, but stood waiting in the doorway. Madame Miché had walked to the far end of the gallery, and pretended to be occupied with having a chicken driven from her parterre.[4] Montéclin stood by, exasperated, fuming, ready to burst out.

Athénaïse went and reached for her riding skirt that hung against the wall. She was rather tall, with a figure which, though not robust, seemed perfect in its fine proportions. "La fille de son père,"[5] she was often called, which was a great compliment to Miché. Her brown hair was brushed all fluffily back from her temples and low forehead, and about her features and expression lurked a softness, a prettiness, a dewiness, that were perhaps too childlike, that savored of immaturity.

She slipped the riding-skirt, which was of black alpaca, over her head, and with impatient fingers hooked it at the waist over her pink linen-lawn. Then she fastened on her white sunbonnet and reached for her gloves on the mantelpiece.

"If you don' wan' to go, you know w'at you got to do, 'Thénaïse," fumed Montéclin. "You don' set yo' feet back on Cane River, by God, unless you want to,—not w'ile I'm alive."

[4] Flower bed.
[5] "Her father's daughter."

Cazeau looked at him as if he were a monkey whose antics fell short of being amusing.

Athénaïse still made no reply, said not a word. She walked rapidly past her husband, past her brother; bidding good-bye to no one, not even to her mother. She descended the stairs, and without assistance from any one mounted the pony, which Cazeau had ordered to be saddled upon his arrival. In this way she obtained a fair start of her husband, whose departure was far more leisurely, and for the greater part of the way she managed to keep an appreciable gap between them. She rode almost madly at first, with the wind inflating her skirt ballon-like about her knees, and her sunbonnet falling back between her shoulders.

At no time did Cazeau make an effort to overtake her until traversing an old fallow meadow that was level and hard as a table. The sight of a great solitary oak-tree, with its seemingly immutable outlines, that had been a landmark for ages—or was it the odor of elderberry stealing up from the gully to the south? or what was it that brought vividly back to Cazeau, by some association of ideas, a scene of many years ago? He had passed that old live-oak hundreds of times, but it was only now that the memory of one day came back to him. He was a very small boy that day, seated before his father on horse-back. They were proceeding slowly, and Black Gabe was moving on before them at a little dog-trot. Black Gabe had run away, and had been discovered back in the Gotrain swamp. They had halted beneath this big oak to enable the negro to take breath; for Cazeau's father was a kind and considerate master, and everyone had agreed at the time that Black Gabe was a fool, a great idiot indeed, for wanting to run away from him.

The whole impression was for some reason hideous, and to dispel it Cazeau spurred his horse to a swift gallop. Overtaking his wife, he rode the remainder of the way at her side in silence.

It was late when they reached home. Félicité was standing on the grassy edge of the road, in the moonlight, waiting for them.

Cazeau once more ate his supper alone; for Athénaïse went to her room, and there she was crying again.

III

Athénaïse was not one to accept the inevitable with patient resignation, a talent born in the souls of many women;
neither was she the one to accept it with philosophical resignation, like her husband. Her sensibilities were alive and keen
and responsive. She met the pleasurable things of life with
frank, open appreciation, and against distasteful conditions
she rebelled. Dissimulation was as foreign to her nature as
guile to the breast of a babe, and her rebellious outbreaks, by
no means rare, had hitherto been quite open and aboveboard.
People often said that Athénaïse would know her own mind
some day, which was equivalent to saying that she was at
present unacquainted with it. If she ever came to such
knowledge, it would be by no intellectual research, by no
subtle analyses or tracing the motives of actions to their
source. It would come to her as the song to the bird, the perfume and color to the flower.

Her parents had hoped—not without reason and justice—
that marriage would bring the poise, the desirable pose, so
glaringly lacking in Athénaïse's character. Marriage they
knew to be a wonderful and powerful agent in the development and formation of a woman's character; they had seen
its effect too often to doubt it.

"And if this marriage does nothing else," exclaimed Miché
in an outburst of sudden exasperation, "it will rid us of
Athénaïse; for I am at the end of my patience with her! You
have never had the firmness to manage her,"—he was speaking to his wife,—"I have not had the time, the leisure, to devote to her training; and what good we might have accomplished, that maudit Montéclin—Well, Cazeau is the one! It
takes just such a steady hand to guide a disposition like
Athénaïse's, a master hand, a strong will that compels obedience."

And now, when they had hoped for so much, here was
Athénaïse, with gathered and fierce vehemence, beside which
her former outbursts appeared mild, declaring that she would
not, and she would not, and she would not continue to enact
the role of wife to Cazeau. If she had had a reason! as
Madame Miché lamented; but it could not be discovered that
she had any sane one. He had never scolded, or called names,
or deprived her of comforts, or been guilty of any of the
many reprehensible acts commonly attributed to objectionable

husbands. He did not slight nor neglect her. Indeed, Cazeau's chief offense seemed to be that he loved her, and Athénaïse was not the woman to be loved against her will. She called marriage a trap set for the feet of unwary and unsuspecting girls, and in round, unmeasured terms reproached her mother with treachery and deceit.

"I told you Cazeau was the man," chuckled Miché, when his wife had related the scene that had accompanied and influenced Athénaïse's departure.

Athénaïse again hoped, in the morning, that Cazeau would scold or make some sort of a scene, but he apparently did not dream of it. It was exasperating that he should take her acquiescence so for granted. It is true he had been up and over the fields and across the river and back long before she was out of bed, and he may have been thinking of something else, which was no excuse, which was even in some sense an aggravation. But he did say to her at breakfast, "That brother of yo's, that Montéclin, is unbearable."

"Montéclin? Par exemple!"

Athénaïse, seated opposite to her husband, was attired in a white morning wrapper. She wore a somewhat abused, long face, it is true,—an expression of countenance familiar to some husbands,—but the expression was not sufficiently pronounced to mar the charm of her youthful freshness. She had little heart to eat, only playing with the food before her, and she felt a pang of resentment at her husband's healthy appetite.

"Yes, Montéclin," he reasserted. "He's developed into a firs'-class nuisance; an' you better tell him, Athénaïse,—unless you want me to tell him,—to confine his energies after this to matters that concern him. I have no use fo' him or fo' his interference in w'at regards you an' me alone."

This was said with unusual asperity. It was the little breach that Athénaïse had been watching for, and she charged rapidly: "It's strange, if you detes' Montéclin so heartily, that you would desire to marry his sister." She knew it was a silly thing to say, and was not surprised when he told her so. It gave her a little foothold for further attack, however. "I don't see, anyhow, w'at reason you had to marry me, w'en there were so many others," she complained, as if accusing him of persecution and injury. "There was Marianne running after you fo' the las' five years till it was disgraceful; an' any one of the Dortrand girls would have been glad to marry you. But no, nothing would do; you mus' come out on the rigolet fo' me." Her complaint was pathetic, and at the same time so amusing that Cazeau was forced to smile.

"I can't see w'at the Dortrand girls or Marianne have to do with it," he rejoined; adding, with no trace of amusement, "I married you because I loved you; because you were the woman I wanted to marry, an' the only one. I reckon I tole you that befo'. I thought—of co'se I was a fool fo' taking things fo' granted—but I did think that I might make you happy in making things easier an' mo' comfortable fo' you. I expected—I was even that big a fool—I believed that yo' coming yere to me would be like the sun shining out of the clouds, an' that our days would be like w'at the story-books promise after the wedding. I was mistaken. But I can't imagine w'at induced you to marry me. W'atever it was, I reckon you foun' out you made a mistake, too. I don' see anything to do but make the best of a bad bargain, an' shake han's over it." He had arisen from the table, and, approaching, held out his hand to her. What he had said was commonplace enough, but it was significant, coming from Cazeau, who was not often so unreserved in expressing himself.

Athénaïse ignored the hand held out to her. She was resting her chin in her palm, and kept her eyes fixed moodily upon the table. He rested his hand, that she would not touch, upon her head for an instant, and walked away out of the room.

She heard him giving orders to workmen who had been waiting for him out on the gallery, and she heard him mount his horse and ride away. A hundred things would distract him and engage his attention during the day. She felt that he had perhaps put her and her grievance from his thoughts when he crossed the threshold; whilst she—

Old Félicité was standing there holding a shining tin pail; asking for flour and lard and eggs from the storeroom, and meal for the chicks.

Athénaïse seized the bunch of keys which hung from her belt and flung them at Félicité's feet.

"Tiens! tu vas les garder comme tu as jadis fait. Je ne veux plus de ce train là, moi!"[6]

The old woman stooped and picked up the keys from the floor. It was really all one to her that her mistress returned

---

[6]"You are going to keep them as you did in the past. I don't want any more of this nonsense."

them to her keeping, and refused to take further account of the ménage.[7]

IV

It seemed now to Athénaïse that Montéclin was the only friend left to her in the world. Her father and mother had turned from her in what appeared to be her hour of need. Her friends laughed at her, and refused to take seriously the hints which she threw out,—feeling her way to discover if marriage were as distasteful to other women as to herself. Montéclin alone understood her. He alone had always been ready to act for her and with her, to comfort and solace her with his sympathy and his support. Her only hope for rescue from her hateful surroundings lay in Montéclin. Of herself she felt powerless to plan, to act, even to conceive a way out of this pitfall into which the whole world seemed to have conspired to thrust her.

She had a great desire to see her brother, and wrote asking him to come to her. But it better suited Montéclin's spirit of adventure to appoint a meeting-place at the turn of the lane, where Athénaïse might appear to be walking leisurely for health and recreation, and where he might seem to be riding along, bent on some errand of business or pleasure.

There had been a shower, a sudden downpour, short as it was sudden, that had laid the dust in the road. It had freshened the pointed leaves of the live-oaks, and brightened up the big fields of cotton on either side of the lane till they seemed carpeted with green, glittering gems.

Athénaïse walked along the grassy edge of the road, lifting her crisp skirts with one hand, and with the other twirling a gay sunshade over her bare head. The scent of the fields after the rain was delicious. She inhaled long breaths of their freshness and perfume, that soothed and quieted her for the moment. There were birds splashing and spluttering in the pools, pluming themselves on the fence-rails, and sending out little sharp cries, twitters, and shrill rhapsodies of delight.

She saw Montéclin approaching from a great distance,—almost as far away as the turn of the woods. But she could not feel sure it was he; it appeared too tall for Montéclin, but that was because he was riding a large horse. She waved her parasol to him; she was so glad to see him. She had never

[7]Housekeeping.

been so glad to see Montéclin before; not even the day when
he had taken her out of the convent, against her parents'
wishes, because she had expressed a desire to remain there no
longer. He seemed to her, as he drew near, the embodiment
of kindness, of bravery, of chivalry, even of wisdom; for she
had never known Montéclin at a loss to extricate himself
from a disagreeable situation.

He dismounted, and, leading his horse by the bridle,
started to walk beside her, after he had kissed her affectionately and asked her what she was crying about. She protested that she was not crying, for she was laughing, though
drying her eyes at the same time on her handkerchief, rolled
in a soft mop for the purpose.

She took Montéclin's arm, and they strolled slowly down
the lane; they could not seat themselves for a comfortable
chat, as they would have liked, with the grass all sparkling
and bristling wet.

Yes, she was quite as wretched as ever, she told him. The
week which had gone by since she saw him had in no wise
lightened the burden of her discontent. There had even been
some additional provocations laid upon her, and she told Montéclin all about them,—about the keys, for instance, which in a
fit of temper she had returned to Félicité's keeping; and she
told how Cazeau had brought them back to her as if they were
something she had accidentally lost, and he had recovered;
and how he had said, in that aggravating tone of his, that it
was not the custom on Cane river for the negro servants to
carry the keys, when there was a mistress at the head of the
household.

But Athénaïse could not tell Montéclin anything to in-
crease the disrespect which he already entertained for his
brother-in-law; and it was then he unfolded to her a plan
which he had conceived and worked out for her deliverance
from this galling matrimonial yoke.

It was not a plan which met with instant favor, which she
was at once ready to accept, for it involved secrecy and dissimulation, hateful alternatives, both of them. But she was
filled with admiration for Montéclin's resources and wonderful talent for contrivance. She accepted the plan; not with the
immediate determination to act upon it, rather with the intention to sleep and to dream upon it.

Three days later she wrote to Montéclin that she had abandoned herself to his counsel. Displeasing as it might be to her
sense of honesty, it would yet be less trying than to live on

with a soul full of bitterness and revolt, as she had done for
the past two months.

V

When Cazeau awoke, one morning at his usual very early
hour, it was to find the place at his side vacant. This did not
surprise him until he discovered that Athénaïse was not in
the adjoining room, where he had often found her sleeping in
the morning on the lounge. She had perhaps gone out for an
early stroll, he reflected, for her jacket and hat were not on
the rack where she had hung them the night before. But there
were other things absent,—a gown or two from the armoire;
and there was a great gap in the piles of lingerie on the shelf;
and her traveling-bag was missing, and so were her bits of
jewelry from the toilet tray—and Athénaïse was gone!

But the absurdity of going during the night, as if she had
been a prisoner, and he the keeper of a dungeon! So much
secrecy and mystery, to go sojourning out on the Bon Dieu!
Well, the Michés might keep their daughter after this. For
the companionship of no woman on earth would he again undergo the humiliating sensation of baseness that had overtaken him in passing the old oak-tree in the fallow meadow.

But a terrible sense of loss overwhelmed Cazeau. It was
not new or sudden; he had felt it for weeks growing upon
him, and it seemed to culminate with Athénaïse's flight from
home. He knew that he could again compel her return as he
had done once before,—compel her to return to the shelter of
his roof, compel her cold and unwilling submission to his love
and passionate transports; but the loss of self-respect seemed
to him too dear a price to pay for a wife.

He could not comprehend why she had seemed to prefer
him above others; why she had attracted him with eyes, with
voice, with a hundred womanly ways, and finally distracted
him with love which she seemed, in her timid, maidenly fashion, to return. The great sense of loss came from the realization of having missed a chance for happiness,—a chance that
would come his way again only through a miracle. He could
not think of himself loving any other woman, and could not
think of Athénaïse ever—even at some remote date—caring
for him.

He wrote her a letter, in which he disclaimed any further
intention of forcing his commands upon her. He did not
desire her presence ever again in his home unless she came of

her free will, uninfluenced by family or friends; unless she could be the companion he had hoped for in marrying her, and in some measure return affection and respect for the love which he continued and would always continue to feel for her. This letter he sent out to the rigolet by a messenger early in the day. But she was not out on the rigolet, and had not been there.

The family turned instinctively to Montéclin, and almost literally fell upon him for an explanation; he had been absent from home all night. There was much mystification in his answers, and a plain desire to mislead in his assurances of ignorance and innocence.

But with Cazeau there was no doubt or speculation when he accosted the young fellow. "Montéclin, w'at have you done with Athénaïse?" he questioned bluntly. They had met in the open road on horseback, just as Cazeau ascended the river bank before his house.

"W'at have you done to Athénaïse?" returned Montéclin for answer.

"I don't reckon you've considered yo' conduct by any light of decency an' propriety in encouraging yo' sister to such an action, but let me tell you"—

"Voyons! you can let me alone with yo' decency an' morality an' fiddlesticks. I know you mus' 'a' done Athénaïse pretty mean that she can't live with you; an' fo' my part, I'm mighty durn glad she had the spirit to quit you."

"I ain't in the humor to take any notice of yo' impertinence, Montéclin; but let me remine you that Athénaïse is nothing but a chile in character; besides that, she's my wife, an' I hol you responsible fo' her safety an' welfare. If any harm of any description happens to her, I'll strangle you, by God, like a rat, and fling you in Cane river, if I have to hang fo' it!" He had not lifted his voice. The only sign of anger was a savage gleam in his eyes.

"I reckon you better keep yo' big talk fo' the women, Cazeau," replied Montéclin, riding away.

But he went doubly armed after that, and intimated that the precaution was not needless, in view of the threats and menaces that were abroad touching his personal safety.

VI

Athénaïse reached her destination sound of skin and limb, but a good deal flustered, a little frightened, and altogether excited and interested by her unusual experiences.

Her destination was the house of Sylvie, on Dauphine Street, in New Orleans,—a three-story gray brick, standing directly on the banquette, with three broad stone steps leading to the deep front entrance. From the second-story balcony swung a small sign, conveying to passers-by the intelligence that within were *"chambres garnies."*[8]

It was one morning in the last week of April that Athénaïse presented herself at the Dauphine Street house. Sylvie was expecting her, and introduced her at once to her apartment, which was in the second story of the back ell, and accessible by an open, outside gallery. There was a yard below, paved with broad stone flagging; many fragrant flowering shrubs and plants grew in a bed along the side of the opposite wall, and others were distributed about in tubs and green boxes.

It was a plain but large enough room into which Athénaïse was ushered, with matting on the floor, green shades and Nottingham-lace curtains at the windows that looked out on the gallery, and furnished with a cheap walnut suit. But everything looked exquisitely clean, and the whole place smelled of cleanliness.

Athénaïse at once fell into the rocking-chair, with the air of exhaustion and intense relief of one who has come to the end of her troubles. Sylvie, entering behind her, laid the big traveling-bag on the floor and deposited the jacket on the bed.

She was a portly quadroon of fifty or there-about, clad in an ample *volante* of the old-fashioned purple calico so much affected by her class. She wore large golden hoop-earrings, and her hair was combed plainly, with every appearance of effort to smooth out the kinks. She had broad, coarse features, with a nose that turned up, exposing the wide nostrils, and that seemed to emphasize the loftiness and command of her bearing,—a dignity that in the presence of white people assumed a character of respectfulness, but never of obsequiousness. Sylvie believed firmly in maintaining the color line, and

[8]Furnished rooms.

would not suffer a white person, even a child, to call her "Madame Sylvie,"—a title which she exacted religiously, however, from those of her own race.

"I hope you be please' wid yo' room, madame," she observed amiably. "Dat's de same room w'at yo' brother, M'sieur Miché, all time like w'en he come to New Orlean'. He well, M'sieur Miché? I receive' his letter las' week, an' dat same day a gent'man want I give 'im dat room. I say, 'No, dat room already ingage'.' Ev-body like dat room on 'count it so quite (quiet). M'sieur Gouvernail, dere in nax' room, you can't pay 'im! He been stay t'ree year' in dat room; but all fix' up fine wid his own furn'ture an' books, 'tel you can't see! I say to 'im plenty time', 'M'sieur Gouvernail, w'y you don't take dat t'ree-story front, now, long it's empty?' He tells me, 'Leave me 'lone, Sylvie; I know a good room w'en I fine it, me.' "

She had been moving slowly and majestically about the apartment, straightening and smoothing down bed and pillows, peering into ewer and basin, evidently casting an eye around to make sure that everything was as it should be.

"I sen' you some fresh water, madame," she offered upon retiring from the room. "An' w'en you want an't'ing, you jus' go out on de gall'ry an' call Pousette: she year you plain,—she right down dere in de kitchen."

Athénaïse was really not so exhausted as she had every reason to be after that interminable and circuitous way by which Montéclin had seen fit to have her conveyed to that city.

Would she ever forget that dark and truly dangerous midnight ride along the "coast" to the mouth of Cane river! There Montéclin had parted with her, after seeing her aboard the St. Louis and Shreveport packet which he knew would pass there before dawn. She had received instructions to disembark at the mouth of Red river, and there transfer to the first south-bound steamer for New Orleans; all of which instructions she had followed implicitly, even to making her way at once to Sylvie's upon her arrival in the city. Montéclin had enjoined secrecy and much caution; the clandestine nature of the affair gave it a savor of adventure which was highly pleasing to him. Eloping with his sister was only a little less engaging than eloping with some one else's sister.

But Montéclin did not do the *grand seigneur*[9] by halves.

[9] Lord of the manor.

He had paid Sylvie a whole month in advance for Athénaïse's board and lodging. Part of the sum he had been forced to borrow, it is true, but he was not niggardly.

Athénaïse was to take her meals in the house, which none of the other lodgers did; the one exception being that Mr. Gouvernail was served with breakfast on Sunday mornings.

Sylvie's clientèle came chiefly from the southern parishes; for the most part, people spending but a few days in the city. She prided herself upon the quality and highly respectable character of her patrons, who came and went unobtrusively.

The large parlor opening upon the front balcony was seldom used. Her guests were permitted to entertain in this sanctuary of elegance,—but they never did. She often rented it for the night to parties of respectable and discreet gentlemen desiring to enjoy a quiet game of cards outside the bosom of their families. The second-story hall also led by a long window out on the balcony. And Sylvie advised Athénaïse, when she grew weary of her back room, to go and sit on the front balcony, which was shady in the afternoon, and where she might find diversion in the sounds and sights of the street below.

Athénaïse refreshed herself with a bath, and was soon unpacking her few belongings, which she ranged neatly away in the bureau drawers and the armoire.

She had revolved certain plans in her mind during the past hour or so. Her present intention was to live on indefinitely in this big, cool, clean back room on Dauphine street. She had thought seriously, for moments, of the convent, with all readiness to embrace the vows of poverty and chastity; but what about obedience? Later, she intended, in some roundabout way, to give her parents and her husband the assurance of her safety and welfare; reserving the right to remain unmolested and lost to them. To live on at the expense of Montéclin's generosity was wholly out of the question, and Athénaïse meant to look about for some suitable and agreeable employment.

The imperative thing to be done at present, however, was to go out in search of material for an inexpensive gown or two; for she found herself in the painful predicament of a young woman having almost literally nothing to wear. She decided upon pure white for one, and some sort of a sprigged muslin for the other.

VII

On Sunday morning, two days after Athénaïse's arrival in the city, she went in to breakfast somewhat later than usual, to find two covers laid at table instead of the one to which she was accustomed. She had been to mass, and did not remove her hat, but put her fan, parasol, and prayer-book aside. The dining-room was situated just beneath her own apartment, and, like all rooms of the house, was large and airy; the floor was covered with a glistening oil-cloth.

The small, round table, immaculately set, was drawn near the open window. There were some tall plants in boxes on the gallery outside; and Pousette, a little, old, intensely black woman, was splashing and dashing buckets of water on the flagging, and talking loud in her Creole patois to no one in particular.

A dish piled with delicate river-shrimps and crushed ice was on the table; a caraffe of crystal-clear water, a few *hors d'œuvres*, beside a small golden-brown crusty loaf of French bread at each plate. A half-bottle of wine and the morning paper were set at the place opposite Athénaïse.

She had almost completed her breakfast when Gouvernail came in and seated himself at table. He felt annoyed at finding his cherished privacy invaded. Sylvie was removing the remains of a mutton-chop from before Athénaïse, and serving her with a cup of café au lait.

"M'sieur Gouvernail," offered Sylvie in her most insinuating and impressive manner, "you please leave me make you acquaint' wid Madame Cazeau. Dat's M'sieur Miché's sister; you meet 'im two t'ree time', you rec'lec', an' been one day to de race wid 'im. Madame Cazeau, you please leave me make you acquaint' wid M'sieur Gouvernail."

Gouvernail expressed himself greatly pleased to meet the sister of Monsieur Miché, of whom he had not the slightest recollection. He inquired after Monsieur Miché's health, and politely offered Athénaïse a part of his newspaper,—the part which contained the Woman's Page and the social gossip.

Athénaïse faintly remembered that Sylvie had spoken of a Monsieur Gouvernail occupying the room adjoining hers, living amid luxurious surroundings and a multitude of books. She had not thought of him further than to picture him a stout, middle-aged gentleman, with a bushy beard turning gray, wearing large gold-rimmed spectacles, and stooping somewhat from much bending over books and writing material. She had confused him in her mind with the likeness of some literary celebrity that she had run across in the advertising pages of a magazine.

Gouvernail's appearance was, in truth, in no sense striking. He looked older than thirty and younger than forty, was of medium height and weight, with a quiet, unobtrusive manner which seemed to ask that he be let alone. His hair was light brown, brushed carefully and parted in the middle. His mustache was brown, and so were his eyes, which had a mild, penetrating quality. He was neatly dressed in the fashion of the day; and his hands seemed to Athénaïse remarkably white and soft for a man's.

He had been buried in the contents of his newspaper, when he suddenly realized that some further little attention might be due to Miché's sister. He started to offer her a glass of wine, when he was surprised and relieved to find that she had quietly slipped away while he was absorbed in his own editorial on Corrupt Legislation.

Gouvernail finished his paper and smoked his cigar out on the gallery. He lounged about, gathered a rose for his button-hole, and had his regular Sunday-morning confab with Pousette, to whom he paid a weekly stipend for brushing his shoes and clothing. He made a great pretense of haggling over the transaction, only to enjoy her uneasiness and garrulous excitement.

He worked or read in his room for a few hours, and when he quitted the house, at three in the afternoon, it was to return no more till late at night. It was his almost invariable custom to spend Sunday evenings out in the American quarter, among a congenial set of men and women,—*des esprits forts*,[10] all of them, whose lives were irreproachable, yet whose opinions would startle even the traditional "sapeur,"[11] for whom "nothing is sacred." But for all his "advanced" opinions, Gouvernail was a liberal-minded fellow; a man or woman lost nothing of his respect by being married.

When he left the house in the afternoon, Athénaïse had already ensconced herself on the front balcony. He could see her through the jalousies when he passed on his way to the front entrance. She had not yet grown lonesome or homesick; the newness of her surroundings made them sufficiently enter-

[10]Freethinkers.
[11]Rebel.

taining. She found it diverting to sit there on the front balcony watching people pass by, even though there was no one to talk to. And then the comforting, comfortable sense of not being married!

She watched Gouvernail walk down the street, and could find no fault with his bearing. He could hear the sound of her rockers for some little distance. He wondered what the "poor little thing" was doing in the city, and meant to ask Sylvie about her when he should happen to think of it.

VIII

The following morning, towards noon, when Gouvernail quitted his room, he was confronted by Athénaïse, exhibiting some confusion and trepidation at being forced to request a favor of him at so early a stage of their acquaintance. She stood in her doorway, and had evidently been sewing, as the thimble on her finger testified, as well as a long-threaded needle thrust in the bosom of her gown. She held a stamped but unaddressed letter in her hand.

And would Mr. Gouvernail be so kind as to address the letter to her brother, Mr. Montéclin Miché? She would hate to detain him with explanations this morning—another time, perhaps,—but now she begged that he would give himself the trouble.

He assured her that it made no difference, that it was no trouble whatever; and he drew a fountain pen from his pocket and addressed the letter at her dictation, resting it on the inverted rim of his straw hat. She wondered a little at a man of his supposed erudition stumbling over the spelling of "Montéclin" and "Miché."

She demurred at overwhelming him with the additional trouble of posting it, but he succeeded in convincing her that so simple a task as the posting of a letter would not add an iota to the burden of the day. Moreover, he promised to carry it in his hand, and thus avoid any possible risk of forgetting it in his pocket.

After that, and after a second repetition of the favor, when she had told him that she had had a letter from Montéclin, and looked as if she wanted to tell him more, he felt that he knew her better. He felt that he knew her well enough to join her out on the balcony, one night, when he found her sitting there alone. He was not one who deliberately sought the society of women, but he was not wholly a bear. A little commiseration for Athénaïse's aloneness, perhaps some curiosity to know further what manner of woman she was, and the natural influence of her feminine charm were equal unconfessed factors in turning his steps towards the balcony when he discovered the shimmer of her white gown through the open hall window.

It was already quite late, but the day had been intensely hot, and neighboring balconies and doorways were occupied by chattering groups of humanity, loath to abandon the grateful freshness of the outer air. The voices about her served to reveal to Athénaïse the feeling of loneliness that was gradually coming over her. Notwithstanding certain dormant impulses, she craved human sympathy and companionship.

She shook hands impulsively with Gouvernail, and told him how glad she was to see him. He was not prepared for such an admission, but it pleased him immensely, detecting as he did that the expression was as sincere as it was outspoken. He drew a chair up within comfortable conversational distance of Athénaïse, though he had no intention of talking more than was barely necessary to encourage Madame—He had actually forgotten her name!

He leaned an elbow on the balcony rail, and would have offered an opening remark about the oppressive heat of the day, but Athénaïse did not give him the opportunity. How glad she was to talk to some one, and how she talked!

An hour later she had gone to her room, and Gouvernail stayed smoking on the balcony. He knew her quite well after that hour's talk. It was not so much what she had said as what her half saying had revealed to his quick intelligence. He knew that she adored Montéclin, and he suspected that she adored Cazeau without being herself aware of it. He had gathered that she was self-willed, impulsive, innocent, ignorant, unsatisfied, dissatisfied; for had she not complained that things seemed all wrongly arranged in this world, and no one was permitted to be happy in his own way? And he told her he was sorry she had discovered that primordial fact of existence so early in life.

He commiserated her loneliness, and scanned his bookshelves next morning for something to lend her to read, rejecting everything that offered itself to his view. Philosophy was out of the question, and so was poetry; that is, such poetry as he possessed. He had not sounded her literary tastes, and strongly suspected she had none; that she would have reject-

ed The Duchess as readily as Mrs. Humphry Ward. He com-
promised on a magazine.

It had entertained her passably, she admitted, upon returning it. A New England story had puzzled her, it was true, and
a Creole tale had offended her, but the pictures had pleased
her greatly, especially one which had reminded her so strongly of Montéclin after a hard day's ride that she was loath to
give it up. It was one of Remington's Cowboys, and Gouvernail insisted upon her keeping it,—keeping the magazine.

He spoke to her daily after that, and was always eager to
render her some service or to do something towards her entertainment.

One afternoon he took her out to the lake end. She had
been there once, some years before, but in winter, so the trip
was comparatively new and strange to her. The large expanse
of water studded with pleasure-boats, the sight of children
playing merrily along the grassy palisades, the music, all en-
chanted her. Gouvernail thought her the most beautiful
woman he had ever seen. Even her gown—the sprigged
muslin—appeared to him the most charming one imaginable.
Nor could anything be more becoming than the arrangement
of her brown hair under the white sailor hat, all rolled back
in a soft puff from her radiant face. And she carried her
parasol and lifted her skirts and used her fan in ways that
seemed quite unique and peculiar to herself, and which he
considered almost worthy of study and imitation.

They did not dine out there at the water's edge, as they
might have done, but returned early to the city to avoid the
crowd. Athénaïse wanted to go home, for she said Sylvie
would have dinner prepared and would be expecting her. But
it was not difficult to persuade her to dine instead in the quiet
little restaurant that he knew and liked, with its sanded floor,
its secluded atmosphere, its delicious menu, and its obsequi-
ous waiter wanting to know what he might have the honor of
serving to "monsieur et madame." No wonder he made the
mistake, with Gouvernail assuming such an air of proprietorship! But Athénaïse was very tired after it all; the sparkle
went out of her face, and she hung draggingly on his arm in
walking home.

He was reluctant to part from her when she bade him
good-night at her door and thanked him for the agreeable
evening. He had hoped she would sit outside until it was time
for him to regain the newspaper office. He knew that she
would undress and get into her peignoir and lie upon her bed;

and what he wanted to do, what he would have given much to do, was to go and sit beside her, read to her something restful, soothe her, do her bidding, whatever it might be. Of course there was no use in thinking of that. But he was surprised at his growing desire to be serving her. She gave him an opportunity sooner than he looked for.

"Mr. Gouvernail," she called from her room, "will you be so kine as to call Pousette an' tell her she fo'got to bring my ice-water?"

He was indignant at Pousette's negligence, and called severely to her over the banisters. He was sitting before his own door, smoking. He knew that Athénaïse had gone to bed, for her room was dark, and she had opened the slats of the door and windows. Her bed was near a window.

Pousette came flopping up with the ice-water, and with a hundred excuses: "Mo pa oua vou à tab c'te lanuite, mo cri vou pé gagni déja là-bas; parole! Vou pas cri conté ça Madame Sylvie?" She had not seen Athénaïse at table, and thought she was gone. She swore to this, and hoped Madame Sylvie would not be informed of her remissness.

A little later Athénaïse lifted her voice again: "Mr. Gouvernail, did you remark that young man sitting on the opposite side from us, coming in, with a gray coat an' a blue ban' aroun' his hat?"

Of course Gouvernail had not noticed any such individual, but he assured Athénaïse that he had observed the young fellow particularly.

"Don't you think he looked something,—not very much, of co'se,—but don't you think he had a little faux-air of Montéclin?"

"I think he looked strikingly like Montéclin," asserted Gouvernail, with the one idea of prolonging the conversation. "I meant to call your attention to the resemblance, and something drove it out of my head."

"The same with me," returned Athénaïse. "Ah, my dear Montéclin! I wonder w'at he is doing now?"

"Did you receive any news, any letter from him to-day?" asked Gouvernail, determined that if the conversation ceased it should not be through lack of effort on his part to sustain it.

"Not to-day, but yesterday. He tells me that maman was so distracted with uneasiness that finally, to pacify her, he was fo'ced to confess that he knew w'ere I was, but that he was boun' by a vow of secrecy not to reveal it. But Cazeau has not noticed him or spoken to him since he threaten' to throw po' Montéclin in Cane river. You know Cazeau wrote me a letter the morning I lef', thinking I had gone to the rigolet. An' maman opened it, an' said it was full of the mos' noble sentiments, an' she wanted Montéclin to sen' it to me; but Montéclin refuse' poin' blank, so he wrote to me."

Gouvernail preferred to talk of Montéclin. He pictured Cazeau as unbearable, and did not like to think of him.

A little later Athénaïse called out, "Good-night, Mr. Gouvernail."

"Good-night," he returned reluctantly. And when he thought that she was sleeping, he got up and went away to the midnight pandemonium of his newspaper office.

IX

Athénaïse could not have held out through the month had it not been for Gouvernail. With the need of caution and secrecy always uppermost in her mind, she made no new acquaintances, and she did not seek out persons already known to her; however, she knew so few, it required little effort to keep out of their way. As for Sylvie, almost every moment of her time was occupied in looking after her house; and, moreover, her deferential attitude towards her lodgers forbade anything like the gossipy chats in which Athénaïse might have condescended sometimes to indulge with her land-lady. The transient lodgers, who came and went, she never had occasion to meet. Hence she was entirely dependent upon Gouvernail for company.

He appreciated the situation fully; and every moment that he could spare from his work he devoted to her entertainment. She liked to be out of doors, and they strolled together in the summer twilight through the mazes of the old French quarter. They went again to the lake end, and stayed for hours on the water; returning so late that the streets through which they passed were silent and deserted. On Sunday morning he arose at an unconscionable hour to take her to the French market, knowing that the sights and sounds there would interest her. And he did not join the intellectual coterie in the afternoon, as he usually did, but placed himself all day at the disposition and service of Athénaïse.

Notwithstanding all, his manner toward her was tactful, and evinced intelligence and a deep knowledge of her character, surprising upon so brief an acquaintance. For the time he was everything to her that she would have him; he replaced home and friends. Sometimes she wondered if he had ever loved a woman. She could not fancy him loving any one passionately, rudely, offensively, as Cazeau loved her. Once she was so naïve as to ask him outright if he had ever been in love, and he assured her promptly that he had not. She thought it an admirable trait in his character, and esteemed him greatly therefor.

He found her crying one night, not openly or violently. She was leaning over the gallery rail, watching the toads that hopped about in the moonlight, down on the damp flagstones of the courtyard. There was an oppressively sweet odor rising from the cape jassamine. Pousette was down there, mumbling and quarreling with some one, and seeming to be having it all her own way,—as well she might, when her companion was only a black cat that had come in from a neighboring yard to keep her company.

Athénaïse did admit feeling heart-sick, body-sick, when he questioned her; she supposed it was nothing but homesick. A letter from Montéclin had stirred her all up. She longed for her mother, for Montéclin; she was sick for a sight of the cotton-fields, the scent of the ploughed earth, for the dim, mysterious charm of the woods, and the old tumble-down home on the Bon Dieu.

As Gouvernail listened to her, a wave of pity and tenderness swept through him. He took her hands and pressed them against him. He wondered what would happen if he were to put his arms around her.

He was hardly prepared for what happened, but he stood it courageously. She twined her arms around his neck and wept outright on his shoulder; the hot tears scalding his cheek and neck, and her whole body shaken in his arms. The impulse was powerful to strain her to him; the temptation was fierce to seek her lips; but he did neither.

He understood a thousand times better than she herself understood it that he was acting as substitute for Montéclin. Bitter as the conviction was, he accepted it. He was patient; he could wait. He hoped some day to hold her with a lover's arms. That she was married made no particle of difference to Gouvernail. He could not conceive or dream of it making a difference. When the time came that she wanted him,—as he hoped and believed it would come,—he felt he would have a right to her. So long as she did not want him, he had no right to her,—no more than her husband had. It was very hard to

feel her warm breath and tears upon his cheek, and her struggling bosom pressed against him and her soft arms clinging to
him and his whole body and soul aching for her, and yet to
make no sign.

He tried to think what Montéclin would have said and
done, and to act accordingly. He stroked her hair, and held
her in a gentle embrace, until the tears dried and the sobs
ended. Before releasing herself she kissed him against the
neck; she had to love somebody in her own way! Even that
he endured like a stoic. But it was well he left her, to plunge
into the thick of rapid, breathless, exacting work till nearly
dawn.

Athénaïse was greatly soothed, and slept well. The touch
of friendly hands and caressing arms had been very grateful.
Henceforward she would not be lonely and unhappy, with
Gouvernail there to comfort her.

X

The fourth week of Athénaïse's stay in the city was
drawing to a close. Keeping in view the intention which she
had of finding some suitable and agreeable employment, she
had made a few tentatives in that direction. But with the exception of two little girls who had promised to take piano
lessons at a price that would be embarrassing to mention,
these attempts had been fruitless. Moreover, the homesickness
kept coming back, and Gouvernail was not always there to
drive it away.

She spent much of her time weeding and pottering among
the flowers down in the courtyard. She tried to take an interest in the black cat, and a mockingbird that hung in a cage
outside the kitchen door, and a disreputable parrot that belonged to the cook next door, and swore hoarsely all day long
in bad French.

Beside, she was not well; she was not herself, as she told
Sylvie. The climate of New Orleans did not agree with her.
Sylvie was distressed to learn this, as she felt in some
measure responsible for the health and well-being of Monsieur Miché's sister; and she made it her duty to inquire
closely into the nature and character of Athénaïse's malaise.

Sylvie was very wise, and Athénaïse was very ignorant.
The extent of her ignorance and the depth of her subsequent
enlightenment were bewildering. She stayed a long, long time
quite still, quite stunned, after her interview with Sylvie, ex-

cept for the short, uneven breathing that ruffled her bosom. Her whole being was steeped in a wave of ecstasy. When she finally arose from the chair in which she had been seated, and looked at herself in the mirror, a face met hers which she seemed to see for the first time, so transfigured was it with wonder and rapture.

One mood quickly followed another, in this new turmoil of her senses, and the need of action became uppermost. Her mother must know at once, and her mother must tell Montéclin. And Cazeau must know. As she thought of him, the first purely sensuous tremor of her life swept over her. She half whispered his name, and the sound of it brought red blotches into her cheeks. She spoke it over and over, as if it were some new, sweet sound born out of darkness and confusion, and reaching her for the first time. She was impatient to be with him. Her whole passionate nature was aroused as if by a miracle.

She seated herself to write to her husband. The letter he would get in the morning, and she would be with him at night. What would he say? How would he act? She knew that he would forgive her, for had he not written a letter?—and a pang of resentment toward Montéclin shot through her. What did he mean by withholding that letter? How dared he not have sent it?

Athénaïse attired herself for the street, and went out to post the letter which she had penned with a single thought, a spontaneous impulse. It would have seemed incoherent to most people, but Cazeau would understand.

She walked along the street as if she had fallen heir to some magnificent inheritance. On her face was a look of pride and satisfaction that passers-by noticed and admired. She wanted to talk to some one, to tell some person; and she stopped at the corner and told the oyster-woman, who was Irish, and who God-blessed her, and wished prosperity to the race of Cazeaus for generations to come. She held the oyster-woman's fat, dirty little baby in her arms and scanned it curiously and observingly, as if a baby were a phenomenon that she encountered for the first time in life. She even kissed it!

Then what a relief it was to Athénaïse to walk the streets without dread of being seen and recognized by some chance acquaintance from Red river! No one could have said now that she did not know her own mind.

She went directly from the oyster-woman's to the office of

Harding & Offdean, her husband's merchants; and it was with
such an air of partnership, almost proprietorship, that she demanded a sum of money on her husband's account, they gave
it to her as unhesitatingly as they would have handed it over
to Cazeau himself. When Mr. Harding, who knew her, asked
politely after her health, she turned so rosy and looked so
conscious, he thought it a great pity for so pretty a woman to
be such a little goose.

Athénaïse entered a dry-goods store and bought all manner of things,—little presents for nearly everybody she knew.
She bought whole bolts of sheerest, softest, downiest white
stuff; and when the clerk, in trying to meet her wishes, asked
if she intended it for infant's use, she could have sunk
through the floor, and wondered how he might have suspected it.

As it was Montéclin who had taken her away from her
husband, she wanted it to be Montéclin who should take her
back to him. So she wrote him a very curt note,—in fact it
was a postal card,—asking that he meet her at the train on
the evening following. She felt convinced that after what had
gone before, Cazeau would await her at their own home; and
she preferred it so.

Then there was the agreeable excitement of getting ready
to leave, of packing up her things. Pousette kept coming and
going, coming and going; and each time that she quitted the
room it was with something that Athénaïse had given her,—
a handkerchief, a petticoat, a pair of stockings with two tiny
holes at the toes, some broken prayer-beads, and finally a silver dollar.

Next it was Sylvie who came along bearing a gift of what
she called "a set of pattern',"—things of complicated design
which never could have been obtained in any new-fangled ba-
zaar or pattern-store, that Sylvie had acquired of a foreign
lady of distinction whom she had nursed years before at the
St. Charles hotel. Athénaïse accepted and handled them with
reverence, fully sensible of the great compliment and favor,
and laid them religiously away in the trunk which she had
lately acquired.

She was greatly fatigued after the day of unusual exertion,
and went early to bed and to sleep. All day long she had not
once thought of Gouvernail, and only did think of him when
aroused for a brief instant by the sound of his foot-falls on
the gallery, as he passed in going to his room. He had hoped
to find her up, waiting for him.

But the next morning he knew. Some one must have told him. There was no subject known to her which Sylvie hesitated to discuss in detail with any man of suitable years and discretion.

Athénaïse found Gouvernail waiting with a carriage to convey her to the railway station. A momentary pang visited her for having forgotten him so completely, when he said to her, "Sylvie tells me you are going away this morning."

He was kind, attentive, and amiable, as usual, but respected to the utmost the new dignity and reserve that her manner had developed since yesterday. She kept looking from the carriage window, silent, and embarrassed as Eve after losing her ignorance. He talked of the muddy streets and the murky morning, and of Montéclin. He hoped she would find everything comfortable and pleasant in the country, and trusted she would inform him whenever she came to visit the city again. He talked as if afraid or mistrustful of silence and himself.

At the station she handed him her purse, and he bought her ticket, secured for her a comfortable section, checked her trunk, and got all the bundles and things safely aboard the train. She felt very grateful. He pressed her hand warmly, lifted his hat, and left her. He was a man of intelligence, and took defeat gracefully; that was all. But as he made his way back to the carriage, he was thinking, "By heaven, it hurts, it hurts!"

XI

Athénaïse spent a day of supreme happiness and expectancy. The fair sight of the country unfolding itself before her was balm to her vision and to her soul. She was charmed with the rather unfamiliar, broad, clean sweep of the sugar plantations, with their monster sugar-houses, their rows of neat cabins like little villages of a single street, and their impressive homes standing apart amid clusters of trees. There were sudden glimpses of a bayou curling between sunny, grassy banks, or creeping sluggishly out from a tangled growth of wood, and brush, and fern, and poison-vines, and palmettos. And passing through the long stretches of monotonous woodlands, she would close her eyes and taste in anticipation the moment of her meeting with Cazeau. She could think of nothing but him.

It was night when she reached her station. There was

Montéclin, as she had expected, waiting for her with a two-seated buggy, to which he had hitched his own swift-footed, spirited pony. It was good, he felt, to have her back on any terms; and he had no fault to find since she came of her own choice. He more than suspected the cause of her coming; her eyes and her voice and her foolish little manner went far in revealing the secret that was brimming over in her heart. But after he had deposited her at her own gate, and as he continued his way toward the rigolet, he could not help feeling that the affair had taken a very disappointing, an ordinary, a most commonplace turn, after all. He left her in Cazeau's keeping.

Her husband lifted her out of the buggy, and neither said a word until they stood together within the shelter of the gallery. Even then they did not speak at first. But Athénaïse turned to him with an appealing gesture. As he clasped her in his arms, he felt the yielding of her whole body against him. He felt her lips for the first time respond to the passion of his own.

The country night was dark and warm and still, save for the distant notes of an accordion which some one was playing in a cabin away off. A little negro baby was crying somewhere. As Athénaïse withdrew from her husband's embrace, the sound arrested her.

"Listen, Cazeau! How Juliette's baby is crying! Pauvre ti chou,[12] I wonder w'at is the matter with it?"

Written, 1895; published, 1896

---

[12]"Poor little dear."

A Pair of Silk Stockings

LITTLE Mrs. Sommers one day found herself the unexpected possessor of fifteen dollars. It seemed to her a very large amount of money, and the way in which it stuffed and bulged her worn old *porte-monnaie* gave her a feeling of importance such as she had not enjoyed for years.

The question of investment was one that occupied her greatly. For a day or two she walked about apparently in a dreamy state, but really absorbed in speculation and calculation. She did not wish to act hastily, to do anything she might afterward regret. But it was during the still hours of the night when she lay awake revolving plans in her mind that she seemed to see her way clearly toward a proper and judicious use of the money.

A dollar or two should be added to the price usually paid for Janie's shoes, which would insure their lasting an appreciable time longer than they usually did. She would buy so and so many yards of percale for new shirt waists for the boys and Janie and Mag. She had intended to make the old ones do by skilful patching. Mag should have another gown. She had seen some beautiful patterns, veritable bargains in the shop windows. And still there would be left enough for new stockings—two pairs apiece—and what darning that would save for a while! She would get caps for the boys and sailor-hats for the girls. The vision of her little brood looking fresh and dainty and new for once in their lives excited her and made her restless and wakeful with anticipation.

The neighbors sometimes talked of certain "better days" that little Mrs. Sommers had known before she had ever thought of being Mrs. Sommers. She herself indulged in no such morbid retrospection. She had no time—no second of time to devote to the past. The needs of the present absorbed her every faculty. A vision of the future like some dim, gaunt monster sometimes appalled her, but luckily to-morrow never comes.

Mrs. Sommers was one who knew the value of bargains; who could stand for hours making her way inch by inch toward the desired object that was selling below cost. She could elbow her way if need be; she had learned to clutch a piece of goods and hold it and stick to it with persistence and determination till her turn came to be served, no matter when it came.

But that day she was a little faint and tired. She had swallowed a light luncheon—no! when she came to think of it, between getting the children fed and the place righted, and preparing herself for the shopping bout, she had actually forgotten to eat any luncheon at all!

She sat herself upon a revolving stool before a counter that was comparatively deserted, trying to gather strength and courage to charge through an eager multitude that was besieging breast-works of shirting and figured lawn. An all-gone limp feeling had come over her and she rested her hand aimlessly upon the counter. She wore no gloves. By degrees she grew aware that her hand had encountered something very soothing, very pleasant to touch. She looked down to see that her hand lay upon a pile of silk stockings. A placard near by announced that they had been reduced in price from two dollars and fifty cents to one dollar and ninety-eight cents; and a young girl who stood behind the counter asked her if she wished to examine their line of silk hosiery. She smiled, just as if she had been asked to inspect a tiara of diamonds with the ultimate view of purchasing it. But she went on feeling the soft, sheeny luxurious things—with both hands now, holding them up to see them glisten, and to feel them glide serpent-like through her fingers.

Two hectic blotches came suddenly into her pale cheeks. She looked up at the girl.

"Do you think there are any eights-and-a-half among these?"

There were any number of eights-and-a-half. In fact, there were more of that size than any other. Here was a light-blue pair; there were some lavender, some all black and various shades of tan and gray. Mrs. Sommers selected a black pair and looked at them very long and closely. She pretended to be examining their texture, which the clerk assured her was excellent.

"A dollar and ninety-eight cents," she mused aloud. "Well, I'll take this pair." She handed the girl a five-dollar bill and waited for her change and for her parcel. What a very small parcel it was. It seemed lost in the depths of her shabby old shopping-bag.

Mrs. Sommers after that did not move in the direction of the bargain counter. She took the elevator, which carried her to an upper floor into the region of the ladies' waiting-rooms. Here, in a retired corner, she exchanged her cotton stockings for the new silk ones which she had just bought. She was not going through any acute mental process or reasoning with herself, nor was she striving to explain to her satisfaction the motive of her action. She was not thinking at all. She seemed for the time to be taking a rest from that laborious and fatiguing function and to have abandoned herself to some mechanical impulse that directed her actions and freed her of responsibility.

How good was the touch of the raw silk to her flesh! She felt like lying back in the cushioned chair and reveling for a while in the luxury of it. She did for a little while. Then she replaced her shoes, rolled the cotton stockings together and thrust them into her bag. After doing this she crossed straight over to the shoe department and took her seat to be fitted.

She was fastidious. The clerk could not make her out; he could not reconcile her shoes with her stockings, and she was not too easily pleased. She held back her skirts and turned her feet one way and her head another way as she glanced down at the polished, pointed-tipped boots. Her foot and ankle looked very pretty. She could not realize that they belonged to her and were a part of herself. She wanted an excellent and stylish fit, she told the young fellow who served her, and she did not mind the difference of a dollar or two more in the price so long as she got what she desired.

It was a long time since Mrs. Sommers had been fitted with gloves. On rare occasions when she had bought a pair they were always "bargains," so cheap that it would have been preposterous and unreasonable to have expected them to be fitted to the hand.

Now she rested her elbow on the cushion of the glove counter, and a pretty, pleasant young creature, delicate and deft of touch, drew a long-wristed "kid" over Mrs. Sommers' hand. She smoothed it down over the wrist and buttoned it neatly, and both lost themselves for a second or two in admiring contemplation of the little symmetrical gloved hand. But there were other places where money might be spent.

There were books and magazines piled up in the window of a stall a few paces down the street. Mrs. Sommers bought two high-priced magazines such as she had been accustomed to read in the days when she had been accustomed to other pleasant things. She carried them without wrapping. As well as she could she lifted her skirts at the crossings. Her stockings and boots and well-fitting gloves had worked marvels in her bearing—had given her a feeling of assurance, a sense of belonging to the well-dressed multitude.

She was very hungry. Another time she would have stilled the cravings for food until reaching her own home, where she would have brewed herself a cup of tea and taken a snack of anything that was available. But the impulse that was guiding her would not suffer her to entertain any such thought.

There was a restaurant at the corner. She had never entered its doors; from the outside she had sometimes caught glimpses of spotless damask and shining crystal, and soft-stepping waiters serving people of fashion.

When she entered her appearance created no surprise, no consternation, as she had half feared it might. She seated herself at a small table alone, and an attentive waiter at once approached to take her order. She did not want a profusion; she craved a nice and tasty bite—a half dozen blue-points, a plump chop with cress, a something sweet—a crème-frappée, for instance; a glass of Rhine wine, and after all a small cup of black coffee.

While waiting to be served she removed her gloves very leisurely and laid them beside her. Then she picked up a magazine and glanced through it, cutting the pages with a blunt edge of her knife. It was all very agreeable. The damask was even more spotless than it had seemed through the window, and the crystal more sparkling. There were quiet ladies and gentlemen, who did not notice her, lunching at the small tables like her own. A soft, pleasing strain of music could be heard, and a gentle breeze was blowing through the window. She tasted a bite, and she read a word or two, and she sipped the amber wine and wiggled her toes in the silk stockings. The price of it made no difference. She counted the money out to the waiter and left an extra coin on his tray, whereupon he bowed before her as before a princess of royal blood.

There was still money in her purse, and her next temptation presented itself in the shape of a matinée poster.

It was a little later when she entered the theatre, the play had begun and the house seemed to her to be packed. But there were vacant seats here and there, and into one of them she was ushered, between brilliantly dressed women who had gone there to kill time and eat candy and display their gaudy attire. There were many others who were there solely for the play and acting. It is safe to say there was no one present who bore quite the attitude which Mrs. Sommers did to her surroundings. She gathered in the whole—stage and players and people in one wide impression, and absorbed it and enjoyed it. She laughed at the comedy and wept—she and the gaudy woman next to her wept over the tragedy. And they talked a little together over it. And the gaudy woman wiped her eyes and sniffled on a tiny square of filmy, perfumed lace and passed little Mrs. Sommers her box of candy.

The play was over, the music ceased, the crowd filed out. It was like a dream ended. People scattered in all directions. Mrs. Sommers went to the corner and waited for the cable car.

A man with keen eyes, who sat opposite to her, seemed to like the study of her small, pale face. It puzzled him to decipher what he saw there. In truth, he saw nothing—unless he were wizard enough to detect a poignant wish, a powerful longing that the cable car would never stop anywhere, but go on and on with her forever.

Written, 1896; published, 1897

The Storm

A Sequel to "The 'Cadian Ball"

I

THE LEAVES were so still that even Bibi thought it was going to rain. Bobinôt, who was accustomed to converse on terms of perfect equality with his little son, called the child's attention to certain sombre clouds that were rolling with sinister intention from the west, accompanied by a sullen, threatening roar. They were at Friedheimer's store and decided to remain there till the storm had passed. They sat within the door on two empty kegs. Bibi was four years old and looked very wise.

"Mama'll be 'fraid, yes," he suggested with blinking eyes.

"She'll shut the house. Maybe she got Sylvie helpin' her this evenin'," Bobinôt responded reassuringly.

"No; she ent got Sylvie. Sylvie was helpin' her yistiday," piped Bibi.

Bobinôt arose and going across to the counter purchased a can of shrimps, of which Calixta was very fond. Then he returned to his perch on the keg and sat stolidly holding the can of shrimps while the storm burst. It shook the wooden store and seemed to be ripping great furrows in the distant field. Bibi laid his little hand on his father's knee and was not afraid.

II

Calixta, at home, felt no uneasiness for their safety. She sat at a side window sewing furiously on a sewing machine. She was greatly occupied and did not notice the approaching storm. But she felt very warm and often stopped to mop her face on which the perspiration gathered in beads. She unfas-

244

tened her white sacque at the throat. It began to grow dark, and suddenly realizing the situation she got up hurriedly and went about closing windows and doors.

Out on the small front gallery she had hung Bobinôt's Sunday clothes to air and she hastened out to gather them before the rain fell. As she stepped outside, Alcée Laballière rode in at the gate. She had not seen him very often since her marriage, and never alone. She stood there with Bobinôt's coat in her hands, and the big rain drops began to fall. Alcée rode his horse under the shelter of a side projection where the chickens had huddled and there were plows and a harrow piled up in the corner.

"May I come and wait on your gallery till the storm is over, Calixta?" he asked.

"Come 'long in, M'sieur Alcée."

His voice and her own startled her as if from a trance, and she seized Bobinôt's vest. Alcée, mounting to the porch, grabbed the trousers and snatched Bibi's braided jacket that was about to be carried away by a sudden gust of wind. He expressed an intention to remain outside, but it was soon apparent that he might as well have been out in the open: the water beat in upon the boards in driving sheets, and he went inside, closing the door after him. It was even necessary to put something beneath the door to keep the water out.

"My! what a rain! It's good two years sence it rain' like that," exclaimed Calixta as she rolled up a piece of bagging and Alcée helped her to thrust it beneath the crack.

She was a little fuller of figure than five years before when she married; but she had lost nothing of her vivacity. Her blue eyes still retained their melting quality; and her yellow hair, dishevelled by the wind and rain, kinked more stubbornly than ever about her ears and temples.

The rain beat upon the low, shingled roof with a force and clatter that threatened to break an entrance and deluge them there. They were in the dining room—the sitting room—the general utility room. Adjoining was her bed room, with Bibi's couch along side her own. The door stood open, and the room with its white, monumental bed, its closed shutters, looked dim and mysterious.

Alcée flung himself into a rocker and Calixta nervously began to gather up from the floor the lengths of a cotton sheet which she had been sewing.

"If this keeps up, *Dieu sait*[1] if the levees goin' to stan' it!" she exclaimed.

"What have you got to do with the leeves?"

"I got enough to do! An' there's Bobinôt with Bibi out in that storm—if he only didn' left Friedheimer's!"

"Let us hope, Calixta, that Bobinôt's got sense enough to come in out of a cyclone."

She went and stood at the window with a greatly disturbed look on her face. She wiped the frame that was clouded with moisture. It was stiflingly hot. Alcée got up and joined her at the window, looking over her shoulder. The rain was coming down in sheets obscuring the view of far-off cabins and enveloping the distant wood in a gray mist. The playing of the lightning was incessant. A bolt struck a tall chinaberry tree at the edge of the field. It filled all visible space with a blinding glare and the crash seemed to invade the very boards they stood upon.

Calixta put her hands to her eyes, and with a cry, staggered backward. Alcée's arm encircled her, and for an instant he drew her close and spasmodically to him.

"*Bonté*"[2] she cried, releasing herself from his encircling arm and retreating from the window, "the house'll go next! If I only knew w'ere Bibi was!" She would not compose herself; she would not be seated. Alcée clasped her shoulders and looked into her face. The contact of her warm, palpitating body when he had unthinkingly drawn her into his arms, had aroused all the old-time infatuation and desire for her flesh.

"Calixta," he said, "don't be frightened. Nothing can happen. The house is too low to be struck, with so many tall trees standing about. There! aren't you going to be quiet? say, aren't you?" He pushed her hair back from her face that was warm and steaming. Her lips were as red and moist as pomegranate seed. Her white neck and a glimpse of her full, firm bosom disturbed him powerfully. As she glanced up at him the fear in her liquid blue eyes had given place to a drowsy gleam that unconsciously betrayed a sensuous desire. He looked down into her eyes and there was nothing for him to do but to gather her lips in a kiss. It reminded him of Assumption.

"Do you remember—in Assumption, Calixta?" he asked in a low voice broken by passion. Oh! she remembered; for in

[1]God knows.
[2]"Goodness!"

Assumption he had kissed her and kissed and kissed her; until his senses would well nigh fail, and to save her he would resort to a desperate flight. If she was not an immaculate dove in those days, she was still inviolate; a passionate creature whose very defenselessness had made her defense, against which his honor forbade him to prevail. Now—well, now—her lips seemed in a manner free to be tasted, as well as her round, white throat and her whiter breasts.

They did not heed the crashing torrents, and the roar of the elements made her laugh as she lay in his arms. She was a revelation in that dim, mysterious chamber; as white as the couch she lay upon. Her firm, elastic flesh that was knowing for the first time its birthright, was like a creamy lily that the sun invites to contribute its breath and perfume to the undying life of the world.

The generous abundance of her passion, without guile or trickery, was like a white flame which penetrated and found response in depths of his own sensuous nature that had never yet been reached.

When he touched her breasts they gave themselves up in quivering ecstasy, inviting his lips. Her mouth was a fountain of delight. And when he possessed her, they seemed to swoon together at the very borderland of life's mystery.

He stayed cushioned upon her, breathless, dazed, enervated, with his heart beating like a hammer upon her. With one hand she clasped his head, her lips lightly touching his forehead. The other hand stroked with a soothing rhythm his muscular shoulders.

The growl of the thunder was distant and passing away. The rain beat softly upon the shingles, inviting them to drowsiness and sleep. But they dared not yield.

The rain was over; and the sun was turning the glistening green world into a palace of gems. Calixta, on the gallery, watched Alcée ride away. He turned and smiled at her with a beaming face; and she lifted her pretty chin in the air and laughed aloud.

III

Bobinôt and Bibi, trudging home, stopped without at the cistern to make themselves presentable.

"My! Bibi, w'at will yo' mama say! You ought to be ashame'. You oughtn' put on those good pants. Look at 'em! An' that mud on yo' collar! How you got that mud on yo' collar, Bibi? I never saw such a boy!" Bibi was the picture of pathetic resignation. Bobinôt was the embodiment of serious solicitude as he strove to remove from his own person and his son's the signs of their tramp over heavy roads and through wet fields. He scraped the mud off Bibi's bare legs and feet with a stick and carefully removed all traces from his heavy brogans. Then, prepared for the worst—the meeting with an over-scrupulous housewife, they entered cautiously at the back door.

Calixta was preparing supper. She had set the table and was dripping coffee at the hearth. She sprang up as they came in.

"Oh, Bobinôt! You back! My! but I was uneasy. W'ere you been during the rain? An' Bibi? he ain't wet? he ain't hurt?" She had clasped Bibi and was kissing him effusively. Bobinôt's explanations and apologies which he had been composing all along the way, died on his lips as Calixta felt him to see if he were dry, and seemed to express nothing but satisfaction at their safe return.

"I brought you some shrimps, Calixta," offered Bobinôt, hauling the can from his ample side pocket and laying it on the table.

"Shrimps! Oh, Bobinôt! you too good fo' anything!" and she gave him a smacking kiss on the cheek that resounded. "J'vous réponds,[3] we'll have a feas' to-night! umph-umph!"

Bobinôt and Bibi began to relax and enjoy themselves, and when the three seated themselves at table they laughed much and so loud that anyone might have heard them as far away as Laballière's.

IV

Alcée Laballière wrote to his wife, Clarisse, that night. It was a loving letter, full of tender solicitude. He told her not to hurry back, but if she and the babies liked it at Biloxi, to stay a month longer. He was getting on nicely; and though he missed them, he was willing to bear the separation a while longer—realizing that their health and pleasure were the first things to be considered.

[3] "I give you my word."

V

As for Clarisse, she was charmed upon receiving her husband's letter. She and the babies were doing well. The society was agreeable; many of her old friends and acquaintances were at the bay. And the first free breath since her marriage seemed to restore the pleasant liberty of her maiden days. Devoted as she was to her husband, their intimate conjugal life was something which she was more than willing to forego for a while.

So the storm passed and every one was happy.

Written, 1898; published, 1969

Charlie

SIX OF Mr. Laborde's charming daughters had been assembled for the past half hour in the study room. The seventh, Charlotte, or Charlie as she was commonly called, had not yet made her appearance. The study was a very large corner room with openings leading out upon the broad upper gallery.

Hundreds of birds were singing out in the autumn foliage. A little stern-wheeler was puffing and sputtering, making more commotion than a man-o'-war as she rounded the bend. The river was almost under the window—just on the other side of the high green levee.

At one of the windows, seated before a low table covered with kindergarten paraphernalia were the twins, nearing six, Paula and Pauline, who were but a few weeks old when their mother died. They were round-faced youngsters with white pinafores and chubby hands. They peeped out at the little snorting stern-wheeler and whispered to each other about it. The eldest sister, Julia, a slender girl of nineteen, rapped upon her desk. She was diligently reading her English Literature. Her hands were as white as lilies and she wore a blue ring and a soft white gown. The other sisters were Charlotte, the absentee, just past her seventeenth birthday, Amanda, Irene, and Fidelia; girls of sixteen, fourteen and ten who looked neat and trim in their ginghams; with shining hair plaited on either side and tied with large bows of ribbon.

Each girl occupied a separate desk. There was a broad table at one end of the room before which Miss Melvern the governess seated herself when she entered. She was tall, with a refined though determined expression. The "Grandfather's Clock" pointed to a quarter of nine as she came in. Her pupils continued to work in silence while she busied herself in arranging the contents of the table.

The little stern-wheeler had passed out of sight though not out of hearing. But again the attention of the twins was engaged with something outside and again their curly heads met across the table.

"Paula," called Miss Melvern, "I don't think it is quite nice to whisper in that way and interrupt your sisters at their work. What are you two looking at out of the window?"

"Looking at Charlie," spoke Paula quite bravely while Pauline glanced down timidly and picked her fingers. At the mention of Charlie, Miss Melvern's face assumed a severe expression and she cautioned the little girls to confine their attention to the task before them.

The sight of Charlie galloping along the green levee summit on a big black horse, as if pursued by demons, was surely enough to distract the attention of any one from any thing.

Presently there was a clatter of hoofs upon the ground below, the voice of a girl pitched rather high was heard and the apologetic, complaining whine of a young negro.

"I didn' have no time, Miss Charlie. It's hones', I never had no time. I tole Marse Laborde you gwine git mad an' fuss. You c'n ax Aleck."

"Get mad and fuss! Didn't have time! Look at that horse's back—look at it. I'll give you time and something else in the bargain. Just let me catch Tim's back looking like that again, sir."

The twins were plainly agitated, and kept looking alternately at Miss Melvern's imperturbable face and at the door through which they expected their sister to enter.

A quick footstep sounded along the corridor, the door was thrown hurriedly open, and in came Charlie. She looked right up at the clock, uttered an exclamation of disgust, jerked off her little cloth cap and started toward her desk. She was robust and pretty well grown for her age. Her hair was cut short and was so damp with perspiration that it clung to her head and looked almost black. Her face was red and overheated at the moment. She wore a costume of her own devising, something between bloomers and a divided skirt which she called her "trouserlets." Canvas leggings, dusty boots and a single spur completed her costume.

"Charlotte!" called Miss Melvern arresting the girl. Charlie stood still and faced the governess. She felt in both side pockets of her trouserlets for a handkerchief which she finally abstracted from a hip pocket. It was not a very white or fresh looking handkerchief; nevertheless she wiped her face with it.

"If you remember," said Miss Melvern, "the last time you came in late to study—which was only the day before yesterday—I told you that if it occurred again I should have to speak to your father. It's getting to be an almost every day affair, and I cannot consent to have your sisters repeatedly interrupted in this way. Take your books and go elsewhere to study until I can see your father." Charlie was gazing dejectedly at the polished floor and continuing to mop her face with the soiled handkerchief. She started to blurt out an apology, checked herself and crossing over to her desk provided herself with a few books and some scraps of paper.

"I'd rather you wouldn't speak to father this once," she appealed, but Miss Melvern only motioned with her head toward the door and the girl went out; not sullenly, but lugubriously. The twins looked at each other with serious eyes while Irene frowned savagely behind the pages of her geography.

It was not many moments before a young black girl came and thrust her head in at the door, rolling two great eyes which she had under very poor control.

"Miss Charlie 'low, please sen' her pencil w'at she lef' behine; an' if Miss Julia wants to give her some dem smove sheets o' paper; an' she be obleege if Miss Irene len' her de fountain pen, des dis once."

Irene darted forward, but subsided at a glance from Miss Melvern. That lady handed the black emissary a pencil and tablet from the table.

Before very long she was back again interrupting the exercises to lay a bulky wad before the governess. It was an elaborate description of the unavoidable adventures which had retarded Charlie's appearance in the study room.

"That will do, Blossom," said Miss Melvern severely, motioning the girl to be gone.

"She wants me to wait fo' an' answer," responded Blossom settling herself comfortably against the door jamb.

"That will do, Blossom," with distinct emphasis, whereupon Blossom reluctantly took her leave. But before long she was back again, nothing daunted and solemnly placed in Miss Melvern's unwilling hand a single folded sheet. Whereupon she retired with a slow dignity which convinced the twins that a telling and important strike had been accomplished by the absent Charlie. This time it was a poem—an original poem, and it began:

"Relentless Fate, and thou, relentless Friend!"

Its composition had cost Charlie much laborious breathing and some hard wrung drops from her perspiring brow. Charlie had a way, when strongly moved, of expressing herself in verse. She was greatly celebrated for two notable achievements in her life. One was the writing of a lengthy ode upon the occasion of her Grandmother's seventieth birthday; but she was perhaps more distinguished for having once saved the levee during a time of perilous overflow when her father was away. It was a story in which an unloaded revolver played a part, demoralized negroes and earth-filled gunny sacks. It got into the papers and made a heroine of her for a week or two.

On the other hand, it would be difficult to enumerate Charlie's shortcomings. She never seemed to do anything that anyone except her father approved of. Yet she was popularly described as not having a mean bone in her body.

Charlie was seated in a tilted chair, her heels on the rung, and in the intervals of composition her attention was greatly distracted by her surroundings. She sat outside on the brick or "false gallery" that formed a sort of long corridor at the back of the house. There was always a good deal going on out there. The kitchen was a little removed from the house. There was a huge live oak under whose spreading branches a few negro children were always playing—a few clucking chickens always scratching in the dust. People who rode in from the field always fastened their horses there. A young negro was under the tree, sharpening his axe at the grindstone while the big fat cook stood in the kitchen door abusing him in unmeasured terms. He was her own child, so she enjoyed the privilege of dealing with him as harshly as the law allowed.

"W'at you did wid dat gode (gourd) you, demins. You kiar water to de grine stone wid it! I tell you, boy, dey be kiarrin' water in yo' skull time I git tho' wid you. Fetch dat gode back heah whar it b'longs. I gwine break eve'y bone in yo' body, an' I gwine tu'n you over to yo' pa: he make jelly outen yo' hide an taller."

The fat woman's vituperations were interrupted by the shock of a well-aimed missile squarely striking her broad body.

"If there are going to be any bones broken around here, I'll take a hand in it and I'll begin with you, Aunt Maryllis. What do you mean by making such a racket when you see me studying out here?"

"I gwine tell yo' pa, Miss Charlie. Dis time I gwine tell 'im sho'. Marse Laborde ain' gwine let you keep on cripplin' his han's scand'lous like you does. You, Demins! run 'long to de cabin, honey, an' fetch yo' mammy de spirits o' camphire." She turned back in the kitchen bent almost double, holding her hand sprawled over her ponderous side.

It was indeed very trying to Charlie to be thus interrupted in her second stanza as she was vainly striving after a suitable rhyme for "persecution." And again there was Aurendele, the 'Cadian girl, stalking across the yard with a brace of chickens to sell. She had them tied together at the legs with a strip of cotton cloth and they hung from her hand head downward motionless.

"He! what do you want? Aurendele!" Charlie called out. The girl piped shrilly back from the depths of a gingham sun-bonnet.

"I lookin' fo' Ma'me Philomel, see if she want buy couple fine pullets. They fine, yes," she reiterated holding them out for Charlie's inspection. "We raise 'em from that Plymouth Rock. They ain't no Creole chicken, them, they good breed, you c'n see fo' yo'se'f."

"Plymouth fiddlesticks! You'd better hold on to them and try to sell them to the circus as curiosities: 'The feathered skeletons.' Here, Demins! turn these martyrs loose. Give them water and corn and rub some oil on their legs . . .

"No, Aurendele, I was only joking. I don't know how you can part with those Plymouth Rocks; you'll feel the separa-tion and it'll go hard with your mother and the children. What do you want for them?"

Aurendele only wanted a little coffee and flour, a piece of fine soap, some blue ribbon such as her sister Odélia had bought at the store and a yard of "cross-bars" for a sunbon-net for Nannouche.

Charlie directed the girl to Ma'me Philomel. "And you ought to know better," she added, "than to stand here talking when you see I'm busy with my lessons."

"You please escuse me, Miss Charlie, I didn' know you was busy. W'ere you say I c'n fine Ma'me Philomel?"

And Charlie went back to the closing stanza which was something of an exhortation: "Let me not look again upon thy face While frowning mood, of joy usurps the place."

The poem being finished, signed and duly delivered by Blossom, the sister of Demins, Charlie felt that she had brought her intellectual labors to a fitting close.

A moment before, a negro had wheeled into the yard on a

hand-cart Charlie's new bicycle. It had been deposited at the landing by the little stern-wheeler earlier in the morning, and to witness and superintend its debarkation had been the cause of Charlie's tardiness in the class room. Now, with the assistance of Demins and Blossom the wheel was unpacked and adjusted under the live oak. It was a beauty, of very latest construction. Charlie had traded her old wheel with Uncle Ruben for an afflicted pony which she had great hope of saving and training for speed. The discarded bicycle was intended as a gift for Uncle Ruben's bride. Since its presentation the bride had not been seen in public.

Charlie mounted and gave an exhibition of her skill to a delighted audience of negroes, chickens and a few dogs. Then she decided that she would ride out in search of her father. It was not on her own account that she had entreated Miss Melvern's silence, it was on his. She realized that she was a difficult and perhaps annoying problem for him, and did not relish the idea of adding to his perplexity.

As Charlie wheeled past the kitchen she peeped furtively in at the window. Aunt Maryllis was kneading a lump of dough with one hand while the other was still clapped to her side. Charlie felt remorseful and wondered whether Aunt Maryllis would rather have fifty cents or a new bandana! But the gate was open, and away she went, down the long inviting level road that led to the sugar mill.

II

Miss Melvern in a moment of exasperation had once asked Charlie if she were wholly devoid of a moral sense. The expression was rather cruelly forceful, but the provocation had been unusually trying. And Charlie was so far devoid of the sense in question as not to be stung by the implication. She really felt that nothing made much difference so long as her father was happy. Her actions were reprehensible in her own eyes only so far as they interfered with his peace of mind. Therefore a great part of her time was employed in apologetic atonement and the framing of vast and unattainable resolutions.

An easy solution would have been to send Charlie away to boarding school. But upon the point of separation from any of his daughters, Mr. Laborde had set his heart with stubborn determination. He had once vaguely entertained the expedient of a second marriage, but was quite willing to abandon the idea on the strength of a touching petition framed by Charlie and signed by the seven sisters—the twins setting down their marks with heavy emphasis. And then Charlie could ride and shoot and fish; she was untiring and fearless. In many ways she filled the place of that ideal son he had always hoped for and that had never come.

He was standing at the mill holding the bridle of his horse and watching Charlie's approach with complicated interest. He was preposterously young looking—slender, with a clean shaved face and deep set blue eyes like Charlie's, and dark brown hair. The gray hairs on his temples might have been counted and often were, by the twins, perched on either arm of his chair.

"Well, Dad, how do you like it? Isn't it a beaut!" Charlie exclaimed as she flung herself off her wheel and wiped her steaming face with her bended arm. Mr. Laborde took a fresh linen handkerchief from his pocket and passed it over her face as if she had been a little child.

"If I hadn't been down at the landing this morning, goodness knows what they would have done with it. What do you suppose? That idiot of a Lulin swore it wasn't aboard. If I hadn't gone aboard myself and found it—well—that's why I happened to be late again. Miss Melvern is going to speak to you." A grieved and troubled look swept into his face, and was more stinging than if he had upbraided her. This way there was no excuse—no denial that she could make.

"And what are you doing out here now? Why aren't you in with the others at work?" he questioned.

"She sent me away—she's getting tired." Charlie's face was a picture of impotent regret as she looked down and uprooted a clump of grass with the toe of her clumsy boot. "I worked some, though, and then I just *had* to see about the wheel. I couldn't have trusted Demins."

It was one of the occasions when she regretted that her father was not a more talkative man. His silences gave her no opportunity to defend herself. When he rode away and left her there she noticed that he did not hold his chin in the air with his glance directed across the fields as usual, but looked meditatively between his horse's ears. Then she knew that he was perplexed again.

Charlie just wished that Miss Melvern with her rules and regulations was back in Pennsylvania where she came from. What was the use of learning tasks one week only to forget them the next? What was the use of hammering a lot of dates and figures into her head beclouding her intelligence and imagination? Wasn't it enough to have six well educated daughters!

But troubled thoughts, doubts, misgivings found no refuge in Charlie's bosom and they glanced away from her as lightly as winged messengers. Her father was plainly hurt and had not invited her to join him as he sometimes did. Miss Melvern had declined to entertain her apologies and, she knew, would not admit her into the class room. Anyway she felt that God must have intended people to be out of doors on a day like that, or why should he have given it to them? Like many older and more intelligent than herself, Charlie sometimes aspired to a knowledge of God's ways.

Far down the lane on the edge of a field was the Bichous' cabin—the parents of Aurendele, from whom Charlie had that morning purchased the chickens. Youngsters were swarming to their noontide meal and the odor within of frying bacon made Charlie sensible of the fact that she was hungry. She rode into the enclosure with an air of proprietorship which no one ever dreamed of resenting, and informed the Bichou family that she had come to dine with them.

"I thought you was *so* busy, Miss Charlie," remarked Aurendele with fine sarcasm.

"You mustn't think so hard, Aurendele. That's what Tinette's baby died of last week."

Aurendele had obtained the yard of "cross-bar" and was cutting out the sun bonnet for Nannouche who happened to have a good complexion which her relatives thought it expedient to preserve.

"Tinette's baby died o' the measles!" screamed Nannouche who knew everything.

"That's what I said. If she had only thought she didn't have the measles instead of thinking so hard that she did, she wouldn't have died. That's a new religion; but you haven't got sense enough to understand it. You haven't an idea above corn bread and molasses."

Charlie seemed not to have many ideas above corn bread and molasses herself when she sat down to dine with the Bichous. She shared the children's *couche couche* in the homely little yellow bowl like the rest of them—and did not disdain to partake of a goodly share of salt pork and greens with which Father Bichou regaled himself. His wife stood up at the head of the table serving every one with her long bare arms that had a tremendous reach.

Charlie made herself exceedingly entertaining by furnishing a condensed chronicle of the news in the great world, colored by her own lively imagination. They had a way of believing everything she said—which was a powerful temptation that many a sterner spirit would have found difficult to resist.

She was on the most intimate and friendly terms with the children and it was Xenophore who procured a fine hickory stick for her when, after dinner she expressed a desire to have one. She trimmed it down to her liking, seated on the porch rail.

"There are lots of bears where I'm going; maybe tigers," she threw off indifferently as she whittled away.

"W'ere you goin'?" demanded Xenophore with round eyed credulity.

"Yonder in the woods."

"I never yeared they any tigers in the wood. Bears, yes. Mr. Gail killed one w'en I been a baby."

"When you 'been a baby,' what do you call yourself now? But tigers or bears, it's all the same to me. I haven't killed quite as many tigers; but tigers die harder. And then if the stick goes back on me, why, I have my diamond ring."

"Yo' diamon' ring!" echoed Xenophore fixing his eyes solemnly on a shining cluster that adorned Charlie's middle finger.

"You see if I find myself in a tight place all I have to do is to turn the ring three times, repeat a Latin verse, and presto! I disappear like smoke. A tiger wouldn't know me from a hickory sapling."

She got down off the rail, brandished the stick around to test its quality, buckled her belt a bit tighter and announced that she would be off. She asked the Bichous to look after her wheel.

"And don't you attempt to ride it, Aurendele," she cautioned. "You might break your head and you'd be sure to break the wheel."

"I got plenty to do, me, let alone ridin' yo' bicyc'," retorted the girl with lofty indifference.

"It wouldn't matter so much about the head—there are plenty to spare around here—but there isn't another wheel like that in America; and I reckon you heard about Ruben's bride."

"W'at about Ruben's bride?"

"Well, never mind about what, but you keep off that wheel."

Charlie started off down the lane with a brisk step.

"W'ere she goin'?" demanded Mother Bichou looking after her. "My! my! she's a piece, that Charlie! W'ere she goin'?"

"She goin' yonder in the wood," replied Xenophore from the abundance of his knowledge. Ma'me Bichou still gazed after the retreating figure of the girl.

"You better go 'long behine her, you, Xenophore."

Xenophore did not wait to be told twice. In three seconds he was off, after Charlie; his little blue-jeaned legs and brown feet moving rapidly beneath the shade thrown by the circle of his enormous straw hat.

The strip of wood toward which Charlie was directing her steps was by no means of the wild and gloomy character of other woods further away. It was hardly more than a breathing spot, a solemn, shady grove inviting dreams and repose. Along its edge there was a road which led to the station. Charlie had reached the wood before she perceived that Xenophore was at her heels. She turned and seized the youngster by the shoulder giving him a vigorous shake.

"What do you mean by following me? If I was anxious for your company I would have invited you, or I could have stayed at the cabin and enjoyed your society. Speak up, why are you tagging along after me like this?"

"Maman sen' me, it's her sen' me behine you."

"Oh, I see; for an escort, a protector. But tell the truth, Xenophore, you came to see me kill the tigers and bears; own up. And just to punish you I'm not going to disturb them. I'm not even going in the direction where they stay."

Xenophore's face clouded, but he continued to follow, confident that despite her disappointing resolutions in regard to the wild beasts, Charlie would furnish diversion of some sort or other. They walked on for a while in silence and when they came to a fallen tree, Charlie sat herself down and Xenophore flopped himself beside her, his brown little hands folded over the blue jeans, and peeping up at her from under the brim of his enormous hat.

"I tell you what it is Xenophore, usually, when I come in the woods, after slaying a panther or so, I sit down and write a poem or two. There are lots of things troubling me, and nothing comforts me like that. But Tennyson himself couldn't write poetry with a little impish 'Cadian staring at him like this. I tell you what let's do, Xenophore," and she pulled a pad of paper from some depths of her trouserlets. "I think I'll practise my shooting; I'm getting a little rusty; only hit nine alligators out of ten last week in bayou Bonfils."

"It's pretty good, nine out o' ten," proclaimed Xenophore with an appreciative bob.

"Do you think so?" in amazement, "why I never think about the nine, only about the one I missed," and she proceeded to tear into little squares portions of the tablet Miss Melvern had sent her by Blossom in the morning. Handing a slip to Xenophore:

"Go stick this to that big tree yonder, as high as you can reach, and come back here." The youngster obeyed with alacrity. Charlie, taking from her back pocket a small pistol which no one on earth knew she possessed except her sister Irene, began to shoot at the mark, keeping Xenophore trotting back and forth to report results. Some of the shots were wide of the mark, and it was with the utmost reluctance that Xenophore admitted these failures.

There was a sudden loud, peremptory cry uttered near at hand.

"Stop that shooting, you idiots!" A young man came stalking through the bushes as if he had popped out of the ground.

"You young scamp! I'll thrash the life out of you," he exclaimed, mistaking Charlie for a boy at first. "Oh! I beg pardon. This is great sport for a girl, I must say. Don't you know you might have killed me? That last ball passed so near that—that—"

"That it hit you!" cried Charlie perceiving with her quick and practised glance a red blotch on the sleeve of his white shirt, above the elbow. He had been walking briskly and carried his coat across his arm. At her exclamation he looked down, turned pale, and then foolishly laughed at the idea of being wounded and not knowing it, or else in appreciation of his deliverance from an untimely death.

"It's no laughing matter," she said with a proffered motion to be of some assistance.

"It might have been worse," he cheerfully admitted, reaching for his handkerchief. With Charlie's help he bound the ugly gash, for the ball had plowed pretty deep into the flesh.

The girl was conscience stricken and too embarrassed to say much. But she invited the victim of her folly to accompany her to Les Palmiers.

That was precisely his original destination, he was pleased

to tell her. He was on a business mission from a New Orleans firm. The beauty of the day had tempted him to take a short cut through the woods.

His name was Walton—Firman Walton, which information, together with his business card he conveyed to Charlie as they walked along. Xenophore kept well abreast, his little heart fluttering with excitement over the stirring adventure.

Charlie glanced absently at the card, as though it had nothing to do with the situation, and proceeded to roll it into a narrow cylinder while a troubled look spread over her face. "I'm dreadfully sorry," she said. "I'm always getting into trouble, no matter what I do. I don't know what father'll say this time—about the gun, and hitting you and all that. He won't forgive me this time!" Her expression was one of abject wretchedness. He glanced down at her with amused astonishment.

"The hurt wasn't anything," he said. "I shall say nothing about it—absolutely nothing; and we'll give this young man a quarter to hold his tongue." She shook her head hopelessly. "It'll have to be dressed and looked after."

"Please don't think of it," he entreated, "and say nothing more about it."

At half past one the family assembled at dinner. It was always Julia who presided at table. She looked very womanly with her long braid of light-brown hair wound round and round till it formed a coil as large as a dessert plate. Her father sat at the opposite end of the table and the children, the governess and Madame Philomel were dispersed on either side. There were always a few extra places set for unexpected guests. Uncle Ruben, in a white linen apron served the soup and carved the meats at a side table while the plates and dishes were passed around by Demins and a young mulatto girl.

The dining room was on the ground floor and opened upon the false gallery where Charlie had spent a portion of her morning in composition. The absence of that young person from her accustomed place at table was immediately observed and commented upon by her father.

"Where's Charlie," he asked, of everybody—of nobody in particular.

Julia looked a little helpless, the others nonplussed, while Pauline picked her fingers in painful embarrassment. Madame Philomel, who was fat and old fashioned, thought that the new bicycle would easily account for her absence.

"If Charlotte appears befo' sundown, it will be a subjec' of astonishment," she said with an air of conviction and irresponsibility. Every one assumed an air of irresponsibility in regard to Charlie which was annoying to Mr. Laborde as it implied that the whole burden of responsibility lay upon his own shoulders, and he was conscious of not bearing it gracefully. He had spent the half hour before dinner in consultation with Miss Melvern, who prided herself upon her firmness—as if firmness were heaven's first law. Mr. Laborde was in a position to convey to her Charlie's latest resolutions, in which Miss Melvern placed but a small degree of faith. Mr. Laborde himself believed firmly in the ultimate integrity of his daughter's intentions. Miss Melvern's strongest point of objection was the pernicious example which Charlie furnished to her well-meaning sisters, and the interruptions occasioned by her misdirected impulses. Her tardiness of the morning, though not a great fault in itself, was the culmination of a long line of offenses. It might in fact be said that it was the last straw *but one*. Miss Melvern was inclined to think it *was* the last straw. But as hers was not the back which bore the brunt of the burden, she was not wholly qualified to judge. Mr. Laborde began to perceive that there might be a last straw.

Blossom, who assumed the role of a privileged character— the velvet footed Blossom stepped softly into the dining room and spoke, while her glance revolved and fixed itself upon the ceiling.

"Yonder Miss Charlie comin' 'long de fiel' road wid a young gent'man. Nary one ain't ridin' de bicycle—des steppin' out slow a-shovin' it 'long. 'Tain't Mr. Gus an' 'tain't Mr. Joe Slocum. 'Tain't nobody we all knows." Whereupon Blossom withdrew, being less anxious to witness the effect of her announcement than to assist at the arrival of Charlie, the gentleman and the bicycle.

Though accustomed to face situations, this young gentleman exhibited some natural trepidation at being ushered unexpectedly into the bosom of a dining family. He was good looking, intelligent looking. His appearance in itself was a guarantee of his respectability.

"This is Mr. Walton, dad," announced Charlie without preliminary, "he was coming to see you anyhow. He took a short cut through the woods and—and I shot him by mistake in the arm. Better have some antiseptic and stuff on it before he sits down. I had my dinner with the Bichous."

III

There seemed to be a universal, tacit understanding that Charlie was in disgrace, that she herself had deposited the last straw and that there would be results. The silence and outward calm with which her father had met this latest offense were ominous. She was made to stand and deliver her firearm together with her ammunition.

"Take care, father, it's loaded," she cautioned as she placed it upon his writing table.

She was informed that she would not be expected to join the others in the class room and was instructed to go and get her wardrobe in order and to discard her trouserlets as soon as possible.

Mr. Walton was not taken into the family confidence, but he realized that his coming was in the nature of a catastrophe. Having dispatched the business which brought him he would have continued on his way, but the scratch on his arm was rather painful, and that night he had some fever. Mr. Laborde insisted upon his remaining a few days. He knew the young man's people in New Orleans and did business with the firm which he represented.

To young Walton the place seemed charming—like a young ladies' Seminary. And well it might. Madame Philomel taught the girls music and drawing; accomplishments which she had herself acquired at the Ursulines in her youth. During the afternoon hour there was nearly always to be heard the sound of the piano: exercises and scales, interspersed with variations upon the Operas.

"Who is playing the piano?" asked Walton. He leaned against a pillar of the portico, his arm in a sling, and caressing a big dog with the other hand. Charlie sat dejectedly on the step. She still wore the trouserlets, having been unable to procure at so short notice anything that she considered suitable.

"The piano?" she echoed, looking up. "Fidelia, I suppose. It all sounds alike to me except that Fidelia plays the loudest. She's so clumsy and heavy-handed."

Fidelia in fact was thickwaisted and breathed hard. She was given over to afflictions of the throat and made to take exercise which, being lazy, she did not like to do.

"What a lot of you there are," said the young fellow.

"Your eldest sister is beautiful, isn't she! It seems to me she's the most beautiful girl I almost ever saw."

"She has a right to be beautiful. She looks like dad and has a character like Aunt Clementine. Aunt Clementine is a perfect angel. If ever there was a saint on earth—Hi, Pitts! catch 'im! catch 'im Pitts!" The dog bounded away after a pig that had mysteriously escaped from its pen and made its way around to the front, prospecting.

Julia, with Amanda and Irene had driven away a while before in the ample barouche. Nothing could have been daintier than Julia in a soft blue "jaconette" that brightened her color and brought out the blue of her eyes.

"Why didn't you go along driving?" asked Walton when the dog had darted away and he seated himself beside Charlie on the step.

"They're going over to Colimarts to take a dancing lesson."

"Don't you like to dance?"

"I haven't time. Maybe if I liked to, I'd find time. Madame Philomel made a row about me not taking dancing and music and all that, and Dad said I might do as I liked about it. So Ma'me Philo stopped interfering. 'I 'ave nothing to say!' that's her attitude now towards poor me."

"I'm awfully sorry," said the young man earnestly.

"Sorry! about the dancing? pshaw! what difference—"

"No—no sorry about the accident of the other day. I'm afraid, perhaps it's going to get you into trouble."

"It'll get me into trouble all right; I see it coming."

"I hope you'll forgive me," he asked persistently, as though he had been the offender.

"It wasn't your fault," she said with condescension. "If it hadn't been that it would have been something else. I don't know what's going to happen; boarding school I'm afraid."

A small figure came gliding around the corner of the house. It was Xenophore, blue jeans, legs, hat and all. He came quietly and seated himself on a step at some little distance.

"What do you want?" she asked in French.

"Nothing."

They both laughed at the youngster. Far from being offended he smiled and peered slyly up from under his hat.

"Mr. Gus sen' word howdy," piped Xenophore a little later apropos of nothing, breaking right into the conversation.

"W'ere you saw Mr. Gus?" asked Charlie, falling into the

'Cadian speech as she sometimes did when talking to the Bichous.

"He pass yonder by de house on 'is ho'se. He say 'How you come on, Xenophore; w'en you see Miss Charlie?' I say, 'I see Miss Charlie to s'mornin',' an' he say 'Tell Miss Charlie howdy fo' me.'"

Then Xenophore arose and turning mechanically, glided noiselessly around the corner of the house.

It was dusk and the moon was already shining in the river and breaking with a pale glow through the magnolia leaves when the girls came home from their dancing lesson. It was nearing the supper hour so they did not linger, and Charlie went with them into the house, bent upon making a bit of toilet for the evening. She was secretly in hopes that Amanda would lend her a dress. Julia's gowns were quite too young-ladified; they touched the ground, often with a graceful sweep. One of Amanda's would have done nicely. But Amanda looked sidewise from her long, narrow, dark eyes when Charlie approached her with the request and blankly refused. Irene grew excited and indignant.

"Don't ask her, Charlie; why do you ask her? She thinks her clothes are made of diamonds and pearls, too good for Queen Victoria! What about my pink gingham if I ripped out the tucks?"

"Oh! it's no use," wailed Charlie. "There isn't time to rip anything and I could never get into it."

They were in Amanda's room, Irene and Charlie seated on a box lounge and Amanda decorating herself before the mirror. She had laid her own evening toilet on the bed and carefully locked closet, wardrobe and bureau drawers. She always kept things locked and had an ostentatious way of carrying her highly polished keys that were on a ring. Charlie gazed at her sister's reflected image with a sort of despair but with no trace of malice.

"If there's a thing I hate, it's to have people sit and stare when I'm dressing," remarked Amanda. The two girls got up and went out and Amanda locked the door behind them.

"Why not wear your Sunday dress, Charlie?" offered Irene as they walked down the long hall, arm in arm.

"You know what Julia said about its being so short and the sleeves so old fashioned and she wouldn't be seen at church with me if I wore it again. So I gave it to Aurendele the other day."

But it was Julia who came to the rescue. She fastened and

pinned and tucked up one of her own gowns on Charlie and the effect, if not completely happy, could not have been called a distinct failure.

No one remarked upon the metamorphosis when she appeared thus arrayed at table. Miss Melvern and Madame Philomel were far too polite to seem to notice. The twins only beamed their approval and astonishment. Fidelia gasped and stared, closed her lips tight and sought Miss Melvern's glance for direction. Blossom alone expressed herself in a smothered explosion in the door way, and went outside and clung to a post for support.

To Mr. Laborde there was something poignant in the sight of his beloved daughter in this unfamiliar garb. It seemed a dismal part of the unhappy situation which had given him such heartache to solve—for he had solved it. He avoided looking at Charlie and wore an expression which reminded them all of the time he heard of his brother's death in Old Mexico.

Mr. Laborde had that evening reached a conclusion which was communicated to Charlie directly after supper when the others strolled out upon the veranda and she went with him to his study. She was to go to New Orleans and enter a private school noted for its excellent discipline. Two weeks at Aunt Clementine's would enable her to be fitted out as became her age, sex and condition in life. Julia was to go to the city with her, to see that she was properly equipped and later her father would join her and accompany her to the Young Ladies' Seminary.

She fingered the lace ruffle on Julia's sleeve as she looked down and listened to her father's admonitions.

"I'm sorry to give you all this worry, dad," she said, "but I'm not going to make any more promises; it's a farce, the way I've persistently broken them. I hope I shan't give you any more trouble." He took her in his arms, and kissed her fervently. Charlie was exceedingly astonished to discover that the arrangement planned by her father was not so distasteful as it would have seemed a while ago. It was not at all distasteful and she secretly marvelled.

When she and her father rejoined the others on the veranda they found that a visitor had arrived, Mr. Gus Bradley, the son of a neighboring planter and an intimate friend of the family. He had been painfully disconcerted at finding a stranger when he had expected to meet only familiar faces and the effect was not happy. Mr. Gus was so shy that it had never yet been discovered whom his visits at Les Palmiers were intended for. It was, however, generally believed that he favored Charlie on account of the messages which he so often sent her through Xenophore and others. He had given her a fine dog and a riding whip. But he had also made the twins a present of a gentle Shetland pony, and he had sent Amanda his photograph! He was a big fellow and awkward only from shyness and when in company, for in the saddle or out in the road or the fields he had a fine, free carriage. His hair was light and fine and his face smooth and looked as if it belonged to a far earlier period of society and had no connection with the fevered and modern present day.

The moon sent a great flood of light in upon the group—the only shadows were cast by the big round pillars and the fantastic quivering vines. Amanda sat by herself, tip toeing in a hammock and picking a tune on the mandolin. Madame Philomel was telling the twins a marvelous story in French about *Croque Mitaine*.[1] Fidelia was drinking in words of wisdom at Miss Melvern's feet. It was Irene who was entertaining Mr. Gus and endeavoring to account to him in veiled whispers for young Walton's presence on the scene. She might have spoken as loud as she liked for the young gentleman in question was entirely absorbed in Julia's conversation and had ears for nothing else.

"I'm not going to stay," said Mr. Gus, almost apologetically. "I only rode over for a minute. I wanted to see your sister Charlie. I had something important to tell her."

"She'll be out pretty soon; she's inside talking to father."

When Charlie came out she went and seated herself beside Irene on the long bench that stood by the railing. Mr. Gus was near by in a camp chair. He was so flustered at seeing Charlie in frills and furbelows that he could scarcely articulate.

"I didn't know you," he blurted.

"Oh, well, I have to begin some time."

Irene got up and left them alone, remembering Mr. Gus's admission of an important communication for Charlie's ears alone.

"I haven't long to stay," he began. "I heard about Tim's shoulder and brought you a recipe for gall. It's the finest thing ever was. You'll find all the ingredients in your father's workshop, and you'd better mix it yourself; don't trust any

[1] The "Bogeyman."

one else. If you'd like, I'll put it up myself and bring it around tomorrow."

Irene off in the distance was positively agitated. She firmly believed Charlie was receiving her first proposal.

"Thank you, Mr. Gus, but it's no use," said Charlie. "Some one else is going to look after Tim from now on; I'm going away."

"Going away!"

"Yes, going to the Seminary in the city. Dad thinks it's best; I suppose it is."

He found absolutely nothing to say, but his mobile face took on a crestfallen look that the moonlight made pathetic; and Irene from her corner of observation, concluded that he had been rejected as she knew he would.

"I'll send dear old Pitts back. You keep him for me. I reckon they wouldn't let me have him in the Seminary."

"I'll come for him tomorrow," responded Mr. Gus with dreary eagerness. "When do you go?"

"In a day or two. The sooner the better as long as there's no getting out of it."

Two days later Charlie left the plantation accompanied by her sister Julia, young Walton and Madame Philomel. They boarded the little sputtering stern-wheeler about nine in the morning. It seemed as if the whole plantation, blacks and whites, had turned out to bid her *bon voyage*. The sisters were in tears. Even Amanda seemed moved and Irene was frankly hysterical. Miss Melvern was under a big sunshade with Fidelia, and the twins held their father's hands. All the Bichous had come; Aurendele in Charlie's "Sunday dress," Xenophore, round eyed, serious, unable to cry, unable to laugh, apprehending calamity. Mr. Gus galloped up with a huge bouquet of flowers, striving to appear as if it were wholly by accident.

Charlie was completely overcome. She would not go up to the cabin but stayed dejectedly seated on a cotton bale, alternately wiping her eyes and waving her handkerchief until it was too limp to flutter.

IV

The change, or rather the revolution in Charlie's character at this period was so violent and pronounced that for a while it rendered Julia helpless. The trouble which Julia had anticipated was entirely of an opposite nature from the one which confronted her and it took her some time to realize the situation and adjust herself to it. As it happened, the combined efforts of both Aunt Clementine and Julia were insufficient to keep Charlie within bounds; to give her a proper appreciation of values after the feminine instinct had been aroused in her.

The diamond ring she had always with her. It was her mother's engagement ring. Hitherto she had worn it for the tender associations which made her love the bauble. Now she began to look upon it as an adornment. She possessed a round gold locket containing her mother's and father's pictures. This she suspended from her neck by a long thin gold chain. Such family jewels as had by inheritance descended to her, seemed to the young thing insufficient to proclaim the gentle quality of sex. She would have cajoled her father into extravagances. She wanted lace and embroideries upon her garments; and she longed to bedeck herself with ribbons and *passementeries*[2] which the shops displayed in such tempting array.

Her short cropped hair was a sore grievance to Charlie when she viewed herself in the mirror and she resorted to the disfiguring curling irons with results which were, to say the least, appalling to Julia who came in one afternoon and discovered her entertaining young Walton with her head looking like a prize chrysanthemum.

"I can't understand her, Aunt," Julia confided to her Aunt Clementine with tears in her blue eyes. "It's bad enough as it is, but just imagine what a spectacle she would make of herself if we permitted it. I'm afraid she's a little out of her senses. I'd almost rather think that than to believe she could develop such vulgar instincts."

Aunt Clementine would do no more than shrug her shoulders and look placidly and blamelessly perplexed. She was quite sure that Charlie did not take after any member of her side of the family; so the blame of heredity, if any, had naturally to be traced to other sides of the family.

Through mild and firm coercion Charlie was brought to understand that such excessive ornamentation as she favored would not for a moment be tolerated by the disciplinarians at the Seminary. When finally that young person was admitted to the refined precincts—save for the diamond ring and the locket, in the matter of which she had taken a stubborn stand—no fault could have been found with her appearance

[2] Laces and edgings.

which was in every way consistent with that of the well mannered girl of seventeen.

She had spent a delightful fortnight. Aunt Clementine who was at once a lady of fashion and a person of gentle refinement had provided entertainment such as Charlie had not yet encountered outside of novels of high life: her Aunt Clementine's *ménage*[3] having not before been to her liking.

They drove, they visited and received calls, dined and went to the opera. There was much shopping, perambulating and trying on of gowns and hats. There was a perpetual flutter, and indescribable excitement awaiting her at every turn. Young Walton was persistent in his attentions to the sisters, but as there were other and many claims upon Julia it was oftener Charlie who entertained him, walked abroad with him and even accompanied him on one occasion to Church.

The first moment that Charlie found herself alone in the privacy of her own room at the Seminary, she devoted that moment to unburdening her soul. She sat beside the window and looked out a while. There was not much inspiration to be gathered from the big red brick building opposite. But her inspiration was not dependent upon anything extraneous; it was bubbling up inside of her and generating an energy that found a vent in its natural channel.

Equipped with a very fine pen point and the filmiest sheet of filmy writing paper, Charlie wrote some lines of poetry in the smallest possible cramped hand. She did not hesitate or bite her pen or frown, seeking for words and rhymes. She had made it all up beforehand and its rhythm kept time with the beating of her heart. Poor little thing! Let her alone. It would be cruel to tell the whole story. When the lines were written she folded the sheet over and over and over, making it as flat and thin as possible. Then with her hat pin she picked out the little glass frame that contained her mother's picture in the locket, and laying the scrap of poetry in the cover, replaced the picture.

As the young girls at the Seminary were all of gentle breeding they gave no pronounced exhibition of their astonishment at Charlie's lack of accomplishments. She herself felt her shortcomings keenly and read their guarded wonder. With dogged determination she had made up her mind to transform herself from a hoyden to a fascinating young lady, if persistence and hard work could do it.

[3]Household.

As for hard work, there was enough of it! Hoeing, or chopping cane seemed child's play compared with the excruciating intricacies which the piano offered her. She began to have some respect for Fidelia's ponderous talent and even wondered at the twins. After some lessons in drawing, the instructor disinterestedly advised her to save her money. He was gloomy about it. The spirit of commercialism, he said, had not touched him to the crass extent of countenancing robbery. With some sinking of heart, Charlie let the drawing go, but when it came to dancing, she would yield not an inch. She practised the steps in the narrow confines of her room, and when opportunity favored her, she waltzed and two-stepped up and down the long corridors. Some of the girls took pity and gave her private instructions, for which she offered tempting inducements to their cupidity in the shape of chocolate bon-bons and stick-pins.

She was immensely liked, though they had small respect for her abilities until one day it fell upon them with the startling bewilderment of lightning from a clear sky that Charlie was a poet. It happened in this wise: The fête of the foundress of the Seminary was to be celebrated and the young ladies were desired to write addresses in her honor, the worthiest of these addresses to be selected and delivered in the venerable lady's presence upon the date in question.

It was so much easier for Charlie to write twenty or fifty lines of verse than pages and pages of prose.

When the announcement of the award was made in a most flattering little speech to the assembled classes by the lady directress, the girls were stupefied, and Charlie herself almost as well pleased as if she had been able to play a minuet upon the piano or go through the figures of a dance without blundering.

"Did you ever!" "Well, I knew there was something in her!"

"I told you she wasn't as stupid as she looks!"

"Why didn't she say so!" were a few of the comments passed upon Charlie's suddenly unearthed talent.

A group besieged her in her room that afternoon.

"Out with them!" cried the spokesman, armed with a box of chocolate creams, "every last of them. Where do you keep them? Hand over the key of that desk. You're a barefaced impostor, if you want to know it."

They seated themselves on chairs, stools, the lounge, the

floor and the bed—as many as could crowd in a row, and awaited with the pleased expectancy of girls ready to extract entertainment from any situation that presents itself.

Charlie had no thought of reluctance. She brought forth the mass of manuscript and delivered it over to the chocolate bearer who had a sonorous voice and a reputation as an elocutionist.

One by one the poems were read, with fictitious fire, with melting pathos as the occasion called for, while silently the chocolates were passed around and around.

Charlie rocked violently and tried to look indifferent. Her hair was long enough to tie back now with a bow of ribbon. On her forehead she wore a few little curls made with the curling irons, and as she glanced in the mirror while she rocked she wondered if her face would ever get beautiful and silky white. Charlie took no part in the athletic sports such as tennis and basket ball, though urged to do so. She was given over to putting some kind of greasy stuff on her hands at night and slept in a pair of her father's old gloves.

"Well," commented the reader, laying down the leaves.

"Moonlight on the Mississippi."

"This is the finest thing I ever read. I wish you'd give me this, I'd like to send it to mother. And all I've got to say for you is that you are a large sized goose. The idea of keeping such poetry as that cooped up here! Why don't you go to work and publish those things in the Magazines, I'd like to know. I tell you, they'd jump at the—well! I like this! Empty! where are all those chocolates gone? The next time I go halves in a box of chocolates you people'll know it!"

It need not be supposed that Charlie saw nothing of her home folks during her stay at the Seminary. They came in squads and detachments. Julia must have been spending much time with her Aunt Clementine, for the two not infrequently drove around in Aunt Clementine's victoria upon which occasions Charlie was very proud of her sister's beauty and air of distinction which the other girls did not fail to observe and rave over.

Amanda and Irene came down from the plantation with their father expressly to see her. The girls who caught a glimpse of them did not hesitate to pronounce Mr. Laborde the handsomest man they had ever set eyes upon; Amanda a most striking and fascinating personality. But of Irene they held their estimate in reserve, as the poor girl had seemed demented, laughing in the midst of tears, weeping to an accompaniment of laughter.

Once Miss Melvern made her appearance with Fidelia. It was a great pleasure to introduce the governess to the faculty and the methods, while Fidelia trod heavily and seriously at her side, crimson under the scrutiny of so many strange eyes.

Last came Madame Philomel one morning with the twins and whom beside but Aurendele and Xenophore! She wore a beautiful new bonnet, a sprigged challie dress with a black mantilla and kid gloves. The young ladies who were growing more and more interested in Charlie's family with every fresh installment, to quote them literally, lost their minds over the twins who were like two chubby rosy-cheeked angels in spotless white.

"It's positively paralyzing!"

"How do you tell them apart?"

"I must have a sketch of them."

"How do they know themselves, which is which?"

"Oh! *we* know them of course," said Charlie with laudable pride, "but strangers can tell by their difference of manner: Pauline is timid and Paula dreadfully mischievous. Would you believe it? She fooled dad one day by hanging her head and picking her fingers when he asked her an embarrassing question. There was no trouble at this juncture in discovering which was which."

Aurendele, still wearing Charlie's "Sunday dress" which was getting sadly small for her and a sailor hat of Irene's, was alert, but overawed and unable to remember the multitude of things she had stored up in her brain to communicate to Charlie. And as for Xenophore, he felt there had been a convulsion of nature and he was powerless to place the responsibility. To be sitting there in "store clothes," brogans, twirling in his hands a little felt hat no bigger than a plate, Miss Charlie in hair ribbons and dressed like a girl! He was speechless. It was only toward the close of the visit that he uttered his first word.

"Mr. Gus sen' word 'howdy.' "

"W'en you saw Mr. Gus?" asked Charlie laughing.

"He pass by the house an' he say, 'How you come on, Xenophore! w'at you all year f'om Miss Charlie?' I tell 'im I'm goin' to the city to see you an' he say, 'Tell Miss Charlie howdy fo' me.' "

But when her father came alone one morning quite early—he had remained overnight in the city that he might be early—and carried her off with him for the day, her delight knew no bounds. He did not tell her in so many words how hungry he was for her, but he showed it in a hundred ways. He was like a school boy on a holiday; it was like a conspiracy; there was a flavor of secrecy about it too. They did not go near Aunt Clementine's. They saw no one they knew except Young Walton who was busy over accounts in the commission office where Mr. Laborde stopped to supply himself with money enough to pay his way. The young fellow turned crimson with unexpected pleasure when he saw them. He was eager to know if any other members of the family were in the city. He showed a disposition to be excused from the office and to join them, a suggestion which Mr. Laborde did not favor, which rather alarmed him and hurried his departure. Moreover he could see that Charlie did not like the young man, and he could not blame her for that, all things considered! She gave her whole attention to her gloves and the clasp of her parasol while there.

It was well they provided themselves with money. Charlie needed every thing she could think of and what she forgot her father remembered. He carried her jacket and assisted her over the crossing like an experienced cavalier. He helped her to select a new sailor hat and saw that she put it on straight. Not approving of her hat pin he bought her another, besides handkerchiefs, a fan, stick pins, presents for the girls and the favorite teachers, books of poetry, and the latest novels. The maid at the Seminary was kept busy all afternoon carrying in bundles.

They went to the lake to eat breakfast; a second breakfast to be sure, but such exceedingly young persons could not be expected to restrict themselves to the conventional order in the matter of refreshment. It was a great delight to be abroad: the air was soft and moist and the warm sun of early March brought out the scent of the earth and of distant gardens and the weedy smell from the still pools.

They were almost alone at the lake end save for the habitual fishermen and sportsmen, the *restaurateurs* and lazy looking *garçons*. Their small table was out where the capricious breeze beat about them, and they sat looking across the glistening water, watching the slow sails and feeling like a couple of bees in clover.

Charlie drew off a glove, looked at her hand and silently held it out for her father's inspection, right under his eyes.

"What do you think of that, dad?" she asked finally. He

gazed at the hand and rubbed his cheek, meditatively, as he would have pulled his moustache if he had had one.

"Just take a good look at it. Notice anything?" He took her hand, scrutinizing the ring.

"No stones missing, are there?"

"I don't mean the ring, but the hand," turning her palm uppermost. "Feel that. You know what it used to be. Ever feel anything softer than that?"

He held the hand fondly in both of his, but she withdrew it, holding it at arm's length.

"Now, dad, I want your candid opinion; don't say anything you don't believe; but do you think it's as white as—Julia's, for instance?"

He narrowed his eyes, surveying the little hand that gleamed in the sun, like a connoisseur sizing up a picture.

"I don't want to be hasty," he said quizzically. "I'm not too sure that I remember, and I shouldn't like to do Julia's hand an injustice, but my opinion is that yours is whiter."

She threw an arm around his neck and hugged him, to the astonishment of a lame oysterman and a little Brazilian monkey that squealed in his cage with amusement.

"It's all right, Charlie dear, but you know you mustn't think too much about the hands and all that. Take care of the head, too, and the temper."

"Don't fret, dad," tapping her forehead under the rim of the 'sailor,' "the head's coming right up to the front: history, literature, ologies, everything but dates and figures; getting right in here; consumed with ambition. And the girls didn't think I'd ever learn to dance until I gave them a double shuffle and a Coonpine! Now I'm giving lessons. Never mind! some of these days they'll be asking your permission to make me queen of the Carnival. And as for temper! Why, it's ridiculous, dad. I'm beginning to—to bleat!"

Well, it was a day full to the brim. In the afternoon they heard a wonderful pianist play. It gave Charlie a feeling of exaltation, a new insight; the music somehow filled her soul with its power.

It was nearly dark when she embraced her father and bade him good bye. For weeks the memory of that day lasted.

It was in the full flush of April that a telegram came summoning Charlie home at once. Terror seized her like some tangible thing. She feared some one was dead.

Her father had been injured, they told her. Not fatally, but he wanted her.

V

It was one of those terrible catastrophes which seem so impossible, so uncalled for when they come home to us, that stupefy with grief and regret; an accident at the sugar mill; a bit of perilous repairing in which he chose to assume the risk rather than expose others to danger. It was hard to say what had happened to him. He was alive; that was all, but torn, maimed and unconscious. The surgeon, who was coming as fast as steam and the iron wheels could bring him, would tell them more of it. The surgeon was on the train with Charlie and so was the professional nurse. They seemed to her like monsters; because he read a newspaper and conversed with the conductor about crops and the weather; and the other, demure in her grey dress and close bonnet, displayed an interest in a group of children who were traveling with their mother.

Charlie could not speak. Her brain was confused with horror and her thoughts were beyond control. Every thing had lost significance but her grief and nothing was real but her despair. Emotion stupefied her when she thought that he would not be there at the station waiting for her with outstretched arms and beaming visage; that she would perhaps never see him again as he had been that day at the lake, robust and beautiful, clasping her with loving arms when he said good bye in the soft twilight. She became keenly conscious of the rhythm of the iron wheels that seemed to mock her and keep time to the throbbing in her head and bosom.

There was a hush upon the whole plantation. Silent embraces; serious faces and tearful eyes greeted her. It seemed inexpressibly hard that she should be kept from him while the surgeon and the nurse were hurried to his side. A physician was already there, and so was Mr. Gus.

During the hour or more that followed, Charlie sat alone on the upper gallery. Madame Philomel with Julia and Amanda were indoors praying upon their knees. The others were speechless with anxiety. Charlie alone was quiet and dull. It had rained and there was a delicious freshness in the air, the birds were mad with joy among the dripping leaves that glistened with the filtering rays of the setting sun. She sat and stared at the water still pouring from a tin spout.

The twins came and leaned their heads against her. She took Pauline into her lap and fastened the child's shoestring that had come untied. She stared at them both with absent-minded eyes. Then Irene came and led them away. The water had stopped flowing from the spout and Charlie fixed her eyes upon the peacock that moved with low trailing plumage over the wet grass.

There was a sweet, sickening odor stealing from the house, more penetrating than the scent of the rain-washed flowers. She groaned as the fumes of the anesthetic reached her. She leaned her elbows upon the rail and with her head clasped in her hands, stared down at the gravel before the steps.

Someone came out upon the porch and stood beside her; it was Mr. Gus, all his shyness submerged for the moment in quick sympathy.

"Poor old Charlie," he said softly and took her hand.

"Is he dead, Mr. Gus? have they killed him?" she asked dully.

"He isn't dead. He won't die if he can help it."

"What have they done to him?"

"Never mind now, Charlie; just thank God that he is left to us."

A deep prayer of thankfulness went up from every heart. The crushing pressure was lifted, and they rejoiced that it was to be life rather than death—life at any price.

With the changed conditions that so soon make themselves familiar, a new character was stamped upon the family life at Les Palmiers. There was a quiet and unconscious readjustment. The center of responsibility shifted and sought as it were to find lodgment for a time in every individual breast. The family took turns in watching at the bedside after the quiet woman in grey had gone. Then it was that even Demins showed fine mettle in those days. Money might have paid his services, it could never balance his devotion.

Charlie forgot that she was young and that the sun was shining out of doors and the voices of the woods and fields awaited her. But between sick-watches she took again to the task of beautifying her outward and inward being. She sought after becoming arrangements of her hair; over the kitchen fire she mixed ointments for the whitening of her skin; and while committing to memory tasks that filled her sisters with admiration, she polished her pointed nails till they rivalled the pearly rose of the conch-shells which Mme. Philomel kept upon either side of her hearth.

It was getting pretty warm and systematic work in the class

room had been abandoned. Miss Melvern went away on her annual home visit and Aunt Clementine came up to the plantation to condole and to read the riot-act.

Her brother was sufficiently recovered to be scolded, to listen to the truth as Aunt Clementine defined her plain talk. It was high time he gave over thinking he might keep his daughters always like a bouquet of flowers, in a bunch, as it were, on the family hearth. He was not quite equal to the task of disagreeing with her. She had plans for separating these blossoms so that they might disseminate their sweetness even across the seas. Julia and Amanda should accompany her abroad in the Autumn. A winter in Paris and Rome, not to mention Florence, would accomplish more for them than years in the class room. Aunt Clementine saw great possibilities of a fine lady in Amanda. The girl presented more crude, promising material than Julia even. A year at the Seminary for Irene, and Charlie—

"Please leave me out of your calculations, Aunt," said Charlie with a flash of her old rebellious nature. "Dad'll have something to say when he's able to bother about it, and in the meantime I propose to take care of myself and the youngsters and of Dad, and this meeting's got to end right here. When he is strong enough to talk back, Aunt Clementine, you may come and have it out with him." Aunt Clementine had always considered the girl coarse and she surveyed the girl with compassion.

"Charlie, remember to whom you are speaking," said Julia with gentle rebuke. But they all filed out of the sick room, Amanda with a calm exultation in her face—and left Charlie to smoothe the pillow and quiet the nerves of the convalescent.

Julia seemed to be always more than ready to accept an invitation from her aunt. Life in the country began apparently to weary her, and, without too much urging she accompanied Aunt Clementine back to the city.

Young Walton had been up to Les Palmiers on a visit of sympathy and had had a conversation alone with Mr. Laborde which had been to the last degree satisfactory. Charlie wore her pink organdie and her grandmother's pearls during his visit and puffed her hair.

It was a week or so after Julia's departure for the city that the remaining sisters were all assembled on the false gallery one forenoon awaiting the return of Demins with the mail. Twice a day it was Demins' duty to fetch and carry the family mail from and to the station. Amanda's familiarity with keys seemed to entitle her to the office of locking and unlocking the canvas bag and it was she who distributed the mail.

There was a letter from Julia for each one of the sisters, under separate cover; even the twins got one between them. A proceeding so unfamiliar on the part of the undemonstrative Julia caused more than a flutter of wonder and comment. Envelopes were torn open, exclamations followed: rejoicing, dismay, elation, consternation! Engaged! Julia engaged! and the sky still in its place overhead and not crumbling about their ears!

Charlie alone said nothing at first, then in a voice hideous with anger:

"She's a deceitful hypocrite, she's no sister of mine, I hate her!" She turned and went into the house leaving Julia's letter lying upon the bricks. Pauline began to utter little choking sobs at once. Fidelia grew red with indecision and dismay.

"She can't bear him," said Irene with shame-faced apology.

"Charlie's a goose," remarked Amanda picking up the letter and folding it back into its envelope, "let's go and hear what father has to say."

A little later Charlie in her trouserlets, boots and leggings, mounted black Tim and galloped madly away, no one knew where.

"Look like ol' Nick took hol' o' Miss Charlie again," commented Aunt Maryllis leaning from the kitchen window.

"She mad 'cause Miss Julia g'in git ma'rid to de young man w'at she shot," said Blossom. "I yeard 'em. Miss Irene 'low Miss Charlie f'or hate dat man like pizen."

At the sound of Tim's pounding hoofs upon the road, Xenophore darted from the cabin door. And at sight of Charlie rushing past in the old familiar guise of a whirlwind, the youngster threw himself flat down and rolled in the dust with glee, even though he knew his mother would whip the dust from his jeans without the trouble of removing them from his small person.

No one ever knew where Charlie ate her dinner that day. She did not quite kill Tim but it took days of care to set him on his accustomed legs again. She did not join the family at the evening meal and remained apart in her own room, refusing admittance to those who sought to reach her.

In her mad ride Charlie had thrown off the savage impulse which had betrayed itself in such bitter denunciation of her sister. Shame and regret had followed and now she was steeped in humiliation such as she had never felt before. She did not feel worthy to approach her father or her sisters. The girlish infatuation which had blinded her was swept away in the torrents of a deeper emotion, and left her a woman.

It was trivial, perhaps, for her to take the little poem from the back of her mother's miniature and holding it on the point of a hat pin, consume it in the flame of a match.

During the stillness of the night when she could not sleep, she crept out of bed and lit her lamp, shading it so that its glimmer could not be detected from without.

Removing the precious diamond ring from her finger she began to polish and brighten it till the glittering stones were scintillant in their dazzling whiteness. The task over, she put the ring in a little blue velvet cover which she took from her bureau drawer and laid it upon the pin cushion. Then Charlie went back to bed and slept till the sun was high in the heavens.

She had little to say at breakfast the next morning and there was no one who felt privileged to question her. With the others she gathered on the false gallery to wait for the mail as she had done the day before. When her letters were handed to her she also took her father's mail and turned to go with it.

"Girls," she said bravely, half turning. "I want to tell you I am ashamed of what I said yesterday. I hope you'll forget it. I mean to try to make you forget it." That was all. She went on up to her father.

He was stretched upon a cot near the window, like a pale shadow of himself.

"Where have you been all this time, Charlie?" he asked, with reproachful eyes. She stood over his cot couch for a moment silent.

"I've been climbing a high mountain, dad." He was used to her flights of speech when they were alone.

"And what did you see from the top, little girl?" he questioned with a smile.

"I saw the new moon. But here are your letters, dad." She drew a low chair and sat close, close to his bed.

"Isn't Gus coming up?" he asked. Mr. Gus came each morning to offer his services in reading or answering letters.

"I'm jealous of Mr. Gus," she said. "I know as much as he, more perhaps when it comes to writing letters. I know as much about the plantation as you do, dad; you know I do.

And from now on I'm going to be—to be your right hand—your poor right hand," she almost sobbed sinking her face in the pillow. The arm that was left to him he folded around her and pressed his lips to her brow.

"Look, Dad," she exclaimed, cheerfully recovering herself and plunging her hand in her pocket. "What do you think of this for a wedding present for Julia?" She held the open blue velvet case before his eyes.

"You rave! nonsense. I thought you prized it more than any of your possessions; more than Tim even."

"I do. That's why I give it. There'd be no value in giving a thing I didn't prize," she said inconsequentially.

While she was writing out the card of presentation at the table, Mr. Gus came in and Charlie joined him at the bed side.

"This little woman has an idea she can run the plantation, Gus, till I get on my feet," said Mr. Laborde more cheerfully than he had spoken since his accident. "What do you think about it?"

Mr. Gus turned a fine pink under his burned skin.

"If she says so, I don't doubt it," he agreed, "and I'm always ready to lend a hand; you know that. I'm going towards the mill now, and if Charlie cares—I see her horse saddled out there," peering from the window as if the sight of the horse saddled, awaiting its rider, was something he had not perceived before.

"Here are your letters, dad. One of the girls will come up and get them ready for you and when I come back I'll answer them. I'll save Mr. Gus that much."

From his window Mr. Laborde watched the two mount their horses under the live oak tree.

Aunt Maryllis was standing in the kitchen door holding a small tin cup.

"Miss Charlie," she called out, "heah dis heah grease you mix' up fo' yo' han's; w'at I gwine do wid it?"

"Throw it away, Aunt Maryllis," cried Charlie, over her shoulder.

The old woman sniffed at the cup. It smelled good. She thrust the tip of a knotty black finger into the creamy white mixture and rubbed it on her hand. Then she deliberately hid the tin in a piece of newspaper and set it away on the chimney shelf.

There is no telling what would have become of Les Palmiers that summer if it had not been for Charlie and Mr. Gus.

It was precisely a year since Charlie had been hustled away to the boarding school in a state of semi-disgrace. Now, with all the dignity and grace which the term implied, she was mistress of Les Palmiers.

Julia was married and away on her wedding journey prior to making her home in the city. Amanda was qualifying in Paris under the tutelage of Aunt Clementine to enter the lists as a fine lady of fashion. The others were back in the class room with Miss Melvern in her old place. Mr. Laborde had recuperated slowly from the terrible shock to his nervous system six months before; and though he was getting about, he spent much time reclining in the long lounge in the upper hall.

It was a moonlight night and very quiet. He could sometimes faintly hear the lap of the great river, and he caught the low hum of voices below. It was Mr. Gus and Charlie conversing in the lower veranda. Mr. Gus was stripping a long, thin branch of its thorns and leaves and tangling his speech into incoherence.

"There's no hurry. I just mentioned it, Charlie, because I—couldn't help it."

"No, there's no hurry," agreed Charlie leaning back against a pillar and gazing up at the sky. "I couldn't dream of leaving Dad without a right arm."

"Of course not; I couldn't expect it. But then couldn't he have two right arms!"

"And then the twins. I've come to be a sort of mother to them rather than a sister; and you see I'd have to wait till they grew up."

"Yes, I suppose so. About how old are the twins now?"

"Nearly seven. But we'll talk of all that some other time. Didn't you hear Dad cough? That's a sly way he has of attracting my attention. He doesn't like to call me outright." Mr. Gus was beating the switch upon the gravel.

"There's something I wanted to ask you."

"I know. You want to ask me not to call you 'Mr.' Gus any more."

"How did you know?"

"I am a clairvoyant. And besides you want to ask me if I like you pretty well."

"You *are* a clairvoyant!"

"It seems to me I've always liked you better than any one, and that I'll keep on liking you more and more. So there!

Good night." She ran lightly away into the house and left him in an ecstasy in the moonlight.

"Is that you, Charlie?" asked her father at the sound of her light footfall. She came and took his hand, leaning fondly over him as he lay in the soft, dim light.

"Did you want anything, Dad?"

"I only wanted to know if you were there."

Written, 1900; published, 1969

𝒞

SIGNET CLASSICS by American Authors

☐ **THE OCTOPUS by Frank Norris.** The story of a titanic struggle between California farmers and the powerful railroad trust which runs the territory. Afterword by Oscar Cargill. (#CJ1203—$1.95)

☐ **THE HOUSE OF MIRTH by Edith Wharton.** The ironic story of a young woman's downfall in the glittering society of 19th century New York. Afterword by Louis Auchincloss. (#CJ1177—$1.95)*

☐ **THE RISE OF SILAS LAPHAM by William Dean Howells.** The first realistic treatment of an American businessman foreshadowed the work of modern writers. Afterword by Harry T. Moore. (#CW1121—$1.50)

☐ **MAIN STREET by Sinclair Lewis.** The crusade of a doctor's wife against the narrow-minded conventions of a small town. Afterword by Mark Schorer. (#CE1140—$2.25)

☐ **BABBITT by Sinclair Lewis.** The caustic portrayal of an American go-getter, ready and willing to sacrifice his principles to get ahead. Afterword by Mark Schorer. (#CW1097—$1.50)

☐ **SISTER CARRIE by Theodore Dreiser.** The story of a woman's spectacular rise from poverty to stage fame through the aid of her lovers. Afterword by Willard Thorp, Princeton University. (#CE1206—$1.75)*

* Not available in Canada

To order these titles,

please use coupon on the

last page of this book.

More Novels from the SIGNET CLASSIC Library

☐ **BILLY BUDD and Other Tales by Herman Melville.** The title story and other outstanding short stories, including the **Piazza Tales**, by the author of **Moby Dick.** Afterword by William Thorp. (#CE1168—$1.75)

☐ **THE HOUSE OF THE SEVEN GABLES by Nathaniel Hawthorne.** A tale of sinister hereditary influences within an old New England family. Afterword by Edward C. Sampson. (#CY1043—$1.25)

☐ **THE MARBLE FAUN by Nathaniel Hawthorne.** This story, set in Rome, of a murderer, Donatello, and his devoted Miriam, is a penetrating study of the effects of sin. Afterword by Murray Krieger. (#CW1084—$1.50)

☐ **THE ADVENTURES OF TOM SAWYER by Mark Twain.** This classic story of boys growing up on the Mississippi River is part of America's enduring heritage. Afterword by George P. Elliott. (#CY1165—$1.25)

☐ **A CONNECTICUT YANKEE IN KING ARTHUR'S COURT by Mark Twain.** A modern American finds himself among the knights of the Round Table in this biting satire on medieval superstitions. Afterword by Edmund Reiss. (#CY1073—$1.25)

☐ **THE AMBASSADORS by Henry James.** A psychologically penetrating novel showing the conflicting cultures of Europe and America by the famous expatriate author. Afterword by R. W. Stallman. (#CW1205—$1.50)

To order these titles, please

use coupon on next page.

SIGNET CLASSICS by British Authors

☐ **A TALE OF TWO CITIES by Charles Dickens.** Rich characterizations drawn against the dramatic backdrop of the French Revolution's bloody strife by England's popular 19th century author. Afterword by Edgar Johnson.
(#CW1076—$1.50)

☐ **MIDDLEMARCH by George Eliot.** A richly complex novel exploring two unhappy marriages in a provincial Victorian community. Afterword by Frank Kermode.
(#CE1044—$2.25)

☐ **PRIDE AND PREJUDICE by Jane Austen.** The prejudice of a young lady and the pride of the aristocratic hero make this book a masterpiece of gentle humor. Afterword by Joann Morse, Barnard. (#CY1111—$1.25)

☐ **THE RETURN OF THE NATIVE by Thomas Hardy.** A powerful novel by one of England's great novelists, about two men and two women who lived on Egdon Heath, sometimes called the strongest character in the book. Afterword by Horace Gregory. (#CW1091—$1.50)

☐ **HUMPHREY CLINKER by Tobias Smollett.** A mirthful tale of a tour by coach-and-four through the cities and countryside of 18th century England. Foreword by Monroe Engel. (#CJ1103—$1.95)

THE NEW AMERICAN LIBRARY, INC.,
P.O. Box 999, Bergenfield, New Jersey 07621

Please send me the SIGNET CLASSIC BOOKS I have checked above. I am enclosing $_____(please add 50¢ to this order to cover postage and handling). Send check or money order—no cash or C.O.D.'s. Prices and numbers are subject to change without notice.

Name _____

Address _____

City_____ State_____ Zip Code_____
Allow at least 4 weeks for delivery
This offer is subject to withdrawal without notice.